WATTERS · LEYH · LAIHO

LUMBERJANES™

A SUMMER TO REMEMBER

Published by

BOOM! BOX™

BOOM! BOX™

LUMBERJANES Volume Nineteen, August 2021. Published by BOOM! Box, a division of Boom Entertainment, Inc. Lumberjanes is ™ & © 2021 Shannon Watters, Grace Ellis, Noelle Stevenson & Brooklyn Allen. Originally published in single magazine form as LUMBERJANES No. 73-74. ™ & © 2020 Shannon Watters, Grace Ellis, Noelle Stevenson & Brooklyn Allen. All rights reserved. BOOM! Box™ and the BOOM! Box logo are trademarks of Boom Entertainment, Inc., registered in various countries and categories. All characters, events, and institutions depicted herein are fictional. Any similarity between any of the names, characters, persons, events, and/or institutions in this publication to actual names, characters, and persons, whether living or dead, events, and/or institutions is unintended and purely coincidental. BOOM! Box does not read or accept unsolicited submissions of ideas, stories, or artwork.

BOOM! Studios, 5670 Wilshire Boulevard, Suite 400, Los Angeles, CA 90036-5679. Printed in Canada. First Printing.

ISBN: 978-1-68415-699-3, eISBN: 978-1-64668-243-0

THIS LUMBERJANES FIELD MANUAL BELONGS TO:

NAME:_____

TROOP:_____

DATE INVESTED:_____

FIELD MANUAL TABLE OF CONTENTS

LUMBERJANES FIELD MANUAL

For the Advanced Program

Tenth Edition • July 1985

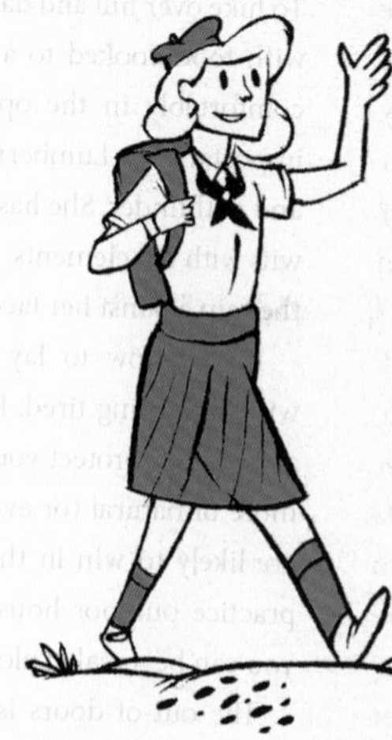

Prepared for the

Miss Qiunzella Thiskwin Penniquiqul Thistle Crumpet's

CAMP FOR [redacted] HARDCORE LADY-TYPES

"Friendship to the Max!"

A MESSAGE FROM THE LUMBERJANES HIGH COUNCIL

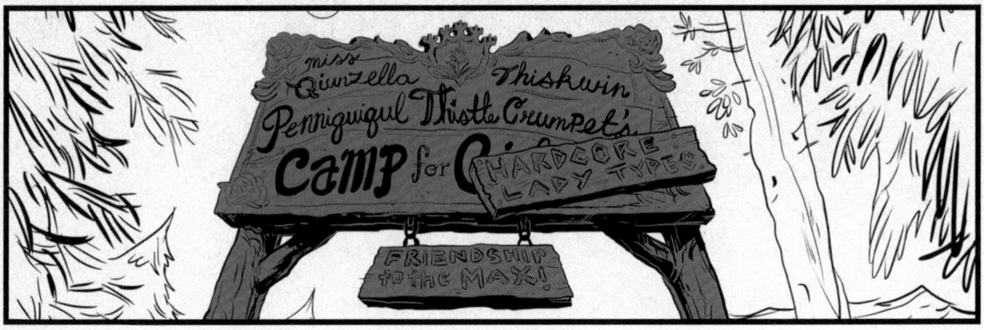
miss Quinzella Thiskwin Penniquiqul Thistle Crumpet's
Camp for
HARDCORE LADY TYPES
FRIENDSHIP to the MAX!

If you have ever been on stage, you have likely heard someone say, "the show must go on." Indeed, whether you've earned your "Tread the Boards" acting badge, or the "Treat the Boards" backstager badge, you may have repeated that old adage yourself, with much the same intent and meaning it is often given, or that your teacher, director, or parent may have suggested it meant. That is, push yourself through the difficulties, whatever they may be, because the play's the thing, and you can rest when it is over.

We of the High Council reject this intent, and its larger implications as well. Certainly, stretching your limits when you want to, or when you are eager to finish an exciting project even if it keeps you up past bedtime is one thing. But for that to be expected, to suggest that your work supersedes yourself, or that problems can be overcome if you simply push yourself harder, without additional support…it leads only to more stress, more struggle, more strife. It teaches both that you, as an individual, are keeping the entire boat afloat, but also that your individual needs are mere inconveniences.

Instead, we suggest: the show must go on... because the show itself is larger than any one person's contribution to it. That when one singer comes down with laryngitis, the entire chorus is there to catch them. That when opening night or deadlines loom, it is perfectly alright to ask for help—the people around you will find workarounds and accommodations, whether that means an understudy going on for a few nights, a second stitcher rushing to help finish sewing the enormous hem of a hoop skirt, or a director focusing on running lines when an actor has twisted an ankle.

When you work with others, you are a part of something larger than yourself. The show will be able to carry on, even if you must stop, take a break, catch your breath. The people who surround you will pick up the slack, knowing that you would do the same for them, when they need it.

THE LUMBERJANES PLEDGE

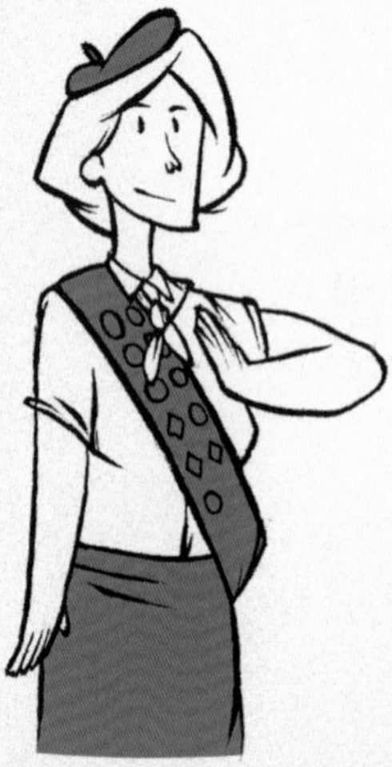

I solemnly swear to do my best
Every day, and in all that I do,
To be brave and strong,
To be truthful and compassionate,
To be interesting and interested,
To pay attention and question
The world around me,
To think of others first,
To always help and protect my friends,
[redacted]
And to make the world a better place
For Lumberjane scouts
And for everyone else.

THEN THERE'S A LINE ABOUT GOD, OR WHATEVER

LUMBERJANES™

A SUMMER TO REMEMBER

Written by
Shannon Watters
& Kat Leyh

Illustrated by
Kat Leyh

Colors by
Maarta Laiho

Letters by
Aubrey Aiese

Cover by
Kat Leyh

Series Designer
Grace Park

Collection Designer
Chelsea Roberts

Editor
Sophie Philips-Roberts

Executive Editor
Jeanine Schaefer

Special thanks to **Kelsey Pate** for giving the Lumberjanes their name.

Created by
Shannon Watters, Grace Ellis, Noelle Stevenson & Brooklyn Allen

LUMBERJANES FIELD MANUAL

CHAPTER
SEVENTY-THREE

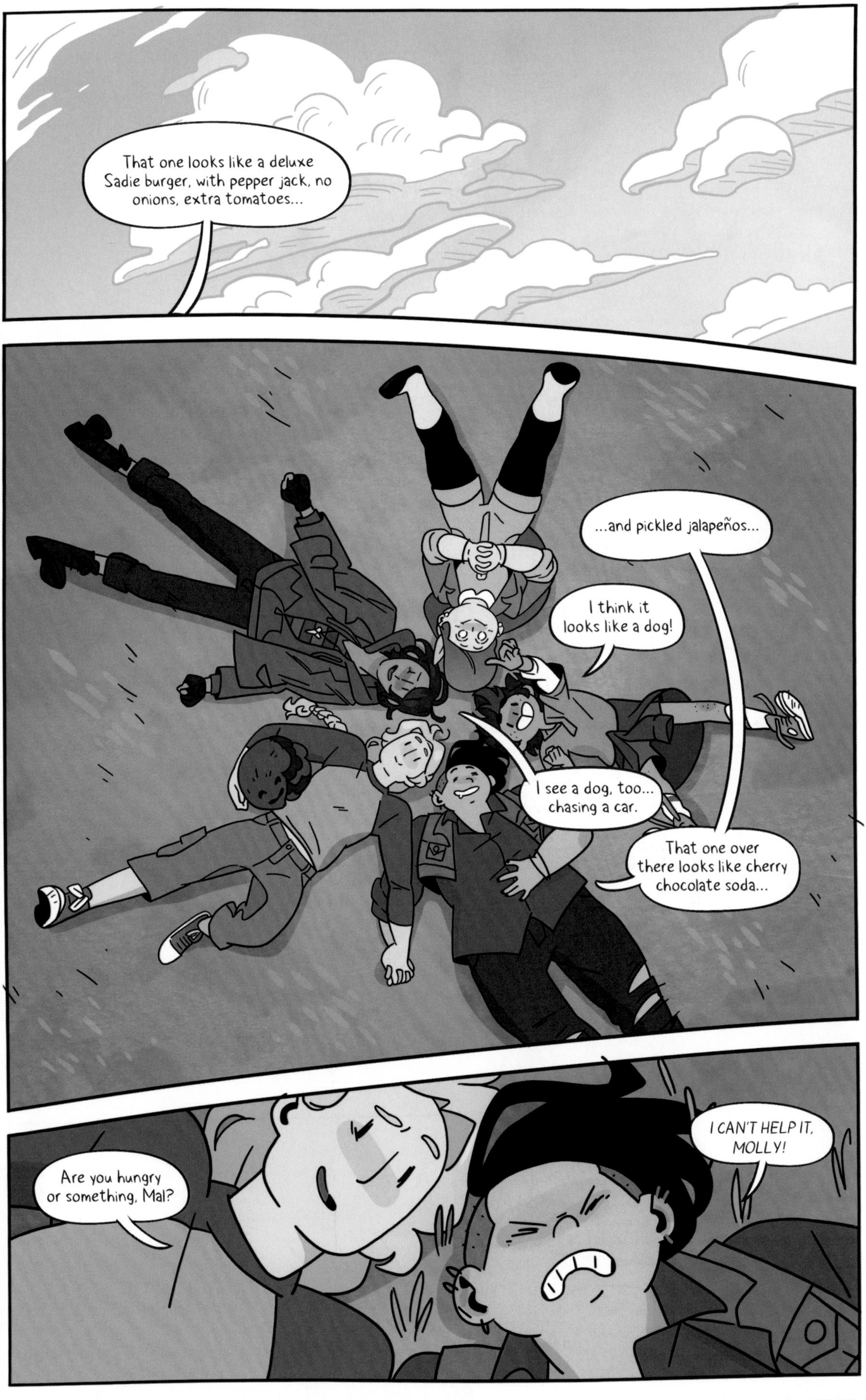
That one looks like a deluxe Sadie burger, with pepper jack, no onions, extra tomatoes...
...and pickled jalapeños...
I think it looks like a dog!
I see a dog, too... chasing a car.
That one over there looks like cherry chocolate soda...
Are you hungry or something, Mal?
I CAN'T HELP IT, MOLLY!

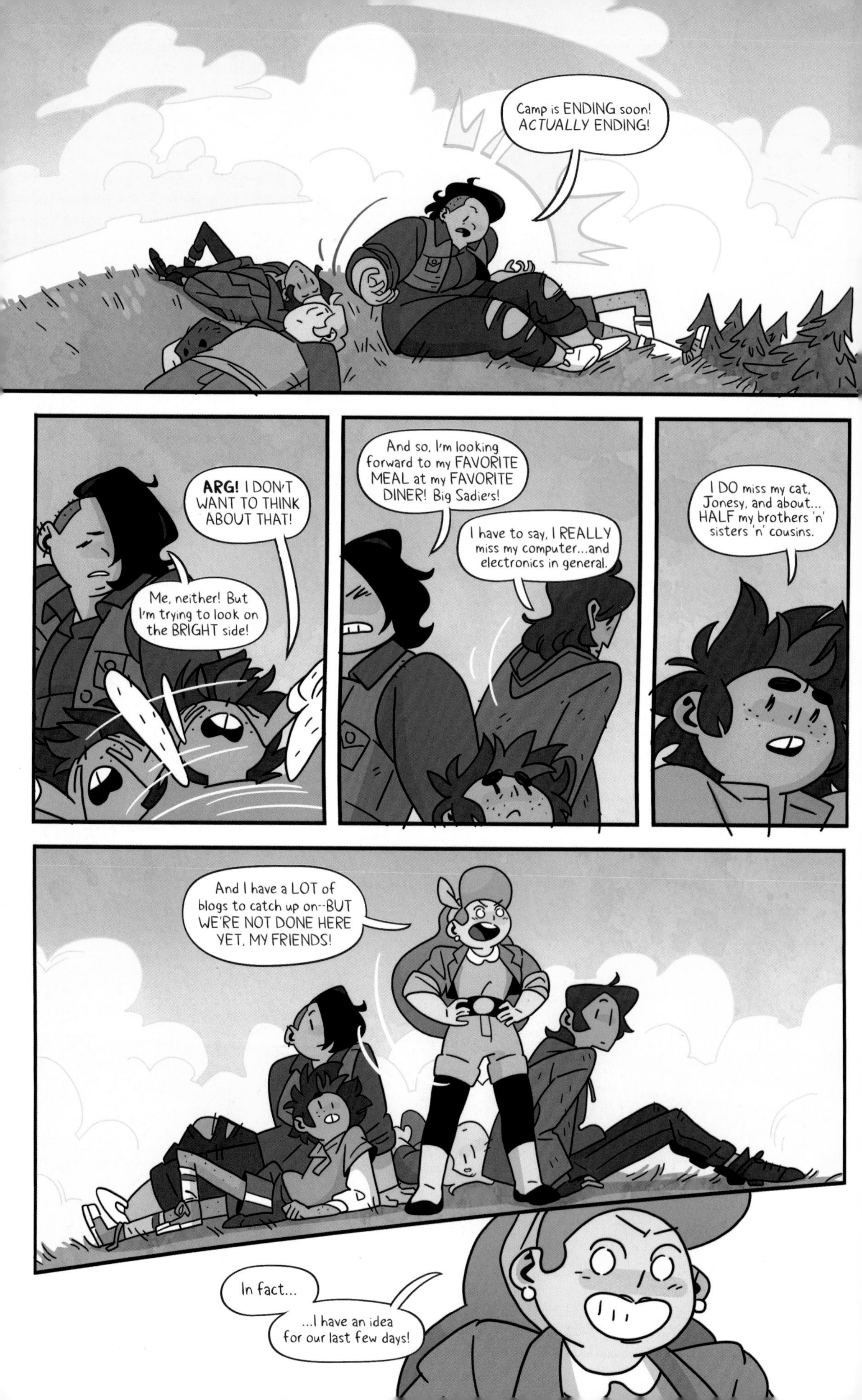

Camp is ENDING soon! ACTUALLY ENDING!
ARG! I DON'T WANT TO THINK ABOUT THAT!
Me, neither! But I'm trying to look on the BRIGHT side!
And so, I'm looking forward to my FAVORITE MEAL at my FAVORITE DINER! Big Sadie's!
I have to say, I REALLY miss my computer...and electronics in general.
I DO miss my cat, Jonesy, and about... HALF my brothers 'n' sisters 'n' cousins.
And I have a LOT of blogs to catch up on--BUT WE'RE NOT DONE HERE YET, MY FRIENDS!
In fact...
...I have an idea for our last few days!

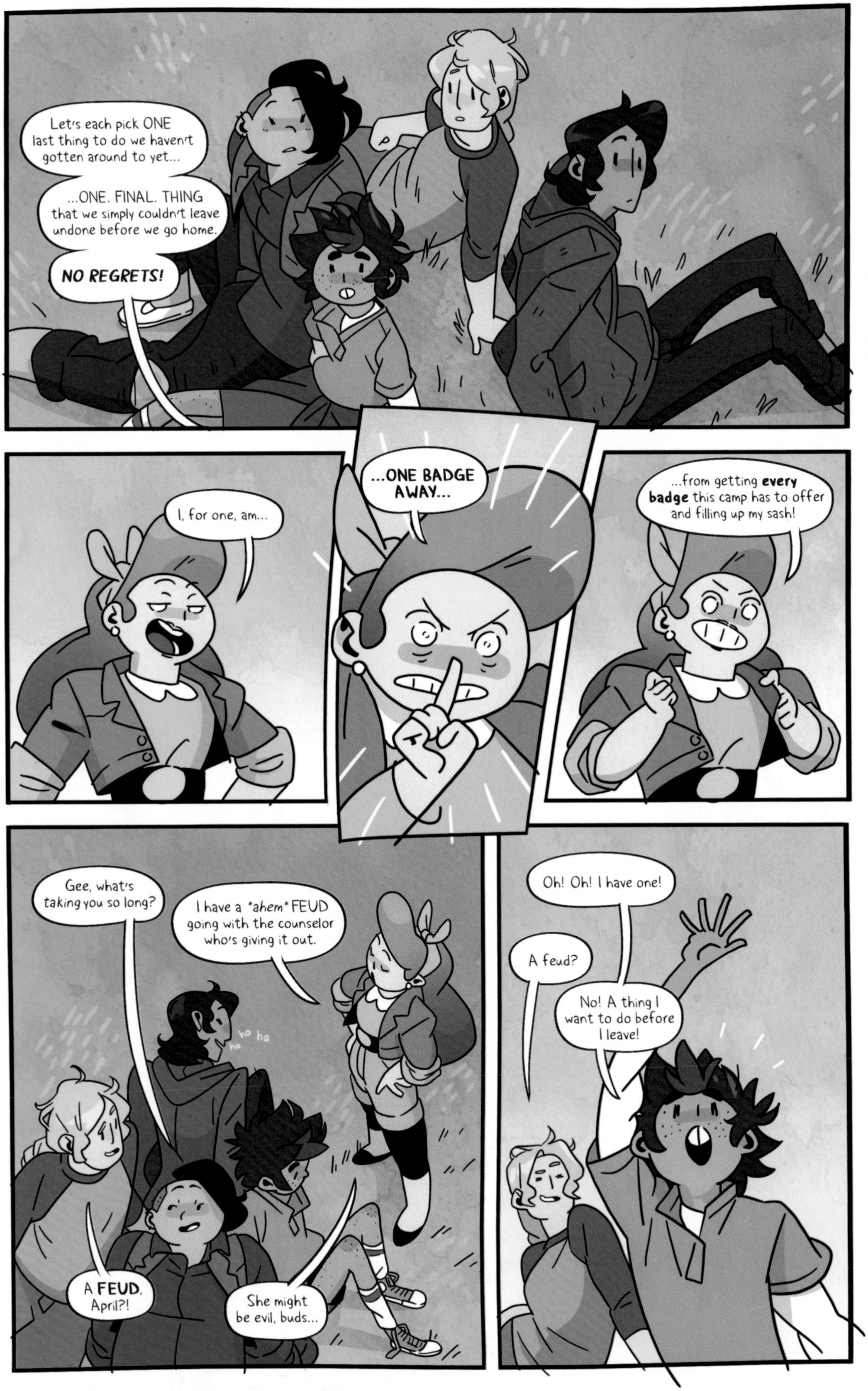
Let's each pick ONE last thing to do we haven't gotten around to yet...
...ONE. FINAL. THING that we simply couldn't leave undone before we go home.
NO REGRETS!
I, for one, am...
...ONE BADGE AWAY...
...from getting **every badge** this camp has to offer and filling up my sash!
Gee, what's taking you so long?
I have a *ahem* FEUD going with the counselor who's giving it out.
ha ho ha
A **FEUD**, April?!
She might be evil, buds...
Oh! Oh! I have one!
A feud?
No! A thing I want to do before I leave!

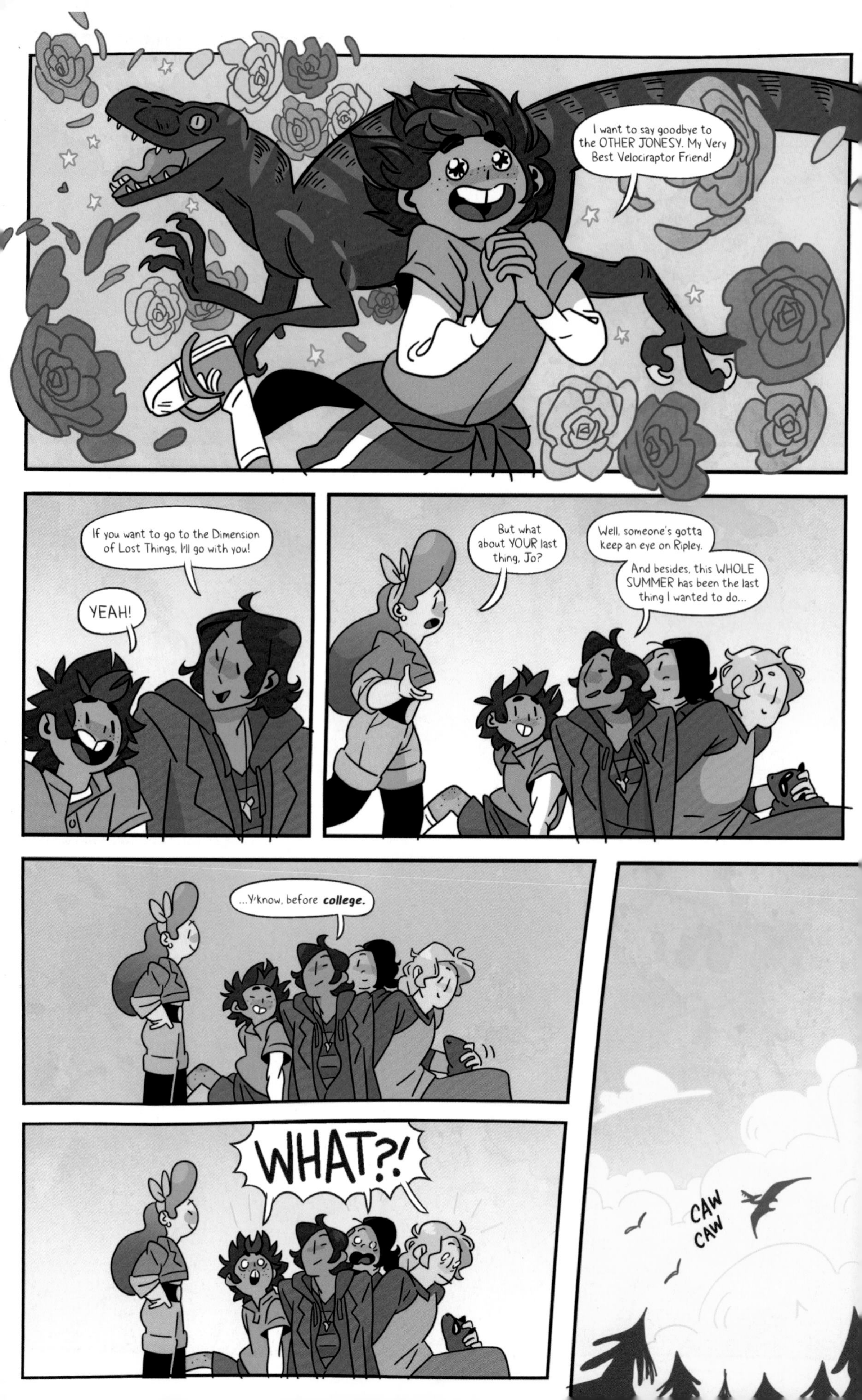
I want to say goodbye to the OTHER JONESY. My Very Best Velociraptor Friend!
If you want to go to the Dimension of Lost Things, I'll go with you!
YEAH!
But what about YOUR last thing, Jo?
Well, someone's gotta keep an eye on Ripley.
And besides, this WHOLE SUMMER has been the last thing I wanted to do...
...Y'know, before **college.**
WHAT?!
CAW CAW

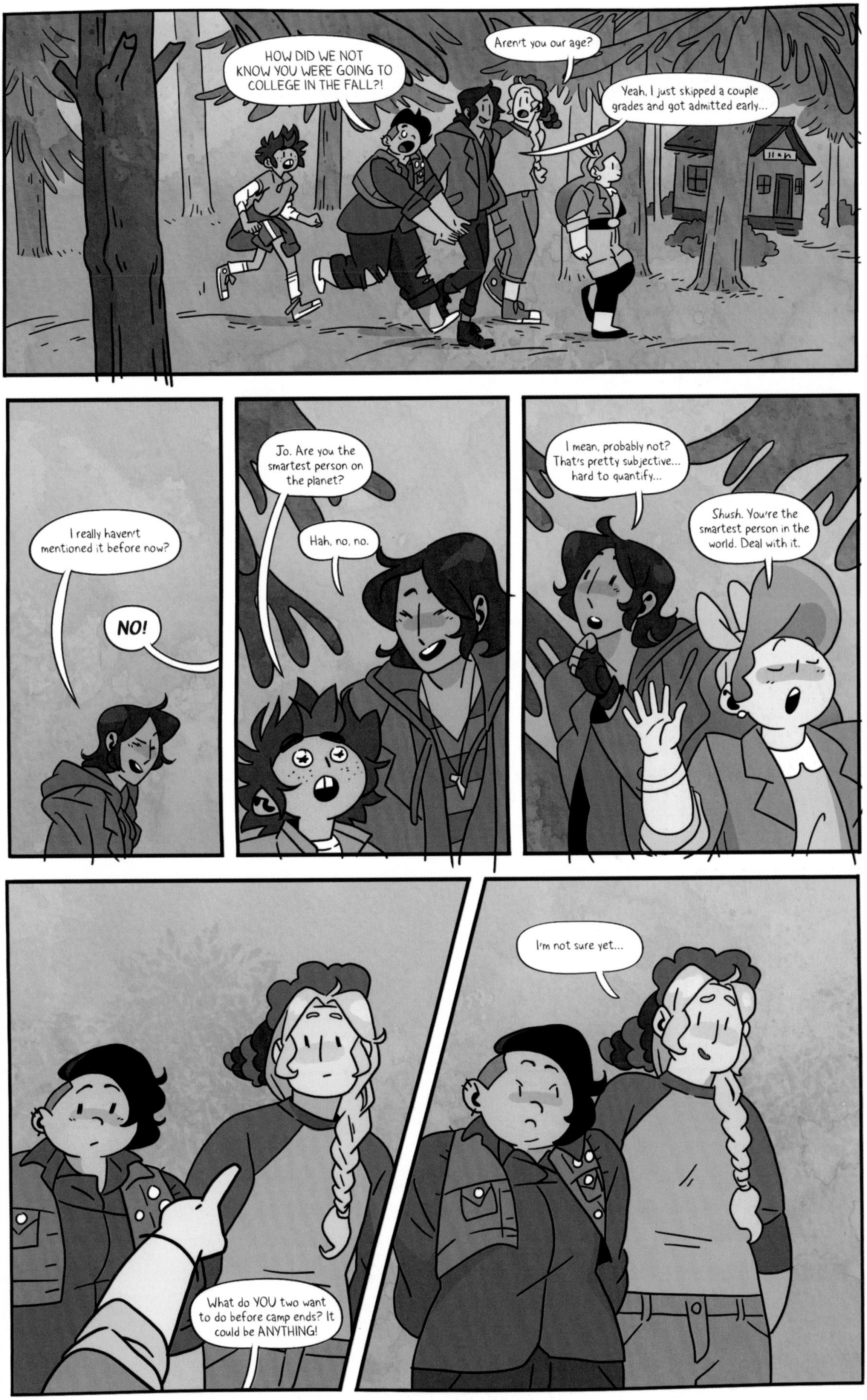
HOW DID WE NOT KNOW YOU WERE GOING TO COLLEGE IN THE FALL?!
Aren't you our age?
Yeah, I just skipped a couple grades and got admitted early...
I really haven't mentioned it before now?
NO!
Jo. Are you the smartest person on the planet?
Hah, no, no.
I mean, probably not? That's pretty subjective... hard to quantify...
Shush. You're the smartest person in the world. Deal with it.
What do YOU two want to do before camp ends? It could be ANYTHING!
I'm not sure yet...

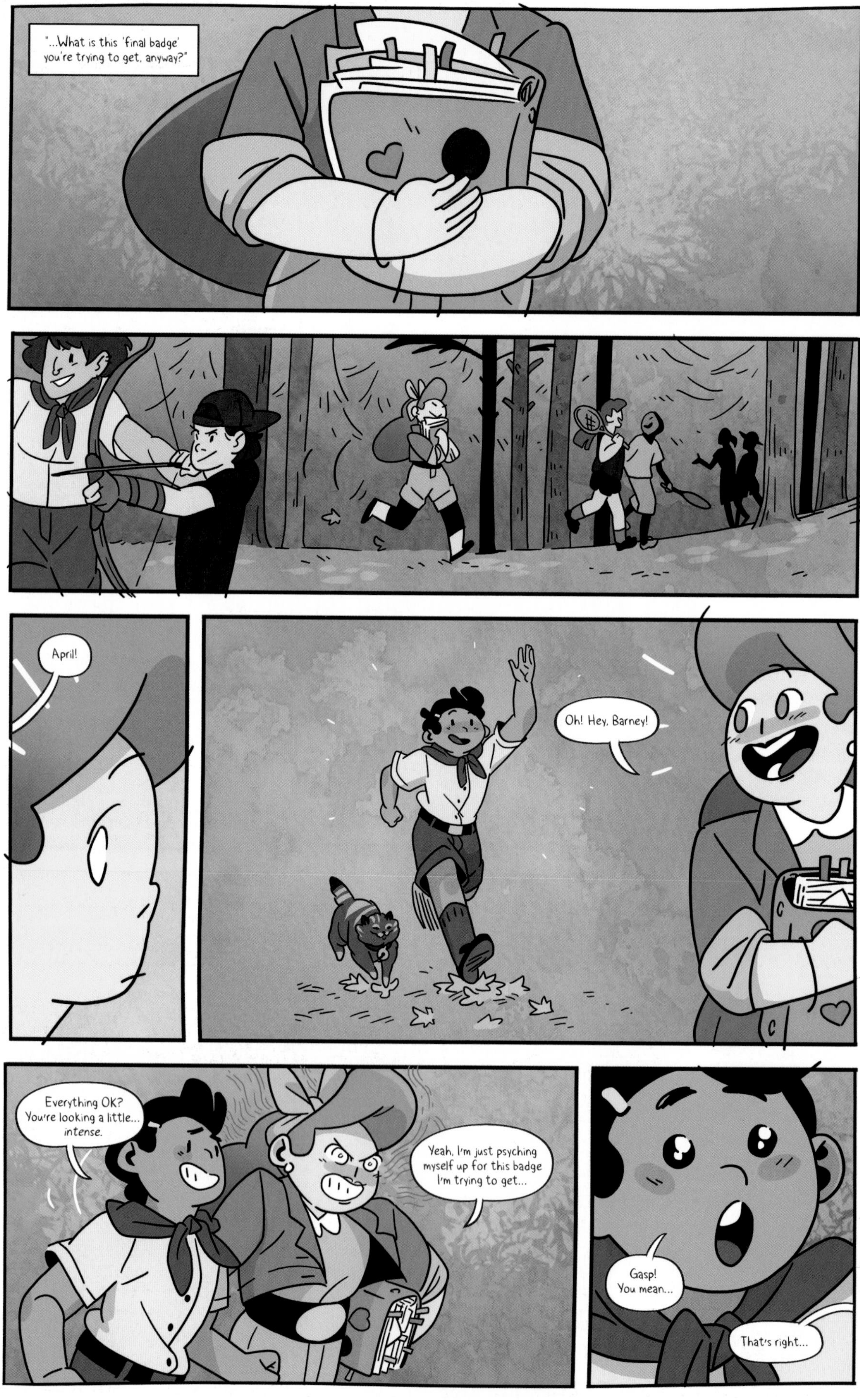
"...What is this 'final badge' you're trying to get, anyway?"
April!
Oh! Hey, Barney!
Everything OK? You're looking a little... *intense.*
Yeah, I'm just psyching myself up for this badge I'm trying to get...
Gasp! You mean...
That's right...

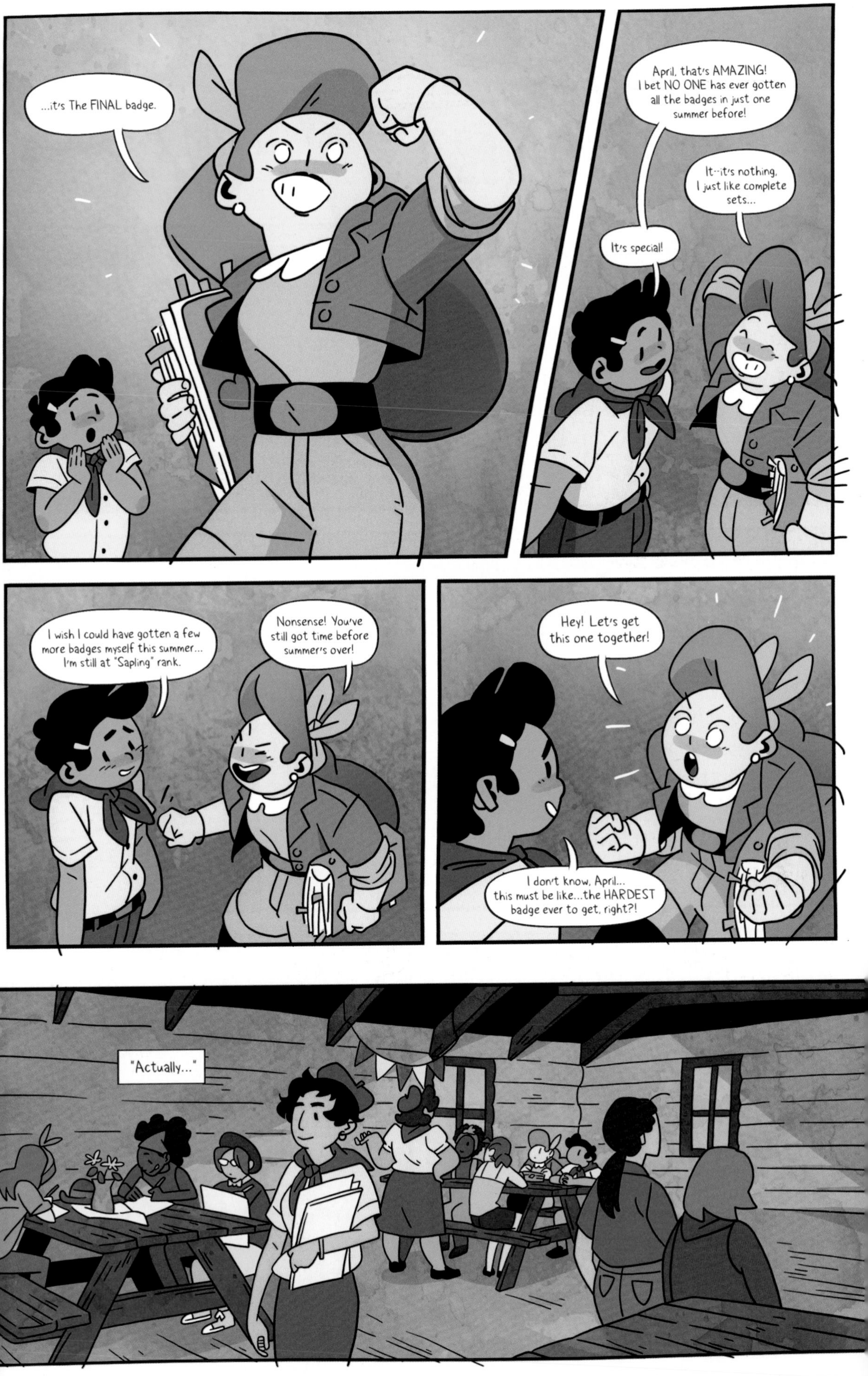
...it's The FINAL badge.
April, that's AMAZING! I bet NO ONE has ever gotten all the badges in just one summer before!
It's special!
It--it's nothing, I just like complete sets...
I wish I could have gotten a few more badges myself this summer... I'm still at "Sapling" rank.
Nonsense! You've still got time before summer's over!
Hey! Let's get this one together!
I don't know, April... this must be like...the HARDEST badge ever to get, right?!
"Actually..."

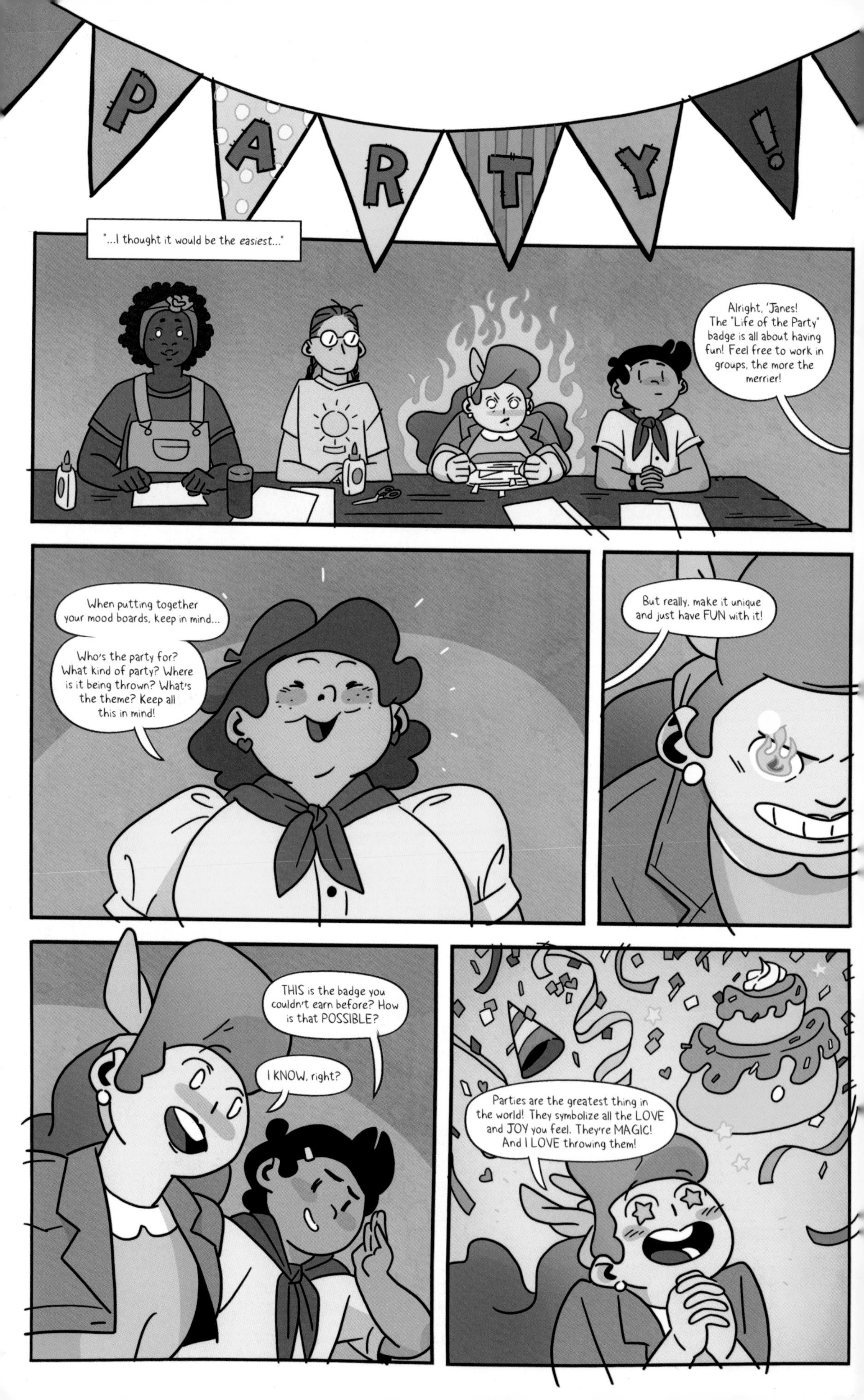
PARTY!
"...I thought it would be the *easiest*..."
Alright, 'Janes! The "Life of the Party" badge is all about having fun! Feel free to work in groups, the more the merrier!
When putting together your mood boards, keep in mind...
Who's the party for? What kind of party? Where is it being thrown? What's the theme? Keep all this in mind!
But really, make it unique and just have FUN with it!
THIS is the badge you couldn't earn before? How is that POSSIBLE?
I KNOW, right?
Parties are the greatest thing in the world! They symbolize all the LOVE and JOY you feel. They're MAGIC! And I LOVE throwing them!

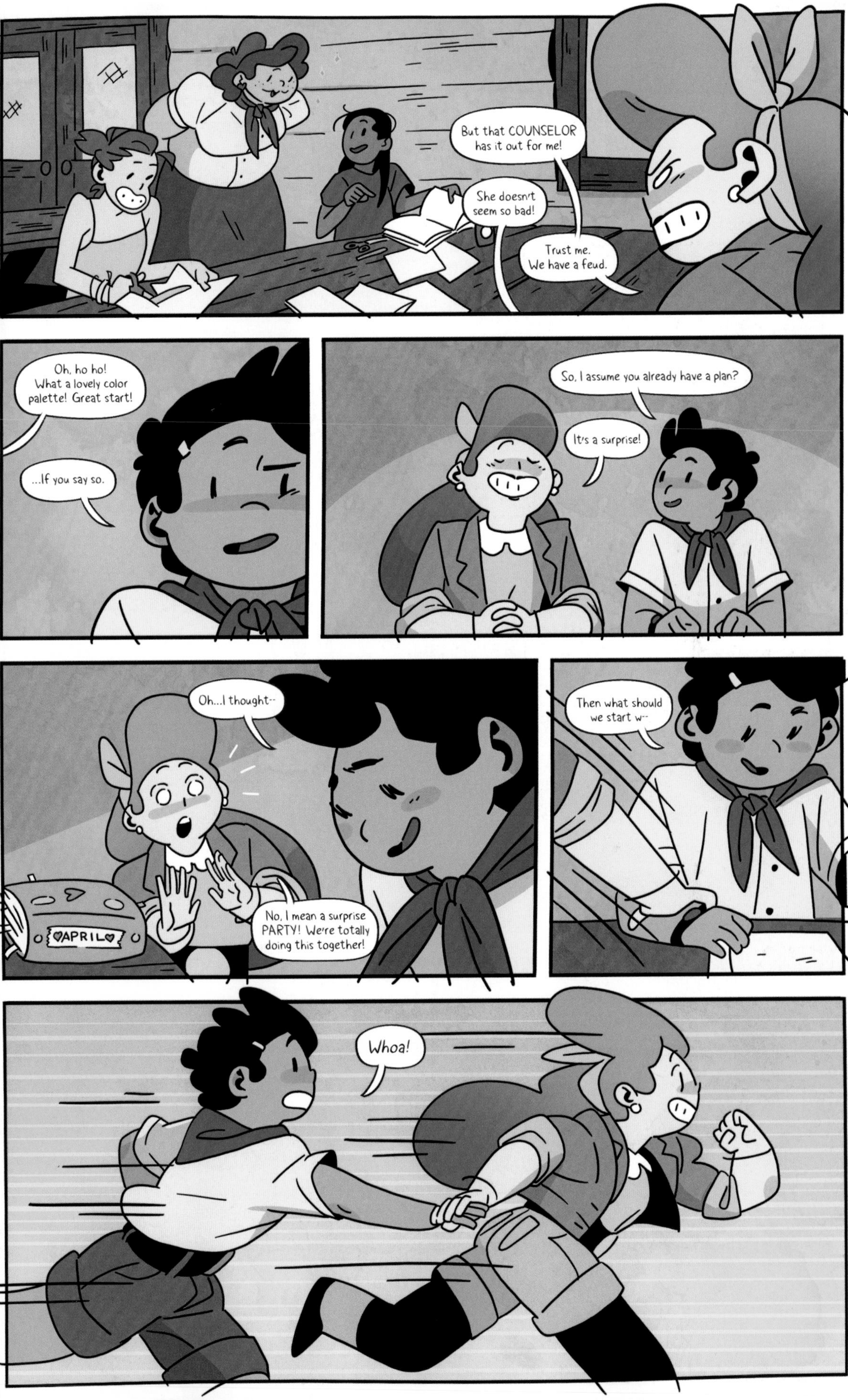
But that COUNSELOR has it out for me!
She doesn't seem so bad!
Trust me. We have a feud.
Oh, ho ho! What a lovely color palette! Great start!
...If you say so.
So, I assume you already have a plan?
It's a surprise!
Oh...I thought--
No, I mean a surprise PARTY! We're totally doing this together!
♥APRIL♥
Then what should we start w--
Whoa!

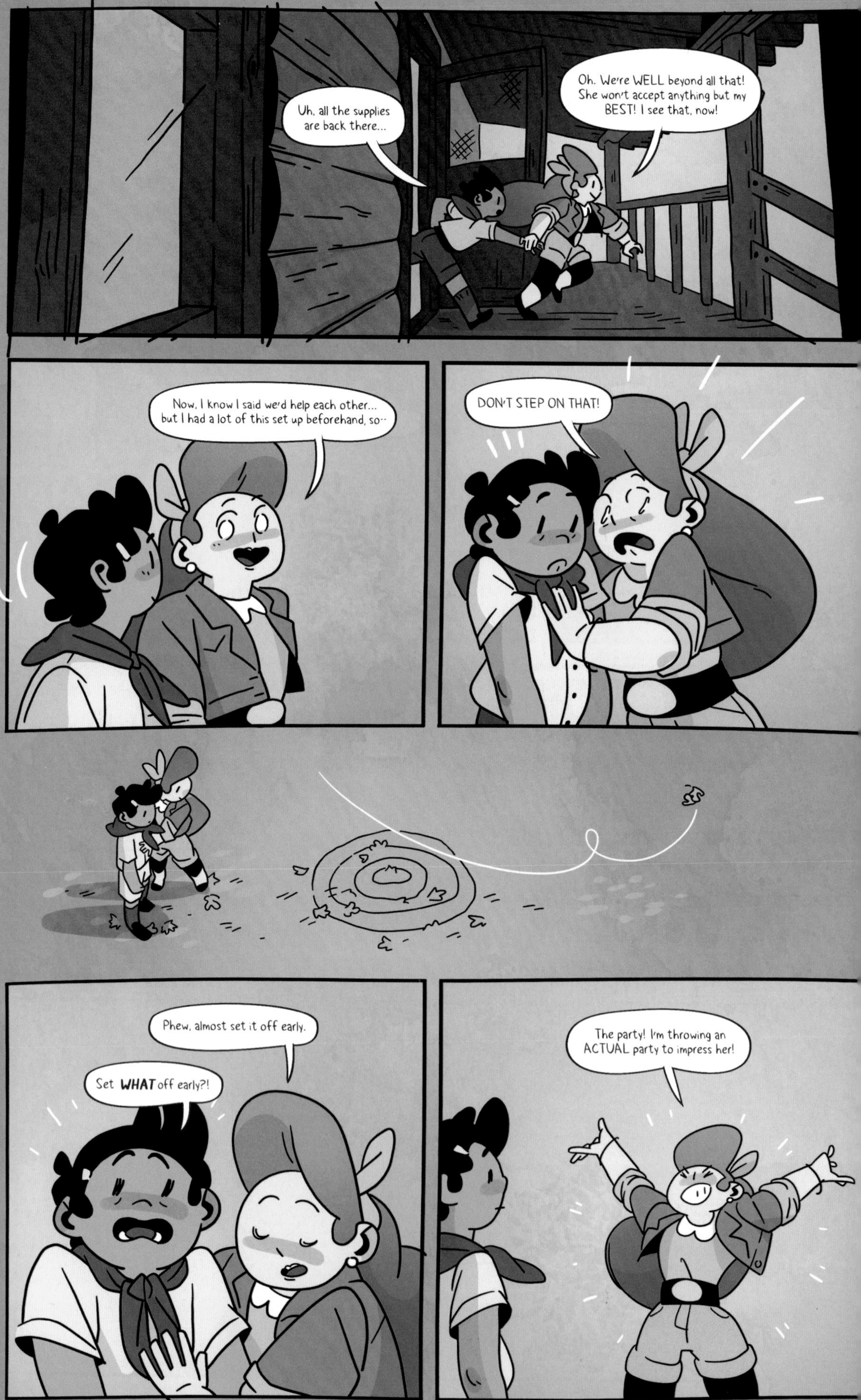
Uh, all the supplies are back there...
Oh. We're WELL beyond all that! She won't accept anything but my BEST! I see that, now!
Now, I know I said we'd help each other... but I had a lot of this set up beforehand, so--
DON'T STEP ON THAT!
Phew, almost set it off early.
Set **WHAT** off early?!
The party! I'm throwing an ACTUAL party to impress her!

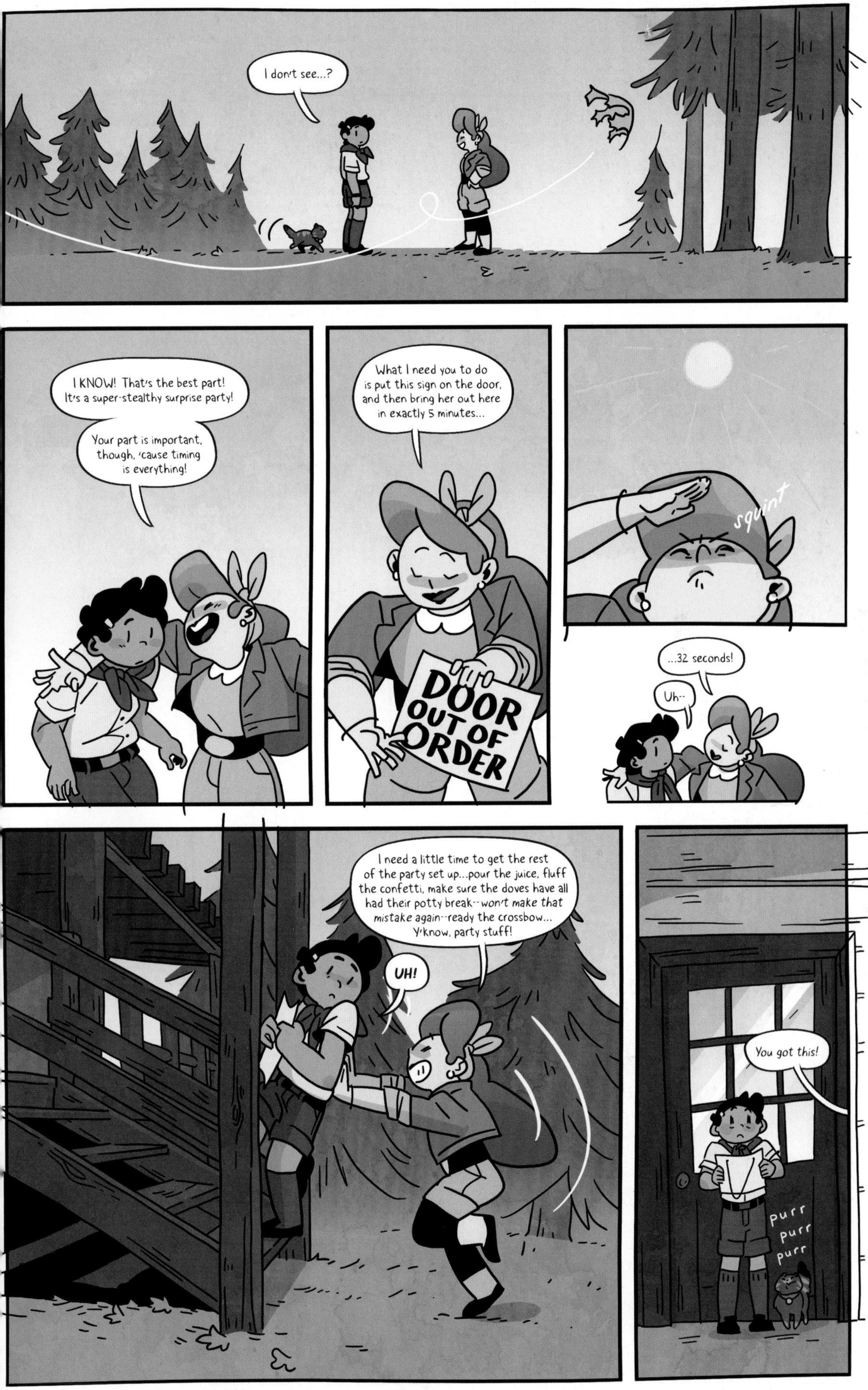
I don't see...?
I KNOW! That's the best part! It's a super-stealthy surprise party!
Your part is important, though, 'cause timing is everything!
What I need you to do is put this sign on the door, and then bring her out here in exactly 5 minutes...
DOOR OUT OF ORDER
squint
...32 seconds!
Uh--
I need a little time to get the rest of the party set up...pour the juice, fluff the confetti, make sure the doves have all had their potty break--won't make that mistake again--ready the crossbow... Y'know, party stuff!
UH!
You got this!
purr purr purr

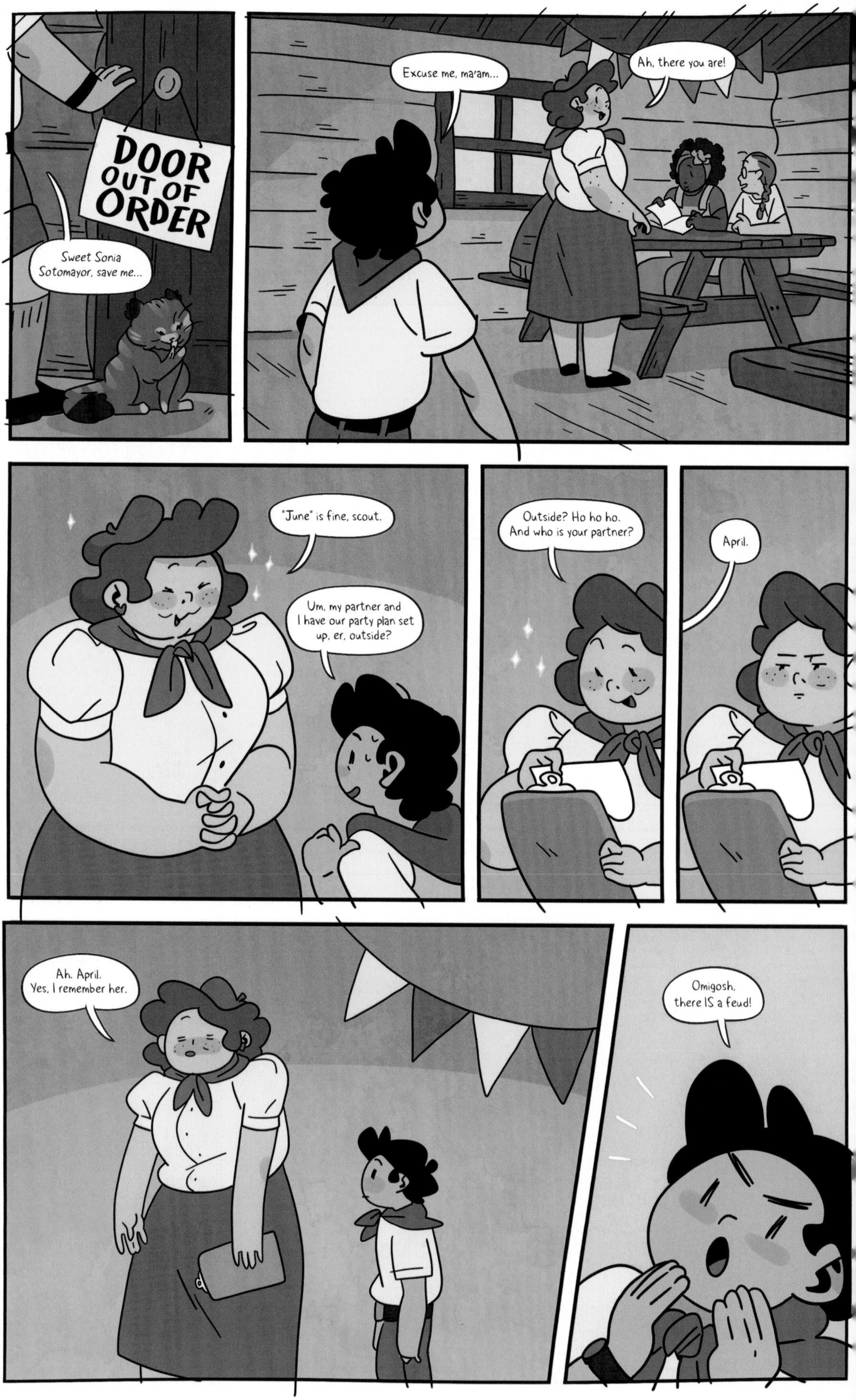
DOOR OUT OF ORDER
Sweet Sonia Sotomayor, save me...
Excuse me, ma'am...
Ah, there you are!
"June" is fine, scout.
Um, my partner and I have our party plan set up, er, outside?
Outside? Ho ho ho. And who is your partner?
April.
Ah. April. Yes, I remember her.
Omigosh, there IS a feud!

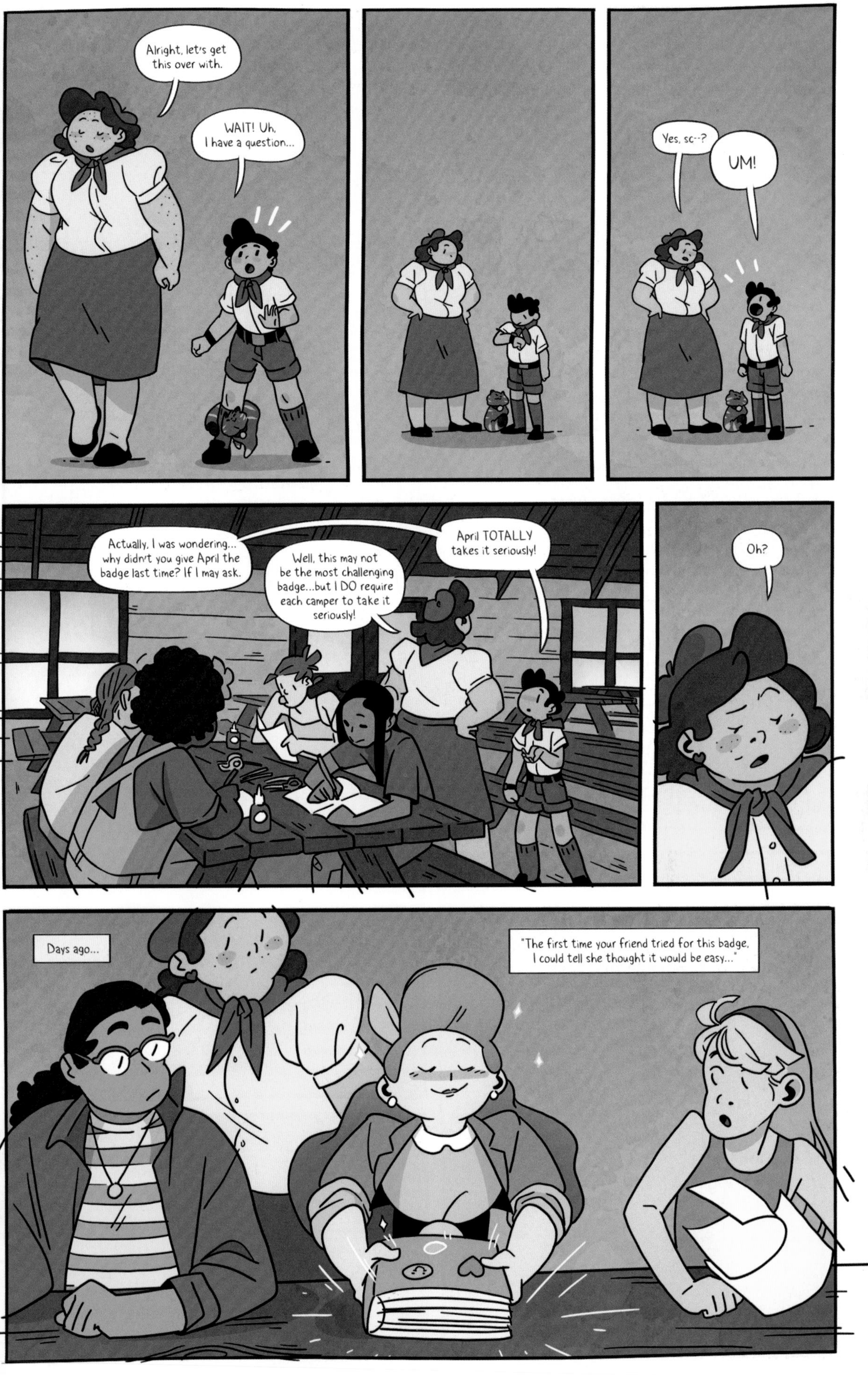
Alright, let's get this over with.
WAIT! Uh, I have a question...
Yes, sc--?
UM!
Actually, I was wondering... why didn't you give April the badge last time? If I may ask.
Well, this may not be the most challenging badge...but I DO require each camper to take it seriously!
April TOTALLY takes it seriously!
Oh?
Days ago...
"The first time your friend tried for this badge, I could tell she thought it would be easy..."

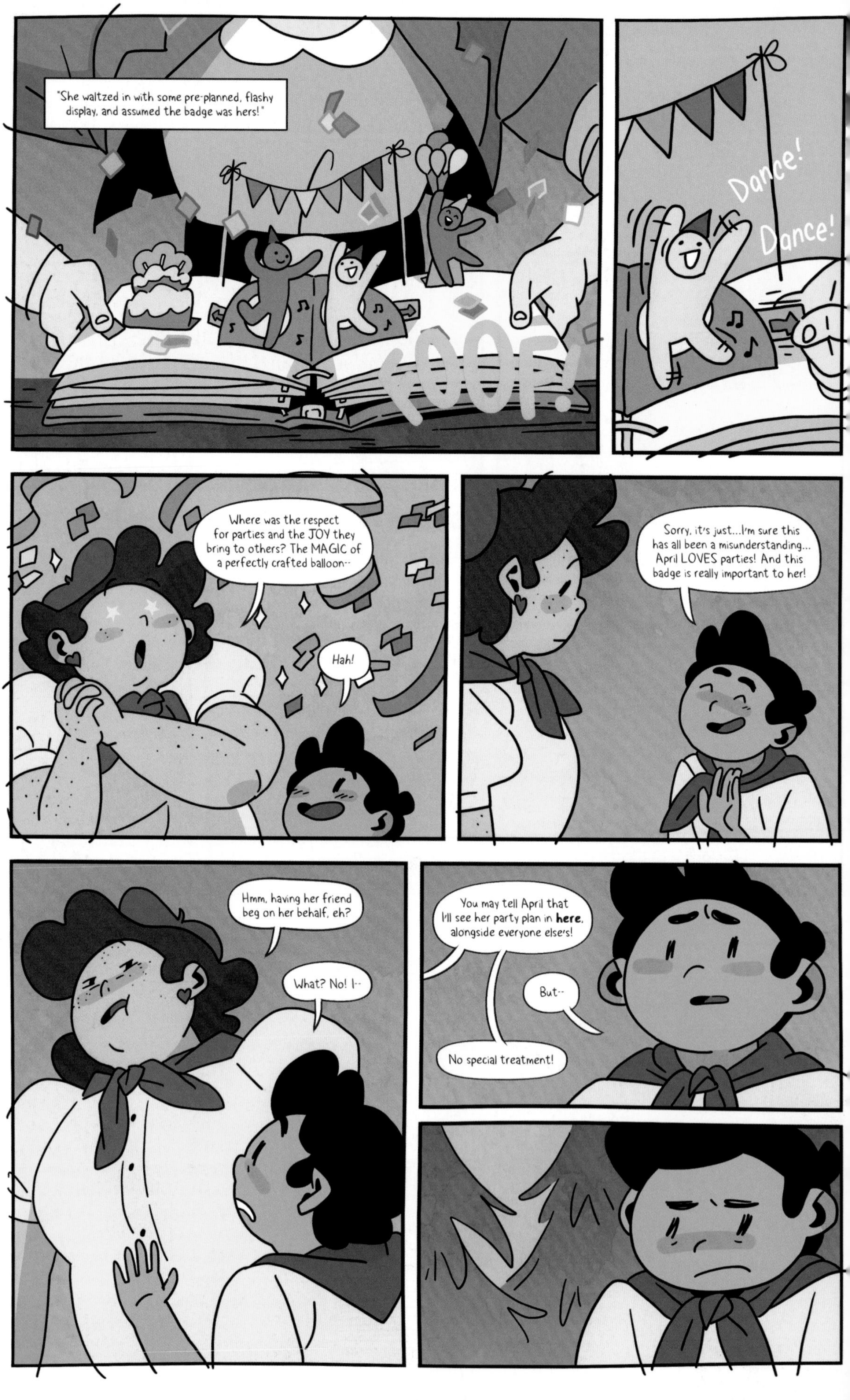
"She waltzed in with some pre-planned, flashy display, and assumed the badge was hers!"
FOOF!
Dance!
Dance!
Where was the respect for parties and the JOY they bring to others? The MAGIC of a perfectly crafted balloon--
Hah!
Sorry, it's just...I'm sure this has all been a misunderstanding... April LOVES parties! And this badge is really important to her!
Hmm, having her friend beg on her behalf, eh?
What? No! I--
You may tell April that I'll see her party plan in **here**, alongside everyone else's!
But--
No special treatment!

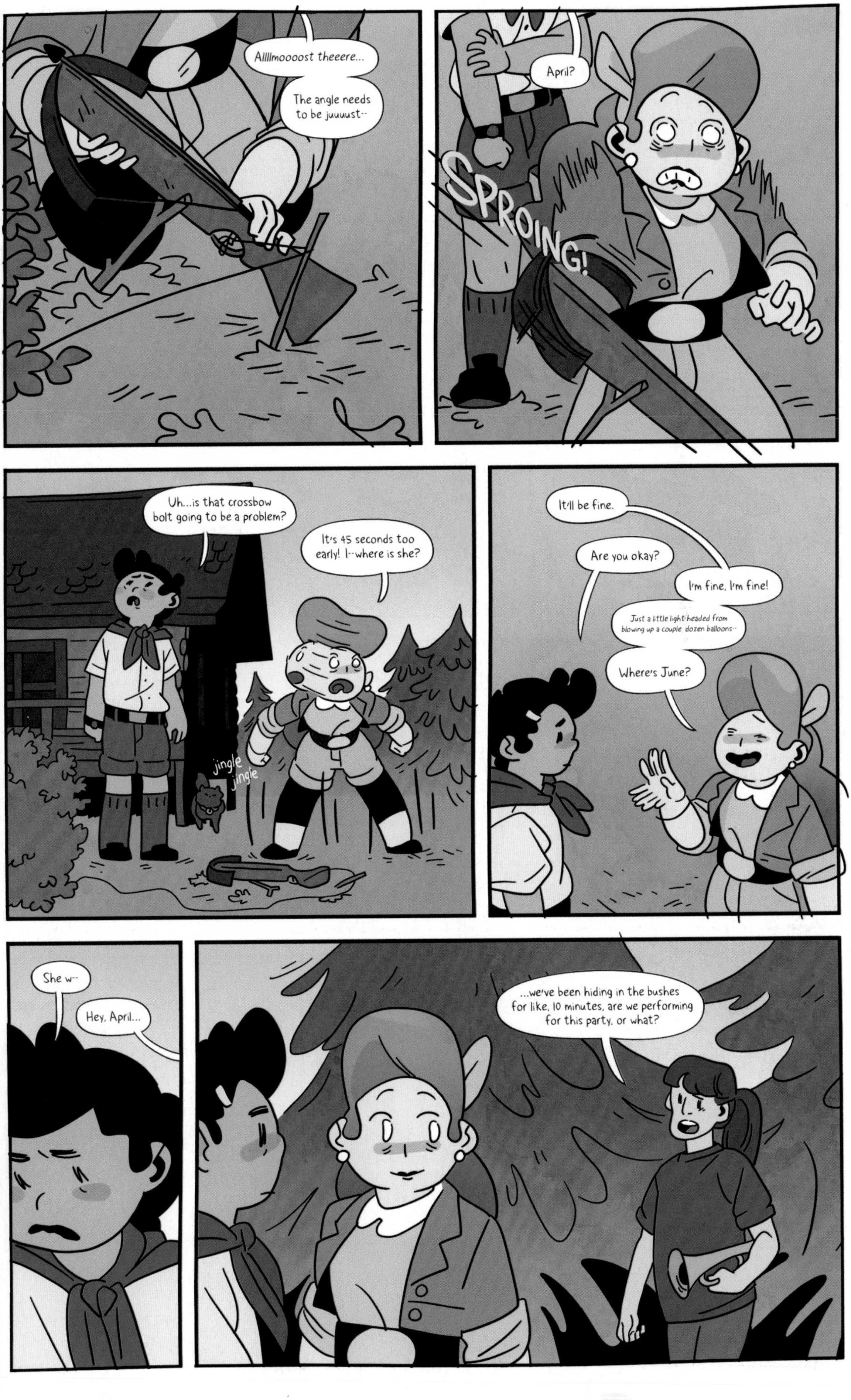
Allllmoooost theeere...
The angle needs to be juuuust--
April?
SPROING!
Uh...is that crossbow bolt going to be a problem?
It's 45 seconds too early! I--where is she?
jingle jingle
It'll be fine.
Are you okay?
I'm fine, I'm fine!
Just a little light-headed from blowing up a couple dozen balloons--
Where's June?
She w--
Hey, April...
...we've been hiding in the bushes for like, 10 minutes, are we performing for this party, or what?

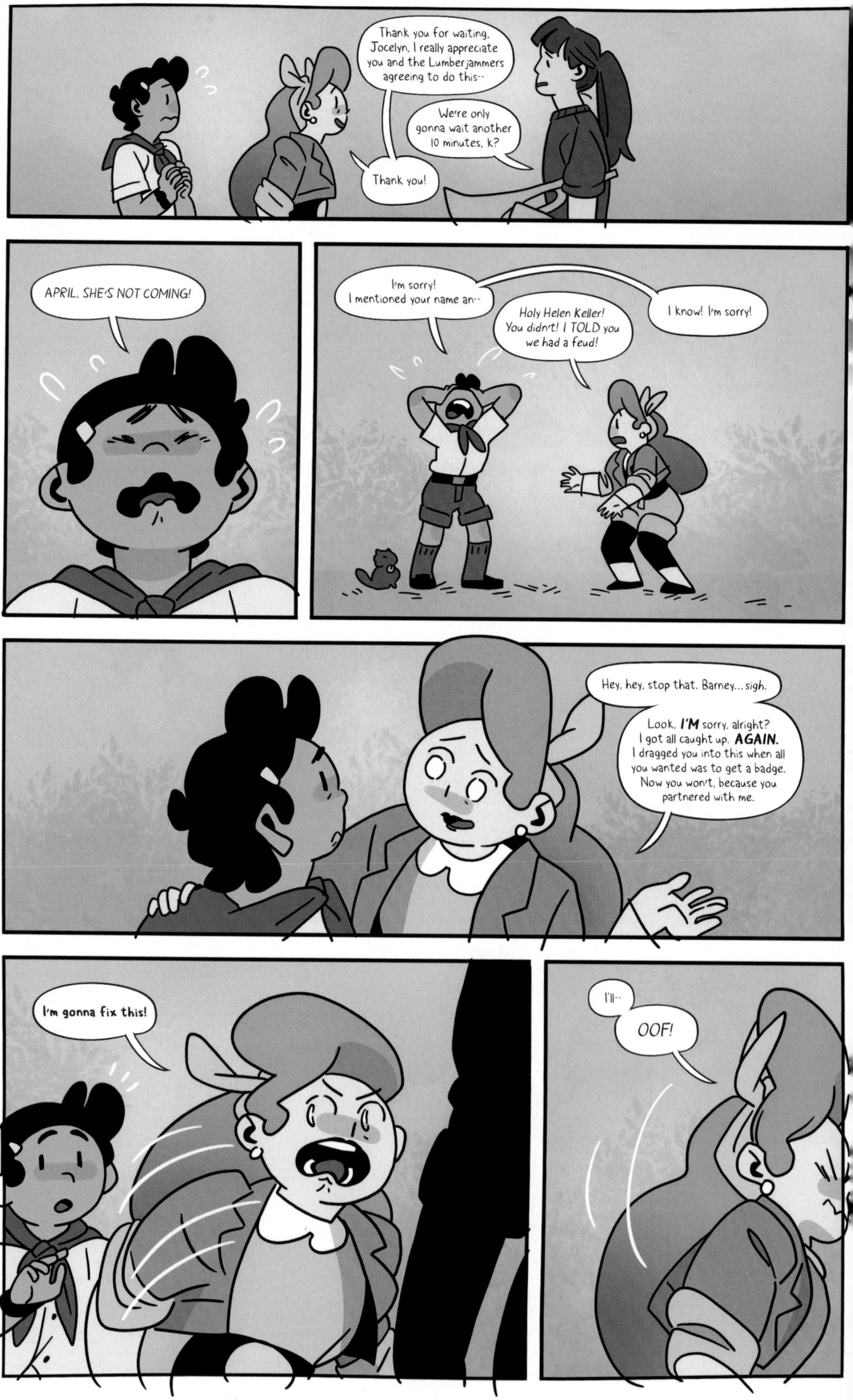
Thank you for waiting, Jocelyn, I really appreciate you and the Lumberjammers agreeing to do this--
We're only gonna wait another 10 minutes, k?
Thank you!
APRIL, SHE'S NOT COMING!
I'm sorry! I mentioned your name an--
Holy Helen Keller! You didn't! I TOLD you we had a feud!
I know! I'm sorry!
Hey, hey, stop that. Barney... sigh.
Look, I'M sorry, alright? I got all caught up. AGAIN. I dragged you into this when all you wanted was to get a badge. Now you won't, because you partnered with me.
I'm gonna fix this!
I'll--
OOF!

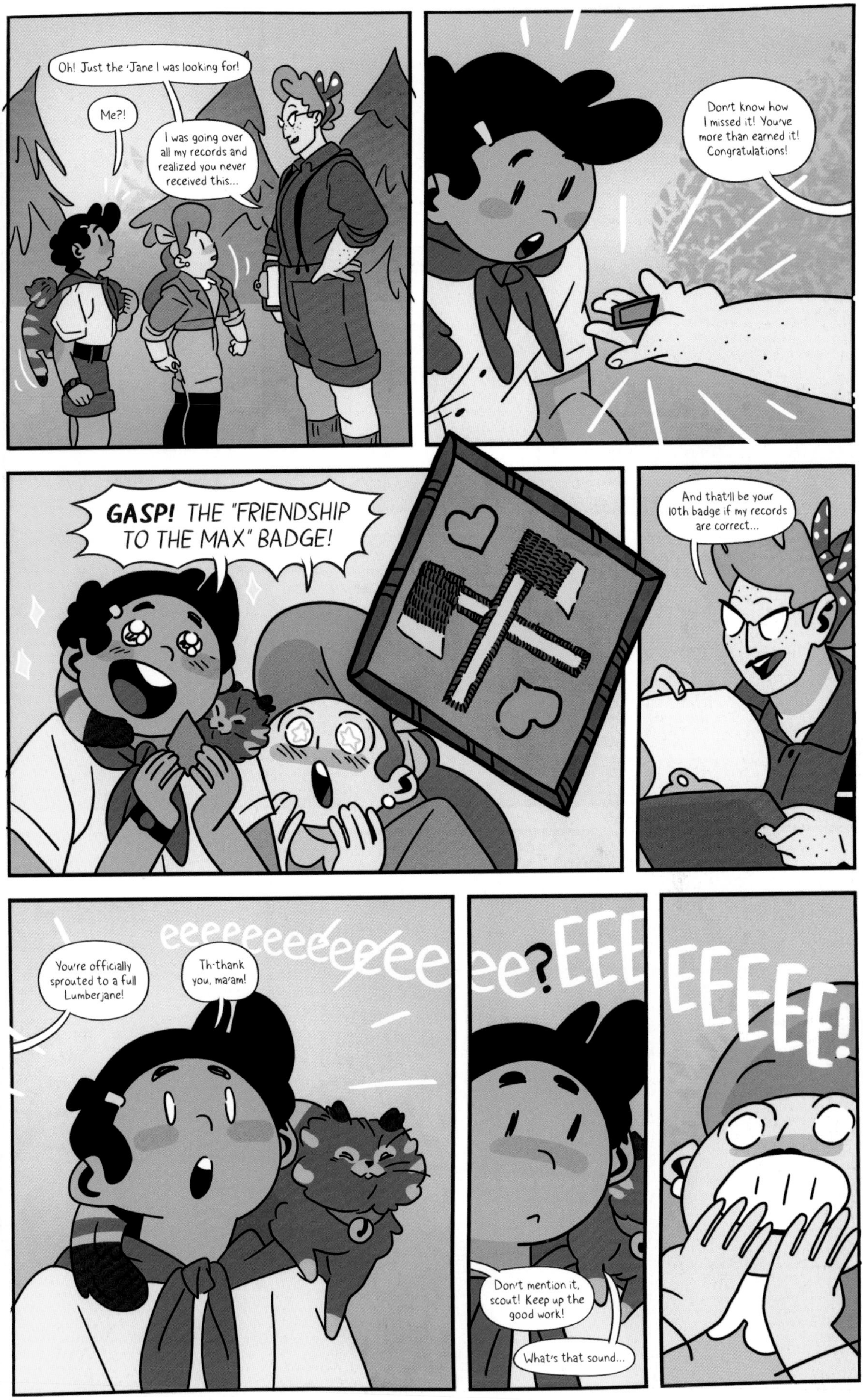
Oh! Just the 'Jane I was looking for!
Me?!
I was going over all my records and realized you never received this...
Don't know how I missed it! You've more than earned it! Congratulations!
GASP! THE "FRIENDSHIP TO THE MAX" BADGE!
And that'll be your 10th badge if my records are correct...
You're officially sprouted to a full Lumberjane!
Th-thank you, ma'am!
eeeeeeeeeeee
ee?EEE
EEEEEE!
Don't mention it, scout! Keep up the good work!
What's that sound...

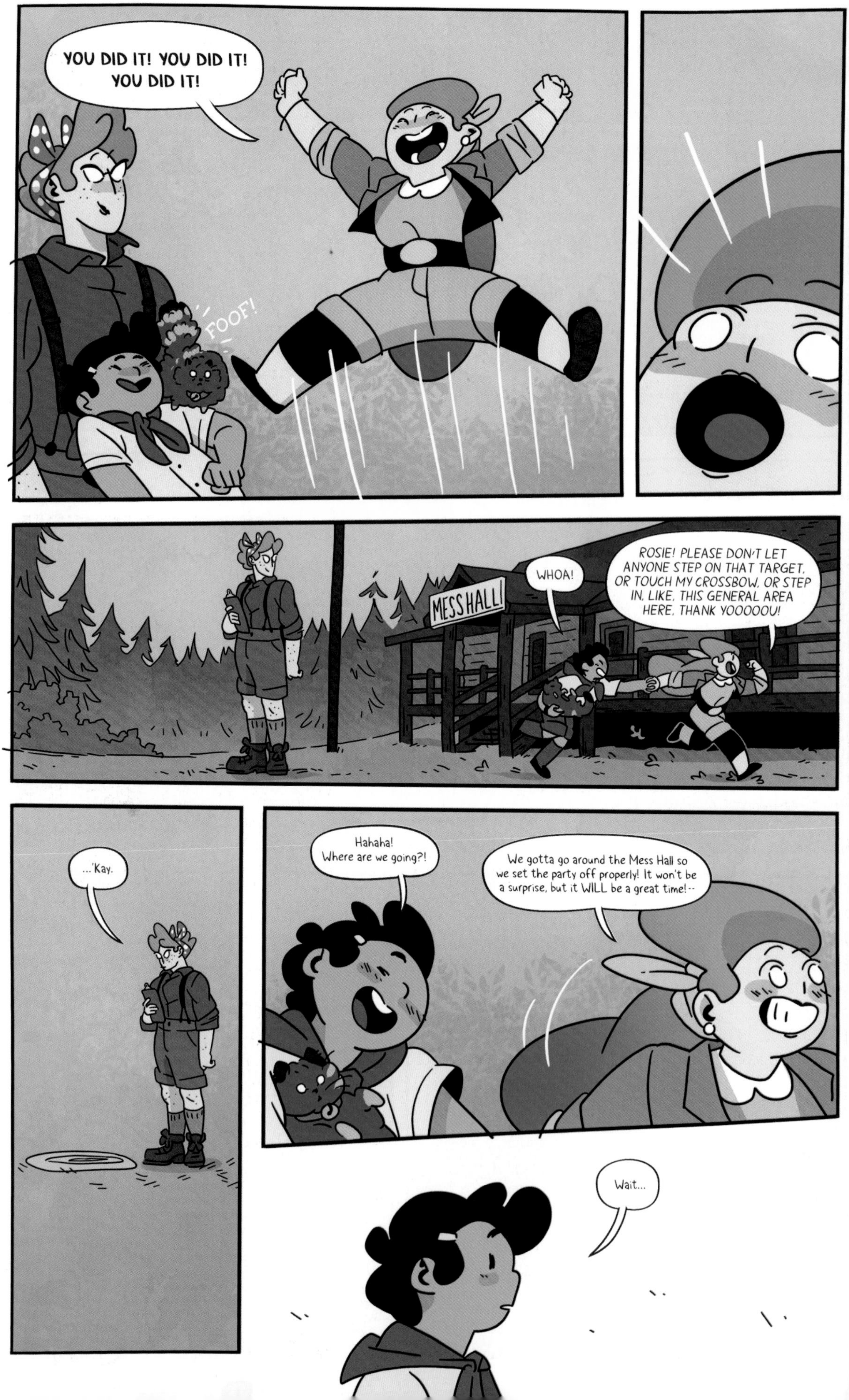
YOU DID IT! YOU DID IT! YOU DID IT!
FOOF!
MESS HALL!
WHOA!
ROSIE! PLEASE DON'T LET ANYONE STEP ON THAT TARGET, OR TOUCH MY CROSSBOW, OR STEP IN, LIKE, THIS GENERAL AREA HERE, THANK YOOOOOU!
...'Kay.
Hahaha! Where are we going?!
We gotta go around the Mess Hall so we set the party off properly! It won't be a surprise, but it WILL be a great time!--
Wait...

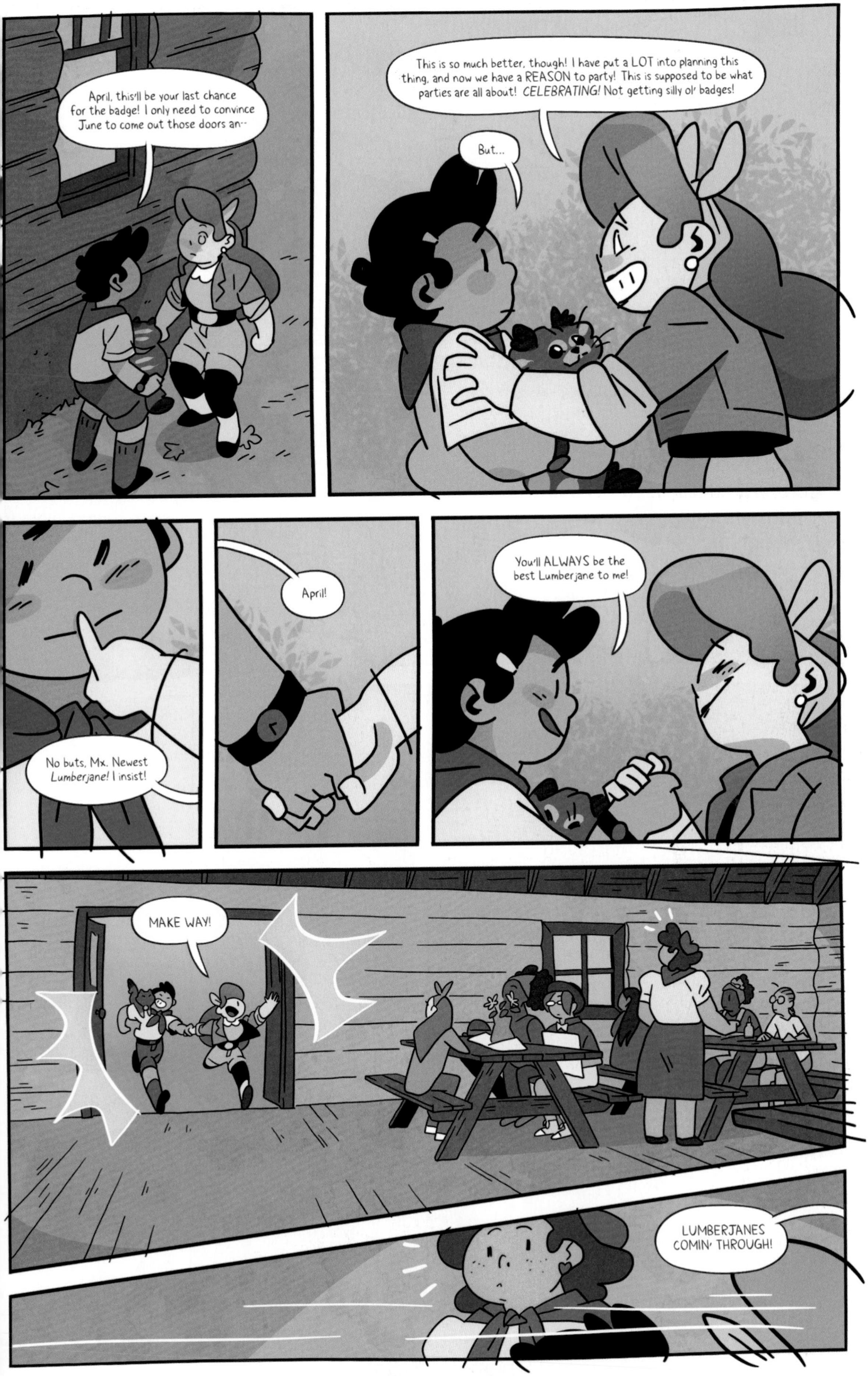
April, this'll be your last chance for the badge! I only need to convince June to come out those doors an--
This is so much better, though! I have put a LOT into planning this thing, and now we have a REASON to party! This is supposed to be what parties are all about! CELEBRATING! Not getting silly ol' badges!
But...
No buts, Mx. Newest Lumberjane! I insist!
April!
You'll ALWAYS be the best Lumberjane to me!
MAKE WAY!
LUMBERJANES COMIN' THROUGH!

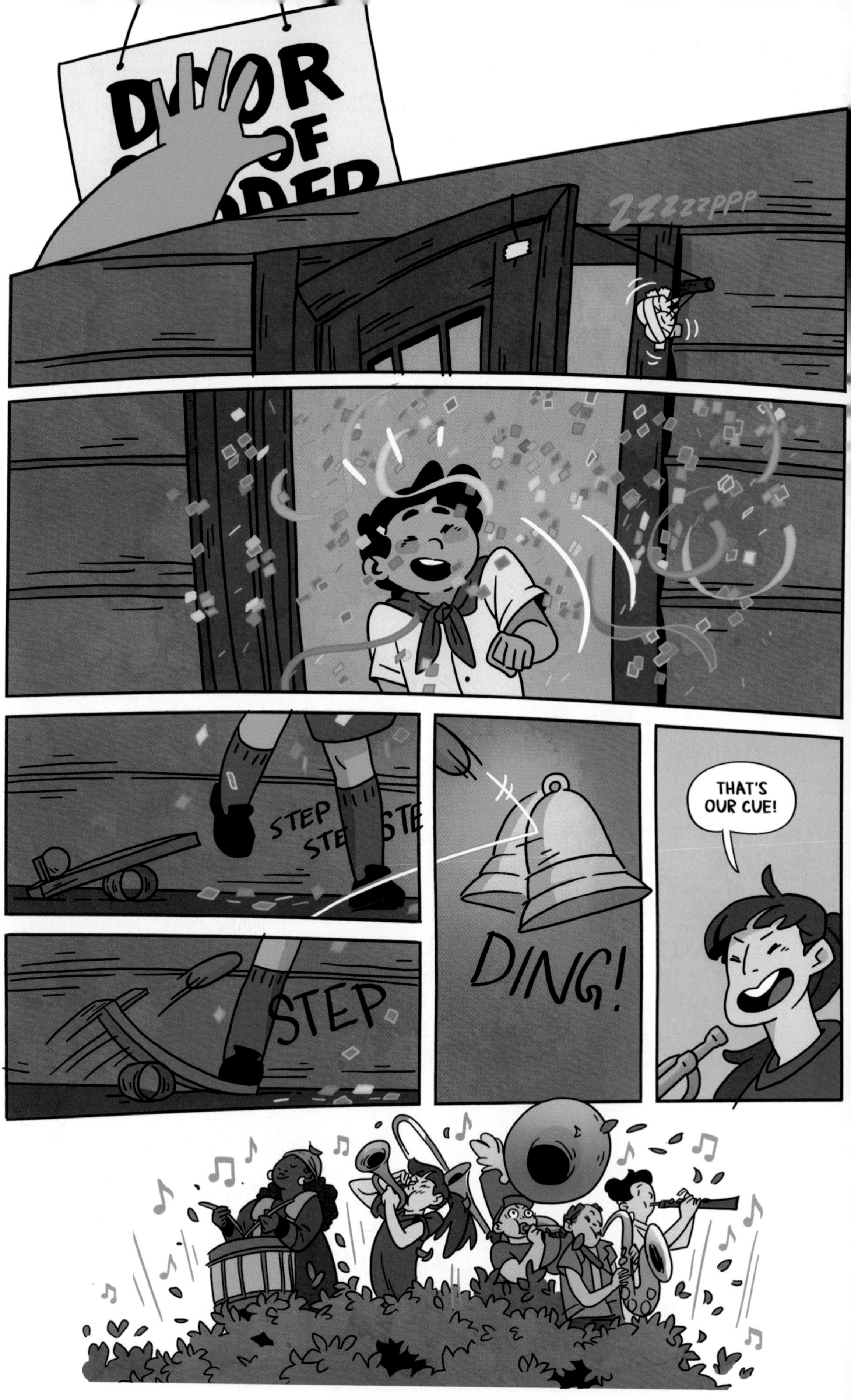
ZZZzzppp
STEP
STEP
STE
STEP
DING!
THAT'S OUR CUE!

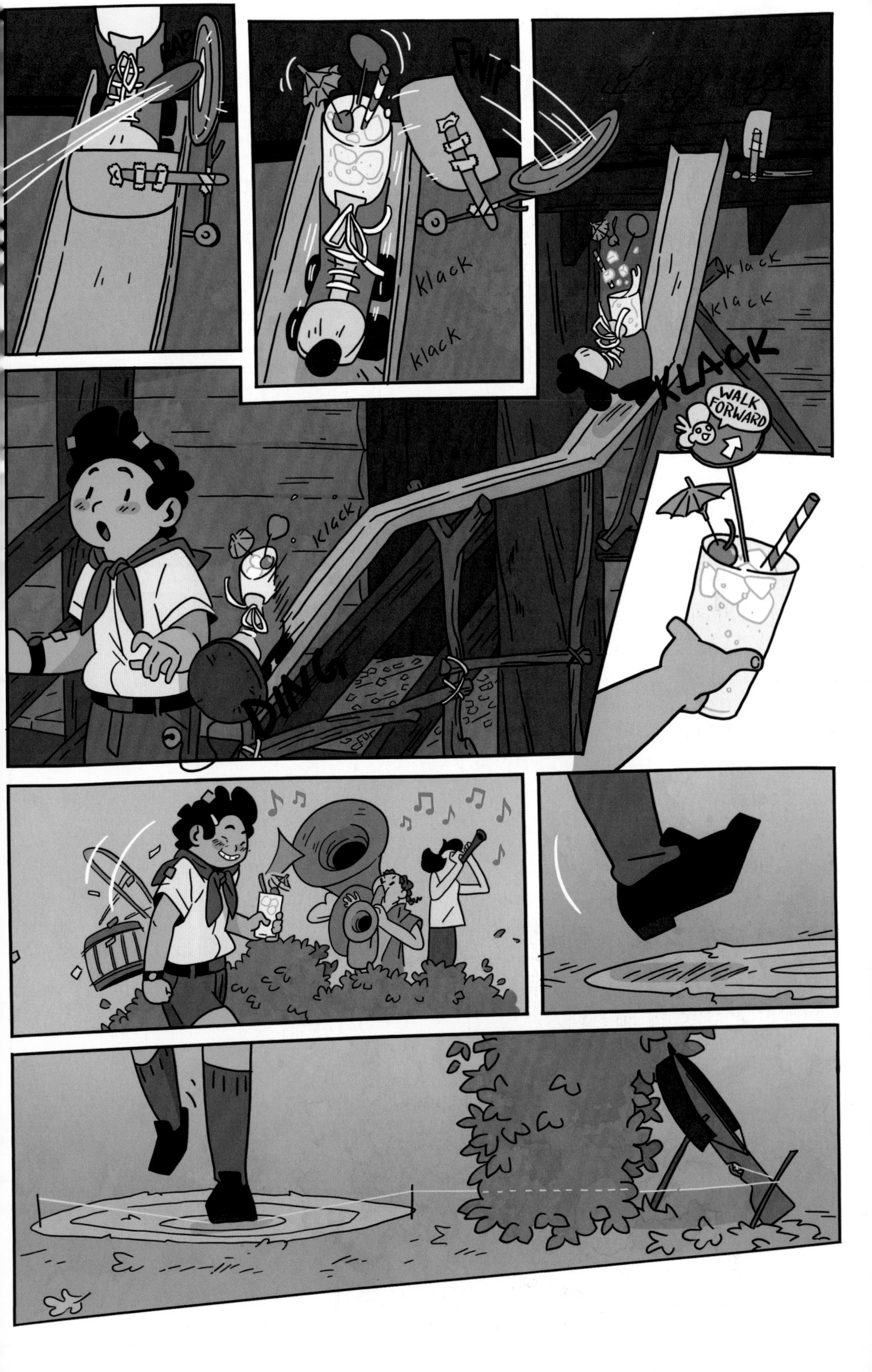

FWIP
klack
klack
klack
klack
KLACK
WALK FORWARD
klack
DING

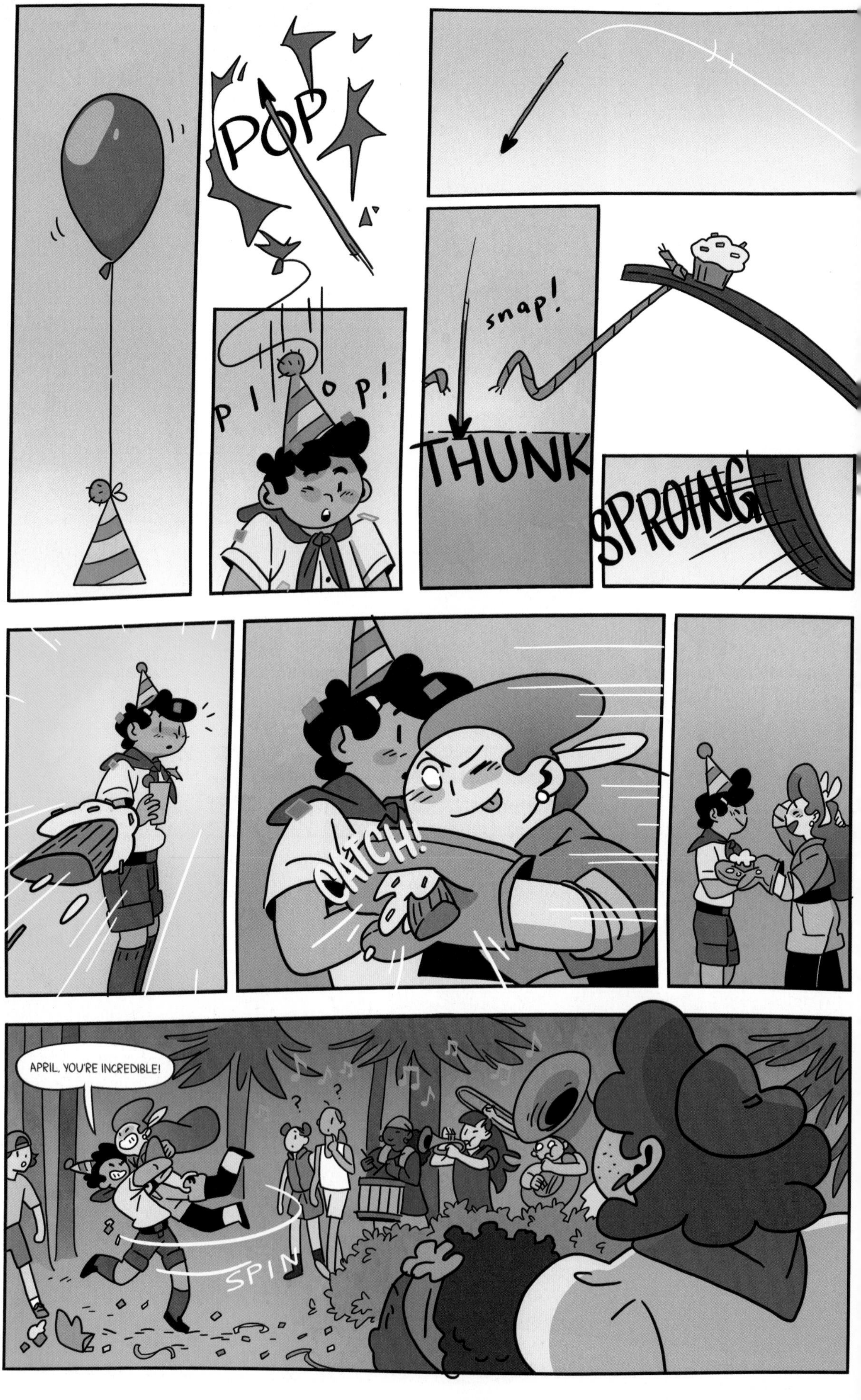
POP
P I O P!
snap!
THUNK
SPROING
CATCH!
APRIL, YOU'RE INCREDIBLE!
SPIN

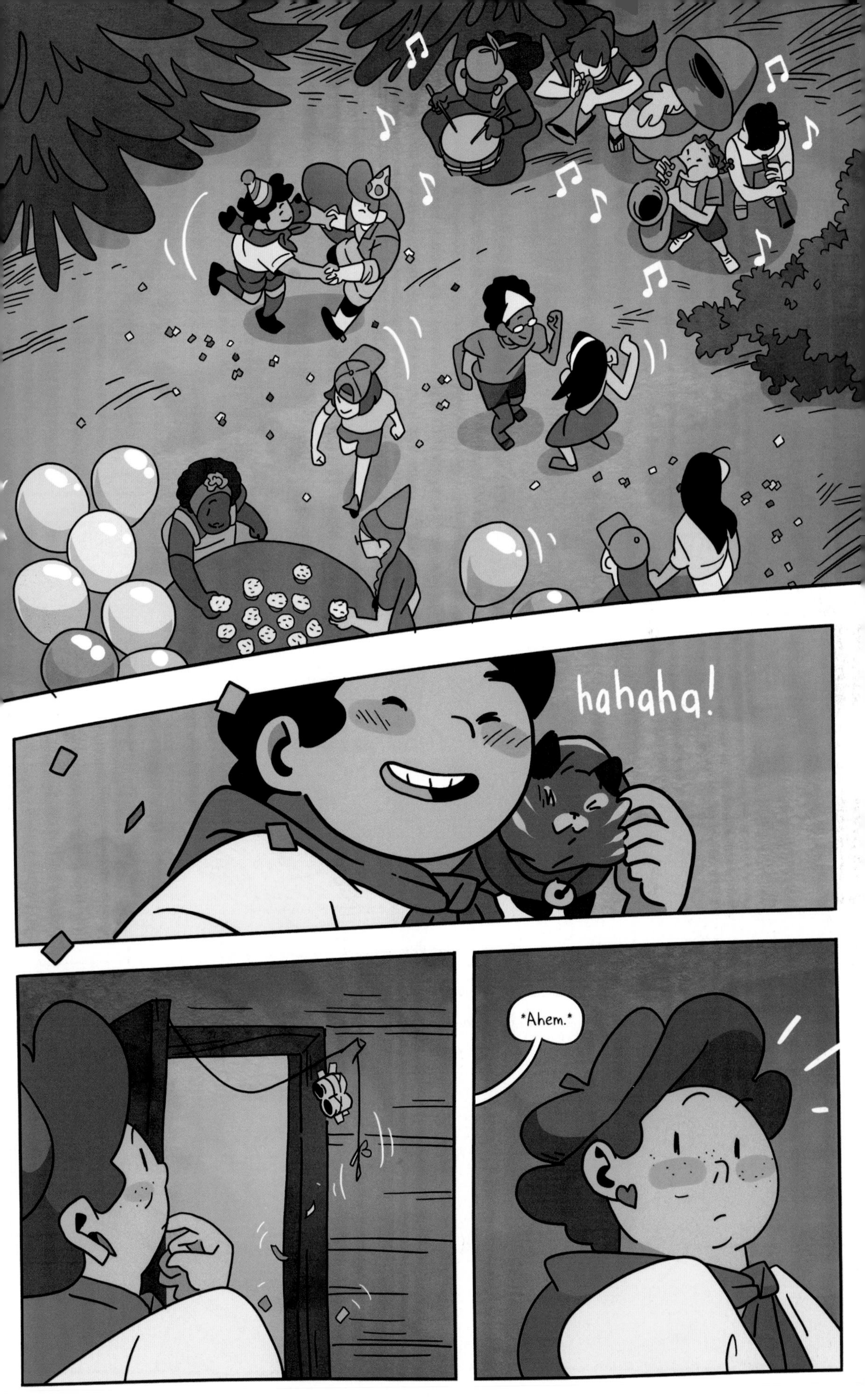
hahaha!
Ahem.

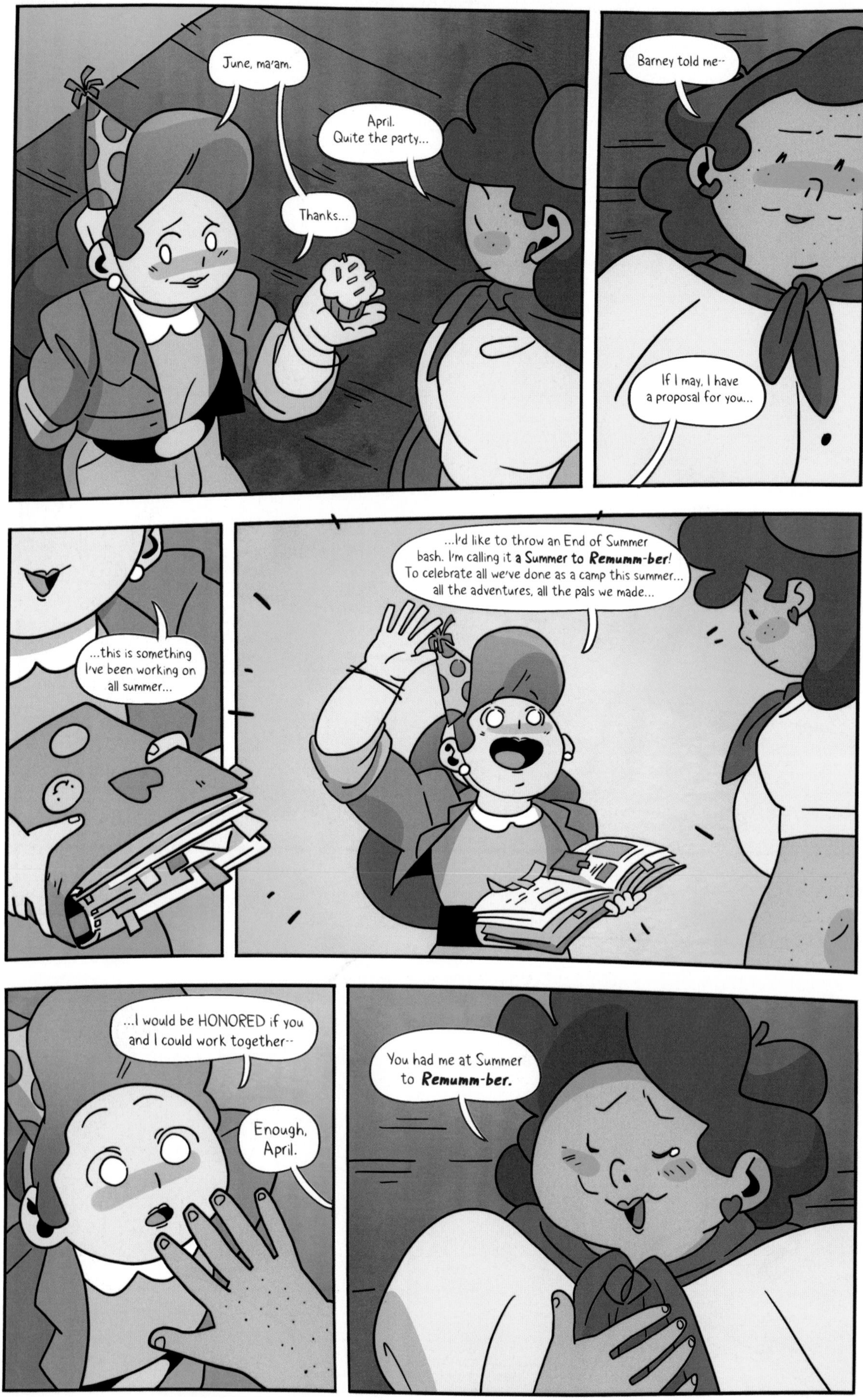
June, ma'am.
April.
Quite the party...
Thanks...
Barney told me--
If I may, I have a proposal for you...
...this is something I've been working on all summer...
...I'd like to throw an End of Summer bash. I'm calling it **a Summer to *Remumm-ber*!** To celebrate all we've done as a camp this summer... all the adventures, all the pals we made...
...I would be HONORED if you and I could work together--
Enough, April.
You had me at Summer to ***Remumm-ber.***

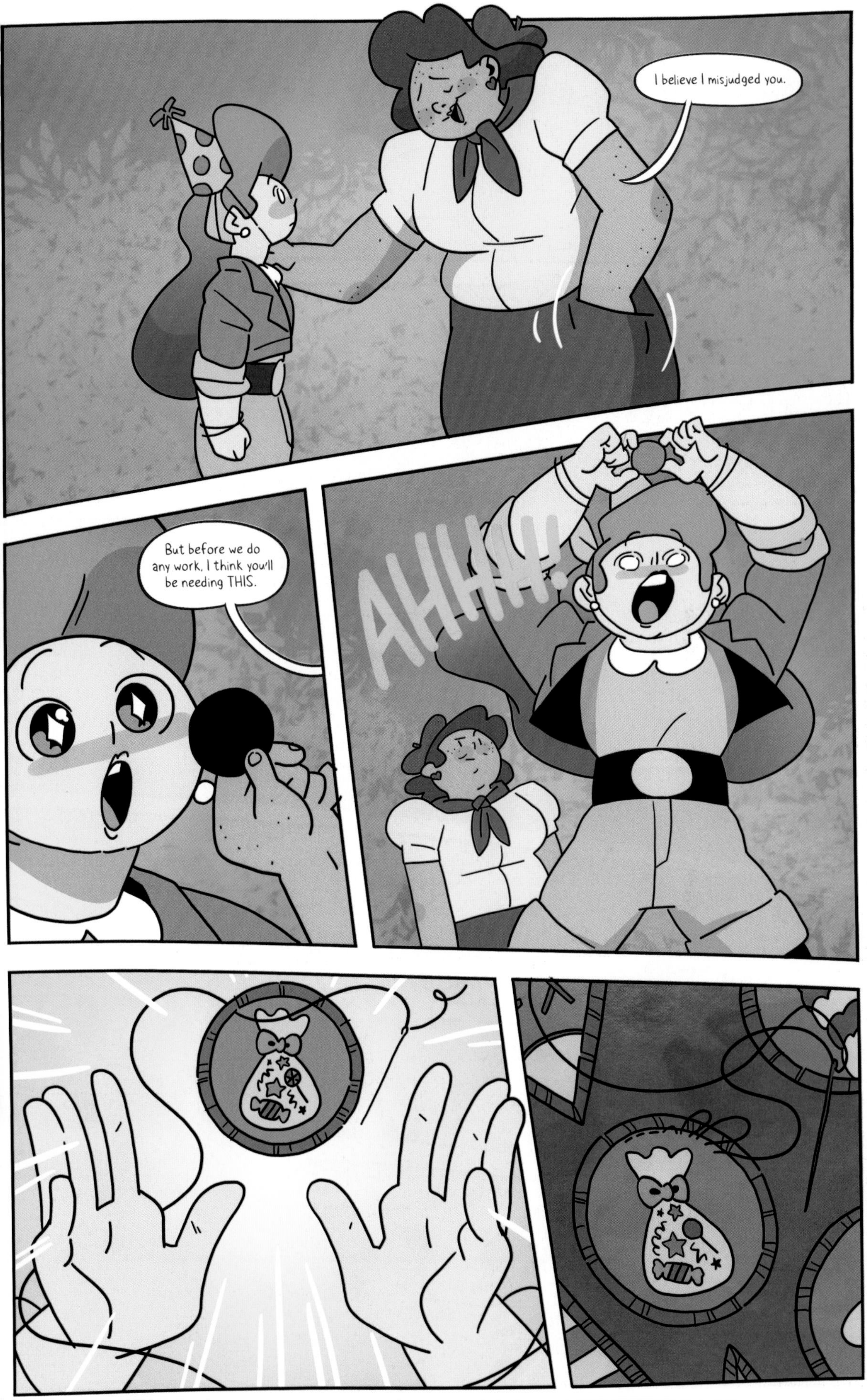
I believe I misjudged you.
But before we do any work, I think you'll be needing THIS.
AHHH!

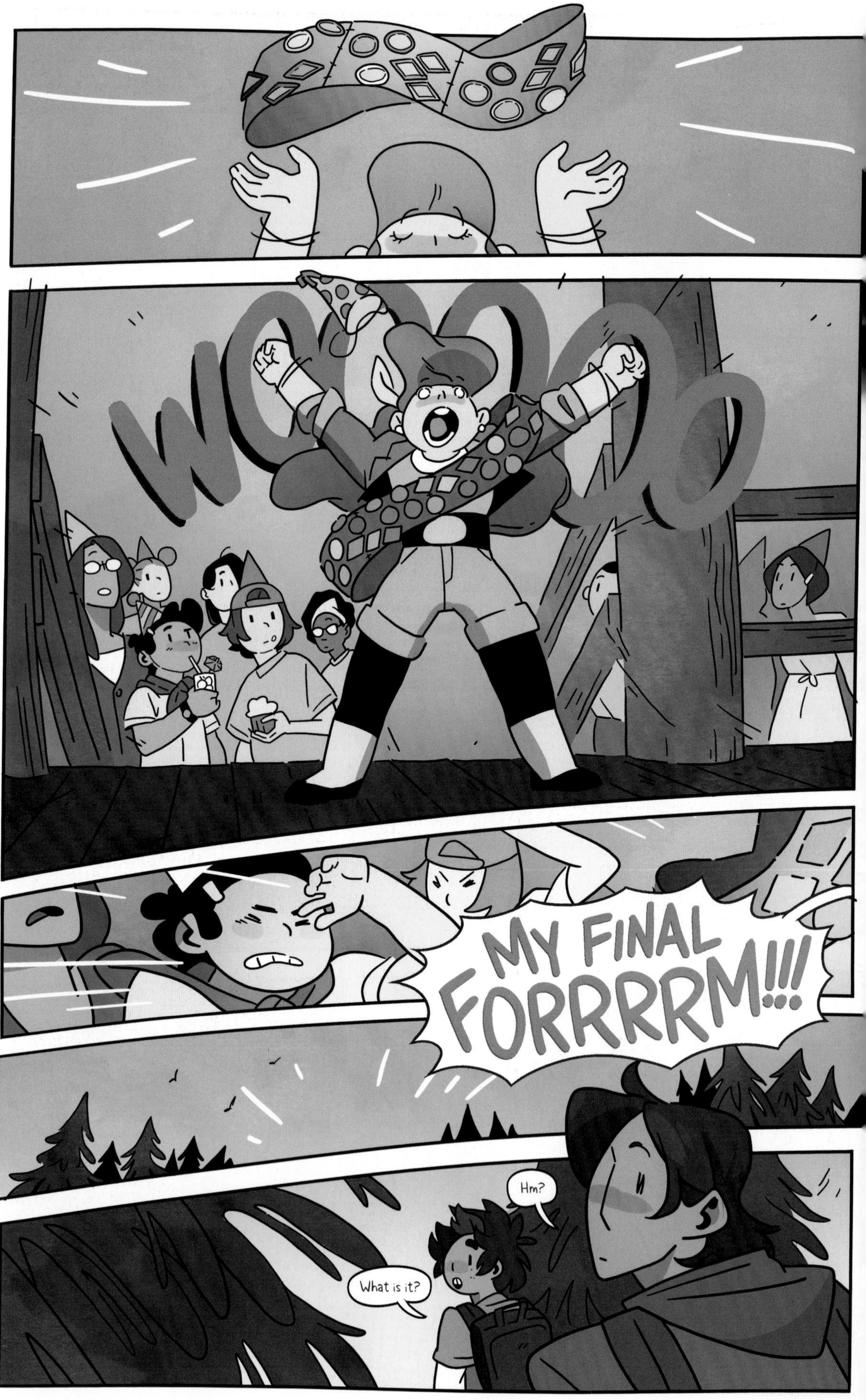
WOOOOO
MY FINAL FORRRRM!!!
Hm?
What is it?

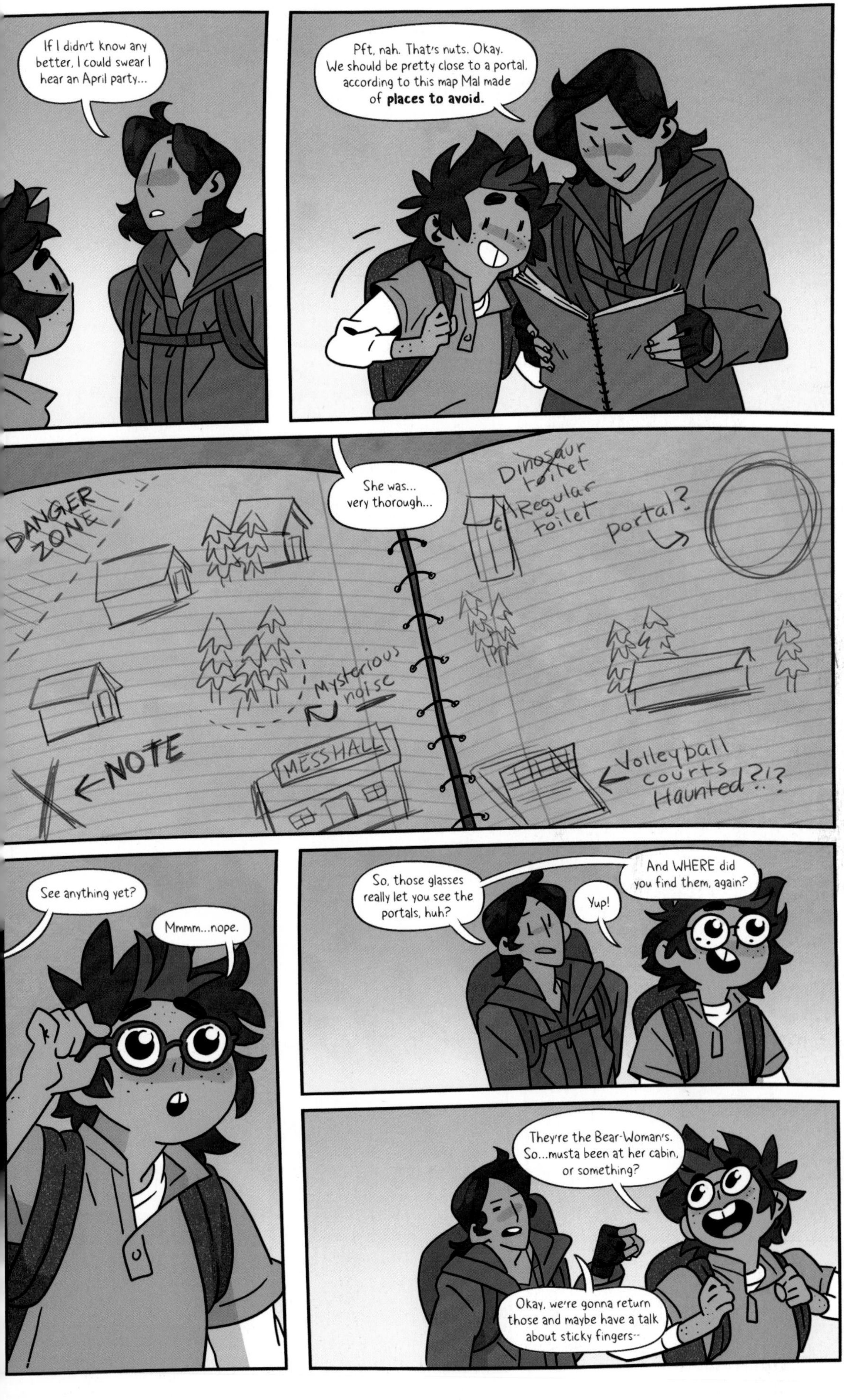
If I didn't know any better, I could swear I hear an April party...
Pft, nah. That's nuts. Okay. We should be pretty close to a portal, according to this map Mal made of **places to avoid.**
She was... very thorough...
DANGER ZONE
Dinosaur toilet
Regular toilet
portal?
Mysterious noise
NOTE
MESSHALL
Volleyball courts Haunted?!?
See anything yet?
Mmmm...nope.
So, those glasses really let you see the portals, huh?
Yup!
And WHERE did you find them, again?
They're the Bear-Woman's. So...musta been at her cabin, or something?
Okay, we're gonna return those and maybe have a talk about sticky fingers--

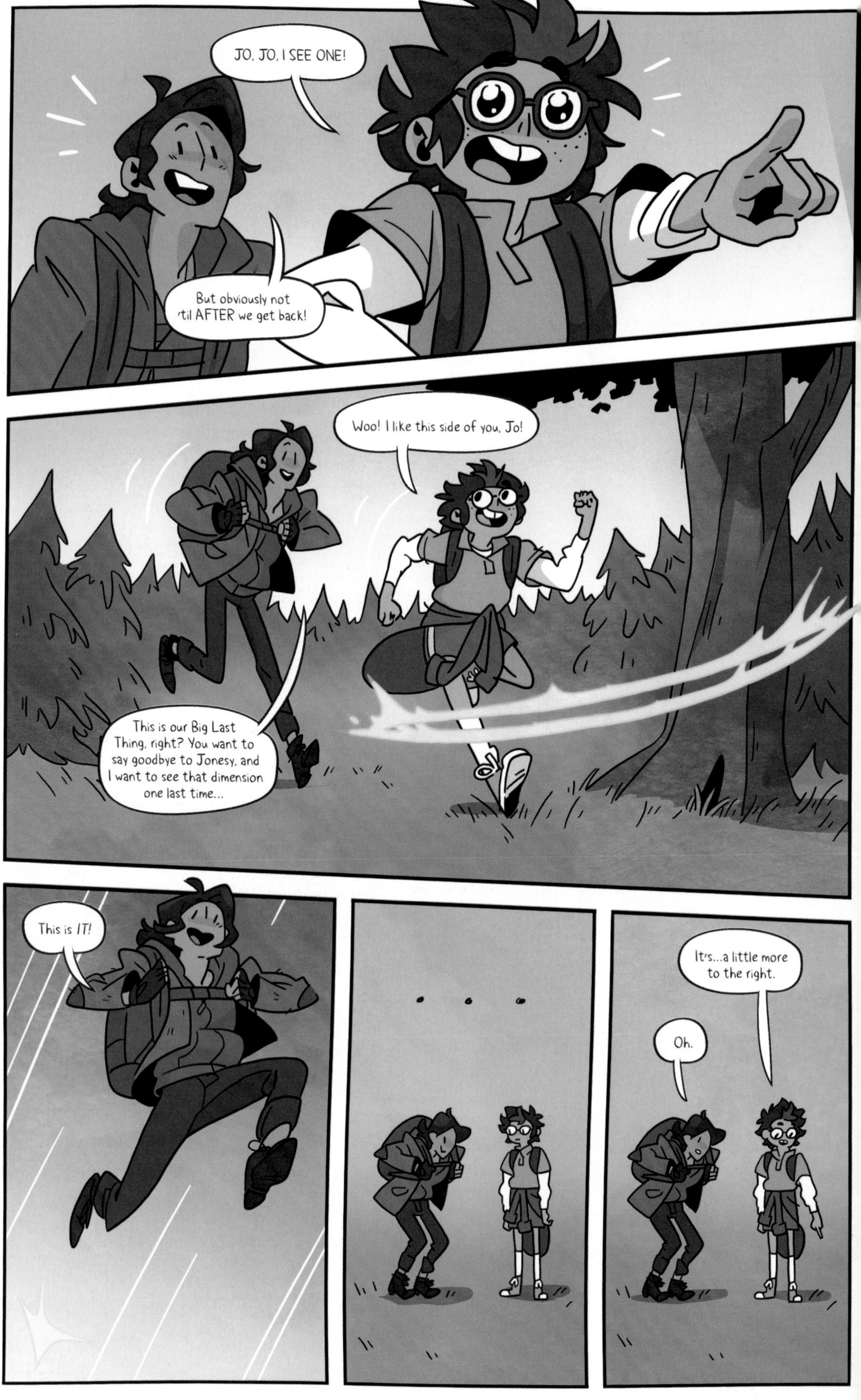
JO, JO, I SEE ONE!
But obviously not 'til AFTER we get back!
Woo! I like this side of you, Jo!
This is our Big Last Thing, right? You want to say goodbye to Jonesy, and I want to see that dimension one last time...
This is IT!
. . .
Oh.
It's...a little more to the right.

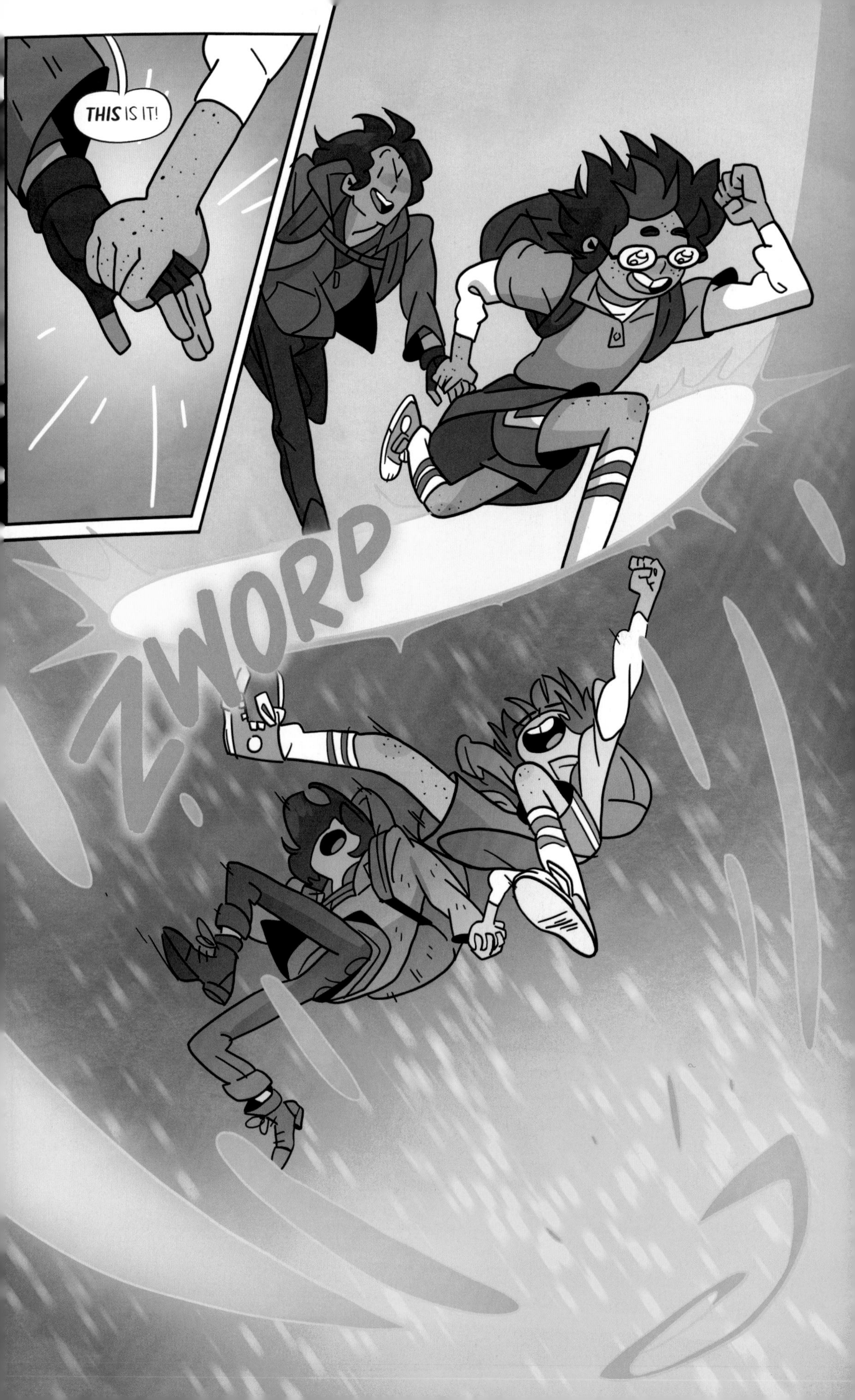
THIS IS IT!
ZWORP

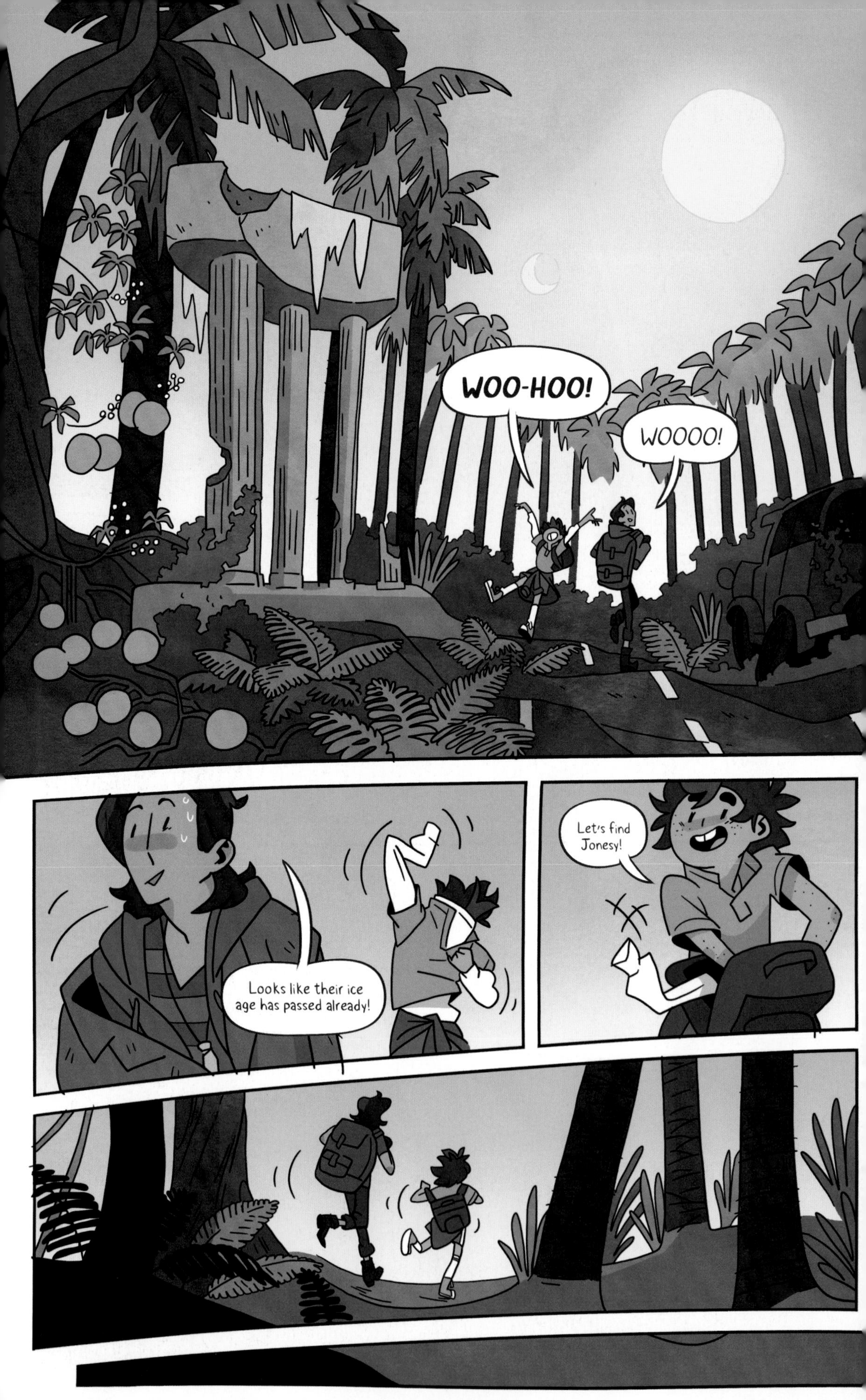
WOO-HOO!
WOOOO!
Looks like their ice age has passed already!
Let's find Jonesy!

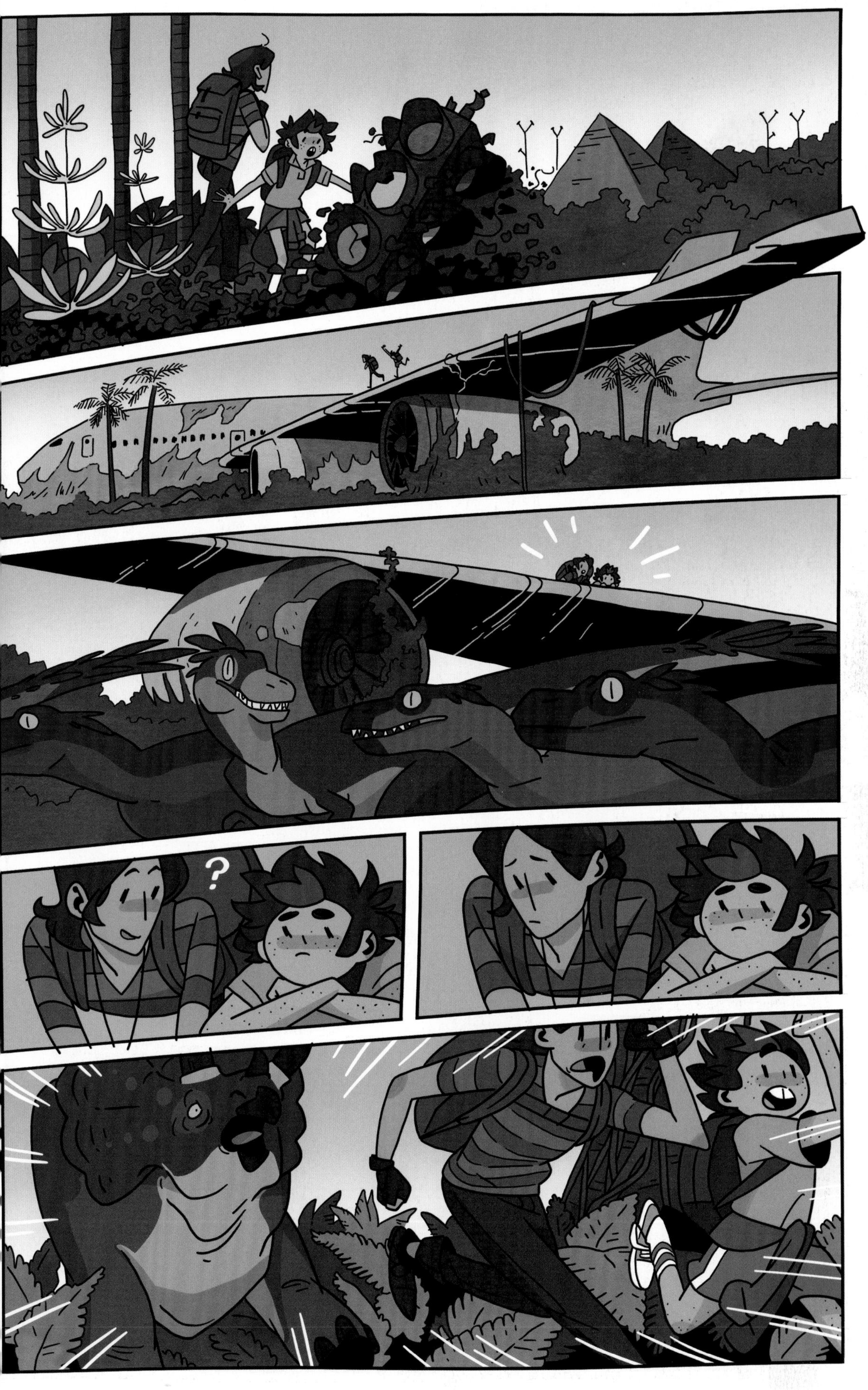
?

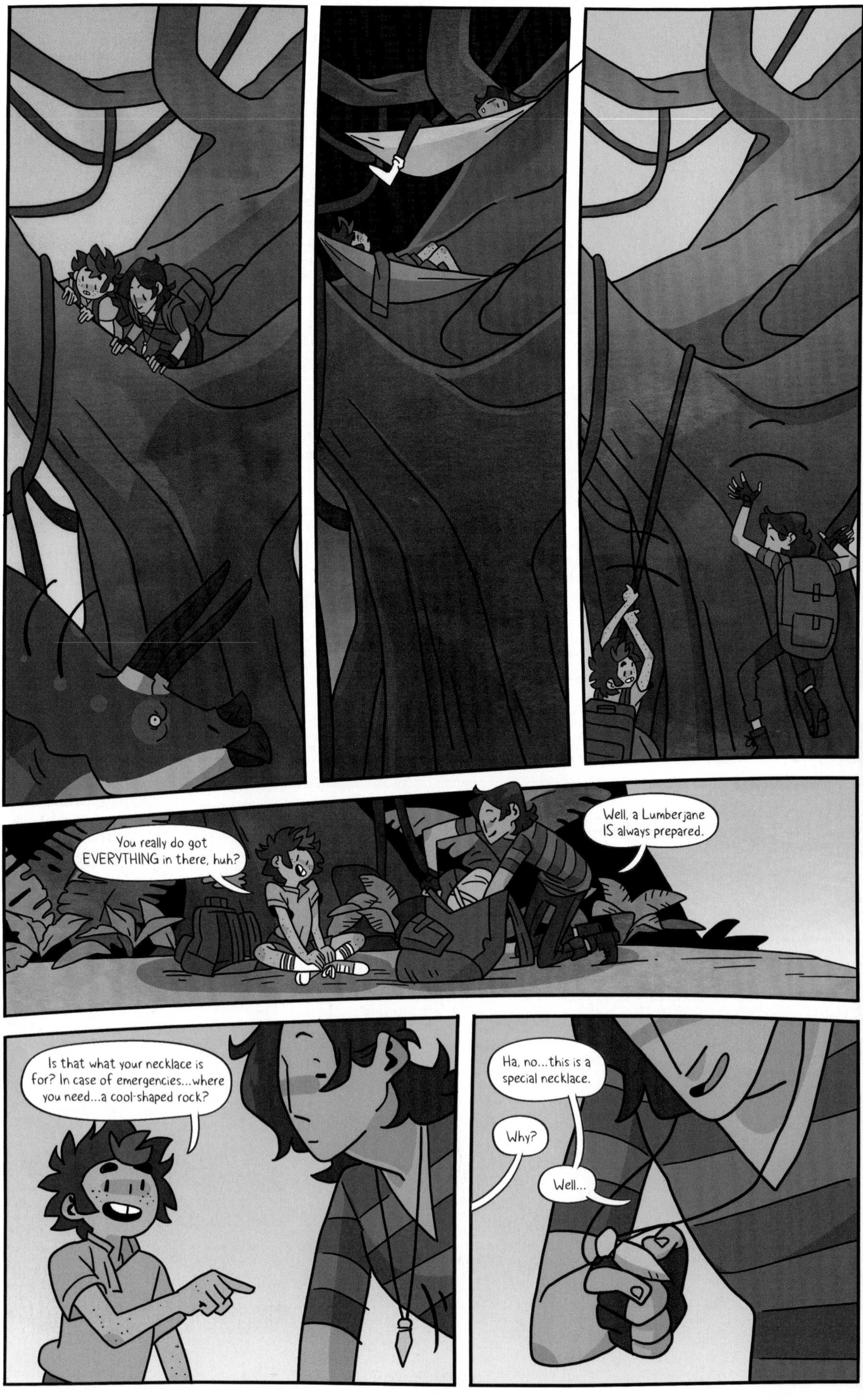
You really do got EVERYTHING in there, huh?
Well, a Lumberjane IS always prepared.
Is that what your necklace is for? In case of emergencies...where you need...a cool-shaped rock?
Ha, no...this is a special necklace.
Why?
Well...

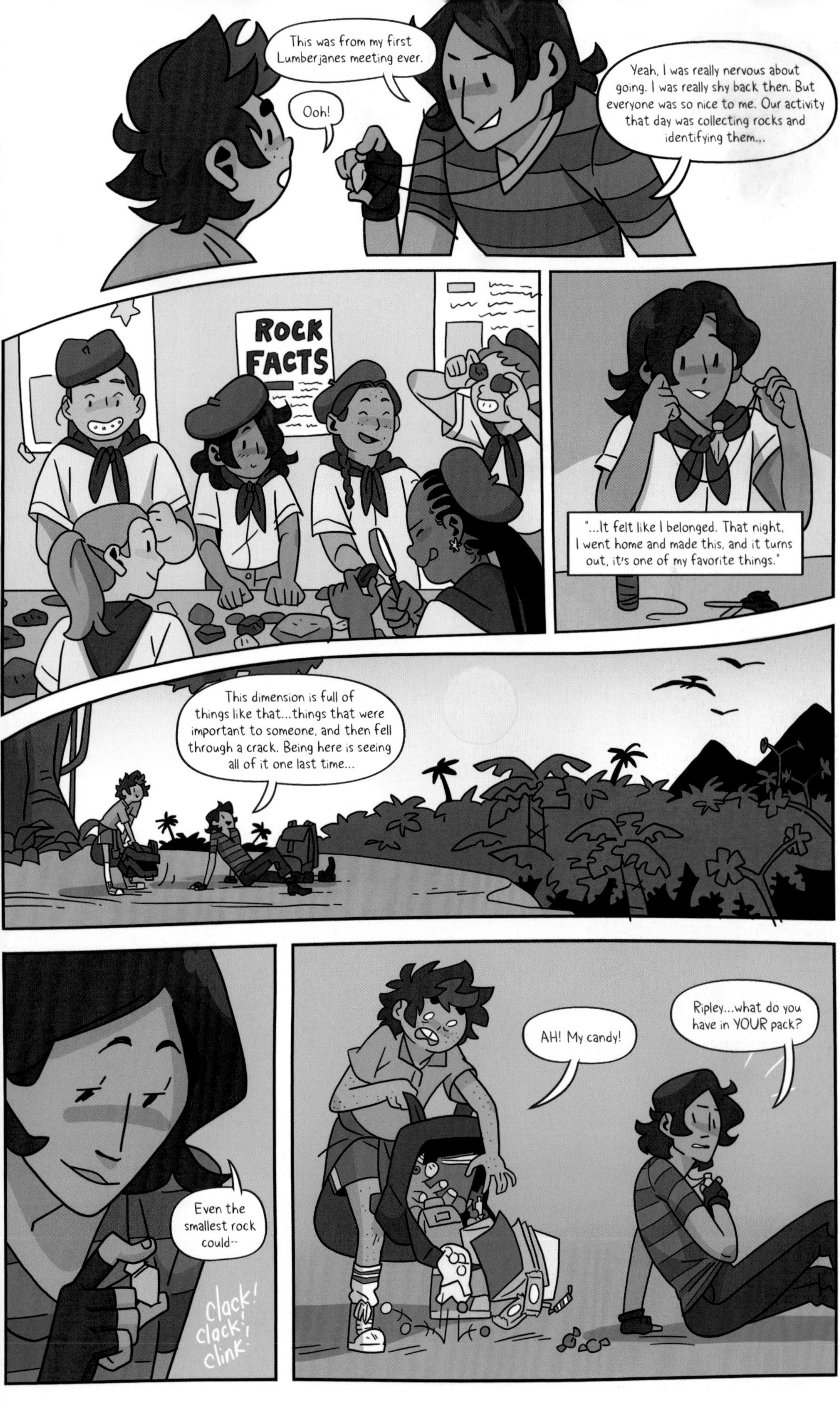
This was from my first Lumberjanes meeting ever.
Ooh!
Yeah, I was really nervous about going. I was really shy back then. But everyone was so nice to me. Our activity that day was collecting rocks and identifying them...
ROCK FACTS
"...It felt like I belonged. That night, I went home and made this, and it turns out, it's one of my favorite things."
This dimension is full of things like that...things that were important to someone, and then fell through a crack. Being here is seeing all of it one last time...
Even the smallest rock could--
clack! clack! clink!
AH! My candy!
Ripley...what do you have in YOUR pack?

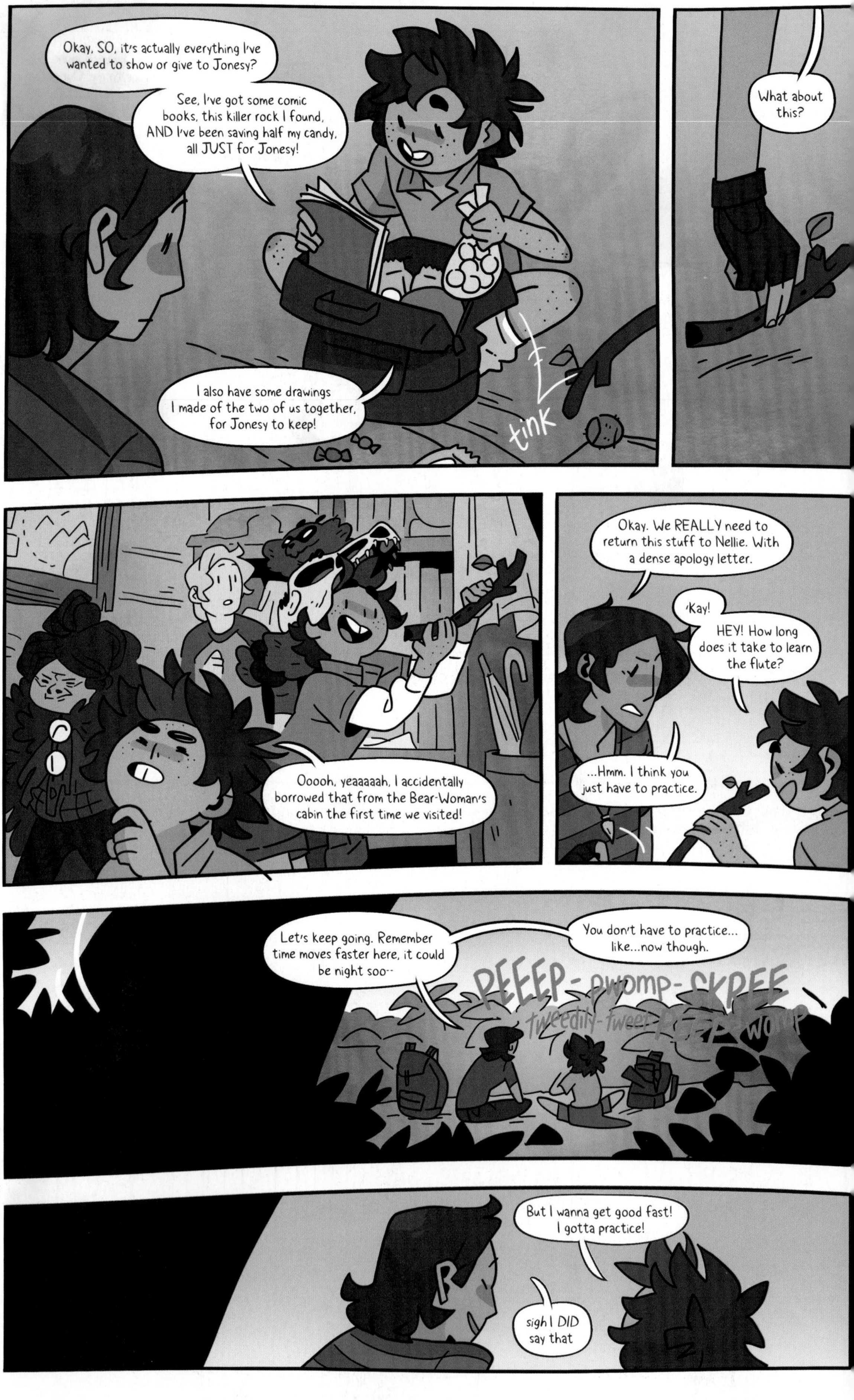
Okay, SO, it's actually everything I've wanted to show or give to Jonesy?
See, I've got some comic books, this killer rock I found, AND I've been saving half my candy, all JUST for Jonesy!
I also have some drawings I made of the two of us together, for Jonesy to keep!
tink
What about this?
Ooooh, yeaaaaah, I accidentally borrowed that from the Bear-Woman's cabin the first time we visited!
Okay. We REALLY need to return this stuff to Nellie. With a dense apology letter.
'Kay!
HEY! How long does it take to learn the flute?
...Hmm. I think you just have to practice.
Let's keep going. Remember time moves faster here, it could be night soo--
You don't have to practice... like...now though.
PEEEP-pwomp-SKREE
tweedily-tweet
womp
But I wanna get good fast! I gotta practice!
sigh I DID say that

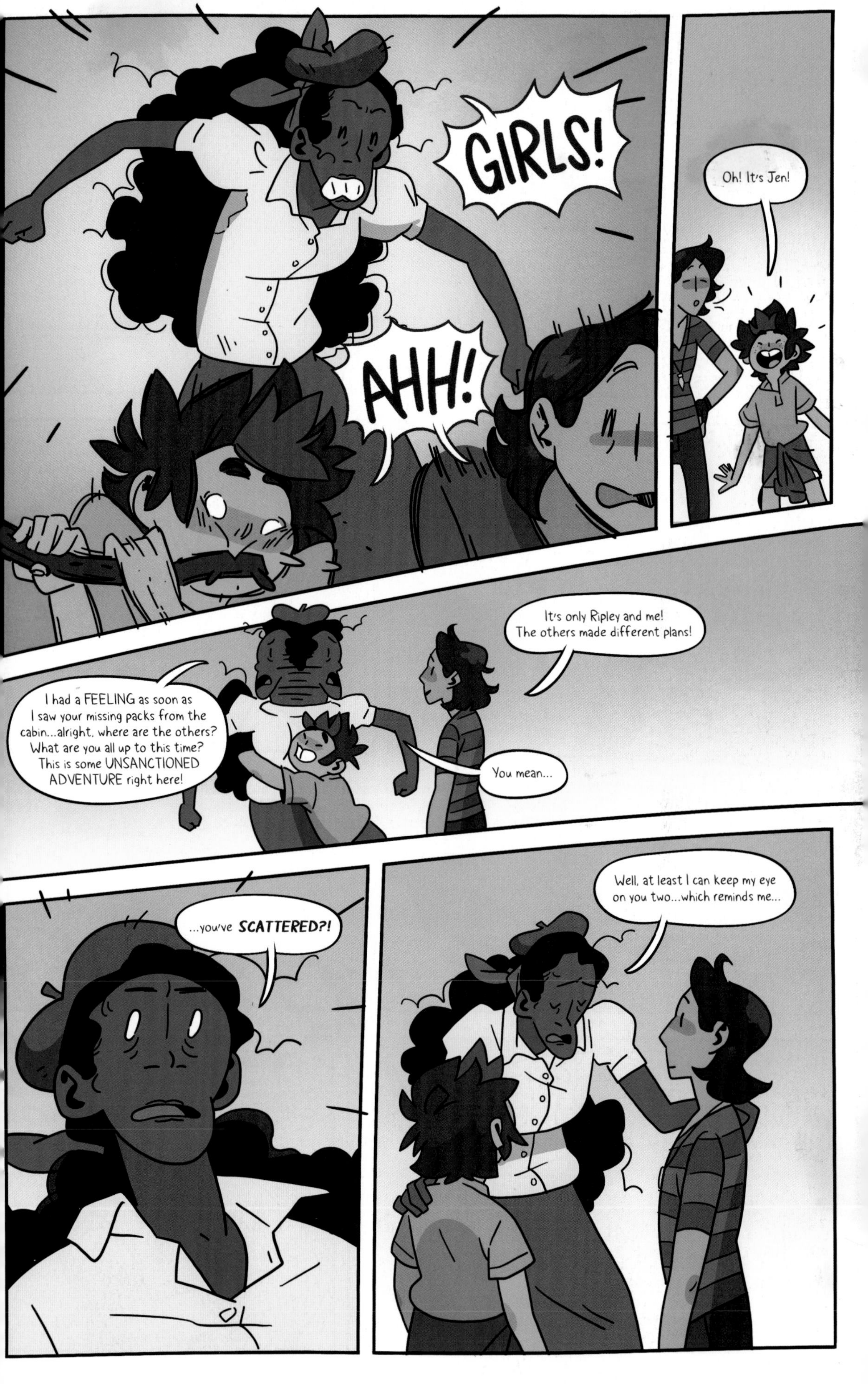
GIRLS!
AHH!
Oh! It's Jen!
It's only Ripley and me!
The others made different plans!
I had a FEELING as soon as I saw your missing packs from the cabin...alright, where are the others? What are you all up to this time? This is some UNSANCTIONED ADVENTURE right here!
You mean...
...you've SCATTERED?!
Well, at least I can keep my eye on you two...which reminds me...

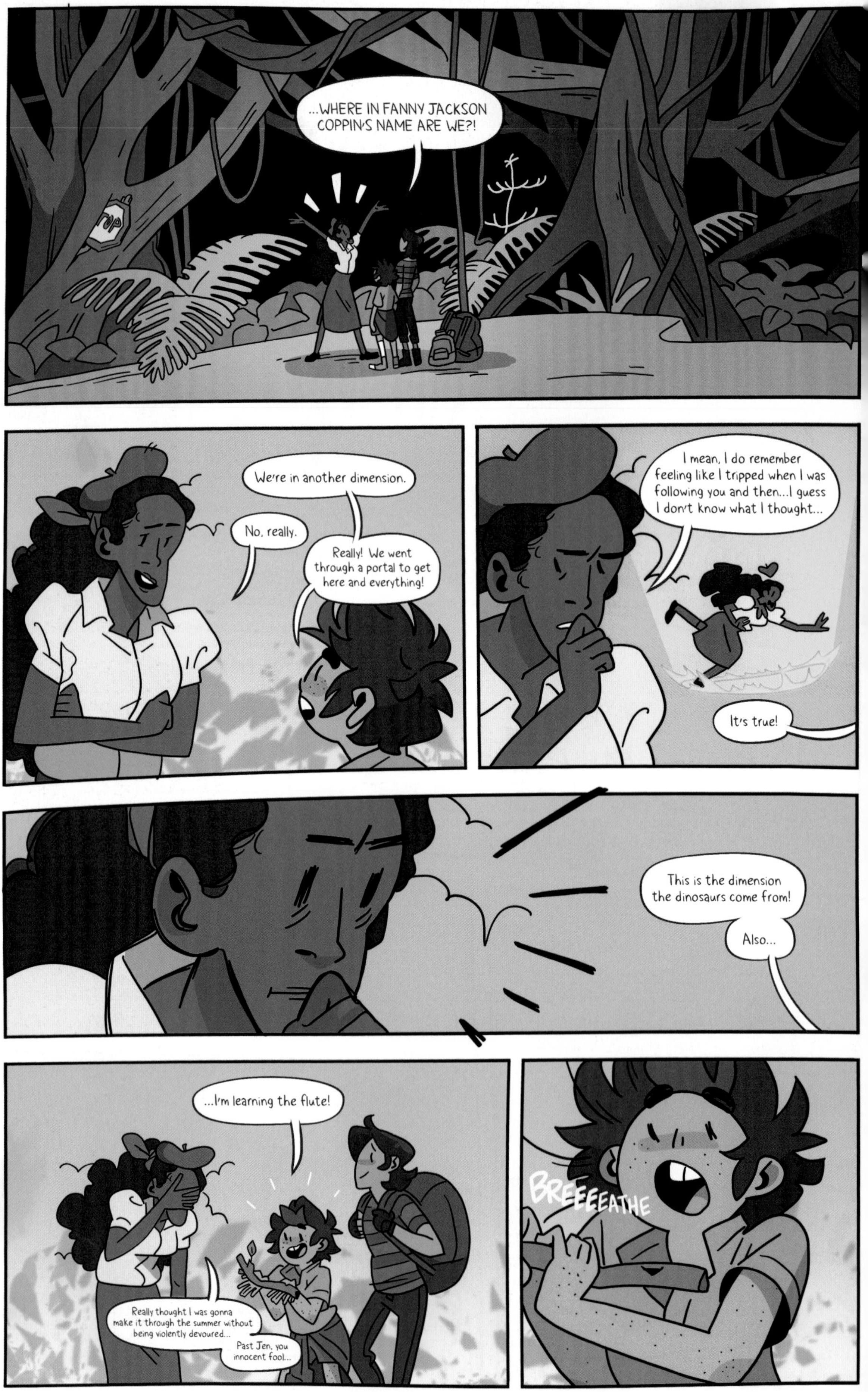
...WHERE IN FANNY JACKSON COPPIN'S NAME ARE WE?!
We're in another dimension.
No, really.
Really! We went through a portal to get here and everything!
I mean, I do remember feeling like I tripped when I was following you and then...I guess I don't know what I thought...
It's true!
This is the dimension the dinosaurs come from!
Also...
...I'm learning the flute!
Really thought I was gonna make it through the summer without being violently devoured...
Past Jen, you innocent fool...
BREEEEEATHE

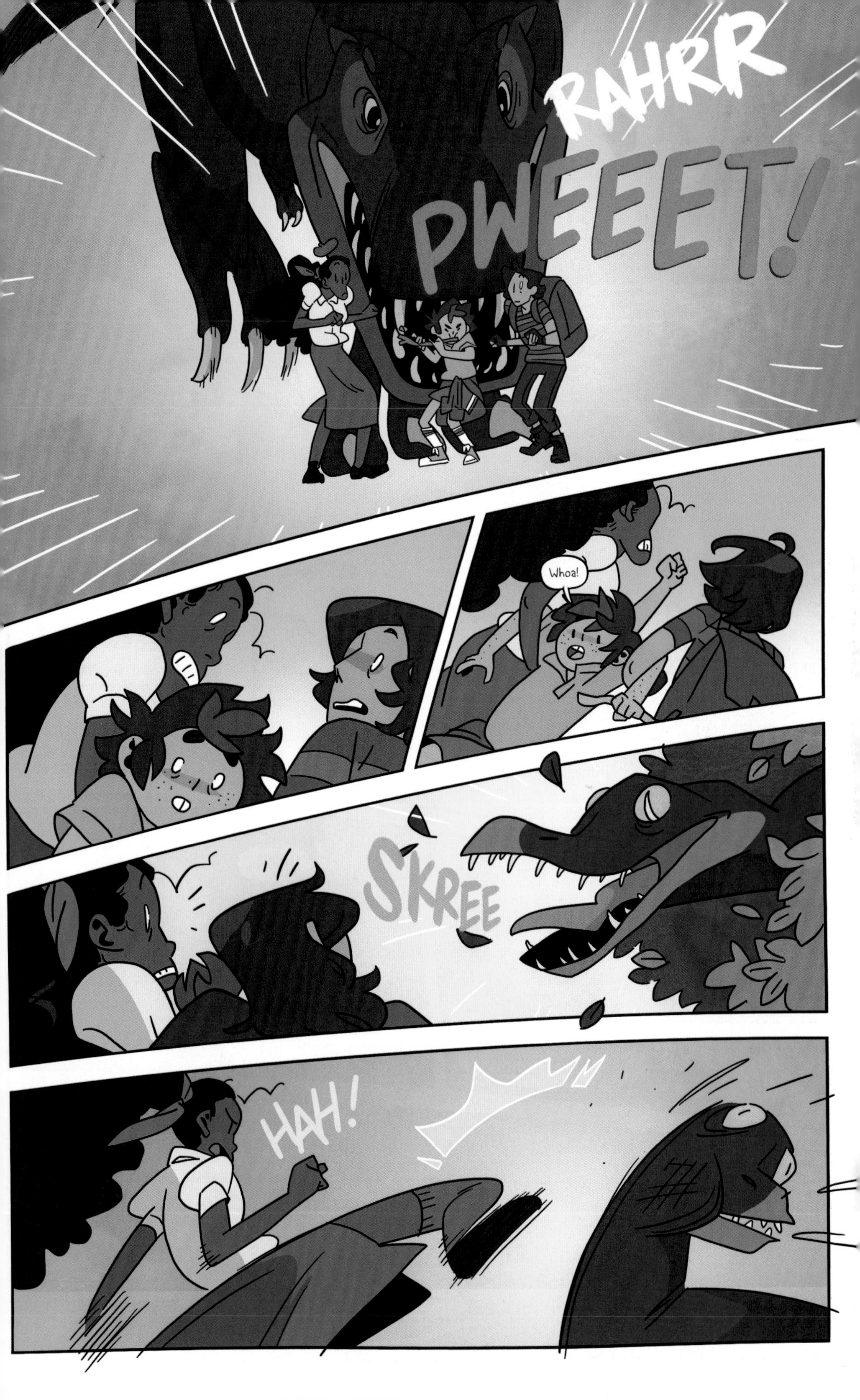
RAHRR
PWEEET!
Whoa!
SKREE
HAH!

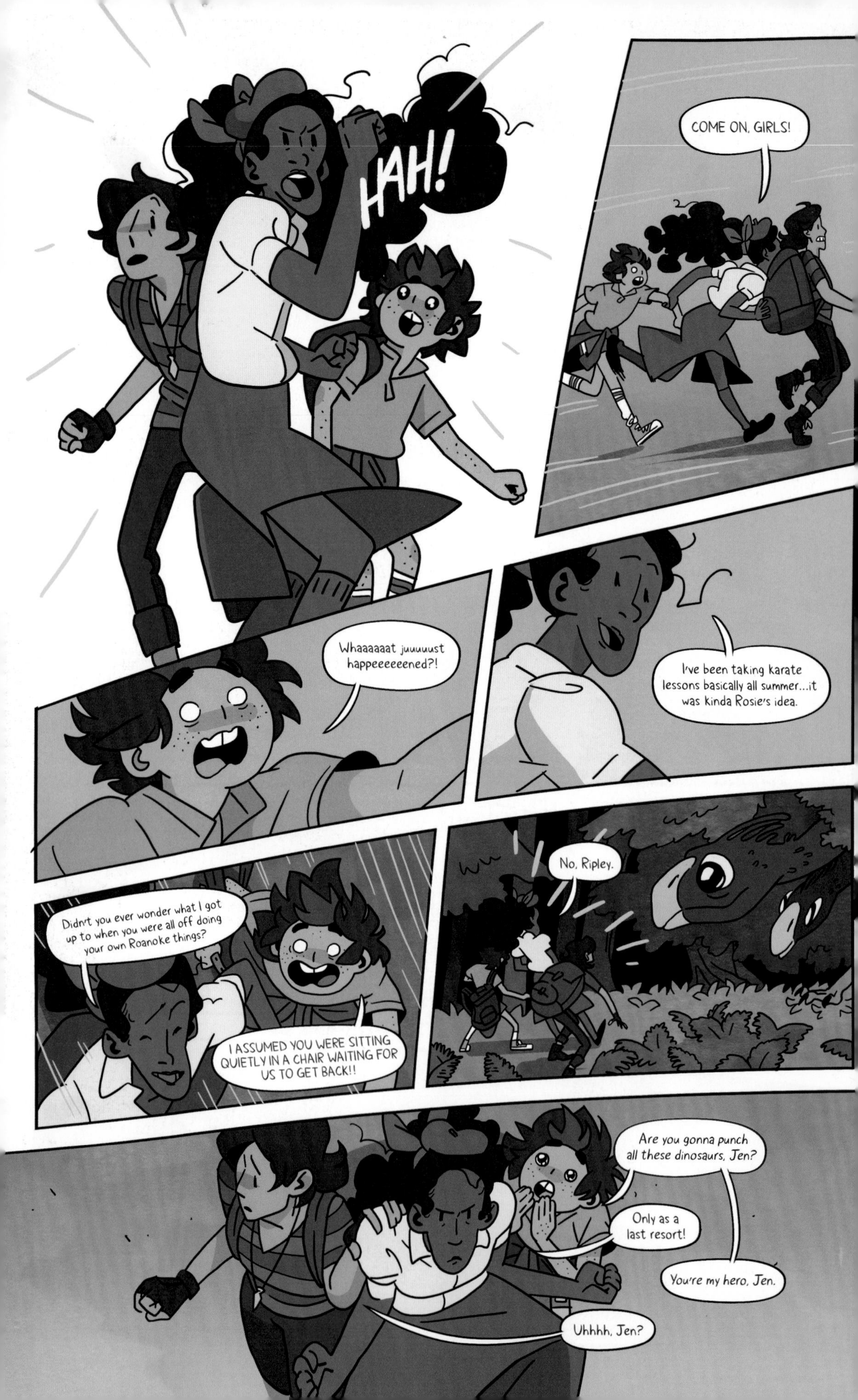
HAH!
COME ON, GIRLS!
Whaaaaaat juuuuust happeeeeeened?!
I've been taking karate lessons basically all summer...it was kinda Rosie's idea.
Didn't you ever wonder what I got up to when you were all off doing your own Roanoke things?
I ASSUMED YOU WERE SITTING QUIETLY IN A CHAIR WAITING FOR US TO GET BACK!!
No, Ripley.
Are you gonna punch all these dinosaurs, Jen?
Only as a last resort!
You're my hero, Jen.
Uhhhh, Jen?

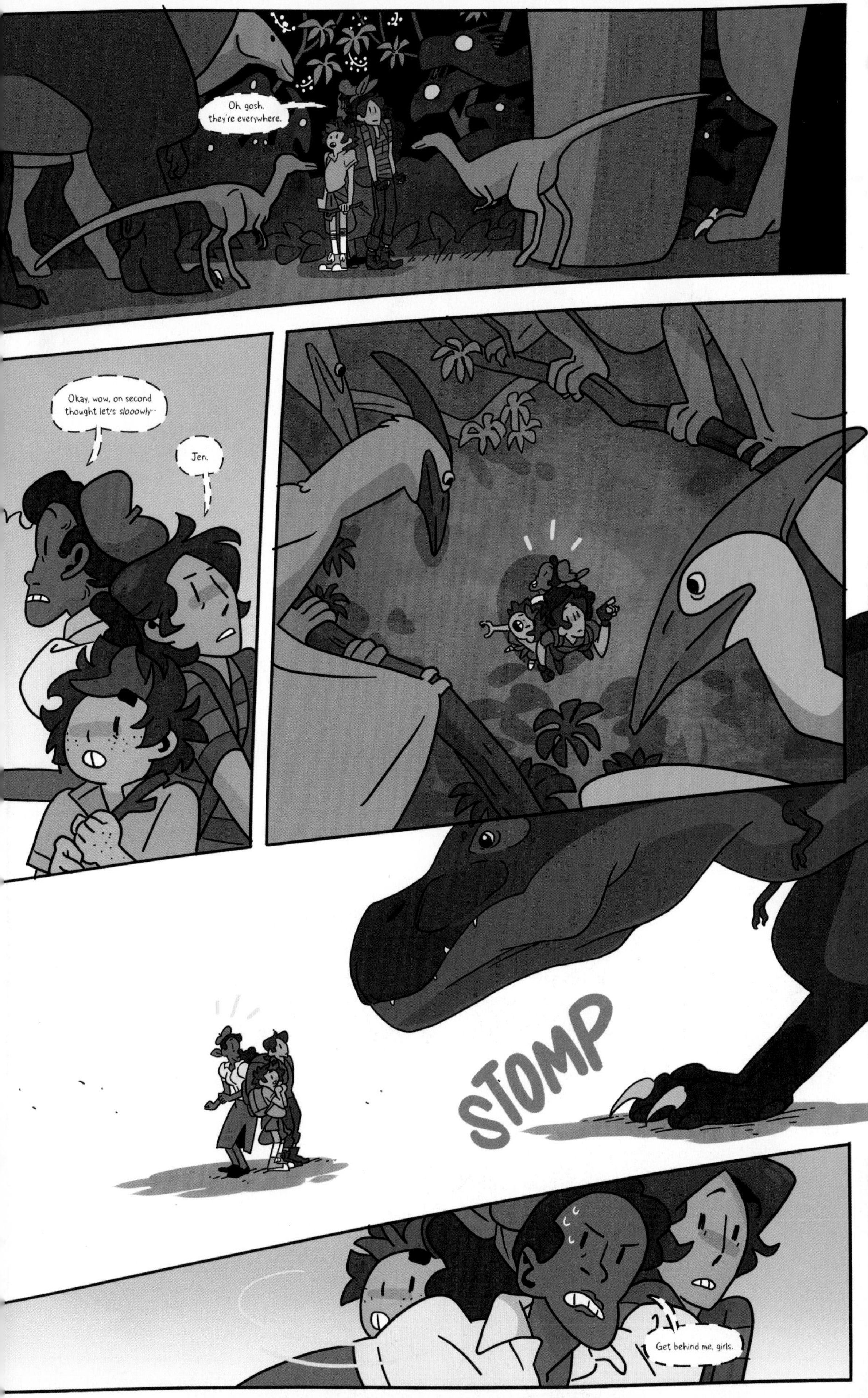
Oh, gosh, they're everywhere.
Okay, wow, on second thought let's slooowly--
Jen.
STOMP
Get behind me, girls.

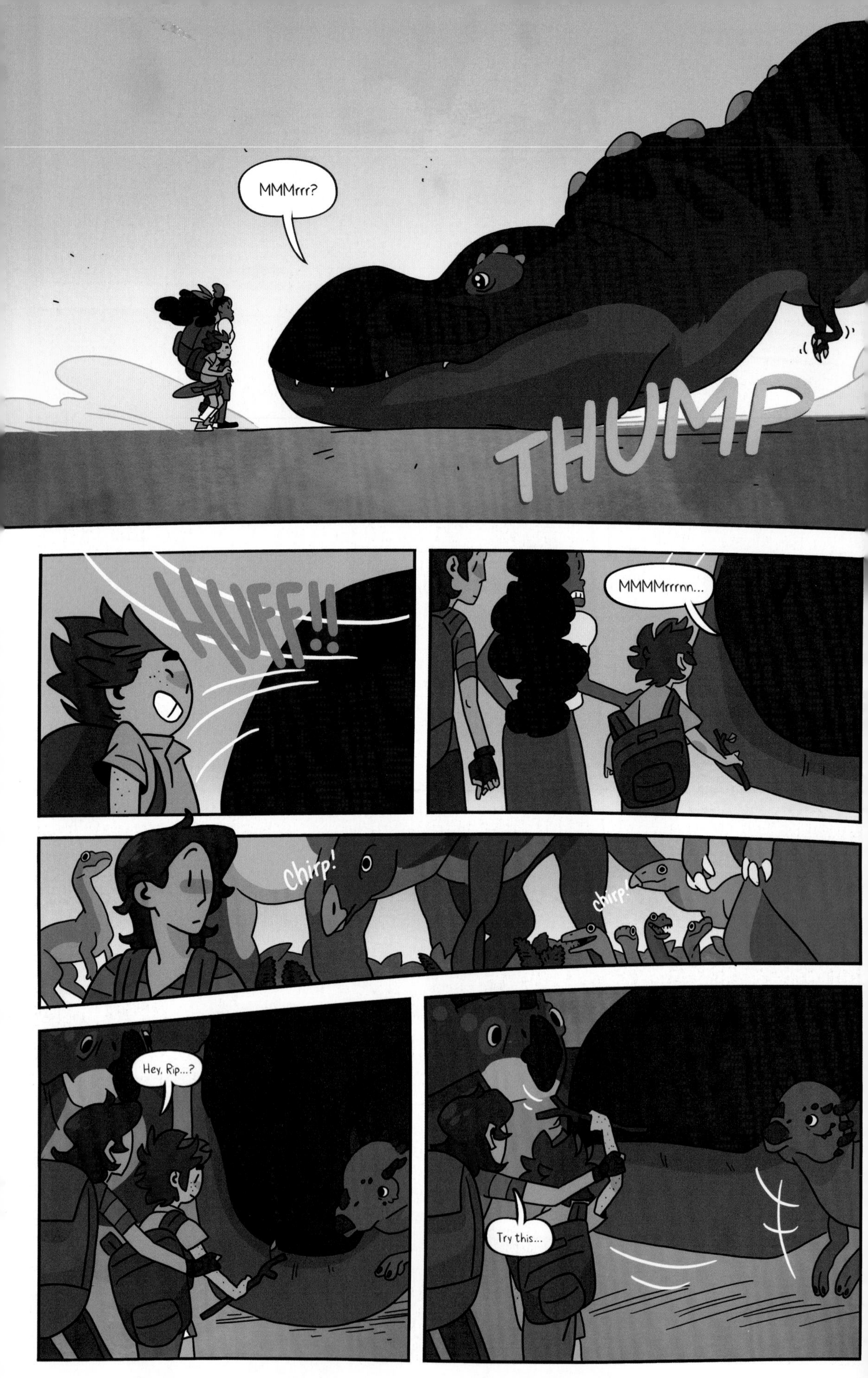
MMMrrr?
THUMP
HUFF!!
MMMMrrrnn...
Chirp!
chirp!
Hey, Rip...?
Try this...

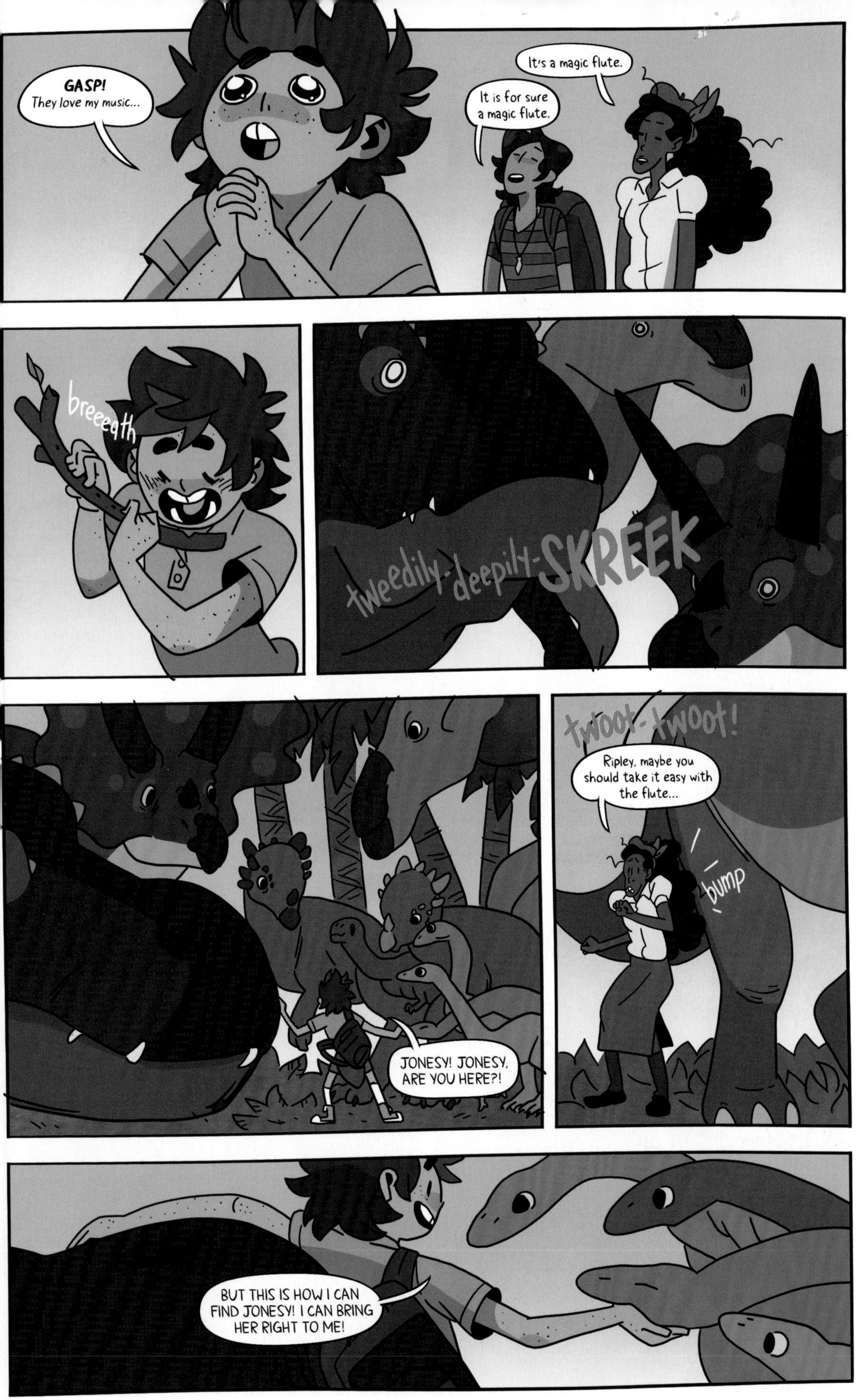
GASP!
They love my music...
It's a magic flute.
It is for sure a magic flute.
breeeath
tweedily-deepily-SKREEK
JONESY! JONESY, ARE YOU HERE?!
twoot-twoot!
Ripley, maybe you should take it easy with the flute...
bump
BUT THIS IS HOW I CAN FIND JONESY! I CAN BRING HER RIGHT TO ME!

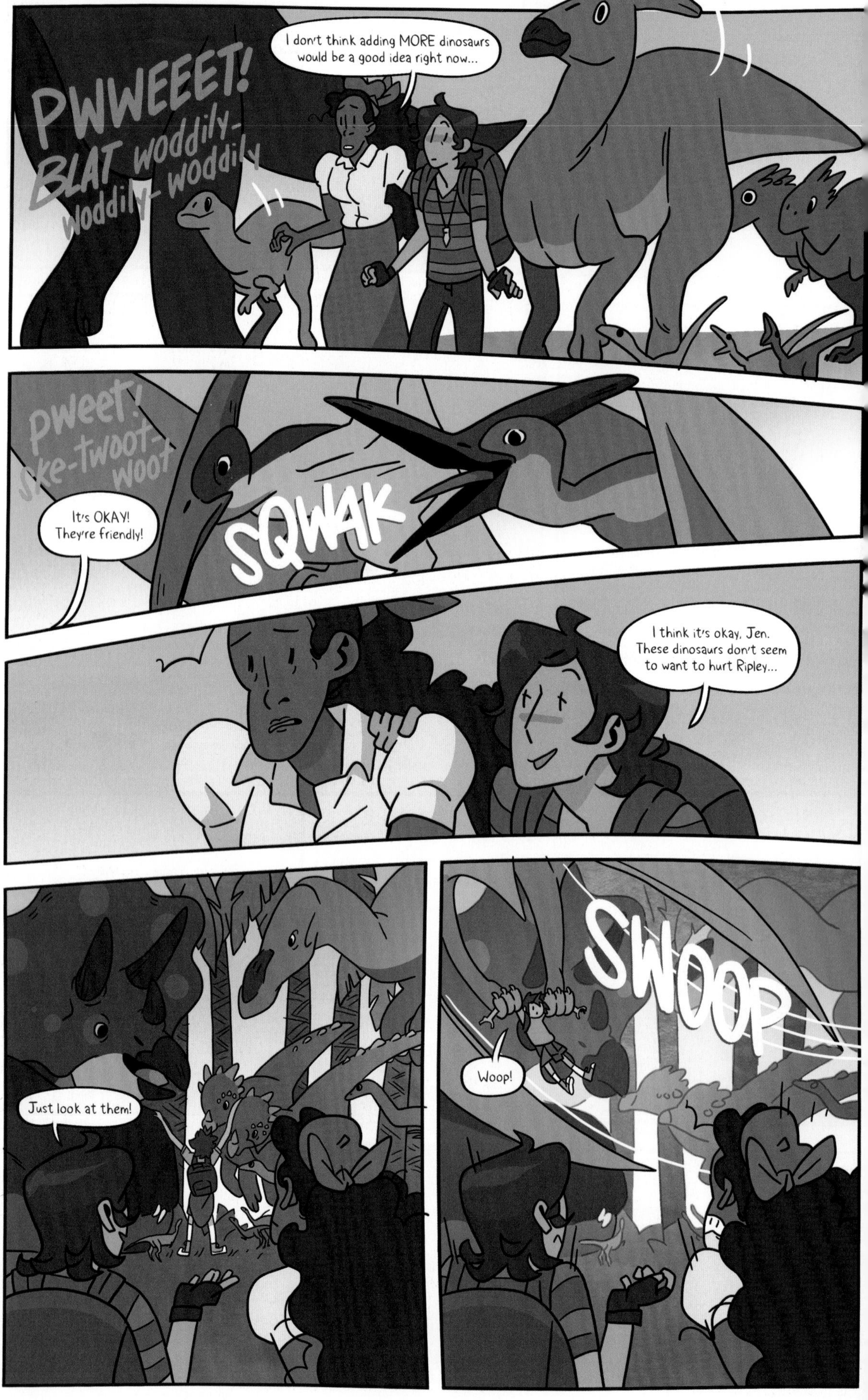
I don't think adding MORE dinosaurs would be a good idea right now...
PWWEEET!
BLAT woddily-woddily-woddily
pweet!
ske-twoot-woot
SQWAK
It's OKAY! They're friendly!
I think it's okay, Jen. These dinosaurs don't seem to want to hurt Ripley...
Just look at them!
SWOOP
Woop!

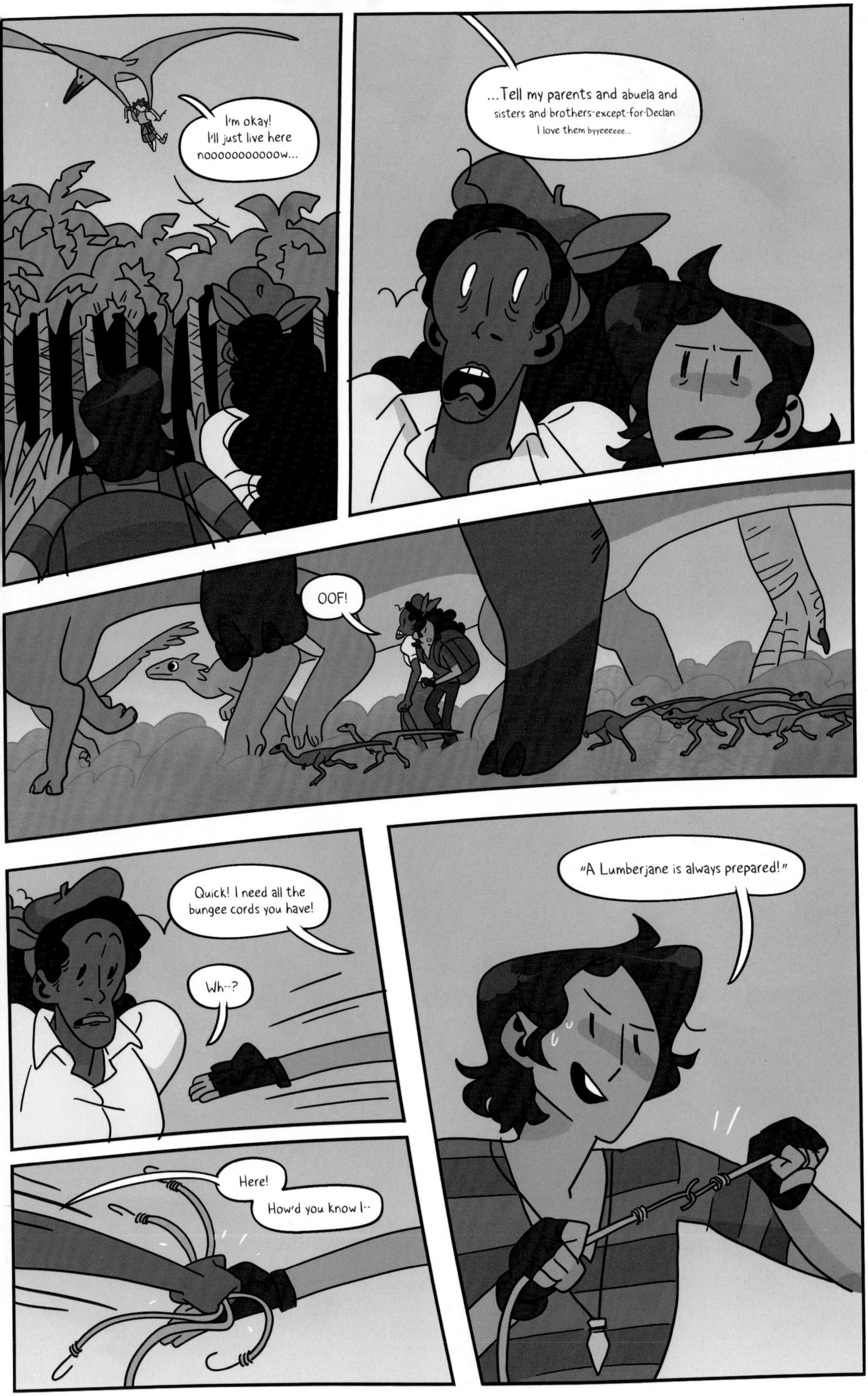
I'm okay!
I'll just live here
noooooooooooow...
...Tell my parents and abuela and
sisters and brothers-except-for-Declan
I love them byyeeeee...
OOF!
Quick! I need all the
bungee cords you have!
Wh--?
"A Lumberjane is always prepared!"
Here!
How'd you know I--

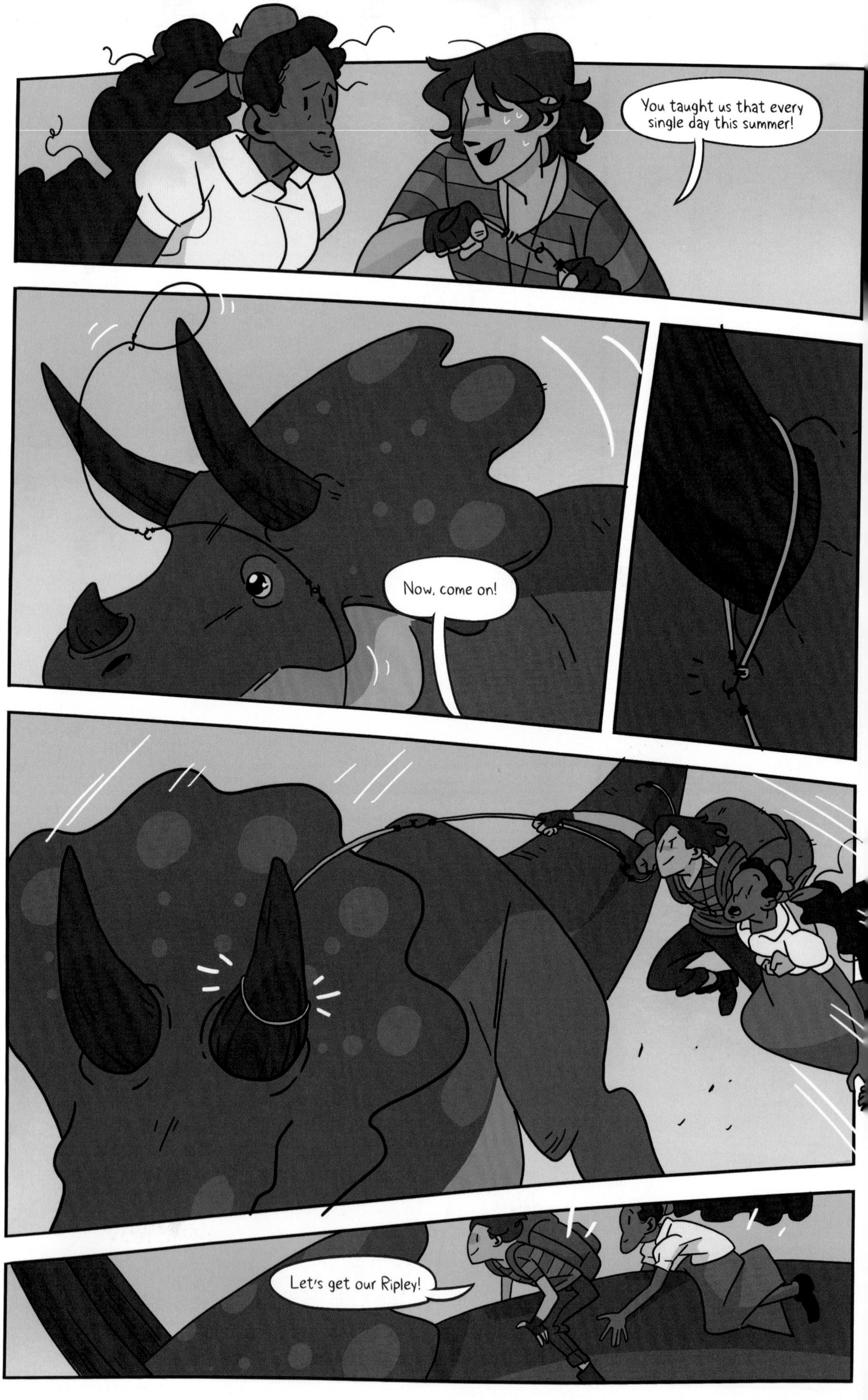
You taught us that every single day this summer!
Now, come on!
Let's get our Ripley!

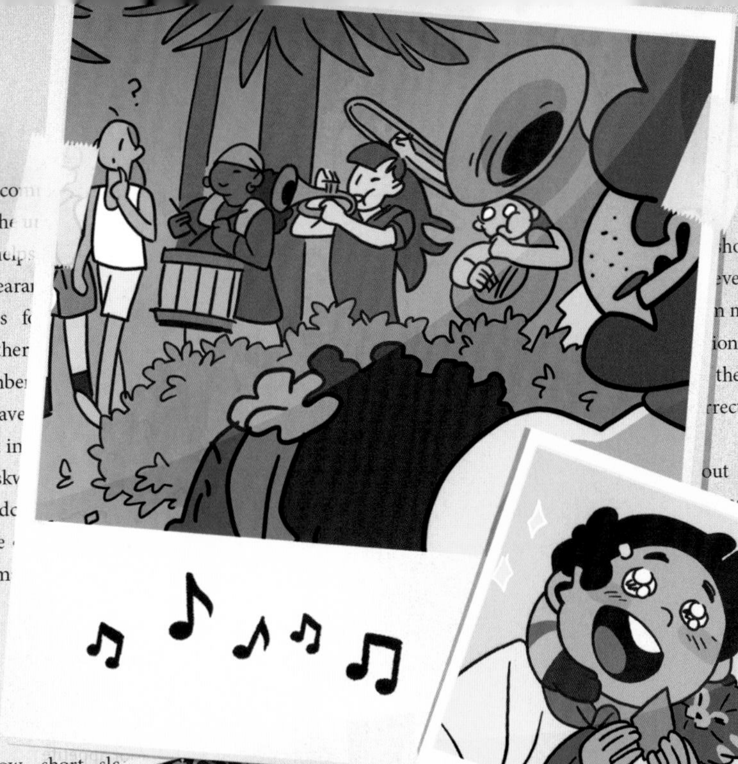
?

will co

The u

It helps

appearan

dress f

Further

Lumbe

to have

part in

Thiskv

Hardc

have

them

HE UNIFORM

should be worn at camp

events when Lumberjanes

n may also be worn at other

ions. It should be worn as a

the uniform dress with

rrect shoes, and stocking or

out grows her uniform or

ther Lumberjane.

a she has

her

f her

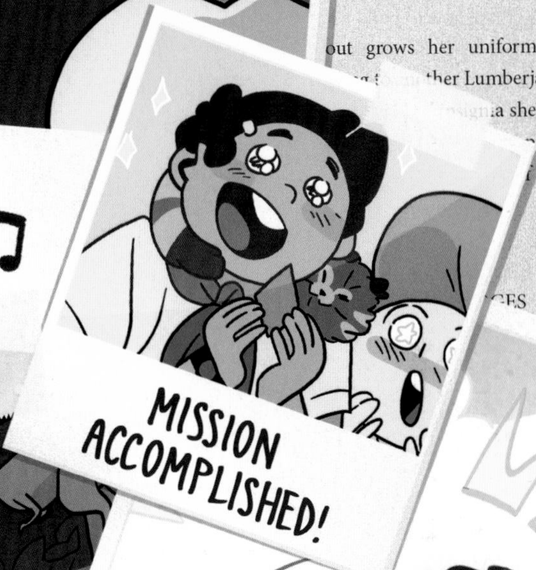
MISSION
ACCOMPLISHED!

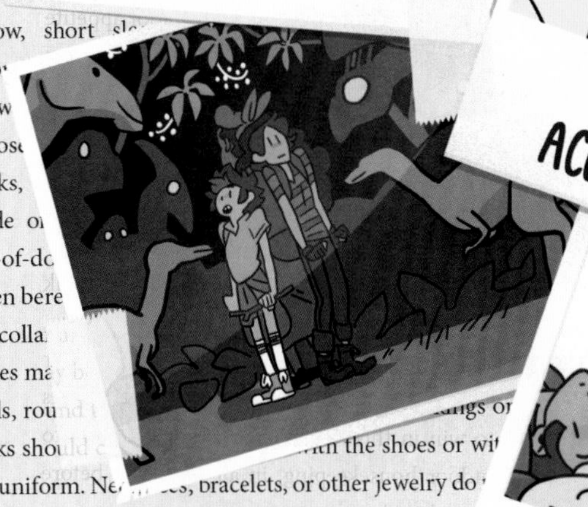

GES

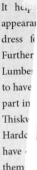

The

yellow, short sl

emb

the w

choose

slacks,

made o

out-of-d

green bere

the colla

Shoes ma

heels, rou ... ings or

socks shou ... with the shoes or wi

the uniform. Ne... bracelets, or other jewelry do

belong with a Lumberjane uniform.

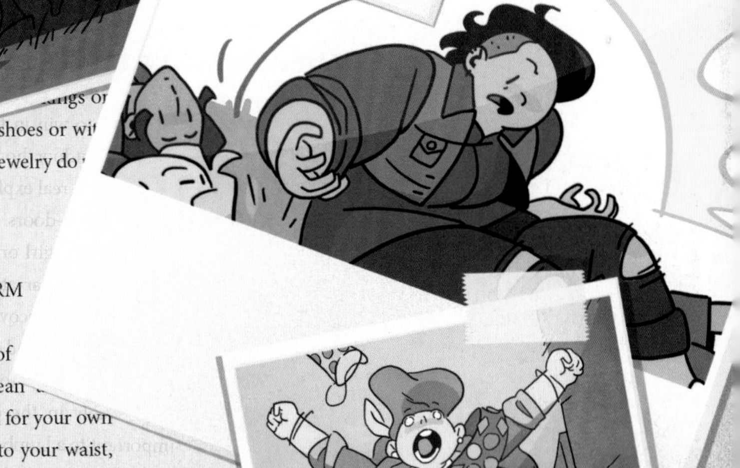

HOW TO WEAR THE UNIFORM

To look well in a uniform demands first of uniform be kept in good condition—clean pressed. See that the skirt is the right length for your own height and build, that the belt is adjusted to your waist, that your shoes and stockings are in keeping with the uniform, that you watch your posture and carry yourself with dignity and grace. If the beret is removed indoors, be sure that your hair is neat and kept in place with an inconspicuous clip or ribbon. When you wear a Lumberjane uniform you are identified as a member of this organization and you should be doubly careful to conduct yourself in a way that will show everyone that courtesy and thoughtfulness are part of being a Lumberjane. People are likely to judge a whole nation by the selfishness of a few individuals, to criticize a whole family because of the misconduct of one member, and to feel unkindly toward an organization because of the

The unifor

helps to cre

in a group.

active life th

another bond

future, and pr

in order to b

Lumberjane pr

Penniquiqul Thi ... ore Lady

Types, but m... will wish to have one. They

can either bu... the uniform, or make it themselves from

materials available at the trading post.

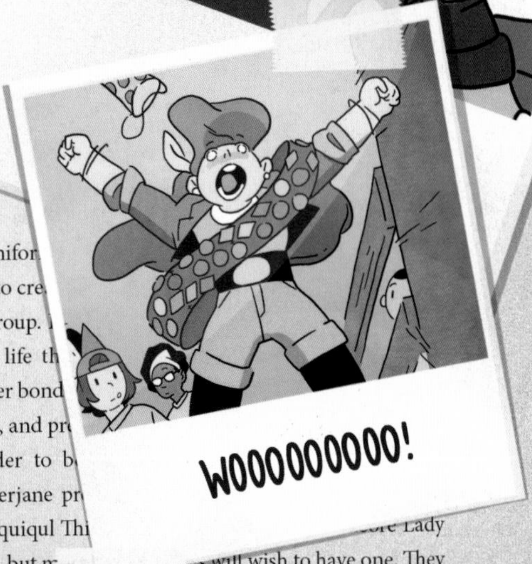
WOOOOOOOOO!

LUMBERJANES FIELD MANUAL

CHAPTER
SEVENTY-FOUR

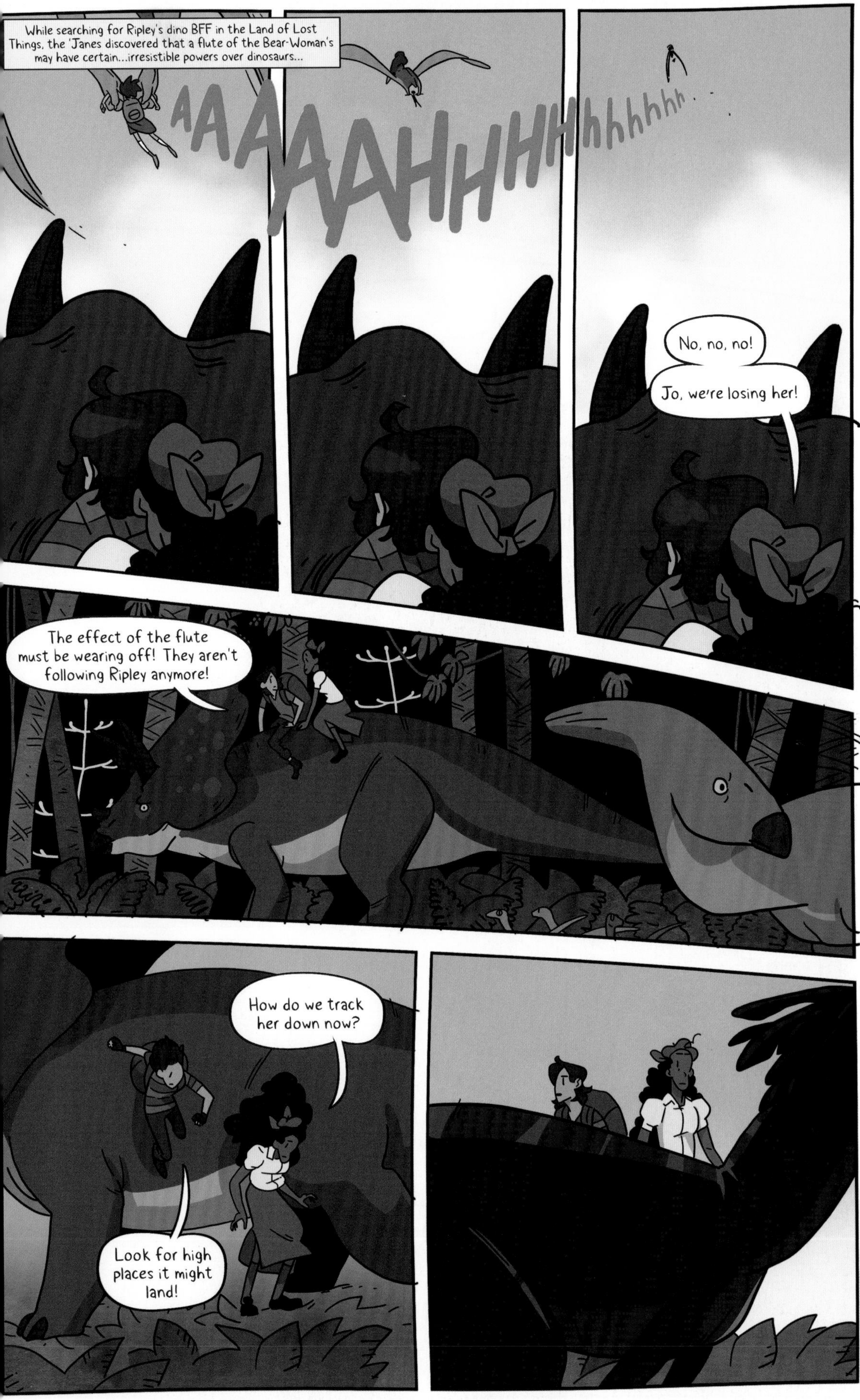
While searching for Ripley's dino BFF in the Land of Lost Things, the 'Janes discovered that a flute of the Bear-Woman's may have certain...irresistible powers over dinosaurs...
AAAAAHHHHhhhhhh...
No, no, no!
Jo, we're losing her!
The effect of the flute must be wearing off! They aren't following Ripley anymore!
How do we track her down now?
Look for high places it might land!

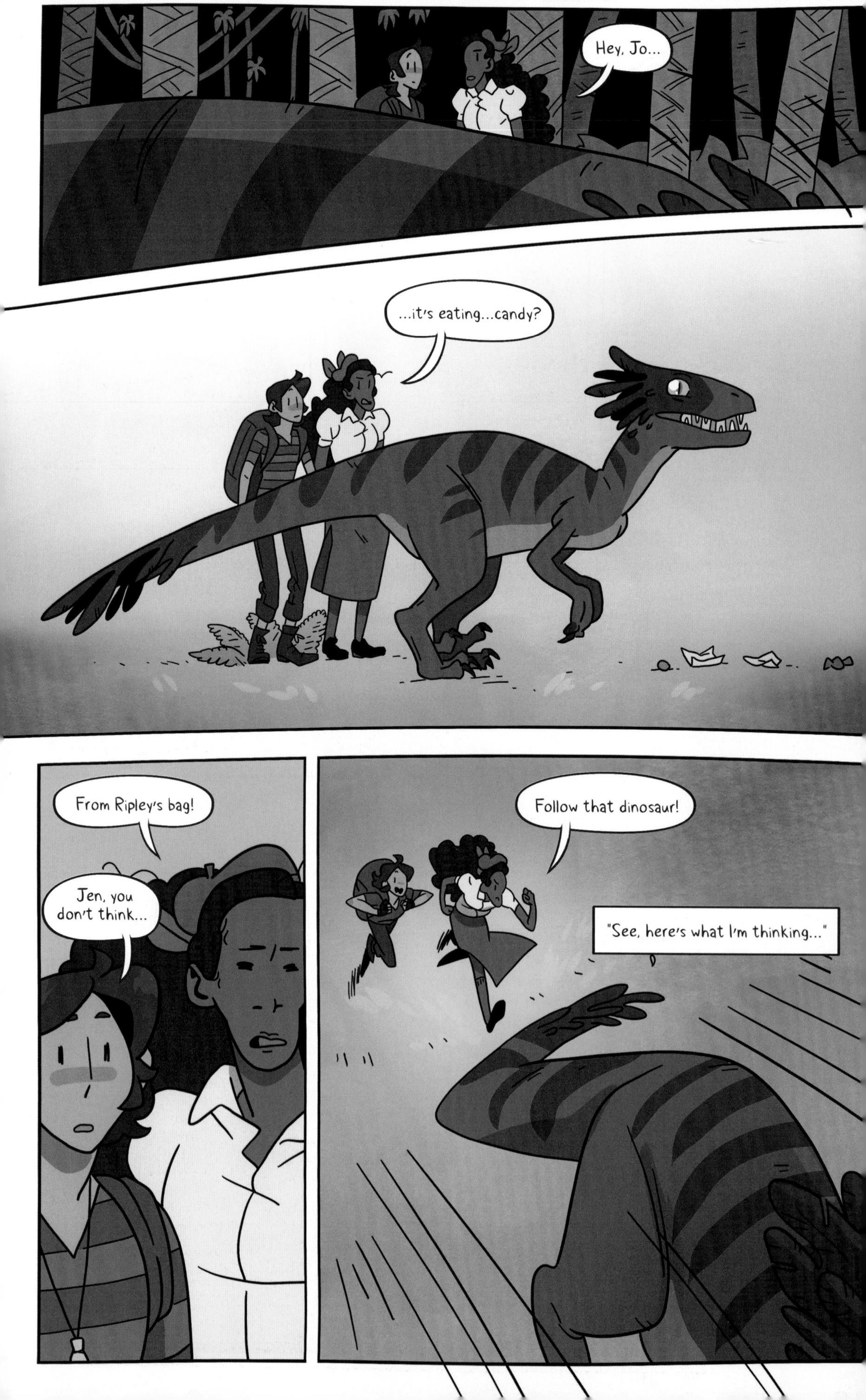
Hey, Jo...
...it's eating...candy?
From Ripley's bag!
Jen, you don't think...
Follow that dinosaur!
"See, here's what I'm thinking..."

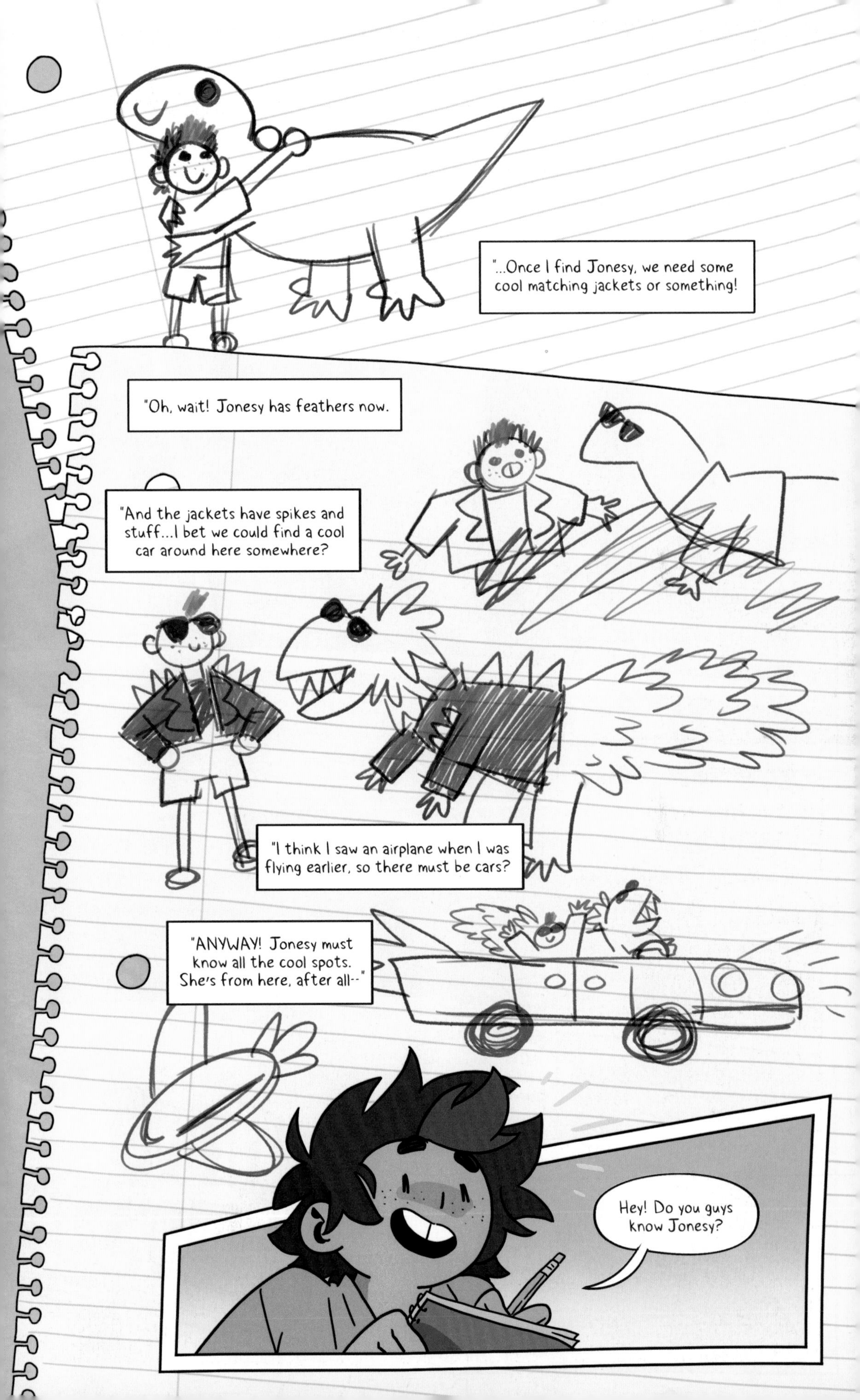
"...Once I find Jonesy, we need some cool matching jackets or something!
"Oh, wait! Jonesy has feathers now.
"And the jackets have spikes and stuff...I bet we could find a cool car around here somewhere?
"I think I saw an airplane when I was flying earlier, so there must be cars?
"ANYWAY! Jonesy must know all the cool spots. She's from here, after all--"
Hey! Do you guys know Jonesy?

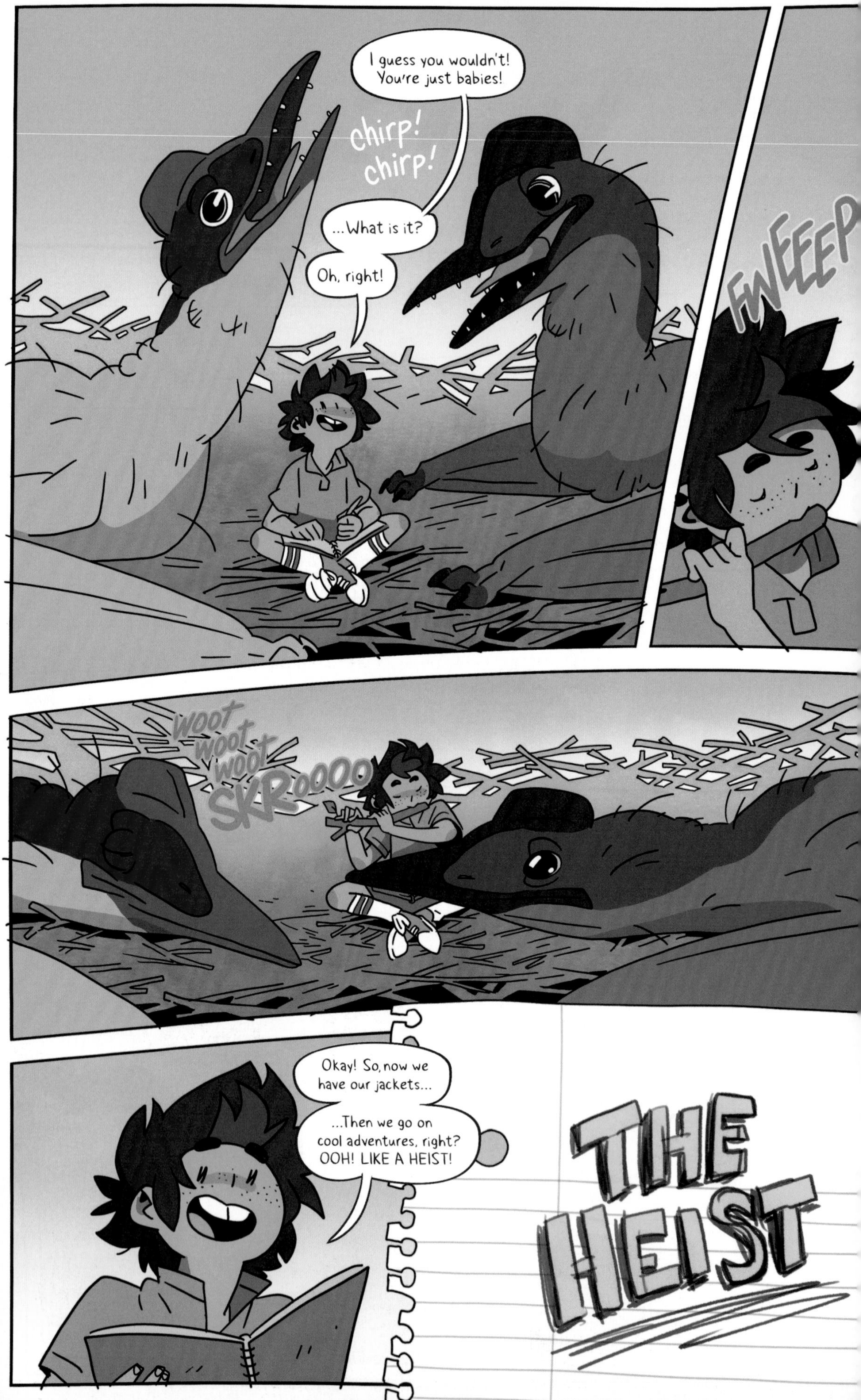
I guess you wouldn't! You're just babies!
chirp! chirp!
...What is it?
Oh, right!
FWEEEP
woot woot woot
SKROOOO
Okay! So, now we have our jackets...
...Then we go on cool adventures, right? OOH! LIKE A HEIST!
THE HEIST

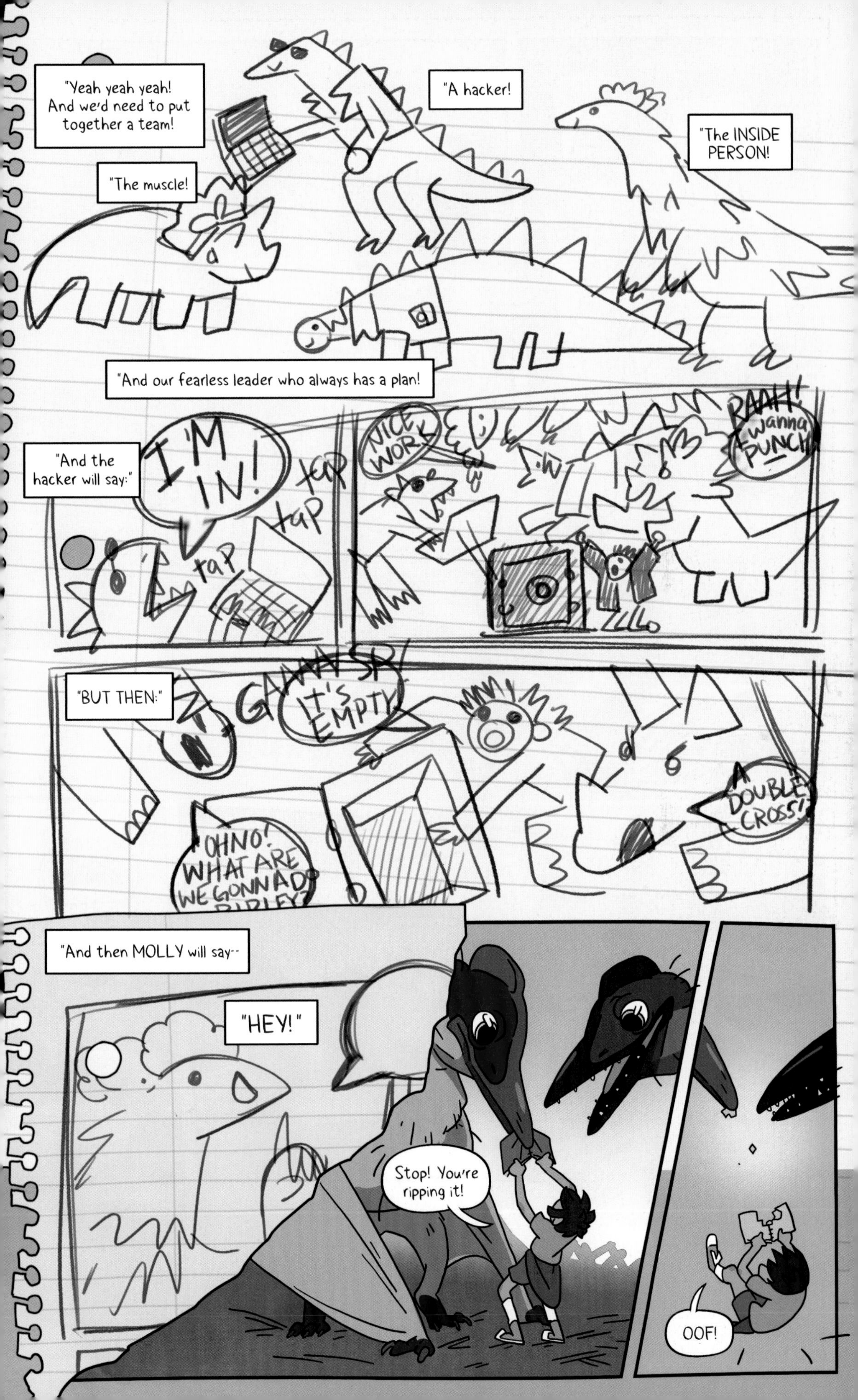

"Yeah yeah yeah! And we'd need to put together a team!
"The muscle!
"A hacker!
"The INSIDE PERSON!
"And our fearless leader who always has a plan!
"And the hacker will say:"
I'M IN!
tap tap tap
NICE WOR
RAAH!
I wanna PUNCH
"BUT THEN:"
GAAASP!
IT'S EMPTY
OH NO! WHAT ARE WE GONNA DO
A DOUBLE CROSS!
"And then MOLLY will say--
"HEY!"
Stop! You're ripping it!
OOF!

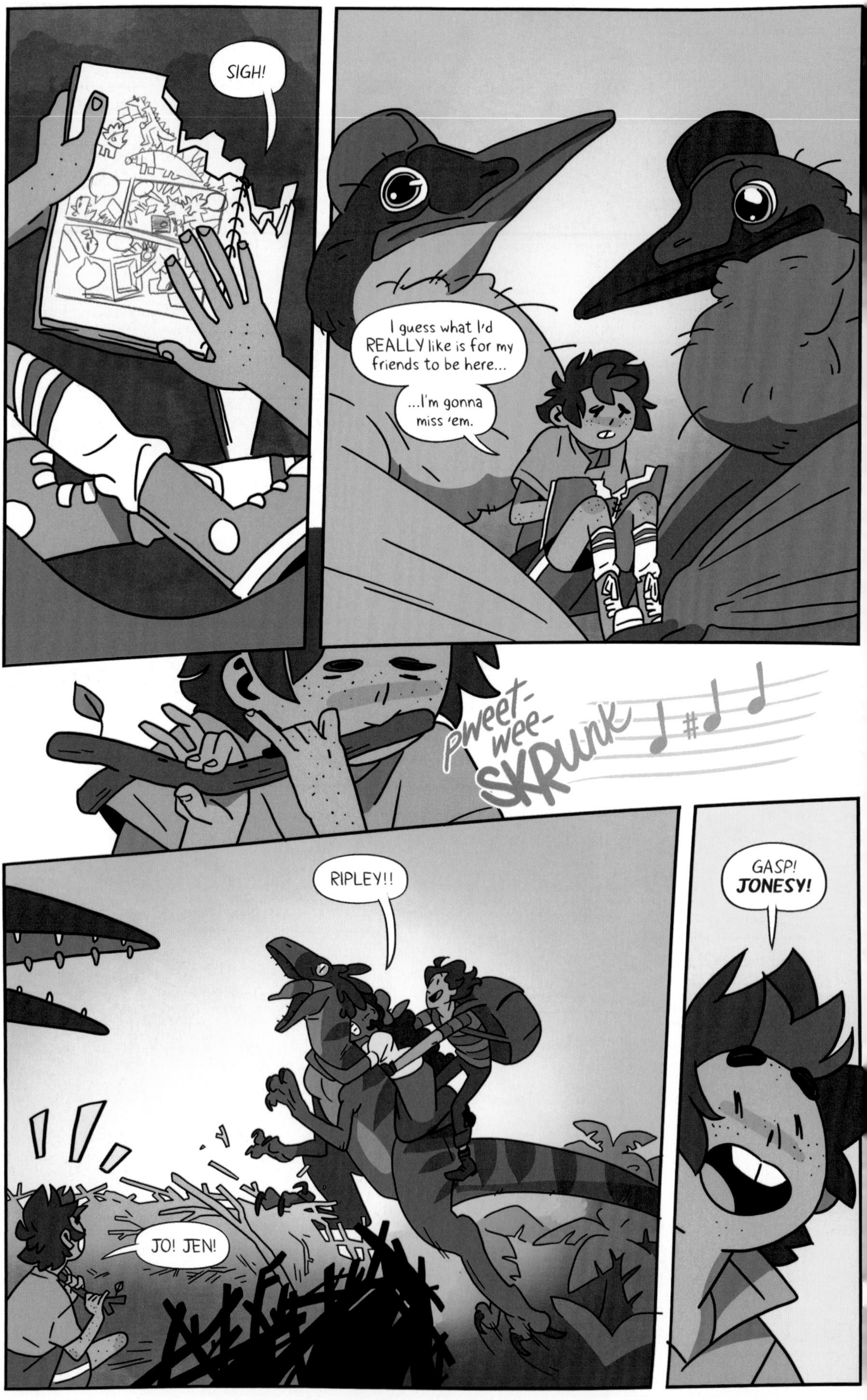
SIGH!
I guess what I'd REALLY like is for my friends to be here...
...I'm gonna miss 'em.
pweet-wee-SKRUNK
RIPLEY!!
JO! JEN!
GASP! **JONESY!**

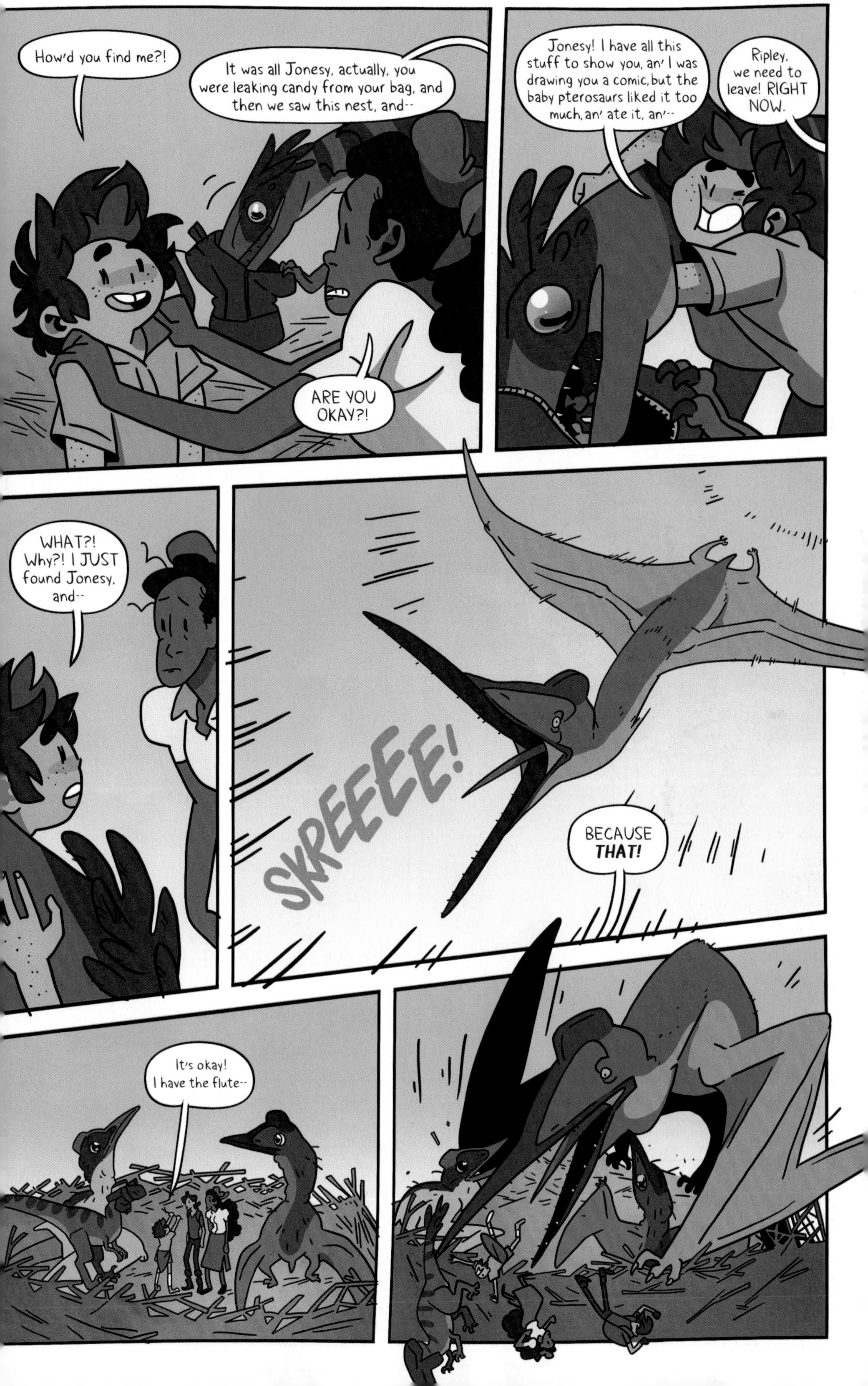
How'd you find me?!
It was all Jonesy, actually, you were leaking candy from your bag, and then we saw this nest, and--
ARE YOU OKAY?!
Jonesy! I have all this stuff to show you, an' I was drawing you a comic, but the baby pterosaurs liked it too much, an' ate it, an'--
Ripley, we need to leave! RIGHT NOW.
WHAT?! Why?! I JUST found Jonesy, and--
SKREEEE!
BECAUSE THAT!
It's okay! I have the flute--

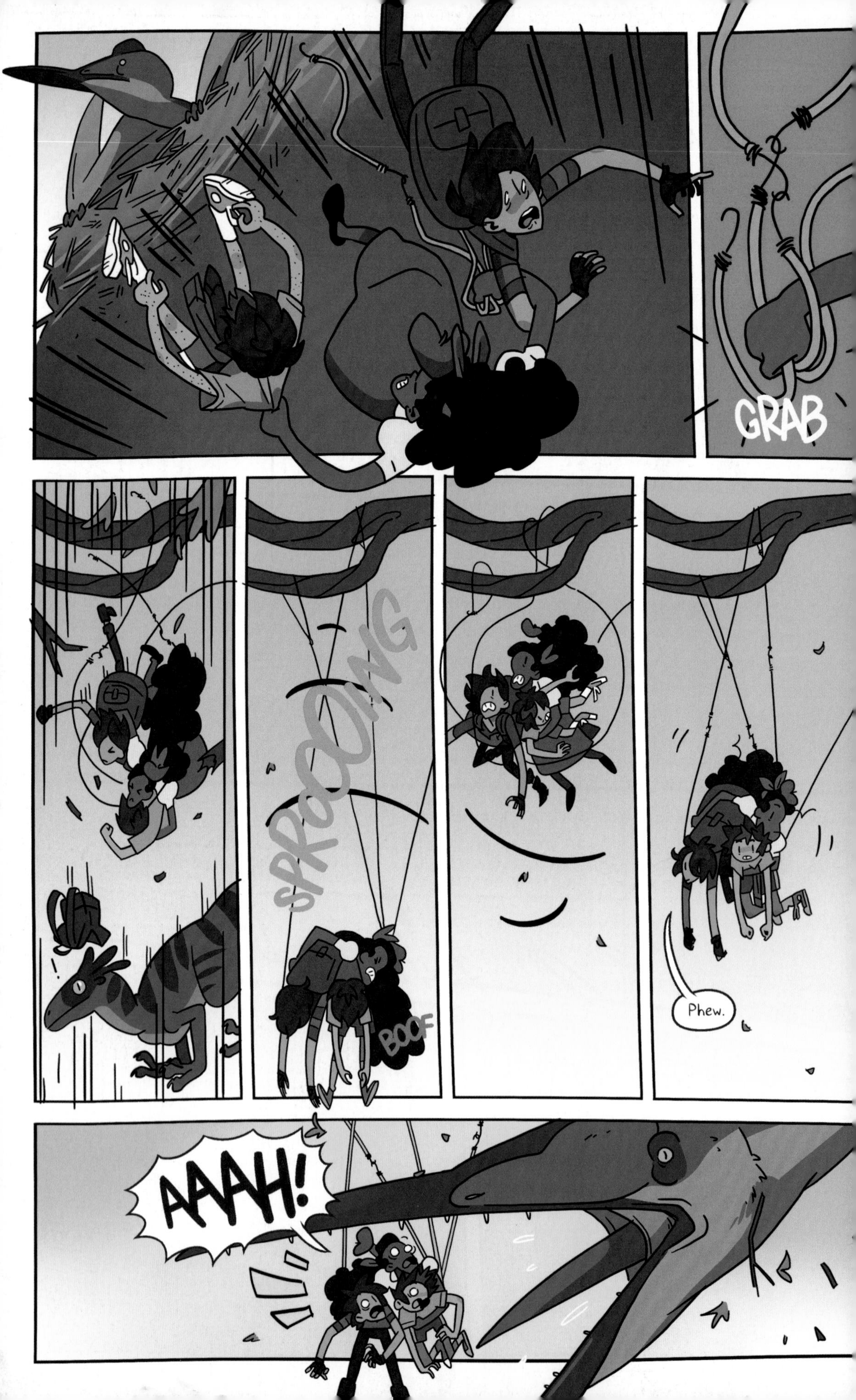
GRAB
SPROOOING
BOOF
Phew.
AAAH!

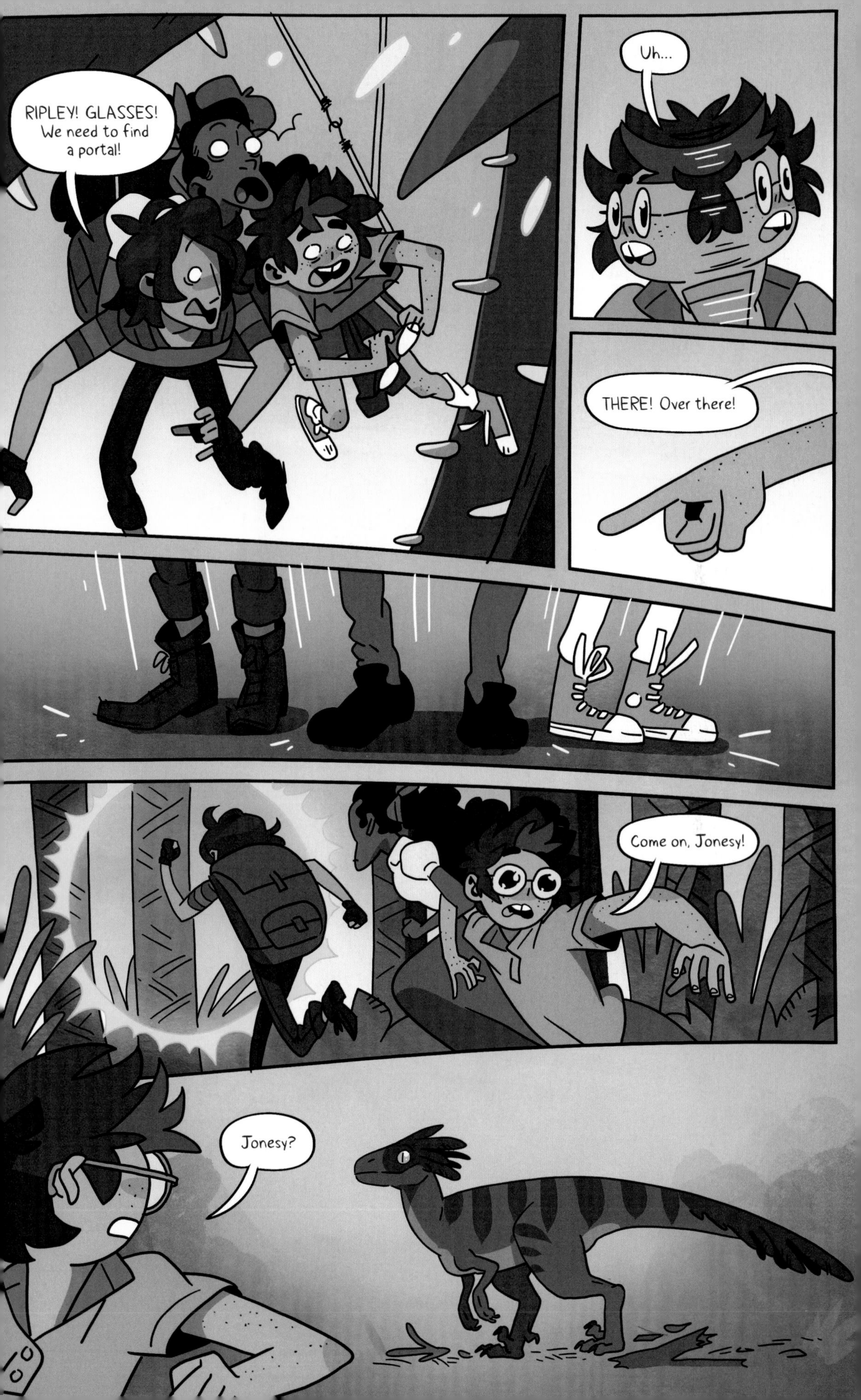
RIPLEY! GLASSES! We need to find a portal!
Uh...
THERE! Over there!
Come on, Jonesy!
Jonesy?

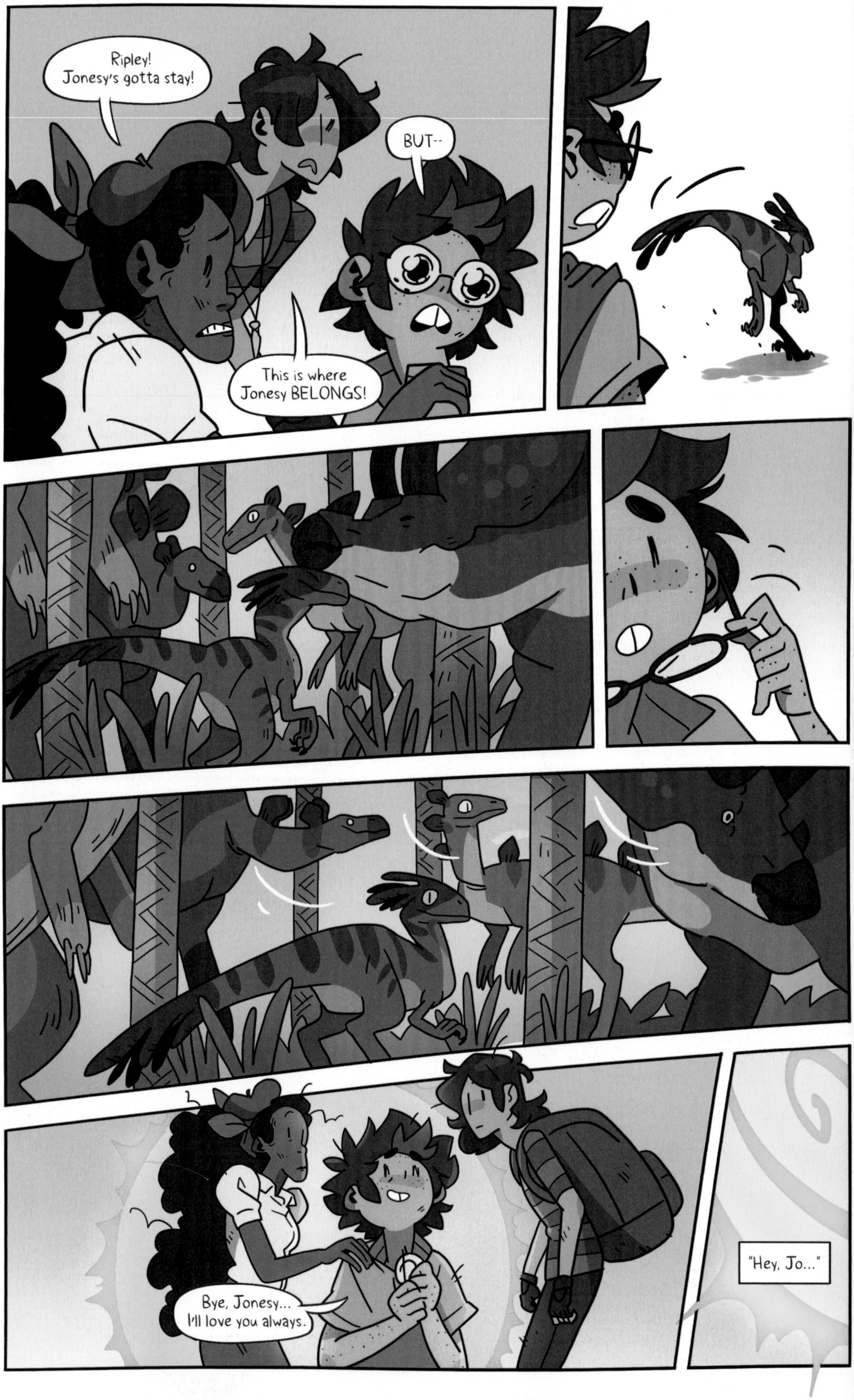
Ripley! Jonesy's gotta stay!
BUT--
This is where Jonesy BELONGS!
Bye, Jonesy... I'll love you always.
"Hey, Jo..."

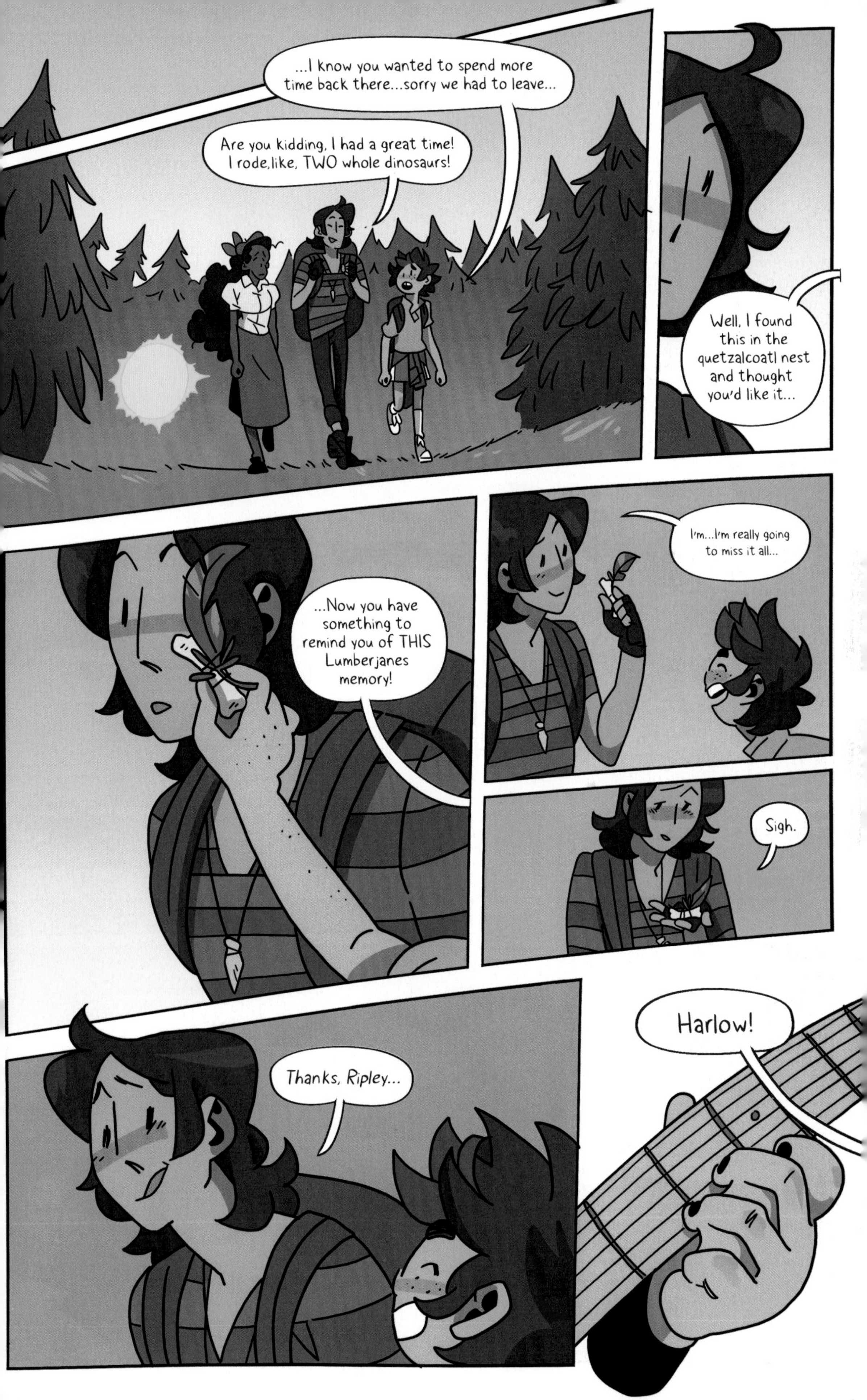
...I know you wanted to spend more time back there...sorry we had to leave...
Are you kidding, I had a great time! I rode,like, TWO whole dinosaurs!
Well, I found this in the quetzalcoatl nest and thought you'd like it...
...Now you have something to remind you of THIS Lumberjanes memory!
I'm...I'm really going to miss it all...
Sigh.
Thanks, Ripley...
Harlow!

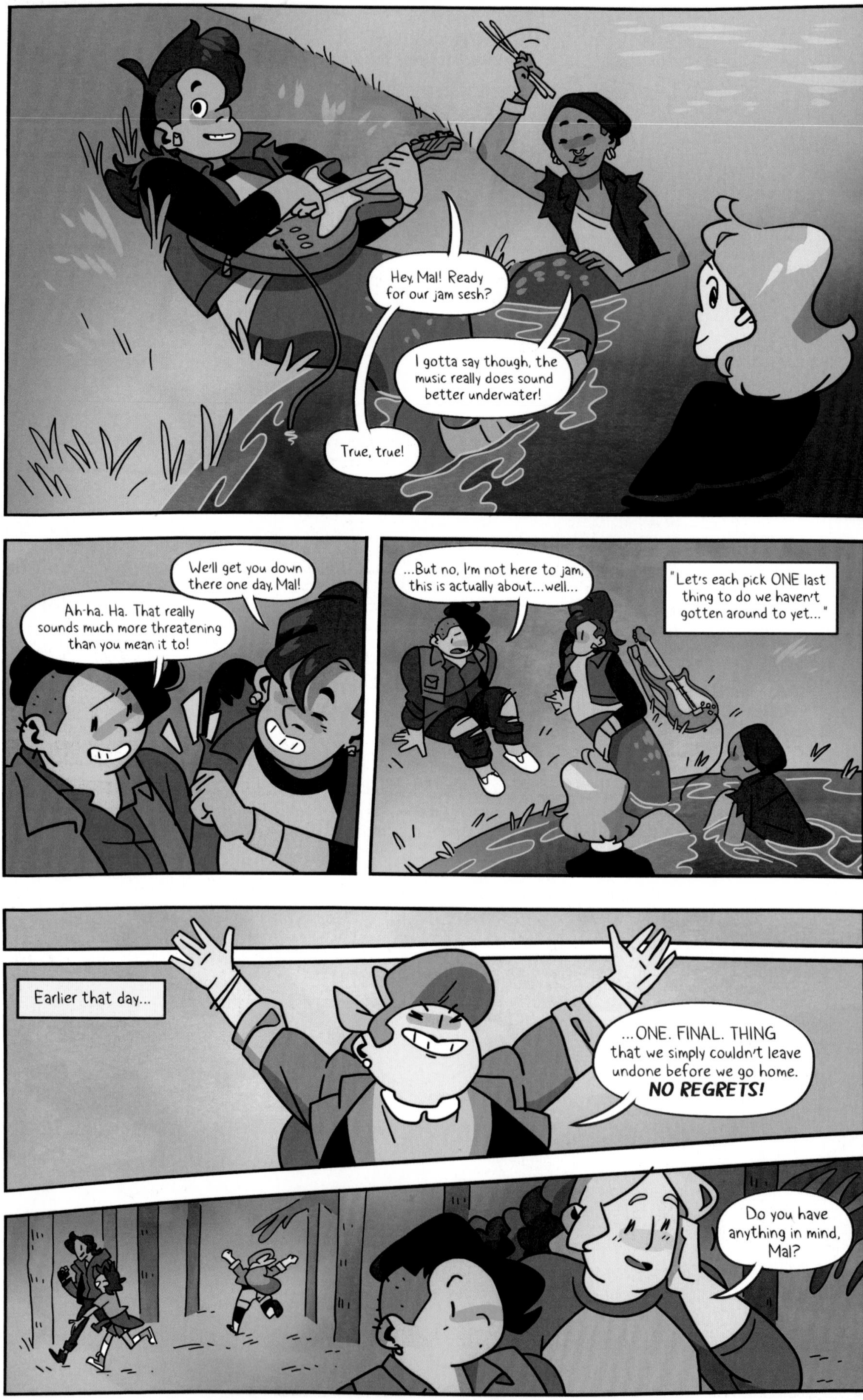
Hey, Mal! Ready for our jam sesh?
I gotta say though, the music really does sound better underwater!
True, true!
We'll get you down there one day, Mal!
Ah-ha. Ha. That really sounds much more threatening than you mean it to!
...But no, I'm not here to jam, this is actually about...well...
"Let's each pick ONE last thing to do we haven't gotten around to yet..."
Earlier that day...
...ONE. FINAL. THING that we simply couldn't leave undone before we go home. NO REGRETS!
Do you have anything in mind, Mal?

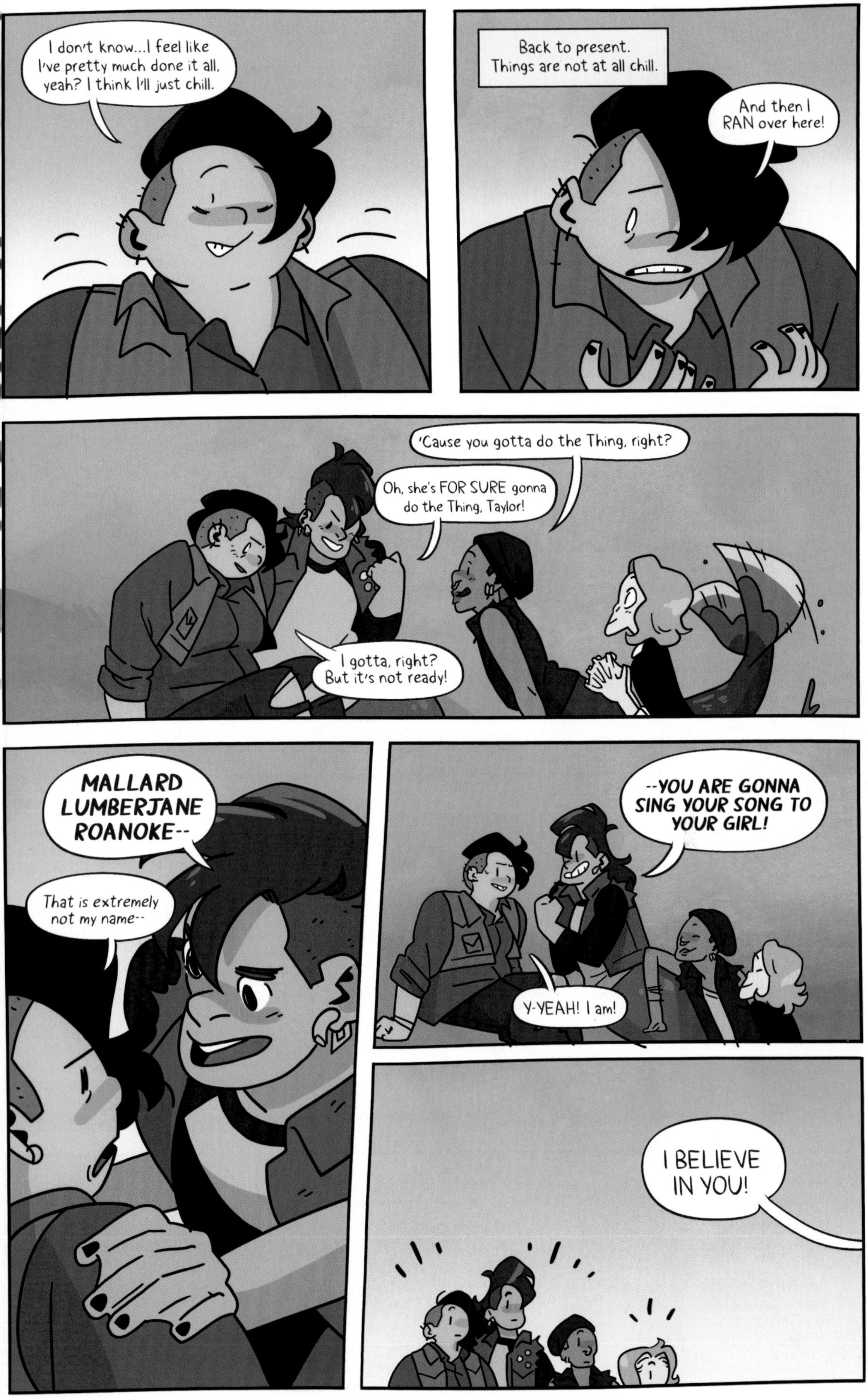
I don't know...I feel like I've pretty much done it all, yeah? I think I'll just chill.
Back to present. Things are not at all chill.
And then I RAN over here!
'Cause you gotta do the Thing, right?
Oh, she's FOR SURE gonna do the Thing, Taylor!
I gotta, right? But it's not ready!
MALLARD LUMBERJANE ROANOKE--
That is extremely not my name--
--YOU ARE GONNA SING YOUR SONG TO YOUR GIRL!
Y-YEAH! I am!
I BELIEVE IN YOU!

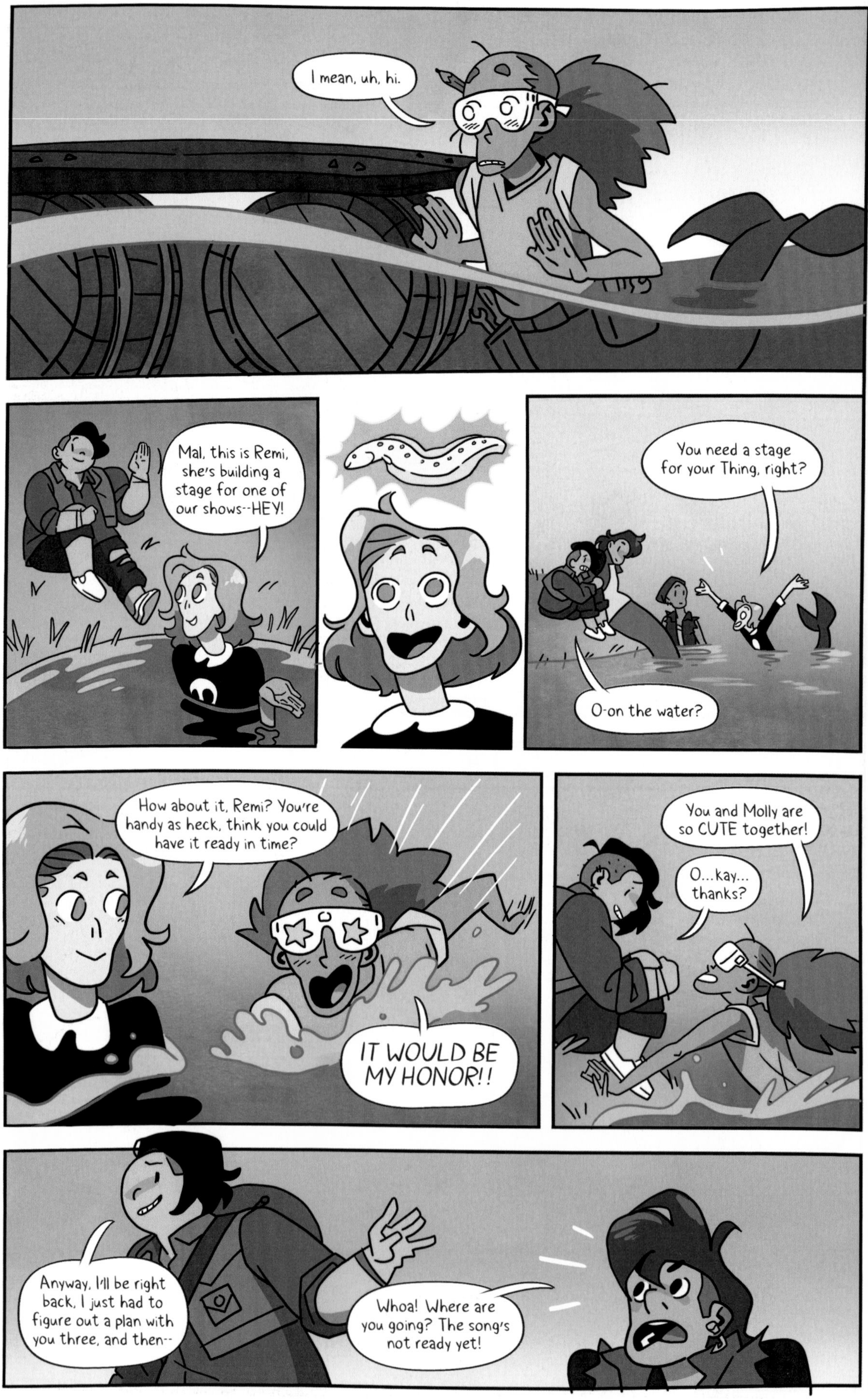
I mean, uh, hi.
Mal, this is Remi, she's building a stage for one of our shows--HEY!
You need a stage for your Thing, right?
O-on the water?
How about it, Remi? You're handy as heck, think you could have it ready in time?
IT WOULD BE MY HONOR!!
You and Molly are so CUTE together!
O...kay... thanks?
Anyway, I'll be right back, I just had to figure out a plan with you three, and then--
Whoa! Where are you going? The song's not ready yet!

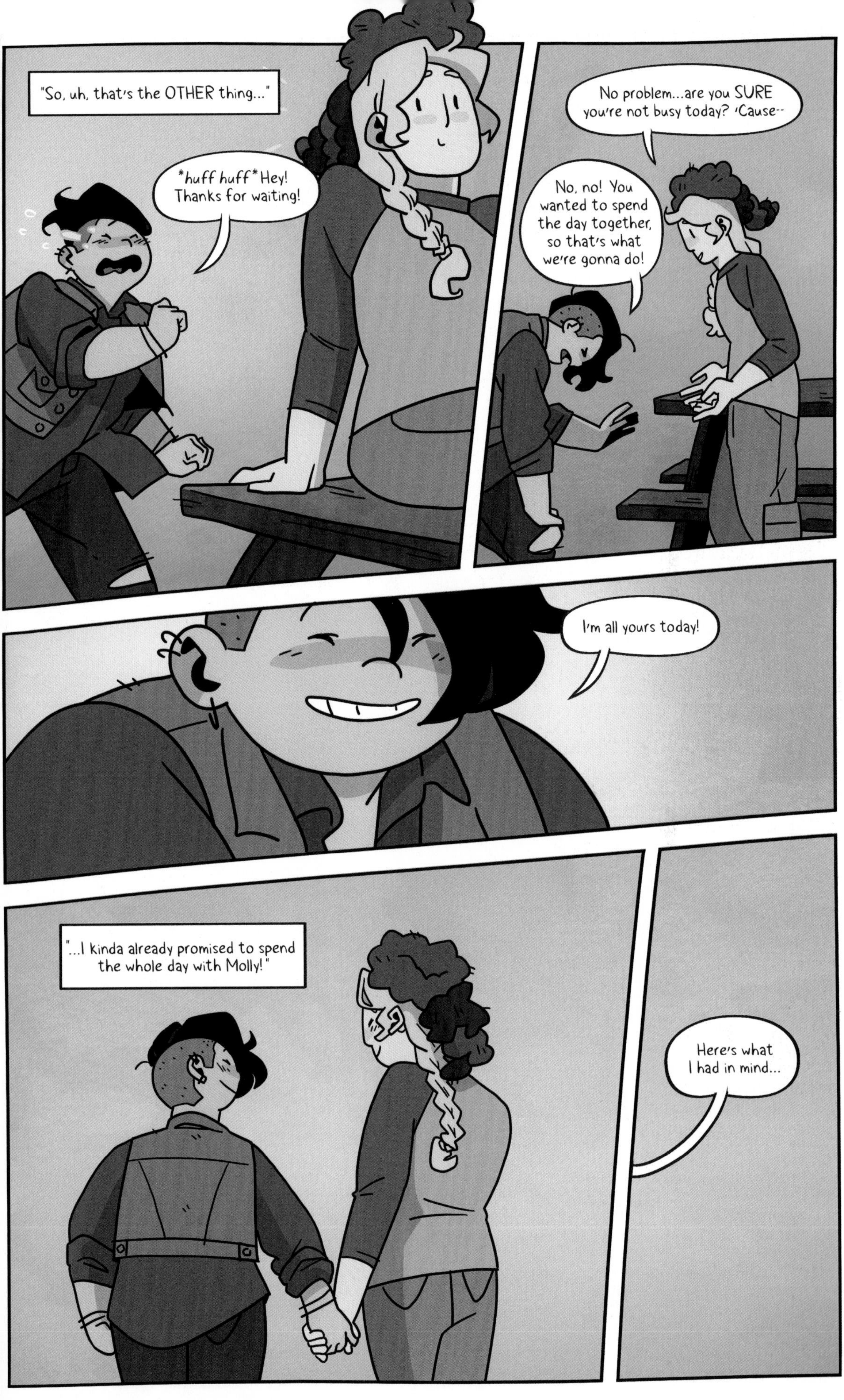
"So, uh, that's the OTHER thing..."
huff huff Hey! Thanks for waiting!
No problem...are you SURE you're not busy today? 'Cause--
No, no! You wanted to spend the day together, so that's what we're gonna do!
I'm all yours today!
"...I kinda already promised to spend the whole day with Molly!"
Here's what I had in mind...

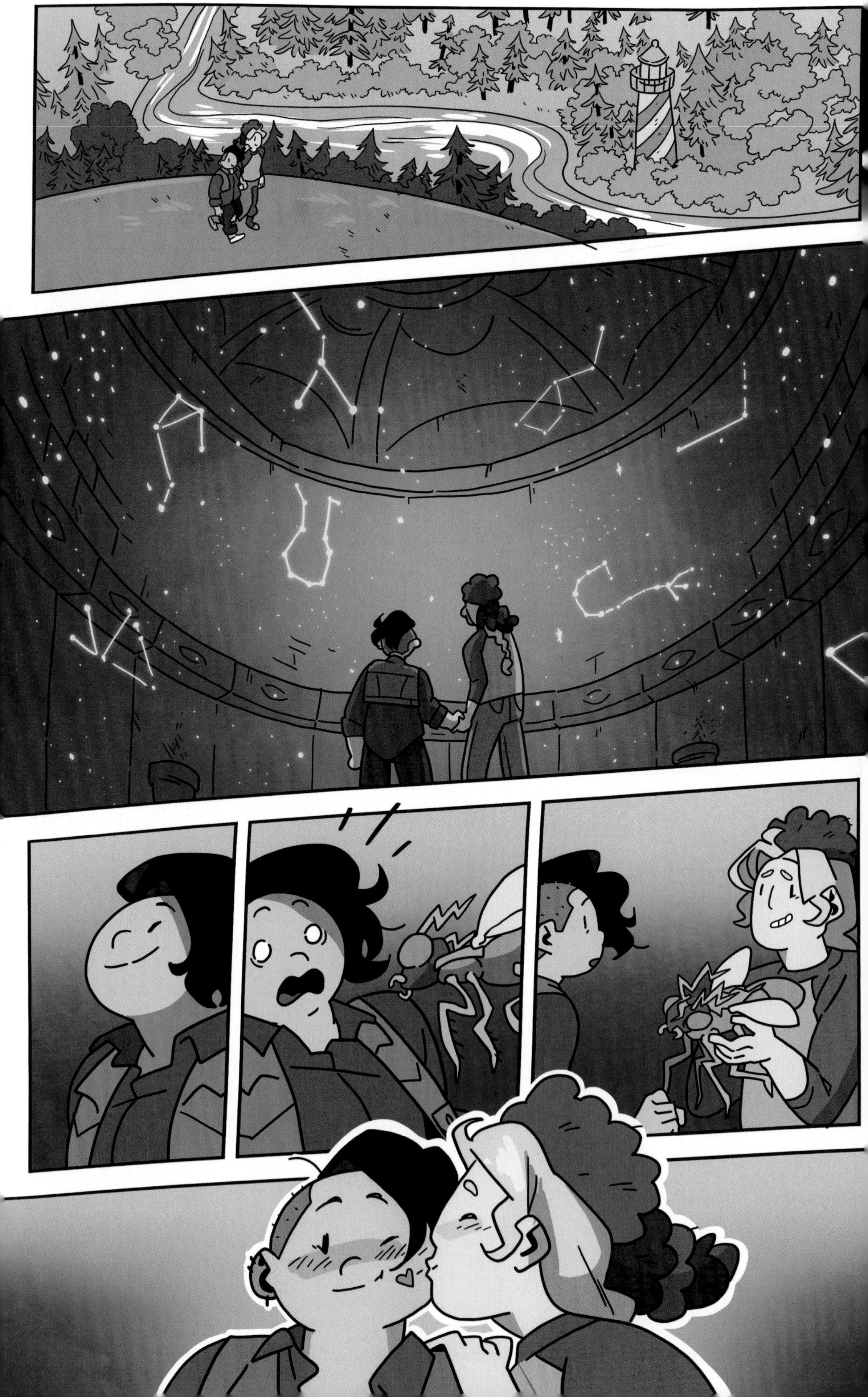

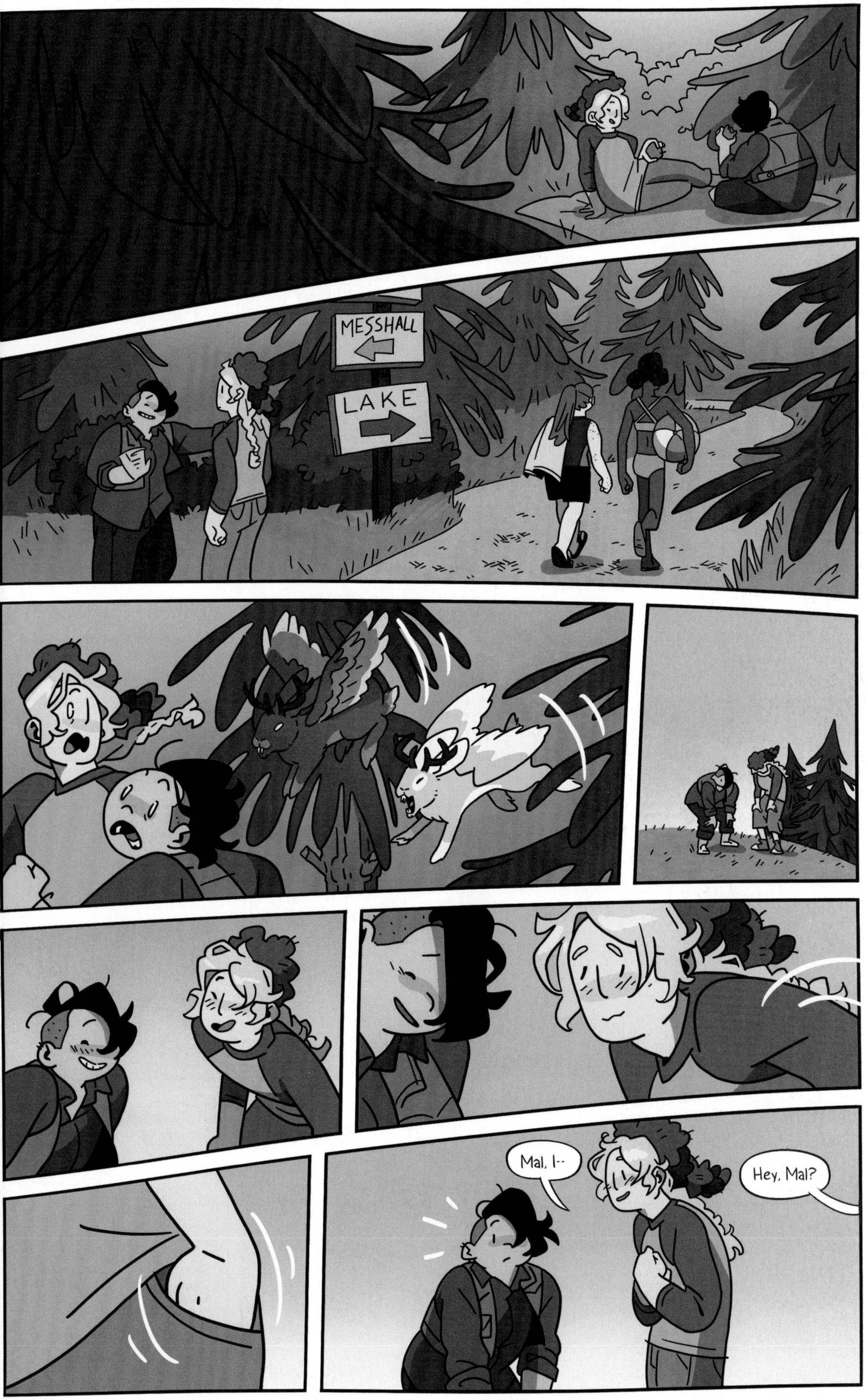
MESSHALL
LAKE
Mal, I--
Hey, Mal?

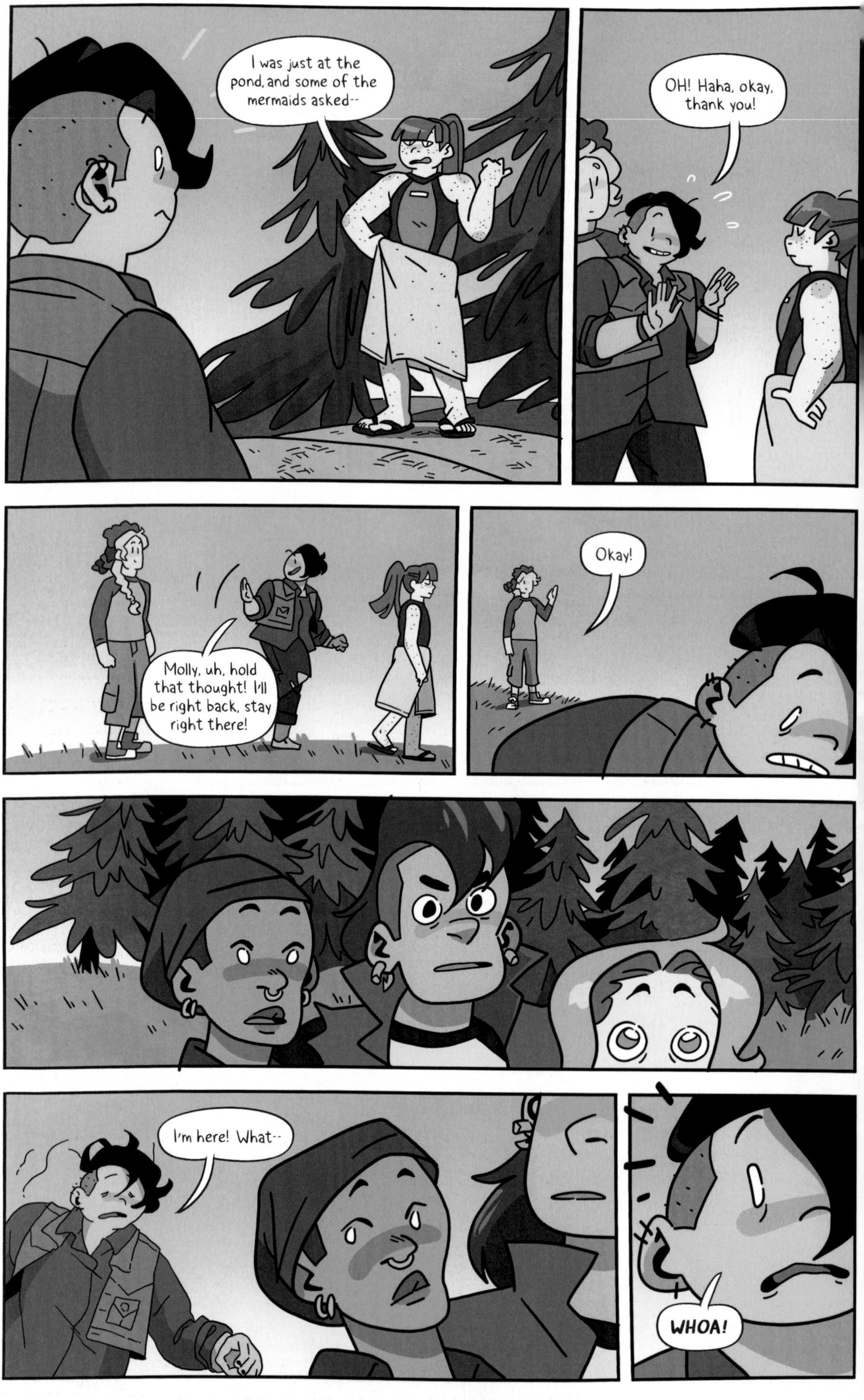
I was just at the pond, and some of the mermaids asked--
OH! Haha, okay, thank you!
Molly, uh, hold that thought! I'll be right back, stay right there!
Okay!
I'm here! What--
WHOA!

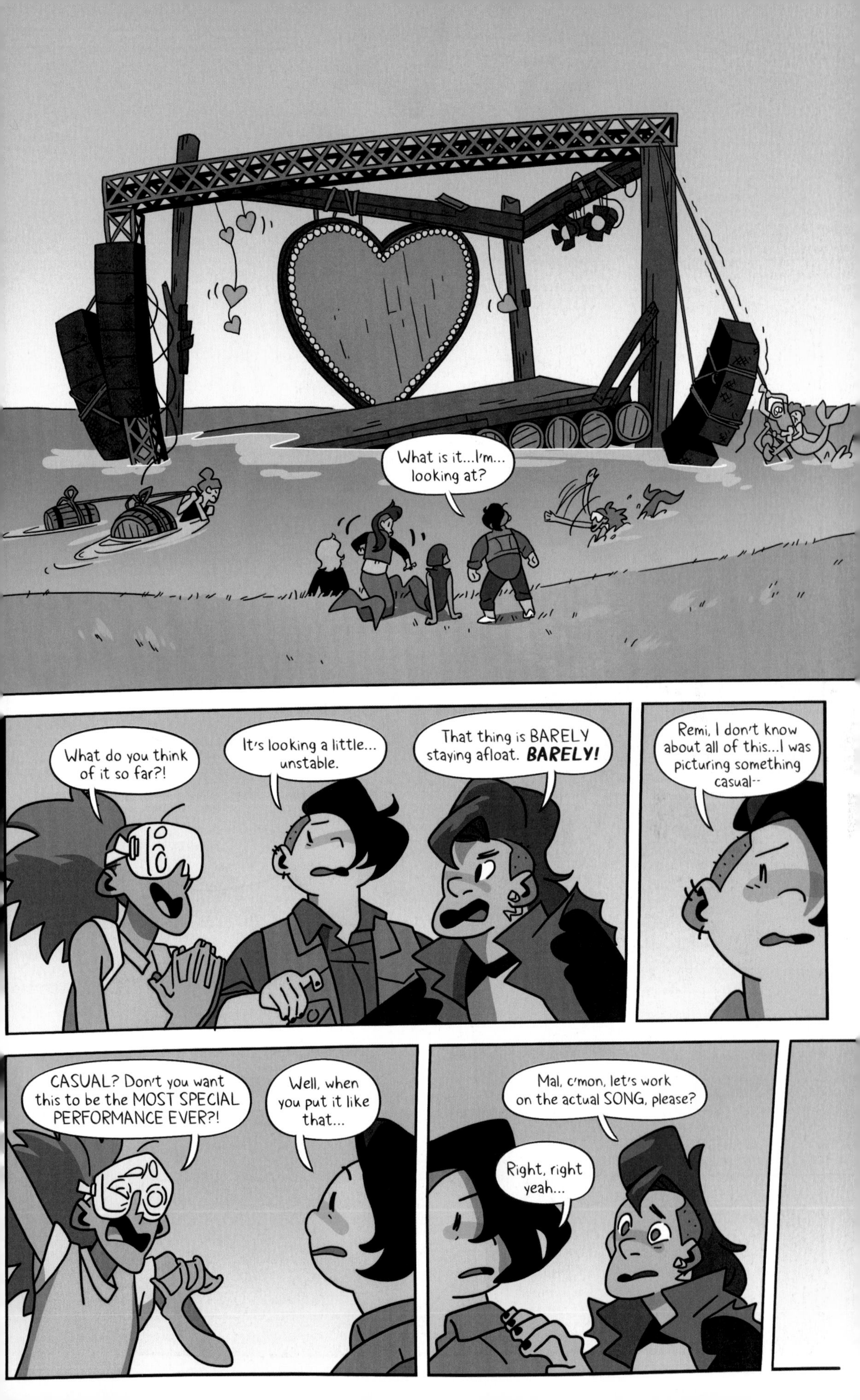
What is it...I'm... looking at?
What do you think of it so far?!
It's looking a little... unstable.
That thing is BARELY staying afloat. **BARELY!**
Remi, I don't know about all of this...I was picturing something casual--
CASUAL? Don't you want this to be the MOST SPECIAL PERFORMANCE EVER?!
Well, when you put it like that...
Mal, c'mon, let's work on the actual SONG, please?
Right, right yeah...

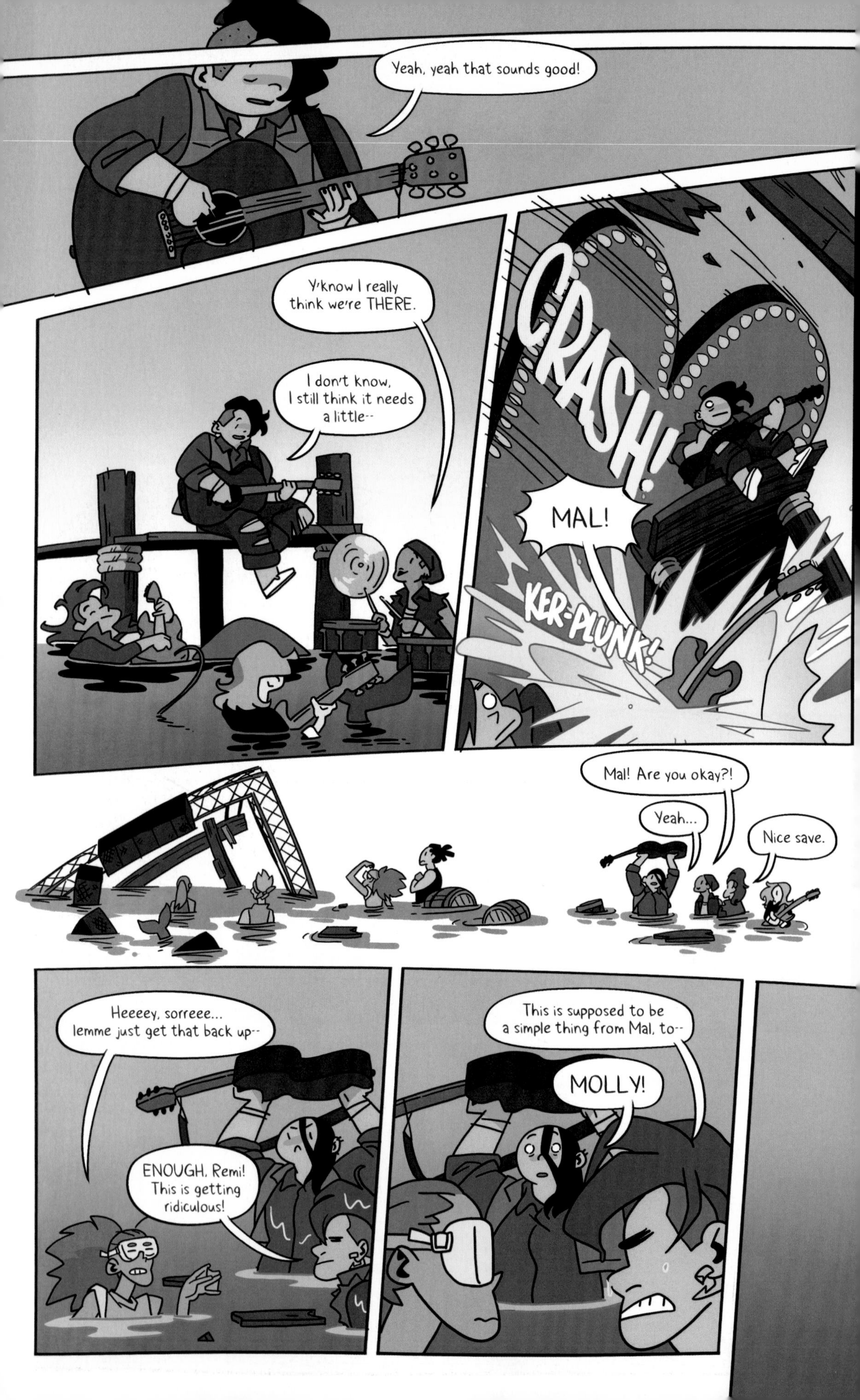
Yeah, yeah that sounds good!
Y'know I really think we're THERE.
I don't know, I still think it needs a little--
CRASH!
MAL!
KER-PLUNK!
Mal! Are you okay?!
Yeah...
Nice save.
Heeeey, sorreee... lemme just get that back up--
ENOUGH, Remi! This is getting ridiculous!
This is supposed to be a simple thing from Mal, to--
MOLLY!

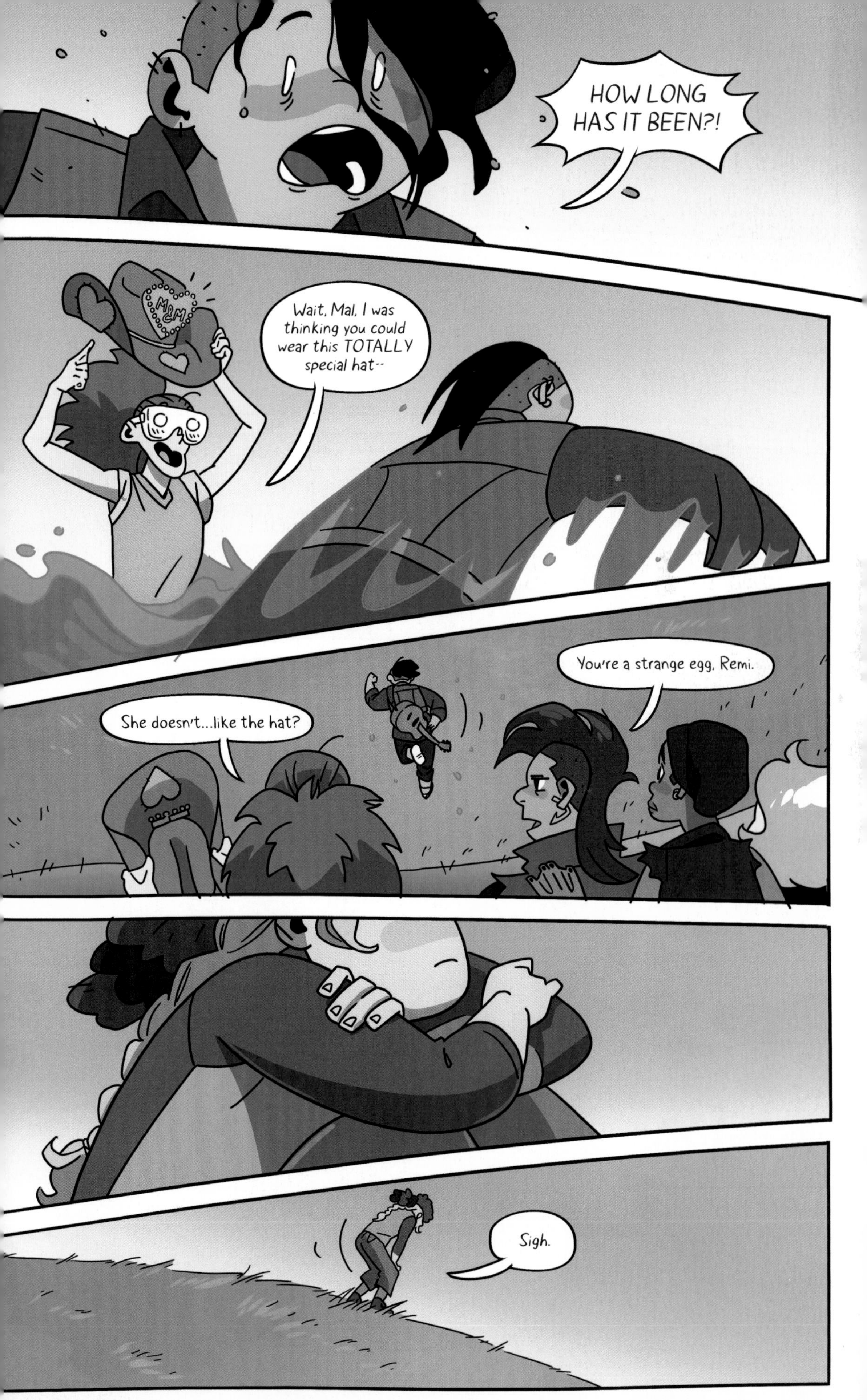
HOW LONG HAS IT BEEN?!
Wait, Mal, I was thinking you could wear this TOTALLY special hat--
M&M
She doesn't...like the hat?
You're a strange egg, Remi.
Sigh.

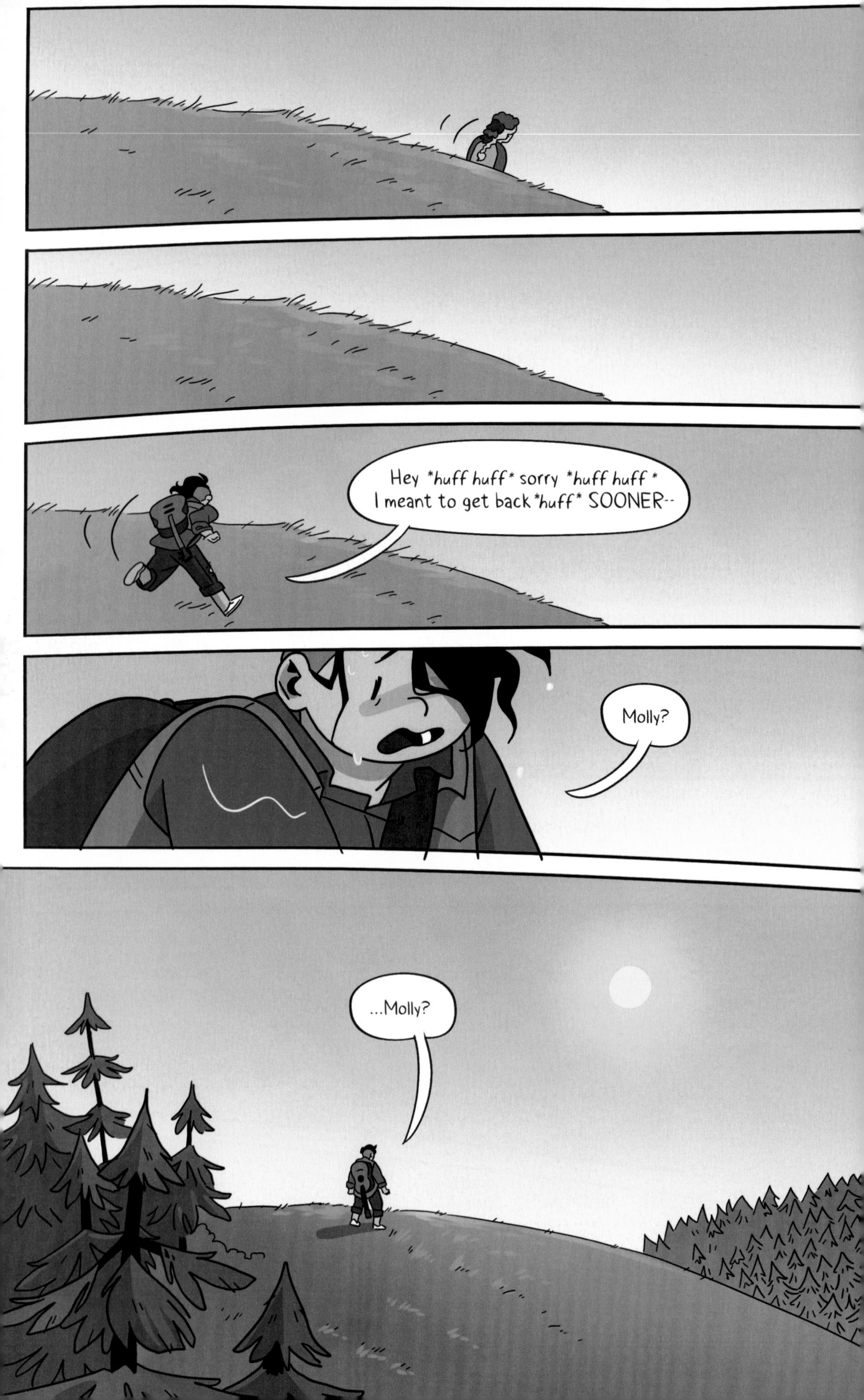
Hey *huff huff* sorry *huff huff *
I meant to get back *huff* SOONER--
Molly?
...Molly?

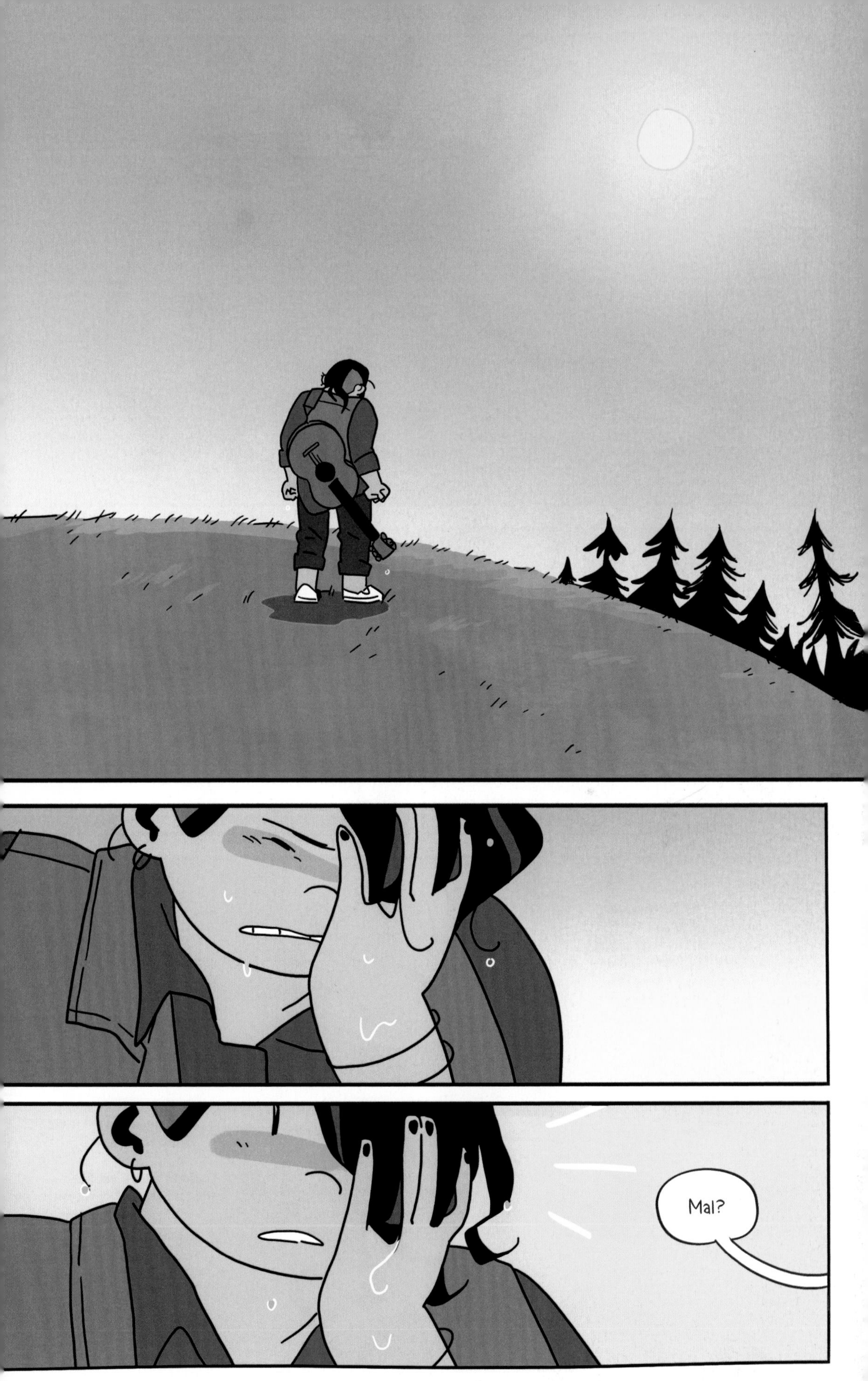
Mal?

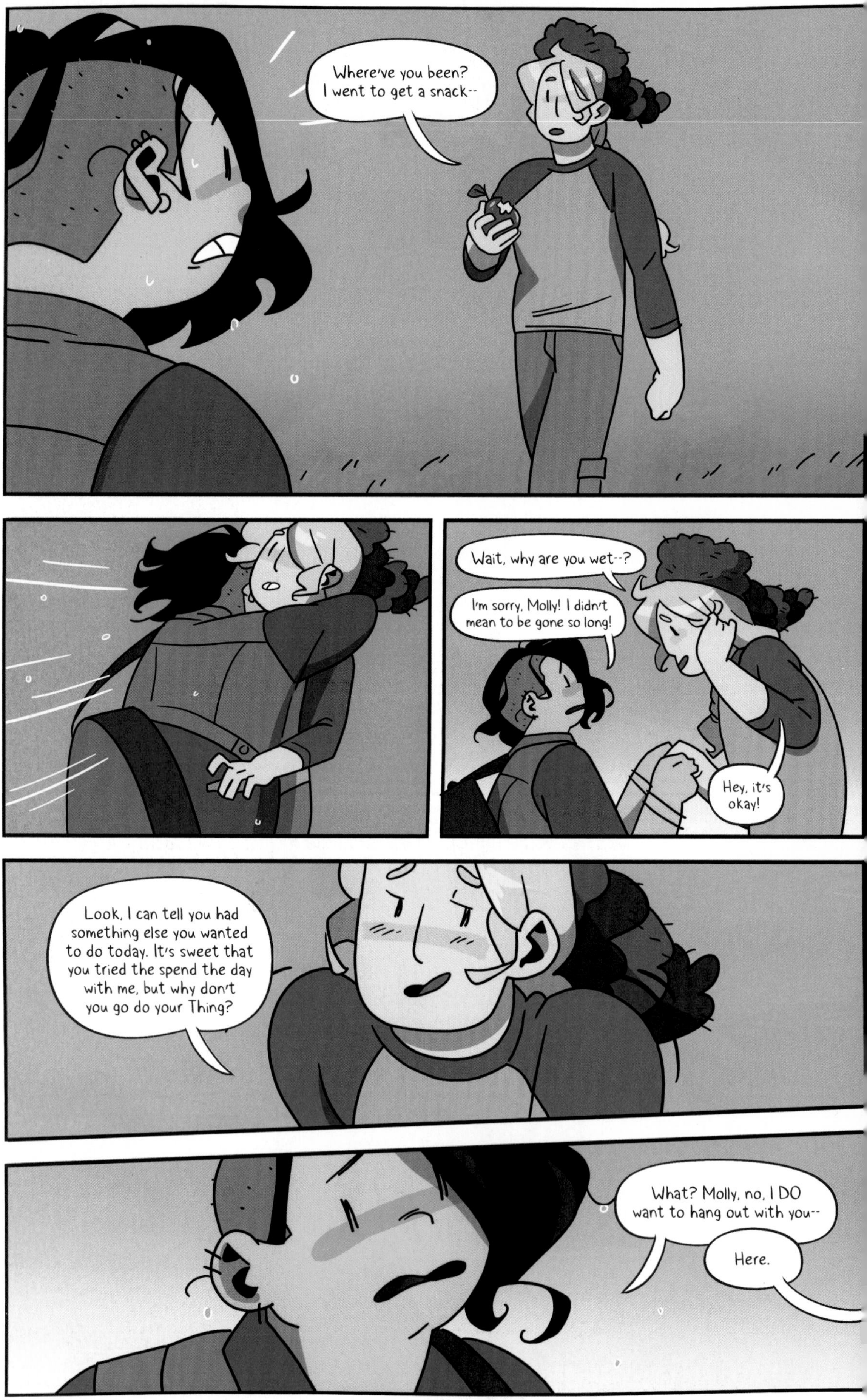
Where've you been? I went to get a snack--
Wait, why are you wet--?
I'm sorry, Molly! I didn't mean to be gone so long!
Hey, it's okay!
Look, I can tell you had something else you wanted to do today. It's sweet that you tried the spend the day with me, but why don't you go do your Thing?
What? Molly, no, I DO want to hang out with you--
Here.

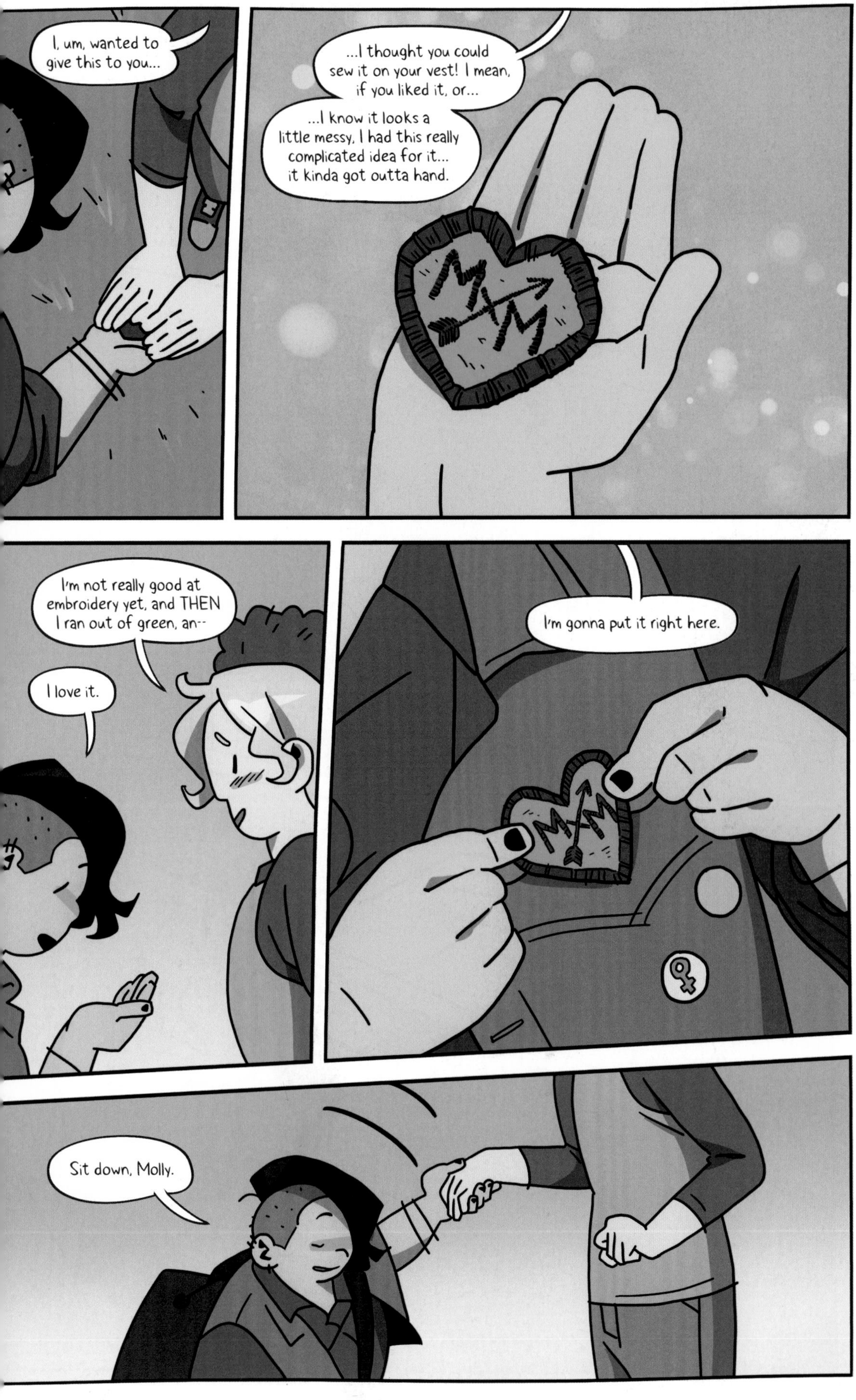
I, um, wanted to give this to you...
...I thought you could sew it on your vest! I mean, if you liked it, or...
...I know it looks a little messy, I had this really complicated idea for it... it kinda got outta hand.
I'm not really good at embroidery yet, and THEN I ran out of green, an--
I love it.
I'm gonna put it right here.
Sit down, Molly.

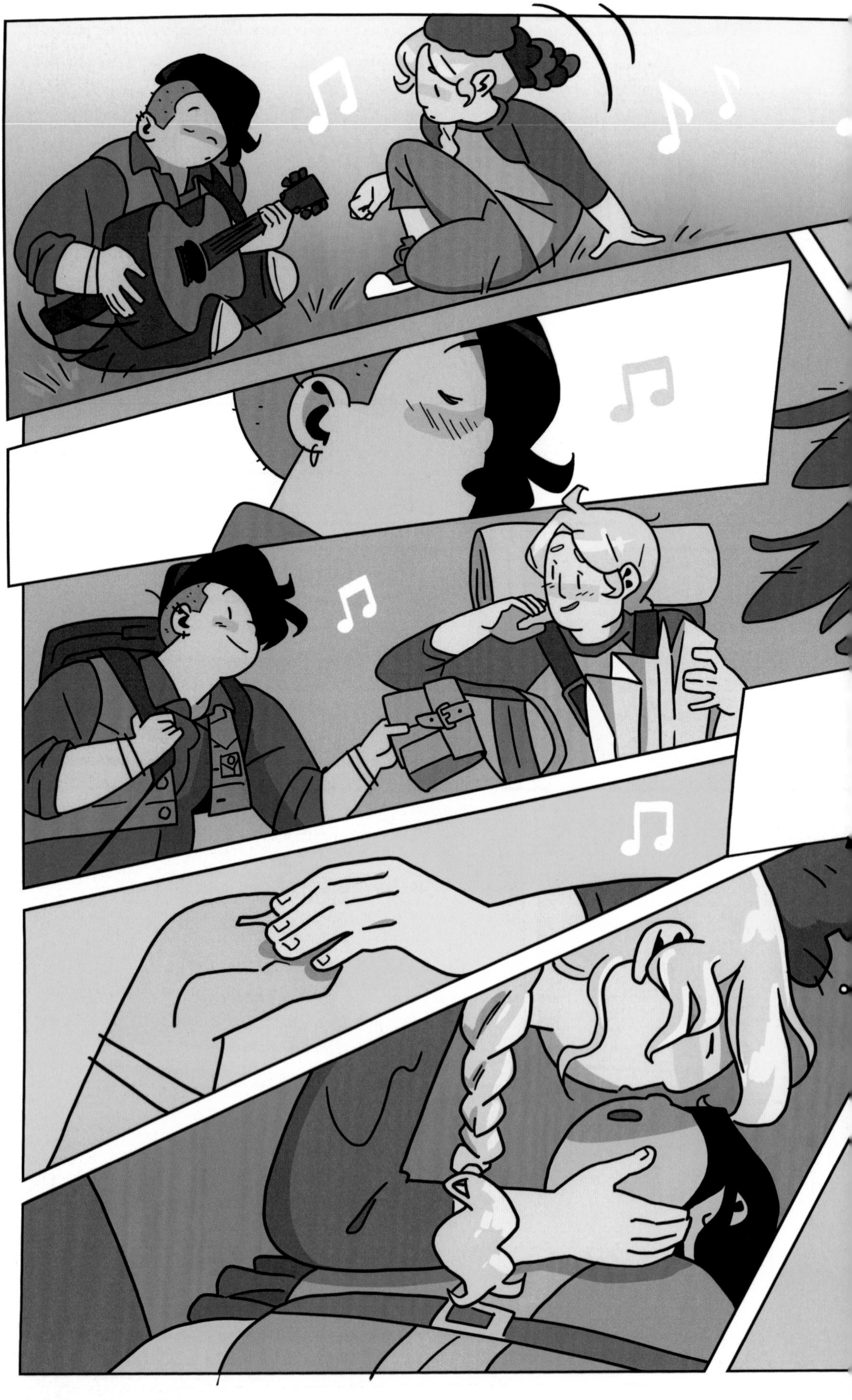

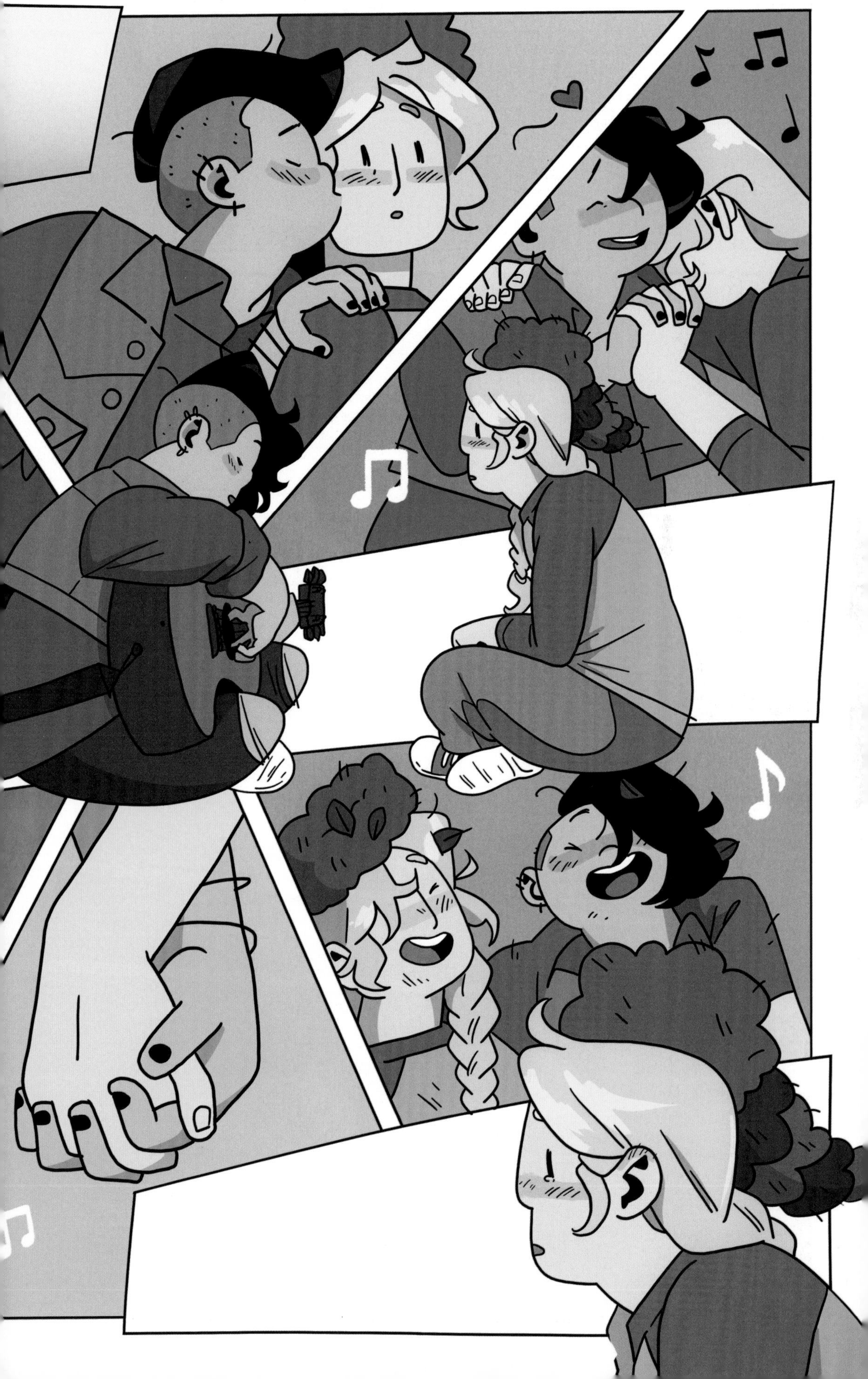

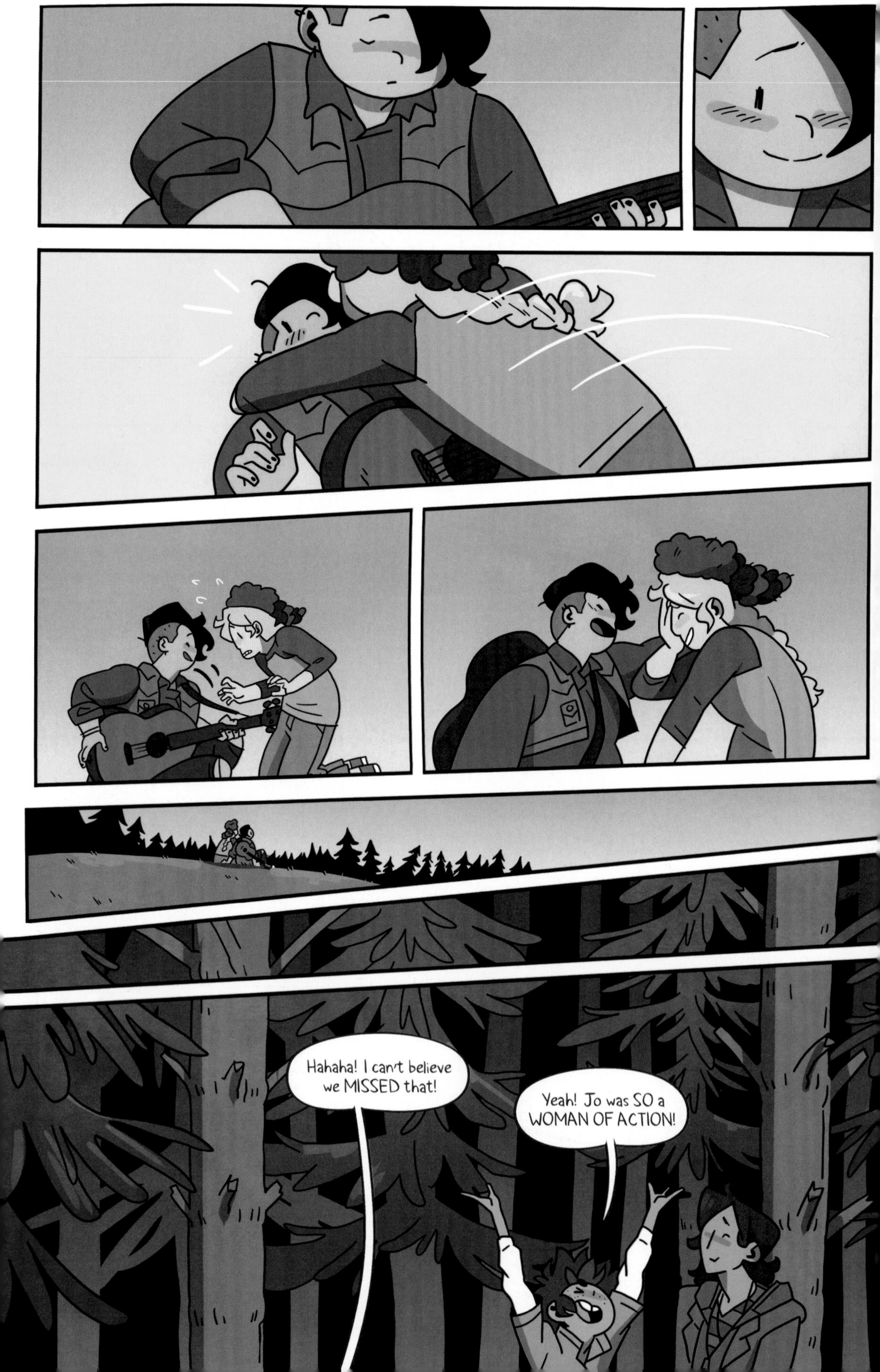
Hahaha! I can't believe we MISSED that!
Yeah! Jo was SO a WOMAN OF ACTION!

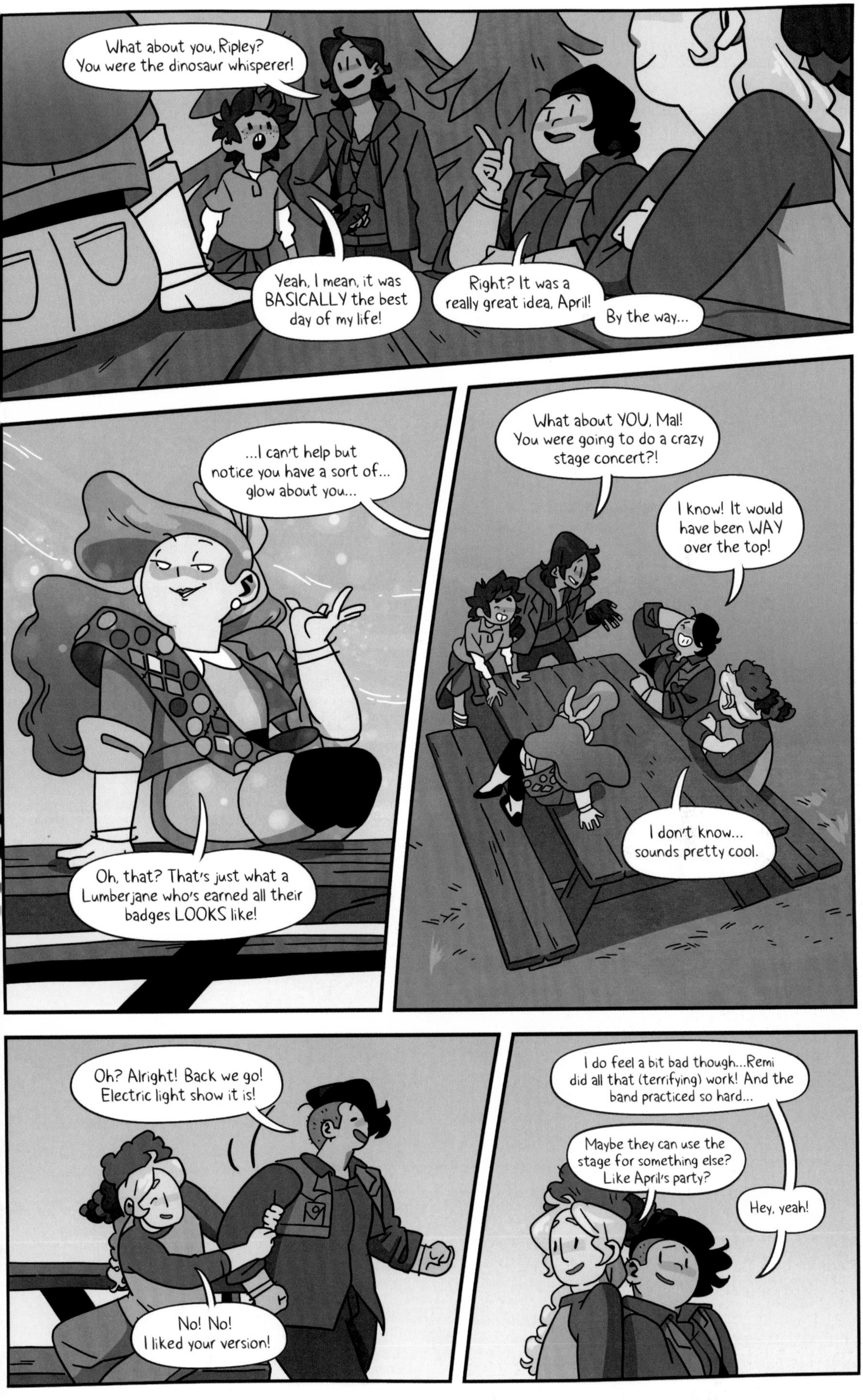
What about you, Ripley? You were the dinosaur whisperer!
Yeah, I mean, it was BASICALLY the best day of my life!
Right? It was a really great idea, April!
By the way...
...I can't help but notice you have a sort of... glow about you...
Oh, that? That's just what a Lumberjane who's earned all their badges LOOKS like!
What about YOU, Mal! You were going to do a crazy stage concert?!
I know! It would have been WAY over the top!
I don't know... sounds pretty cool.
Oh? Alright! Back we go! Electric light show it is!
No! No! I liked your version!
I do feel a bit bad though...Remi did all that (terrifying) work! And the band practiced so hard...
Maybe they can use the stage for something else? Like April's party?
Hey, yeah!

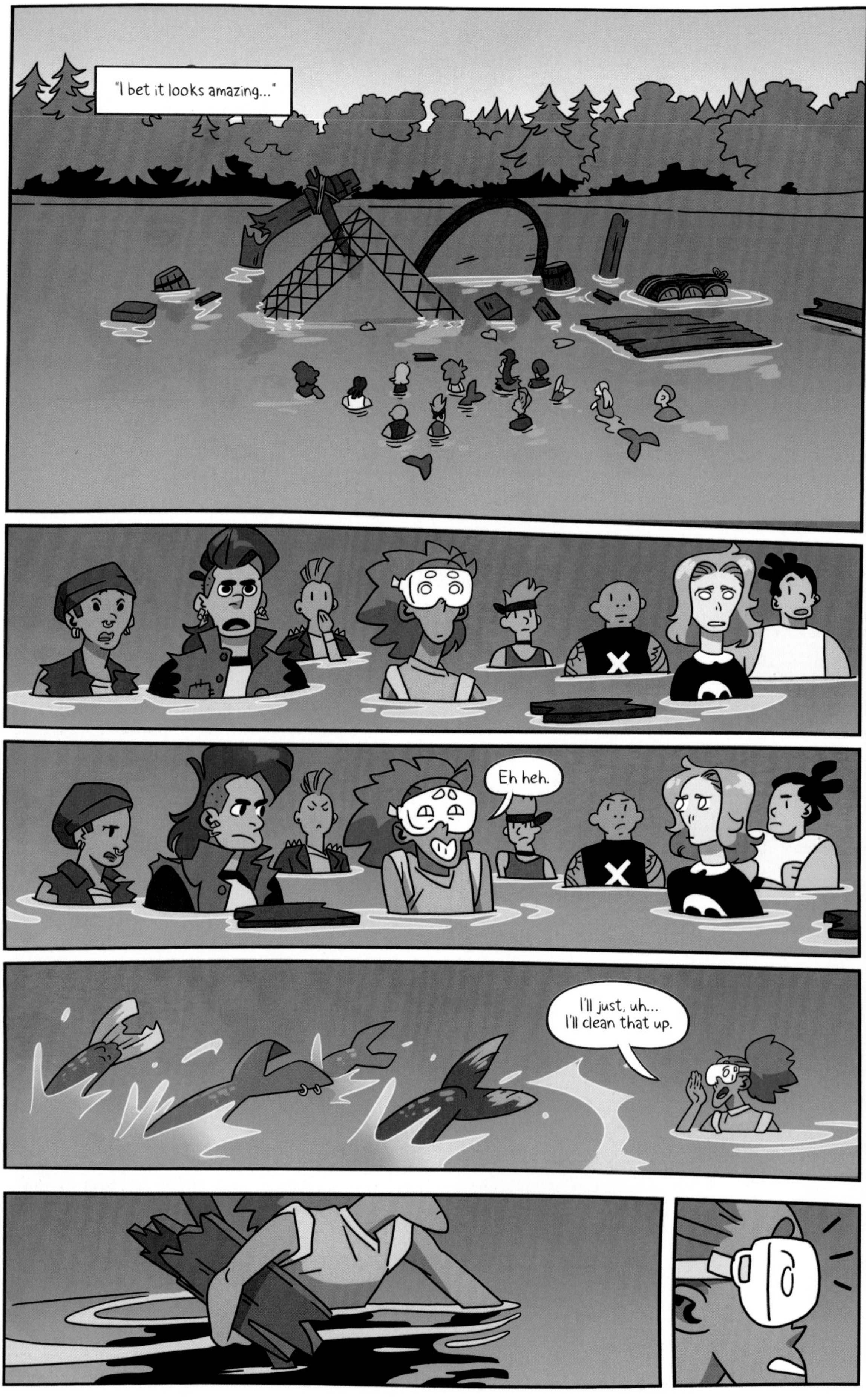
"I bet it looks amazing..."
Eh heh.
I'll just, uh...
I'll clean that up.

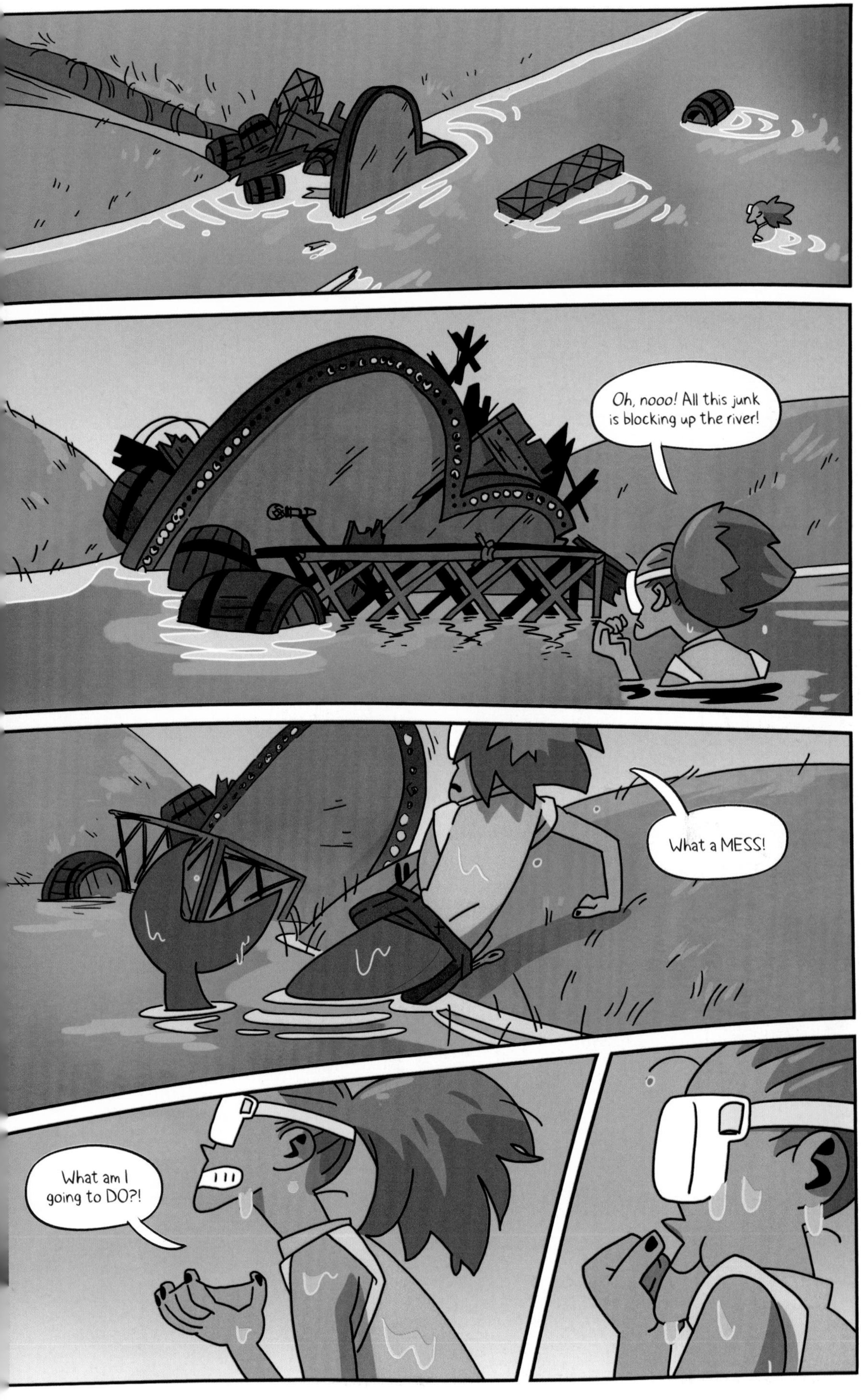
Oh, nooo! All this junk is blocking up the river!
What a MESS!
What am I going to DO?!

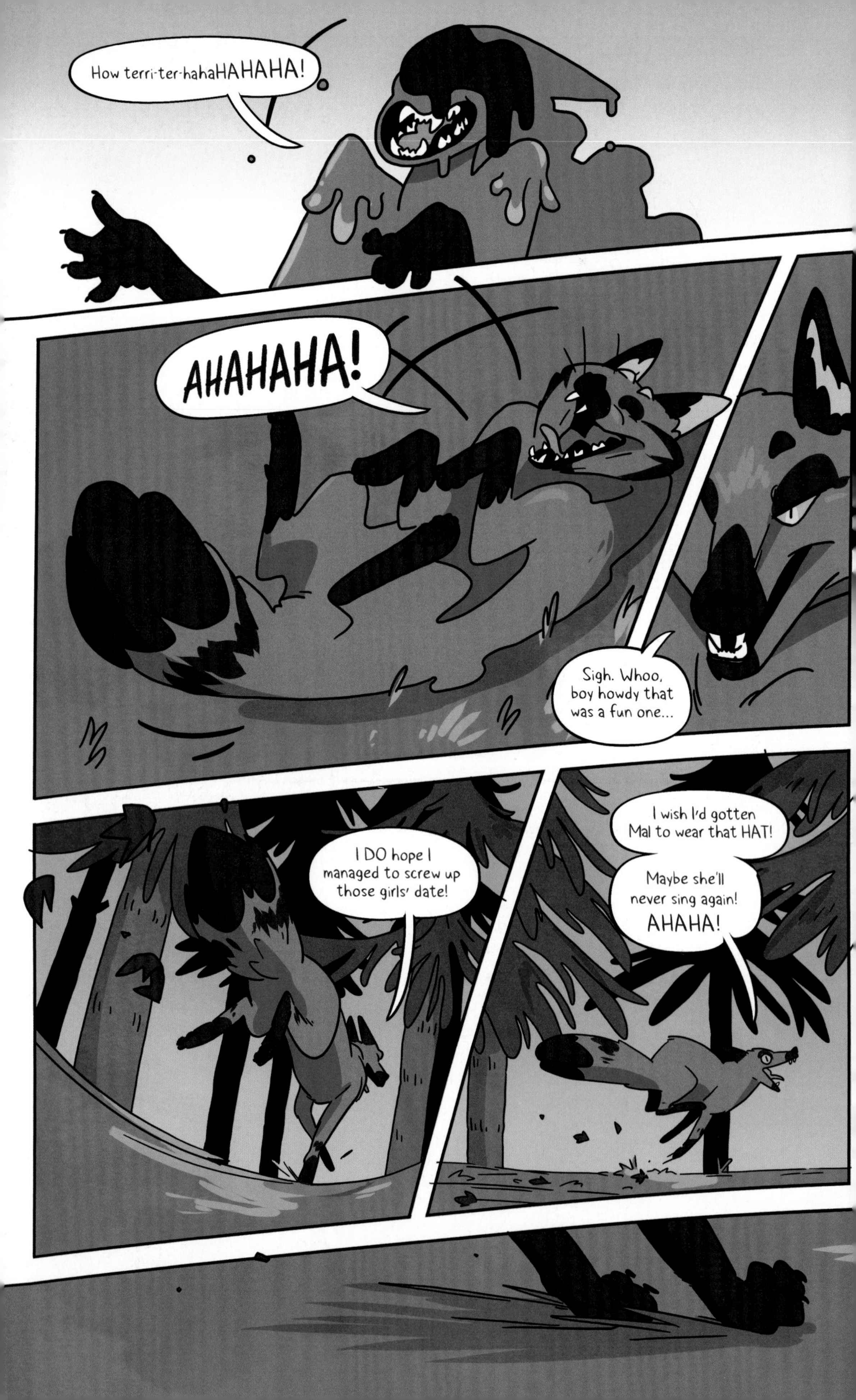
How terri-ter-hahaHAHAHA!
AHAHAHA!
Sigh. Whoo, boy howdy that was a fun one...
I DO hope I managed to screw up those girls' date!
I wish I'd gotten Mal to wear that HAT!
Maybe she'll never sing again! AHAHA!

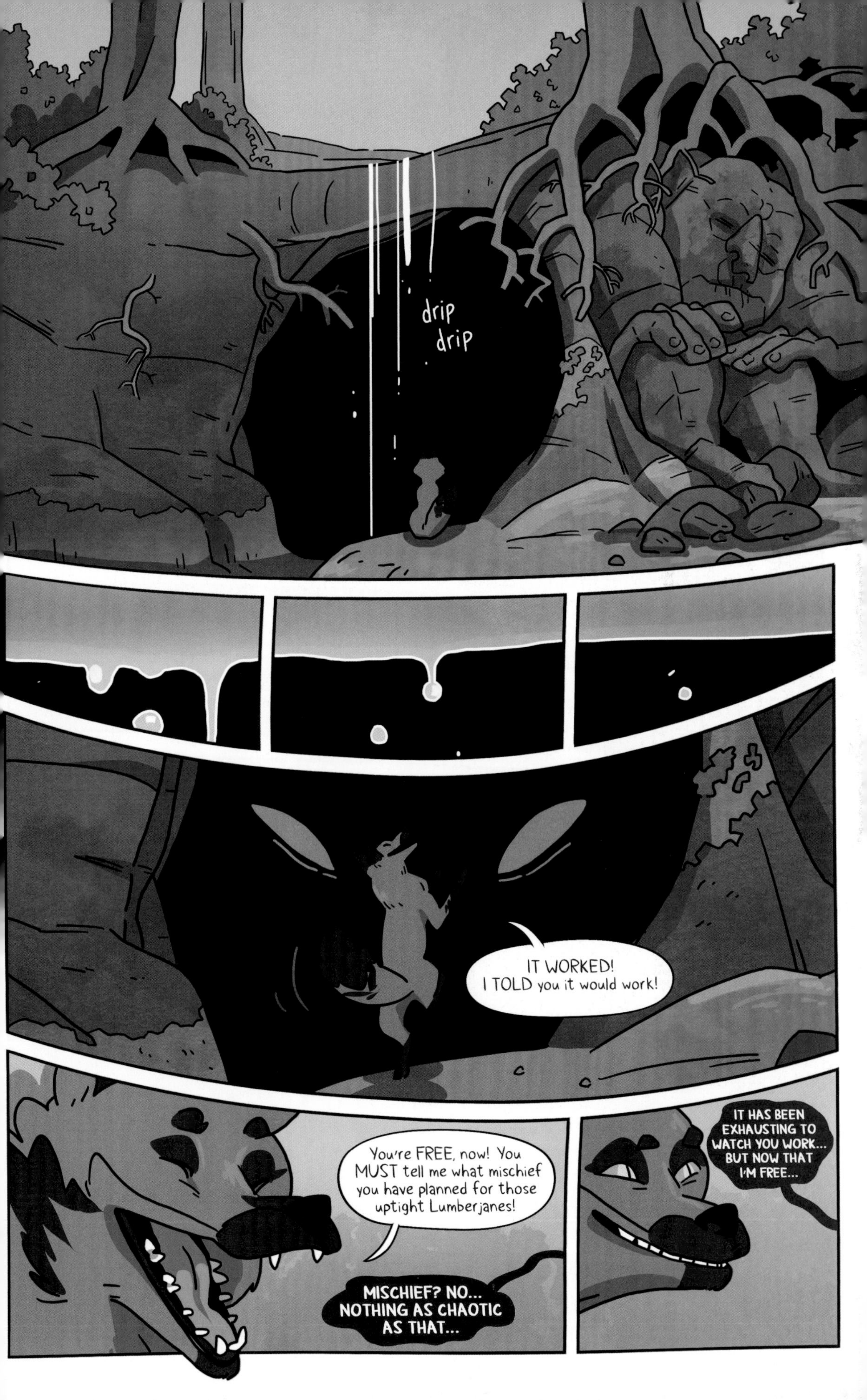
drip
drip
IT WORKED!
I TOLD you it would work!
You're FREE, now! You MUST tell me what mischief you have planned for those uptight Lumberjanes!
MISCHIEF? NO... NOTHING AS CHAOTIC AS THAT...
IT HAS BEEN EXHAUSTING TO WATCH YOU WORK... BUT NOW THAT I'M FREE...

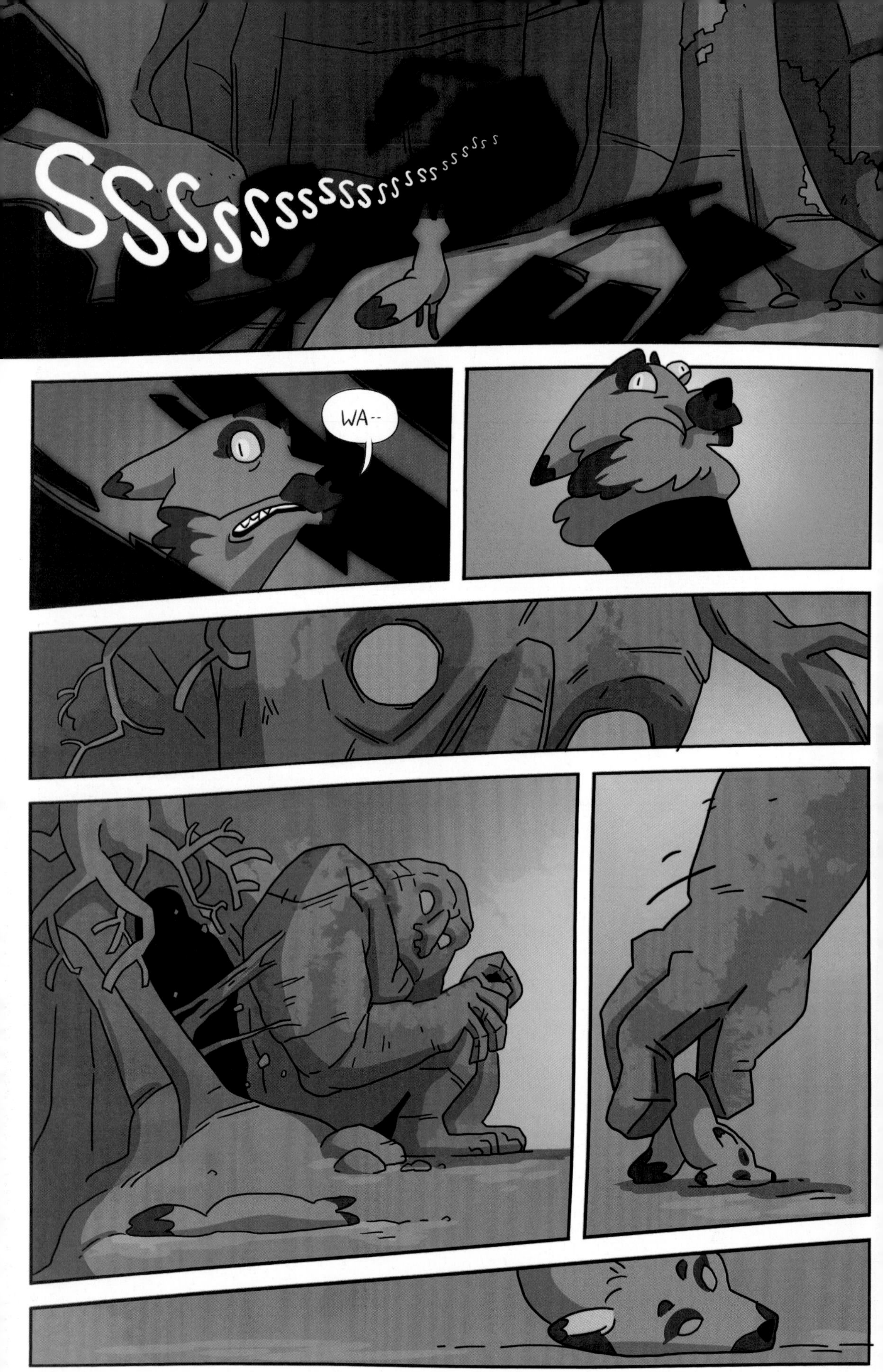
SSSSSSSSSSSSSSSSSSSSSSSSS
WA--

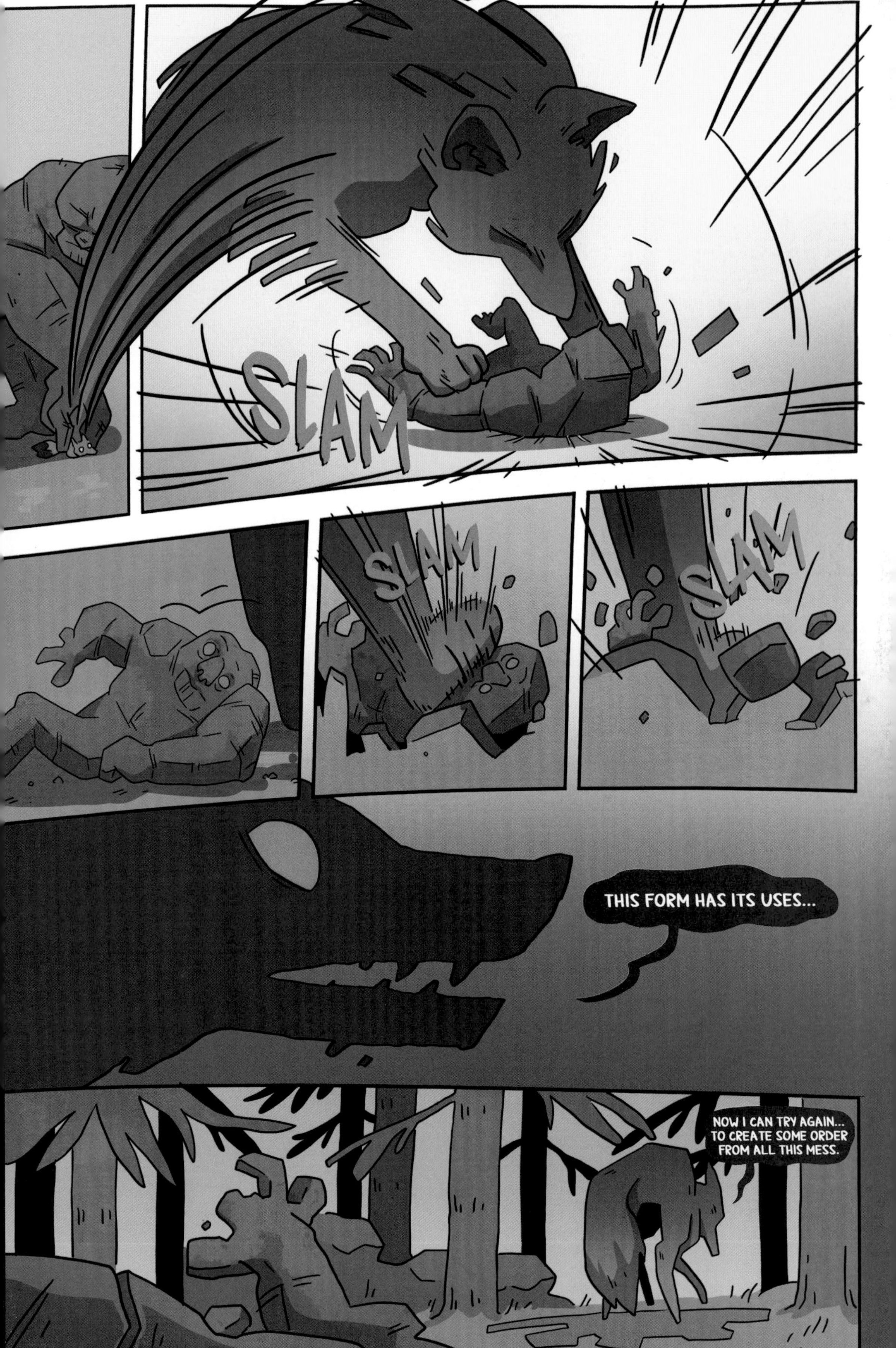
SLAM
SLAM
SLAM
THIS FORM HAS ITS USES...
NOW I CAN TRY AGAIN... TO CREATE SOME ORDER FROM ALL THIS MESS.

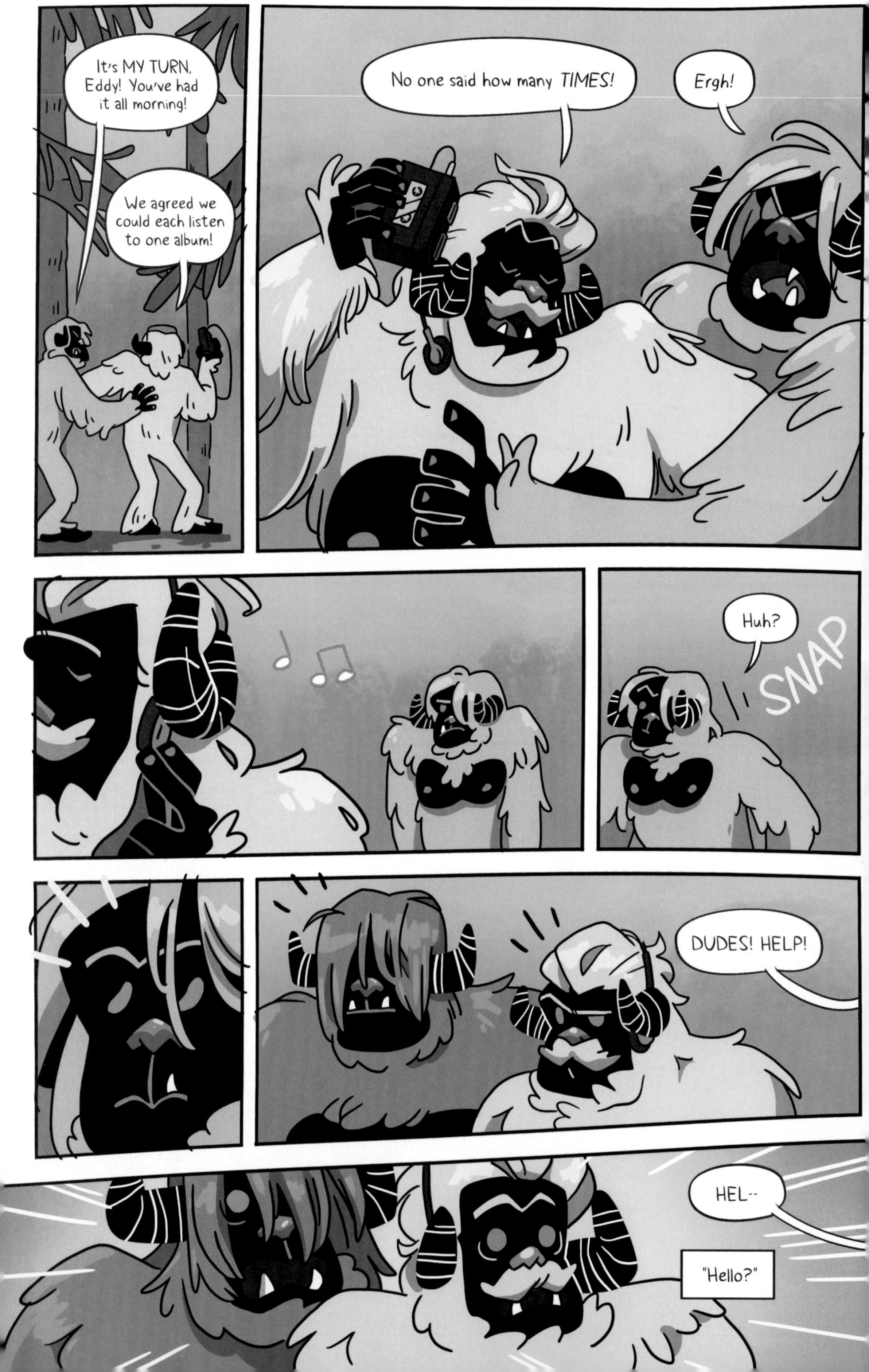
It's MY TURN, Eddy! You've had it all morning!
We agreed we could each listen to one album!
No one said how many TIMES!
Ergh!
Huh?
SNAP
DUDES! HELP!
HEL--
"Hello?"

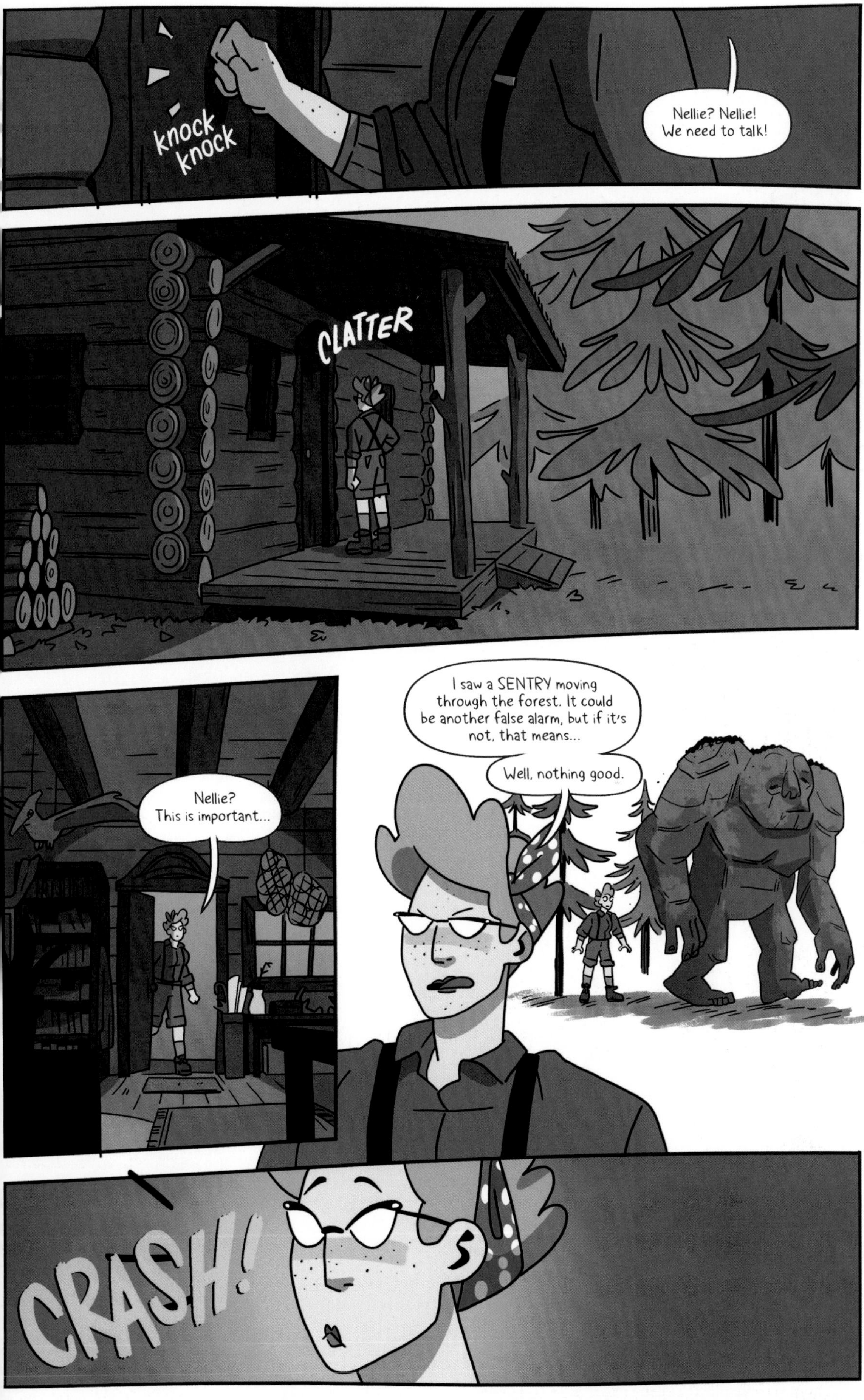
knock knock
Nellie? Nellie! We need to talk!
CLATTER
Nellie? This is important...
I saw a SENTRY moving through the forest. It could be another false alarm, but if it's not, that means...
Well, nothing good.
CRASH!

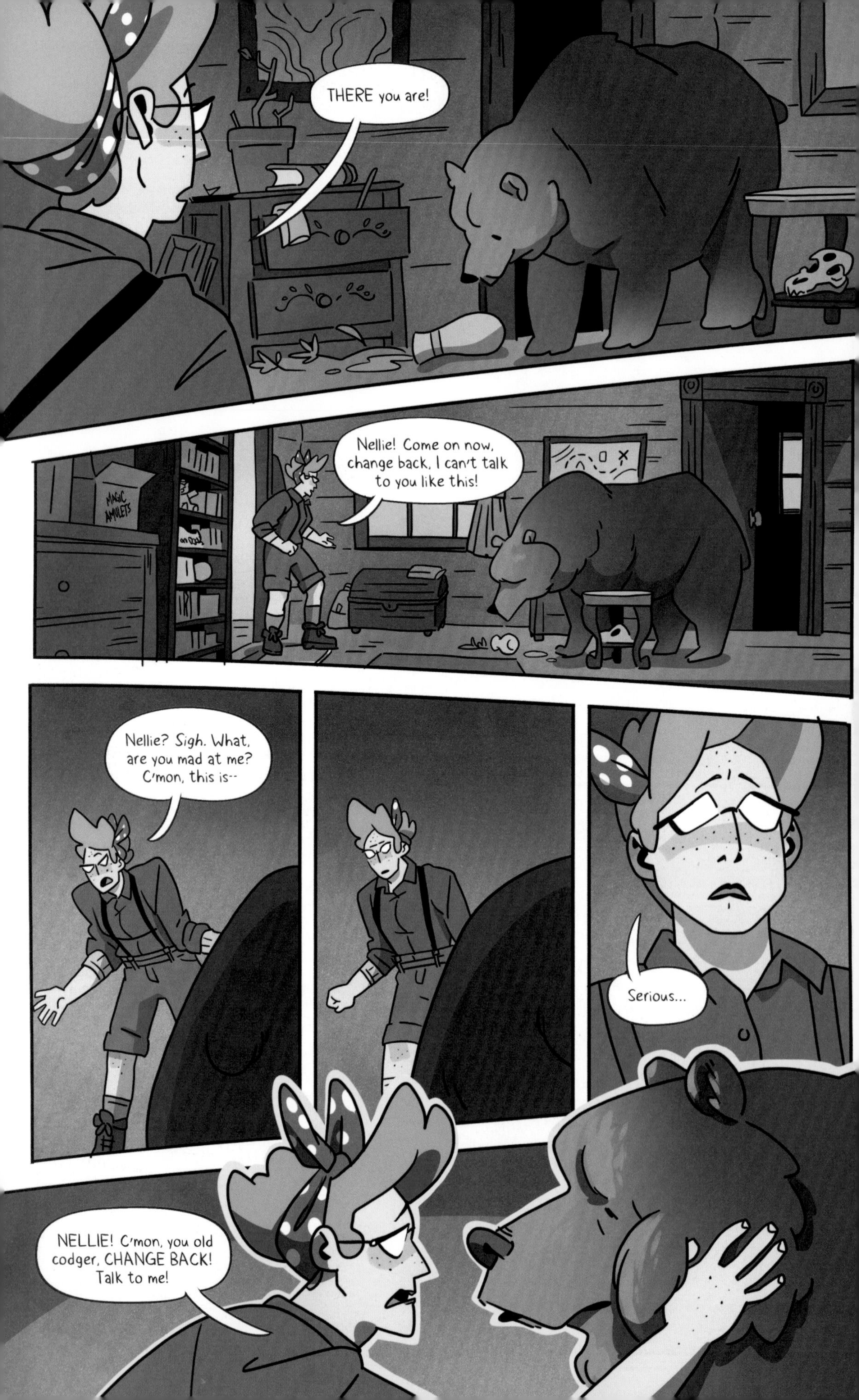
THERE you are!
Nellie! Come on now, change back, I can't talk to you like this!
MAGIC AMULETS
Nellie? *Sigh.* What, are you mad at me? C'mon, this is--
Serious...
NELLIE! C'mon, you old codger, CHANGE BACK! Talk to me!

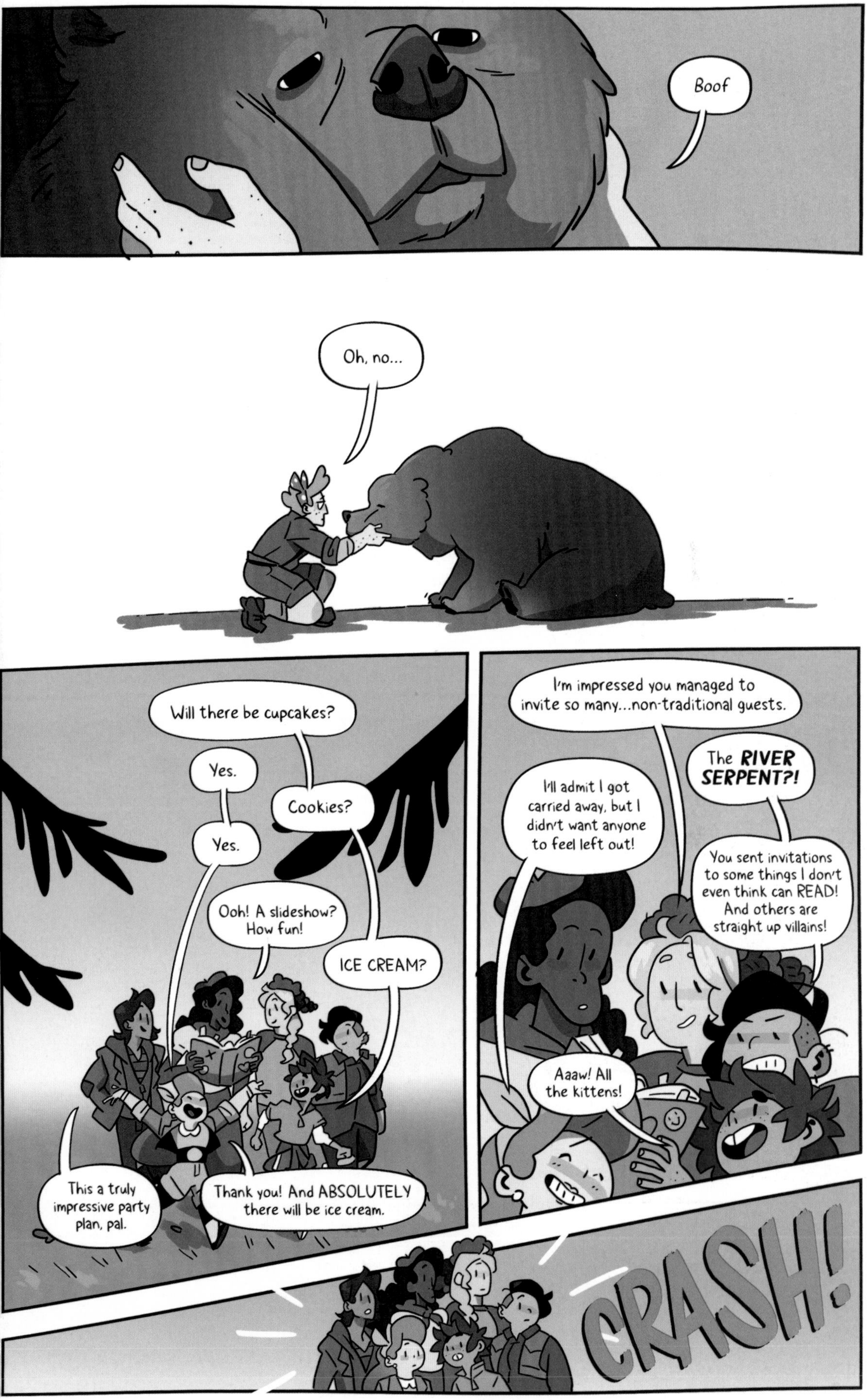

Boof
Oh, no...
Will there be cupcakes?
Yes.
Cookies?
Yes.
Ooh! A slideshow? How fun!
ICE CREAM?
This a truly impressive party plan, pal.
Thank you! And ABSOLUTELY there will be ice cream.
I'm impressed you managed to invite so many...non-traditional guests.
I'll admit I got carried away, but I didn't want anyone to feel left out!
The **RIVER SERPENT?!**
You sent invitations to some things I don't even think can READ! And others are straight up villains!
Aaaw! All the kittens!
CRASH!

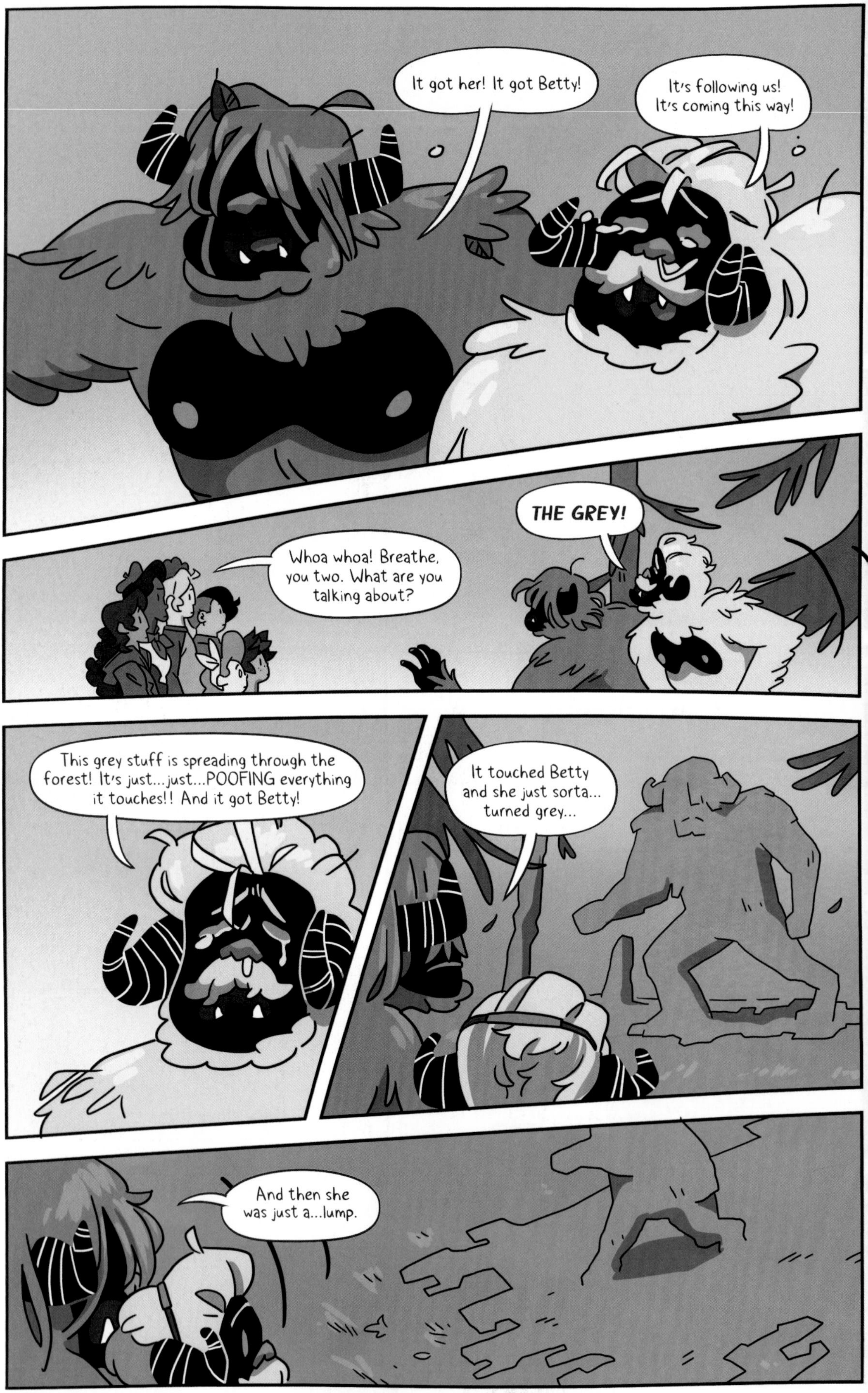
It got her! It got Betty!
It's following us! It's coming this way!
THE GREY!
Whoa whoa! Breathe, you two. What are you talking about?
This grey stuff is spreading through the forest! It's just...just...POOFING everything it touches!! And it got Betty!
It touched Betty and she just sorta... turned grey...
And then she was just a...lump.

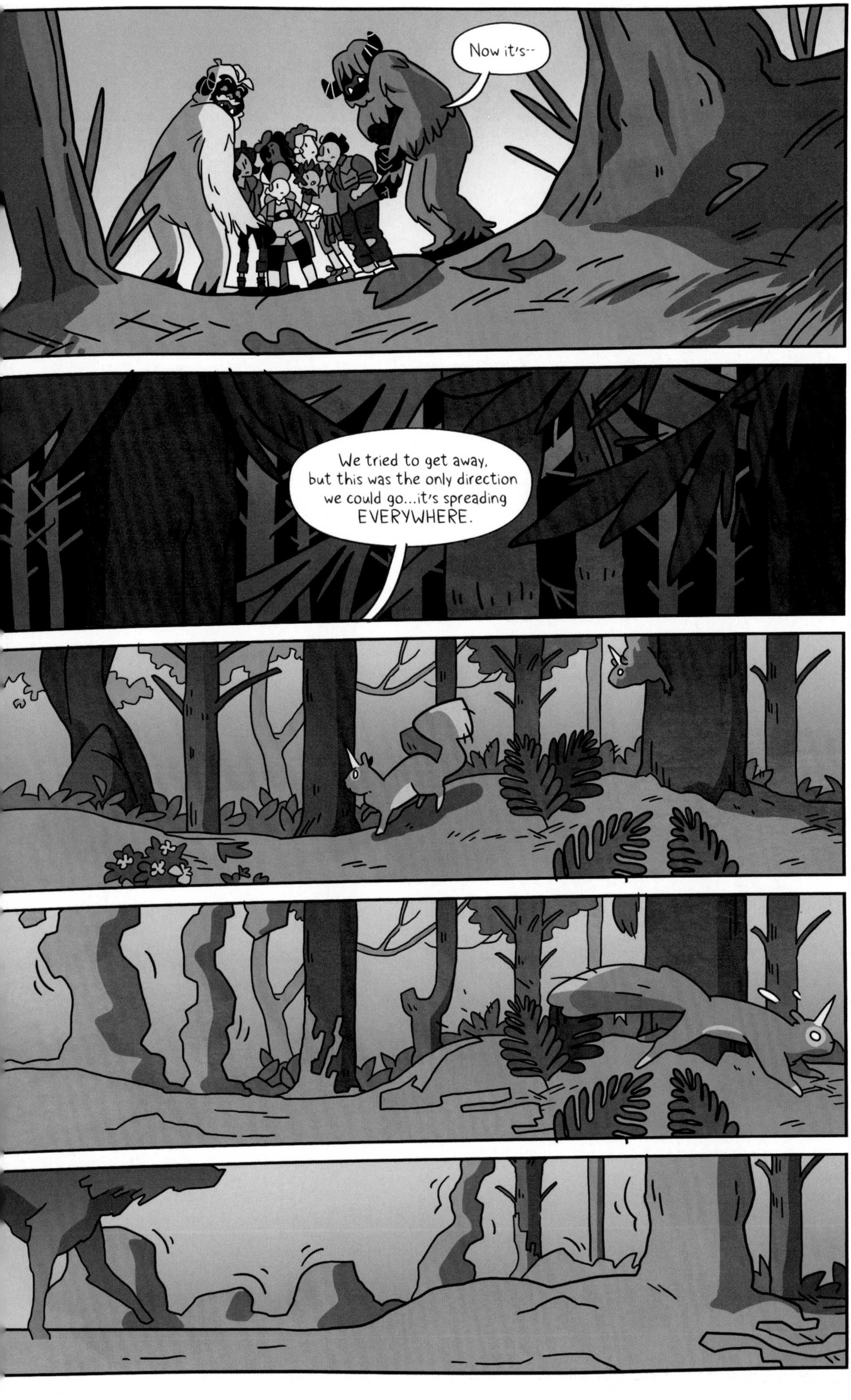
Now it's--
We tried to get away, but this was the only direction we could go...it's spreading EVERYWHERE.

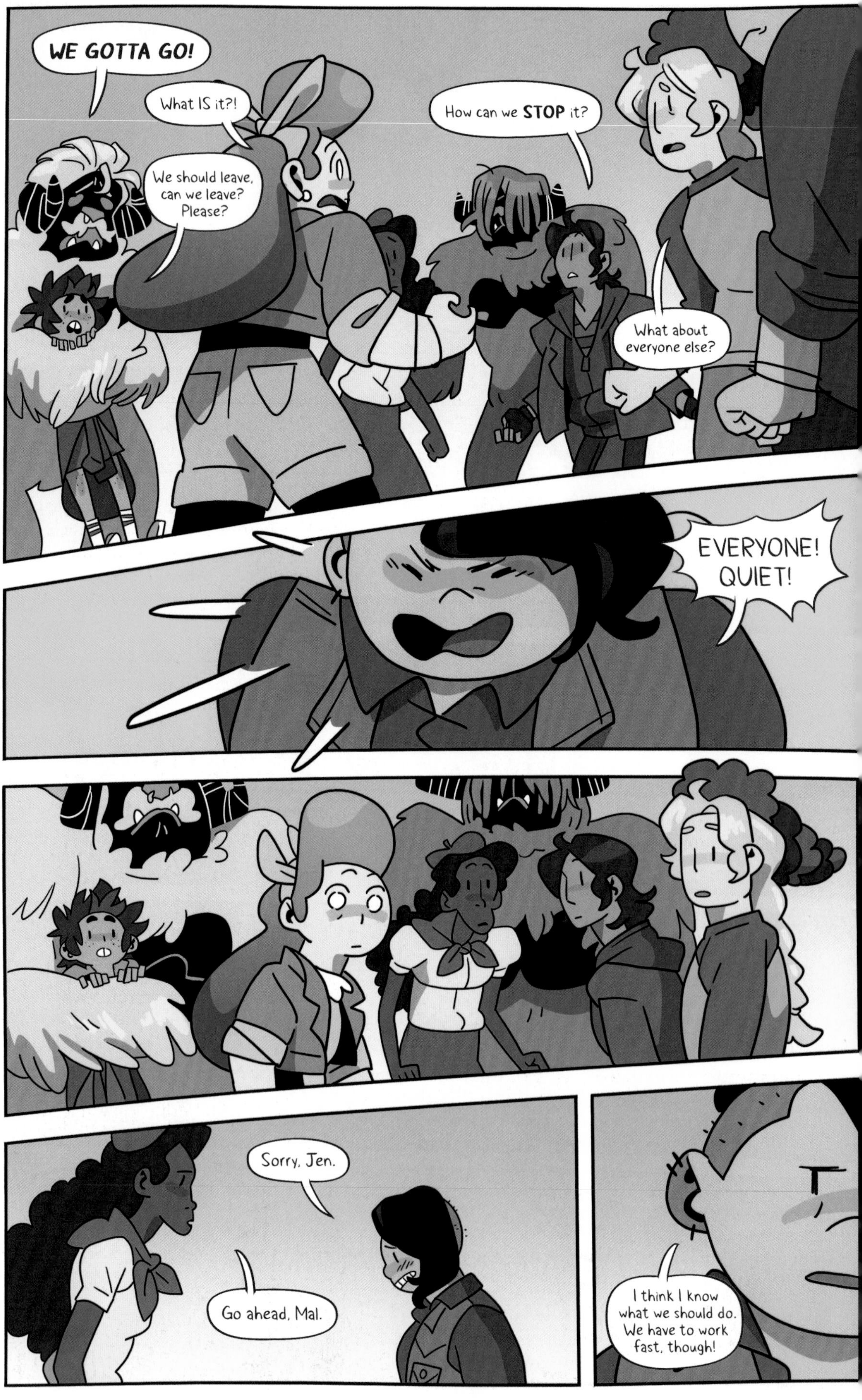
WE GOTTA GO!
What IS it?!
We should leave, can we leave? Please?
How can we STOP it?
What about everyone else?
EVERYONE! QUIET!
Sorry, Jen.
Go ahead, Mal.
I think I know what we should do. We have to work fast, though!

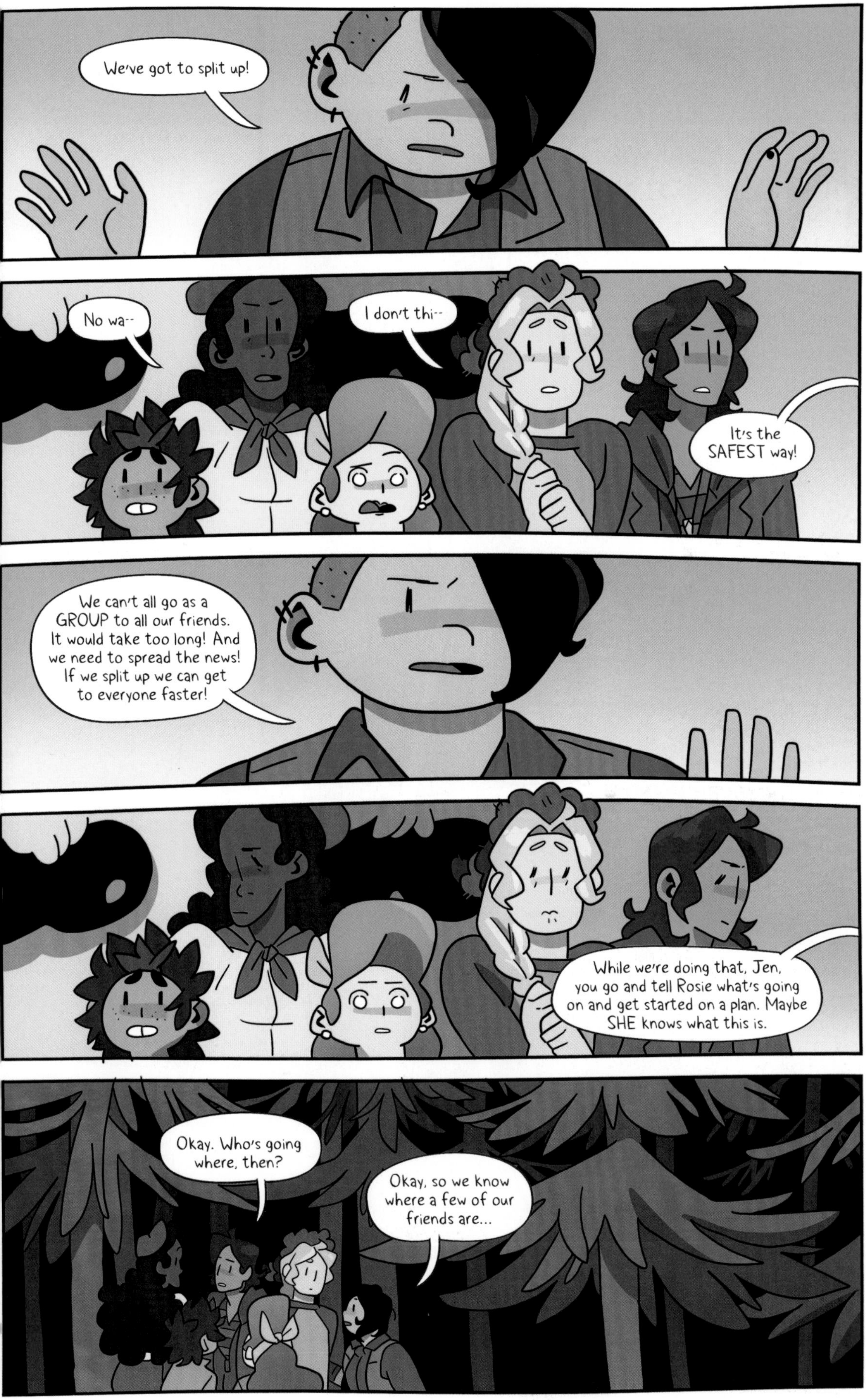
We've got to split up!
No wa--
I don't thi--
It's the SAFEST way!
We can't all go as a GROUP to all our friends. It would take too long! And we need to spread the news! If we split up we can get to everyone faster!
While we're doing that, Jen, you go and tell Rosie what's going on and get started on a plan. Maybe SHE knows what this is.
Okay. Who's going where, then?
Okay, so we know where a few of our friends are...

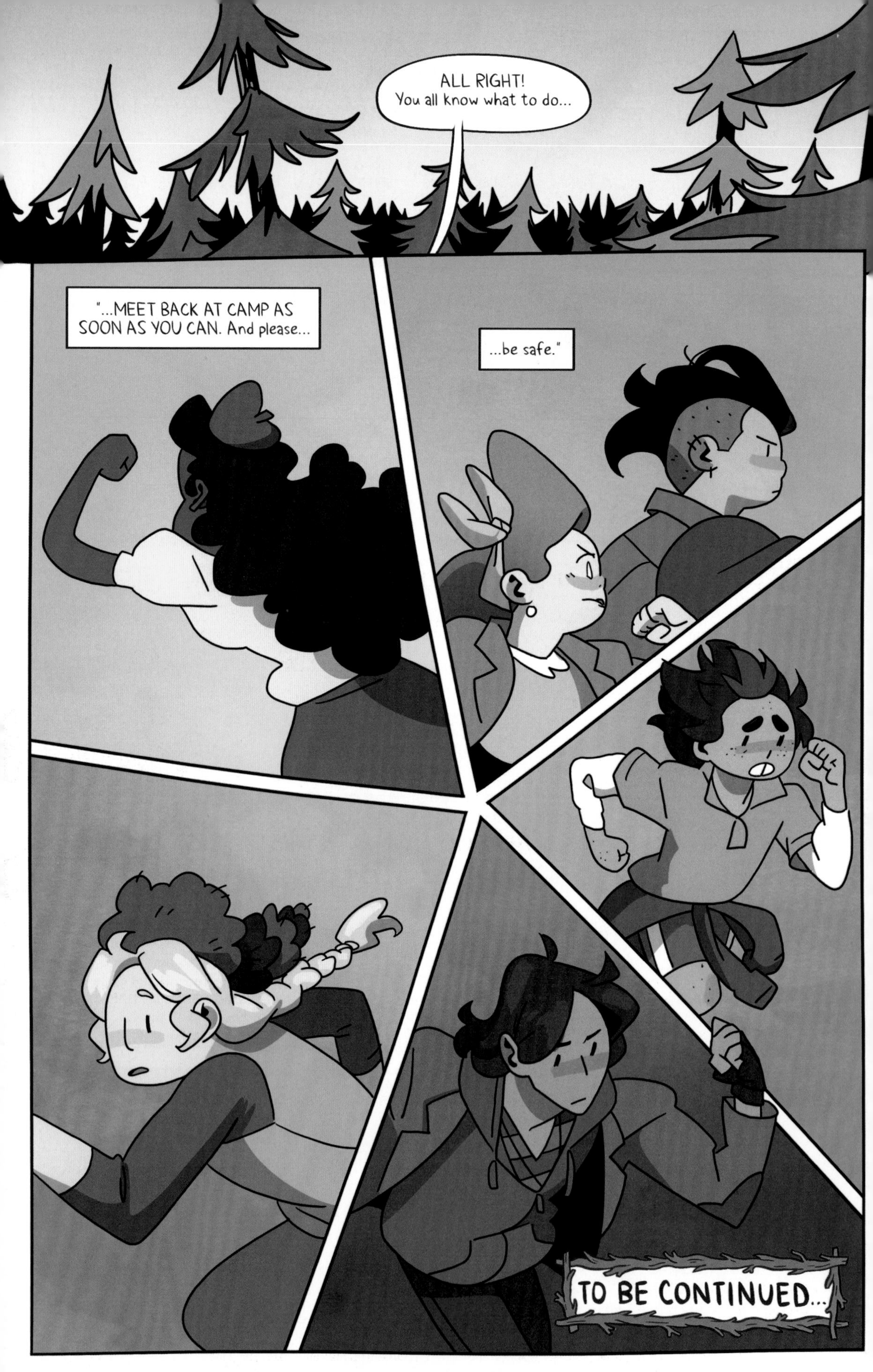
ALL RIGHT!
You all know what to do...
"...MEET BACK AT CAMP AS SOON AS YOU CAN. And please...
...be safe."
TO BE CONTINUED...

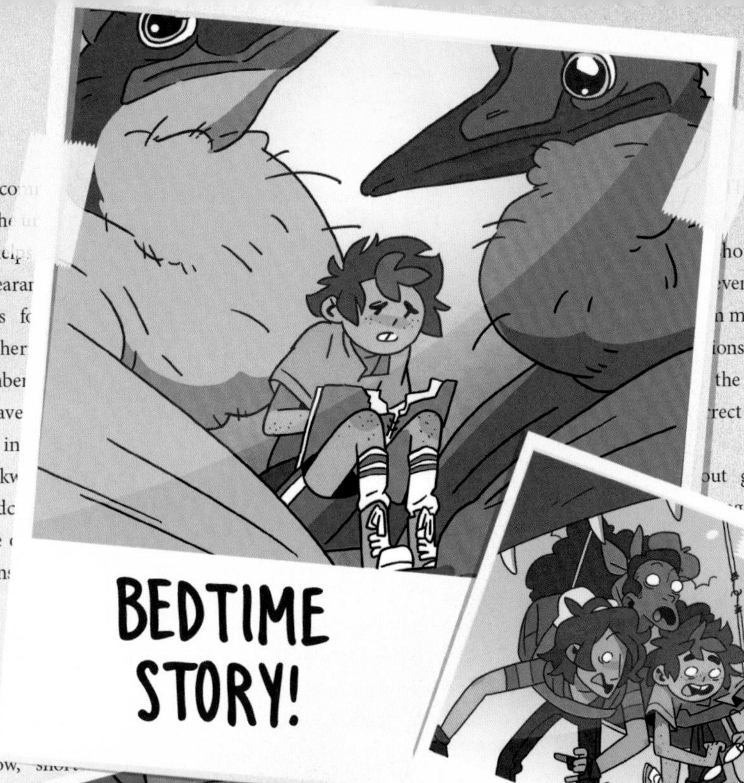
BEDTIME STORY!

will co...

The u...
It he...
appeara...
dress f...
Further...
Lumbe...
to have...
part in...
Thiskw...
Hardc...
have ...
thems...

...HE UNIFORM

...hould be worn at camp
...events when Lumberjanes
...n may also be worn at other
...ions. It should be worn as a
... the uniform dress with
...rrect shoes, and stocking or

...out grows her uniform or
...ther Lumberjane.
...a she has
... her
... her

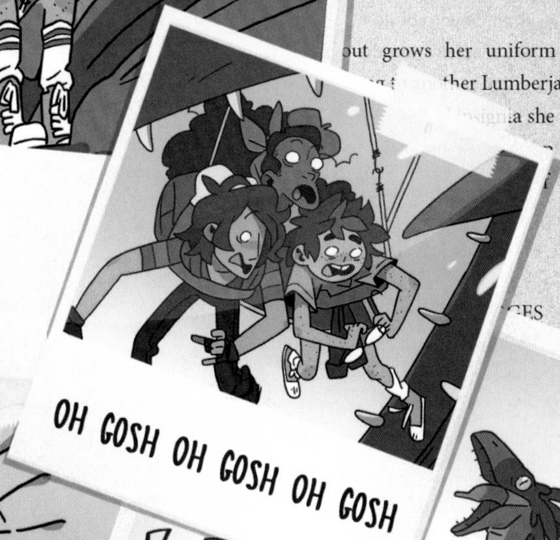
OH GOSH OH GOSH OH GOSH

The ...
yellow, ...
emb...
the w...
choose...
slacks, ...
made o...
out-of-do...
green bere...
the colla...
Shoes ma...
heels, rou... ...kings or
socks shou... ...with the shoes or wi...
the uniform. Ne... ...es, bracelets, or other jewelry do ...
belong with a Lumberjane uniform.

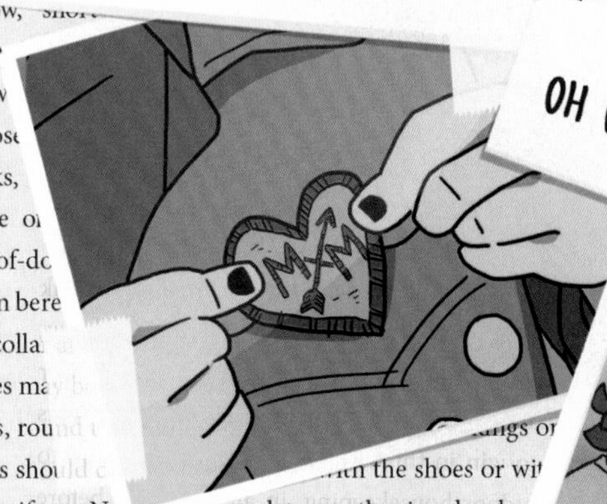

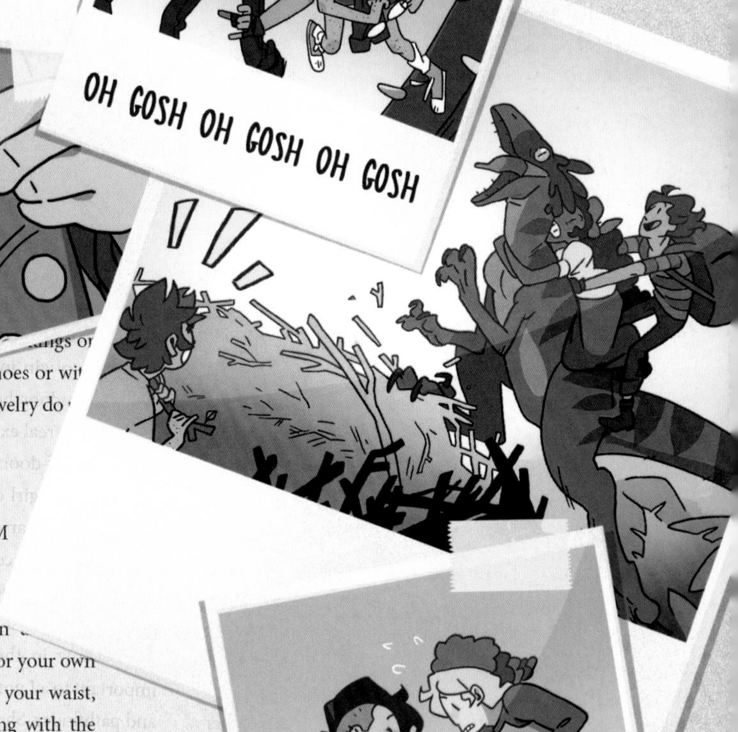

HOW TO WEAR THE UNIFORM

To look well in a uniform demands first of ...
uniform be kept in good condition—clean ...
pressed. See that the skirt is the right length for your own height and build, that the belt is adjusted to your waist, that your shoes and stockings are in keeping with the uniform, that you watch your posture and carry yourself with dignity and grace. If the beret is removed indoors, be sure that your hair is neat and kept in place with an inconspicuous clip or ribbon. When you wear a Lumberjane uniform you are identified as a member of this organization and you should be doubly careful to conduct yourself in a way that will show everyone that courtesy and thoughtfulness are part of being a Lumberjane. People are likely to judge a whole nation by the selfishness of a few individuals, to criticize a whole family because of the misconduct of one member, and to feel unkindly toward an organization because of the

The unifor...
helps to cre...
in a group. ...
active life th...
another bond...
future, and pr...
in order to b...
Lumberjane pr...
Penniquiqul Thi... ...ore Lady
Types, but m... ...es will wish to have one. They
can either bu... ...the uniform, or make it themselves from
materials available at the trading post.

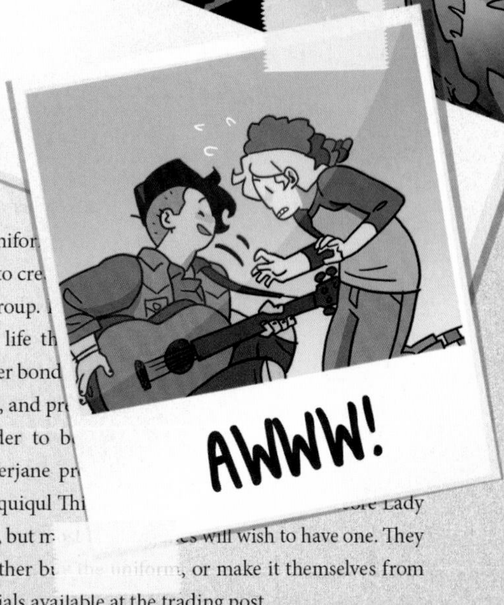
AWWW!

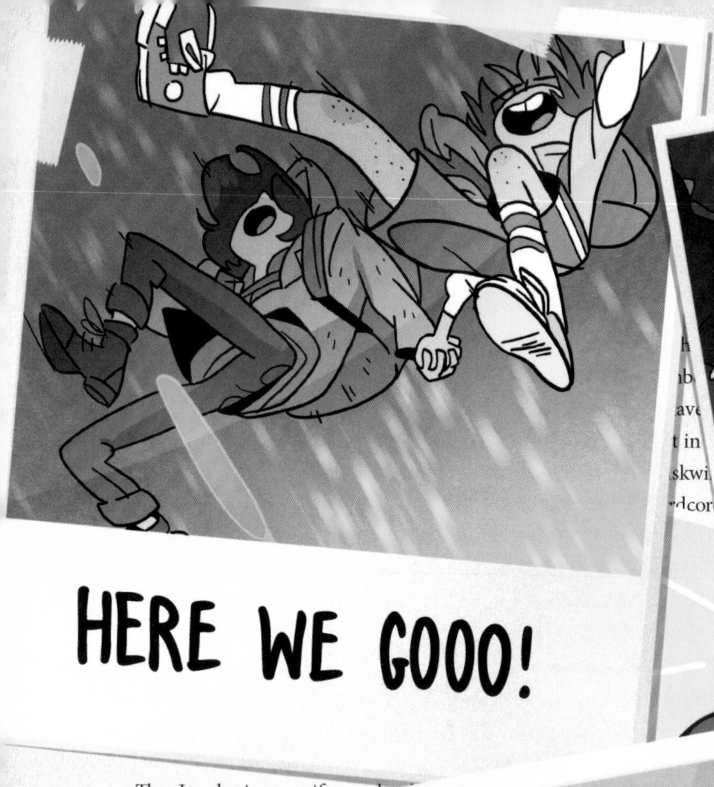
HERE WE GOOO!

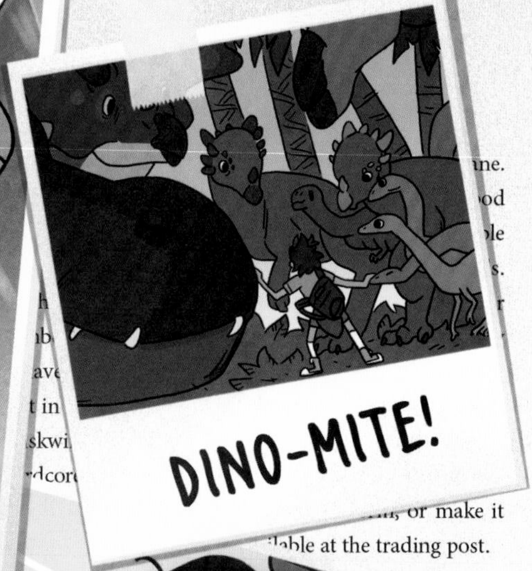
DINO-MITE!

...ane.
...ood
...ple
...s.
...h ...r
...nb...
...ave...
...t in...
...skwi...
...rdcor...
..., or make it
...ilable at the trading post.

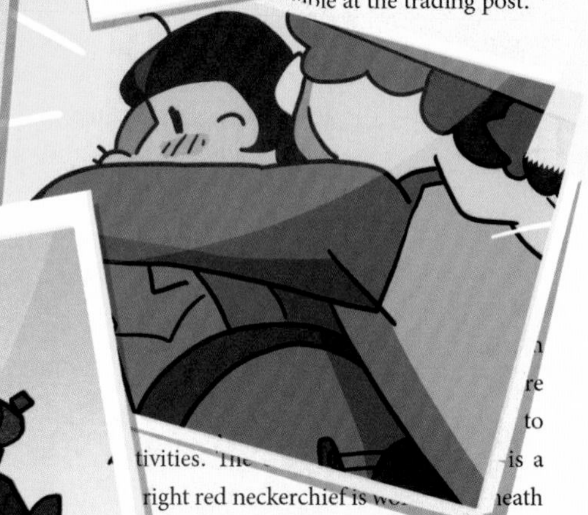

The Lumberjane uniform sh...
meetin...

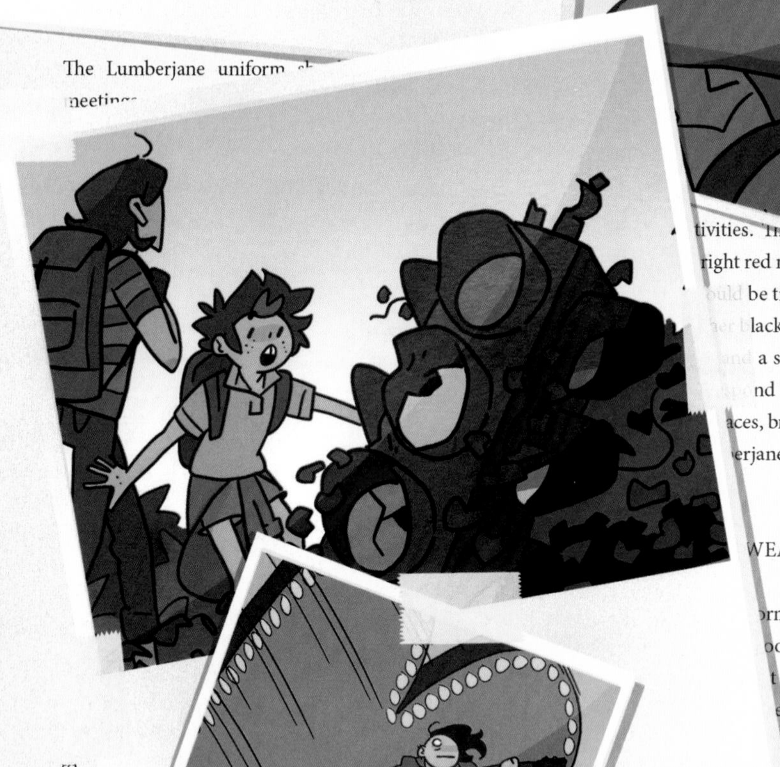

...n
...re
...to
...tivities. The ... is a
...right red neckerchief is wo... ...neath
...ould be tied in a simple friendship knot.
...lack or brown and should have flat
... a straight inner line. Stockings or
...nd in color with the shoes or with
...aces, bracelets, or other jewelry do not
...erjane uniform.

...WEAR THE UNIFORM

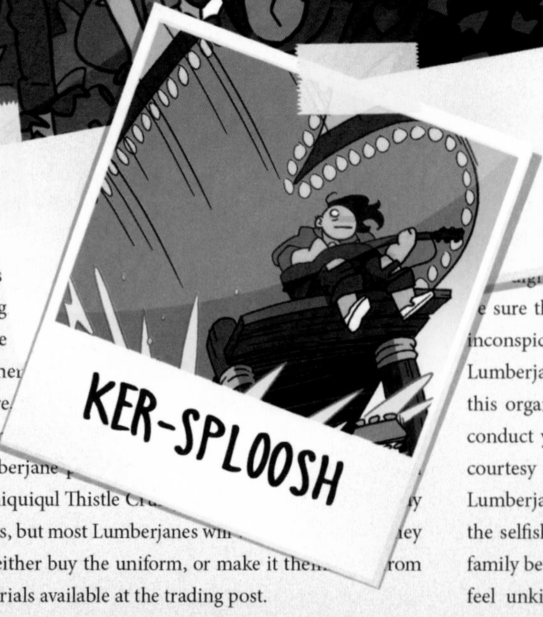
KER-SPLOOSH

The ...
helps ...
in a g...
active ...
another...
future...
in or...
Lumberjane p...
Penniquiqul Thistle Cr... ...y
Types, but most Lumberjanes wi... ...ey
can either buy the uniform, or make it the... ...rom
materials available at the trading post.

...orm demands first of all that the ...ood condition—clean and well ...t is the right length for your own ...e belt is adjusted to your waist, ...kings are in keeping with the ...our posture and carry yourself ...dignity and grace. If the beret is removed indoors, ...e sure that your hair is neat and kept in place with an inconspicuous clip or ribbon. When you wear a Lumberjane uniform you are identified as a member of this organization and you should be doubly careful to conduct yourself in a way that will show everyone that courtesy and thoughtfulness are part of being a Lumberjane. People are likely to judge a whole nation by the selfishness of a few individuals, to criticize a whole family because of the misconduct of one member, and to feel unkindly toward an organization because of the

COVER GALLERY

Lumberjanes "Out-of-Doors" Program Field

DAYLIGHT SAVOR

"Make hay while the sun shines!"

We're losing daylight! There are a few Lumberjanes badges that teach you to seize the day, to make the most of every hour, and strike while the iron is hot! But that is not the Daylight Savor badge—this badge is about the quality of the time spent, rather than the quantity of things you achieve. In many ways, the summers and the afternoons of your youth are your time to do what you will, and we often encourage you Lumberjane scouts to take advantage of the free time you do have, between school and sports and other activities to learn, to explore, to engage in new ideas and interests. And while being interesting and interested are two core values to us as Lumberjanes, we hope that you will take advantage of the Daylight Savor badge to also learn to spend time at rest, as well. To let a piece of chocolate melt in your mouth, rather than biting down and chomping through.

Lie in a patch of sunlight (with adequate protection), breath in the smell of the plants and dirt that surround you, have a nap if you wish. Read a book, pet a cat, do nothing, if that is what you desire.

So often we go, go, go, and this badge is about taking a moment to stop. People often say that you won't know the value of a dollar until you have earned it yourself, but it is also true that you won't know the value of your time until it has been yours to allocate as you will. It is yours to waste, yours let trickle or drip as quickly or as slowly as you like. How long is a minute when you're lying under a tree? How long is it when you are standing on your hands? Time is relative, and when you have the chance, it is always worth it to spend some time…spending time. Reset your internal clock, and remember that not every moment needs to be filled.

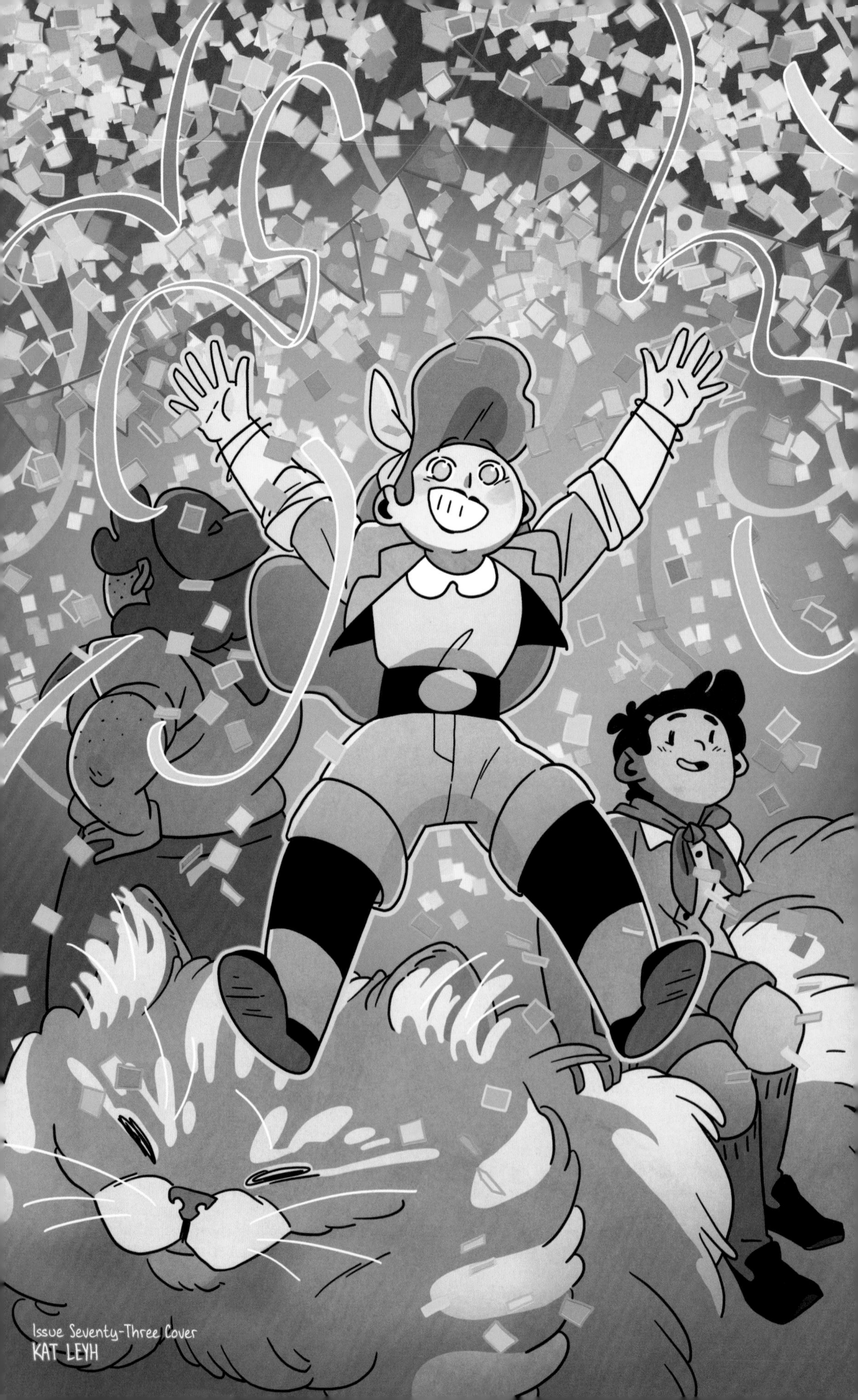
Issue Seventy-Three Cover
KAT LEYH

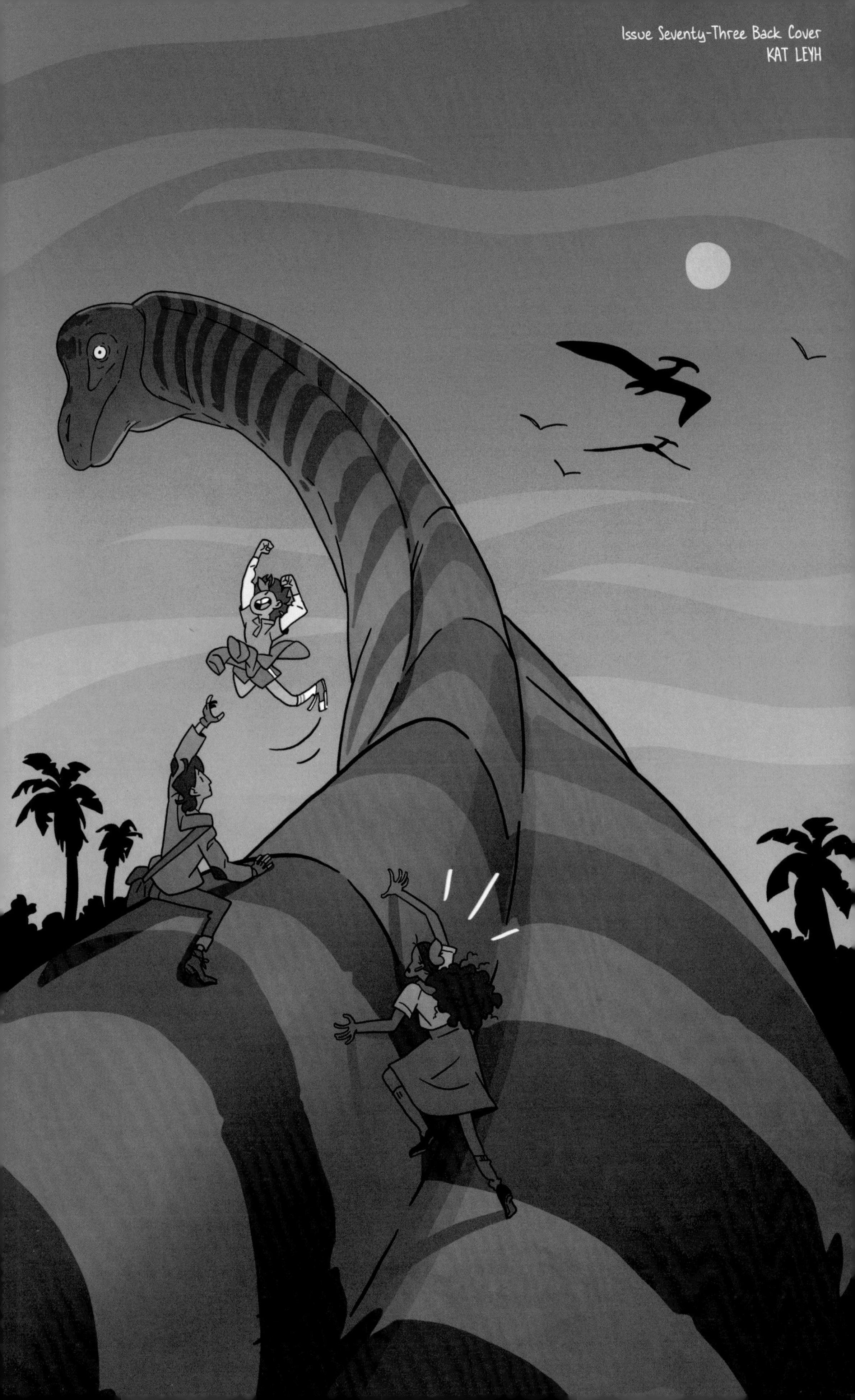
Issue Seventy-Three Back Cover
KAT LEYH

Issue Seventy-Three Preorder Cover
HARRIET MOULTON

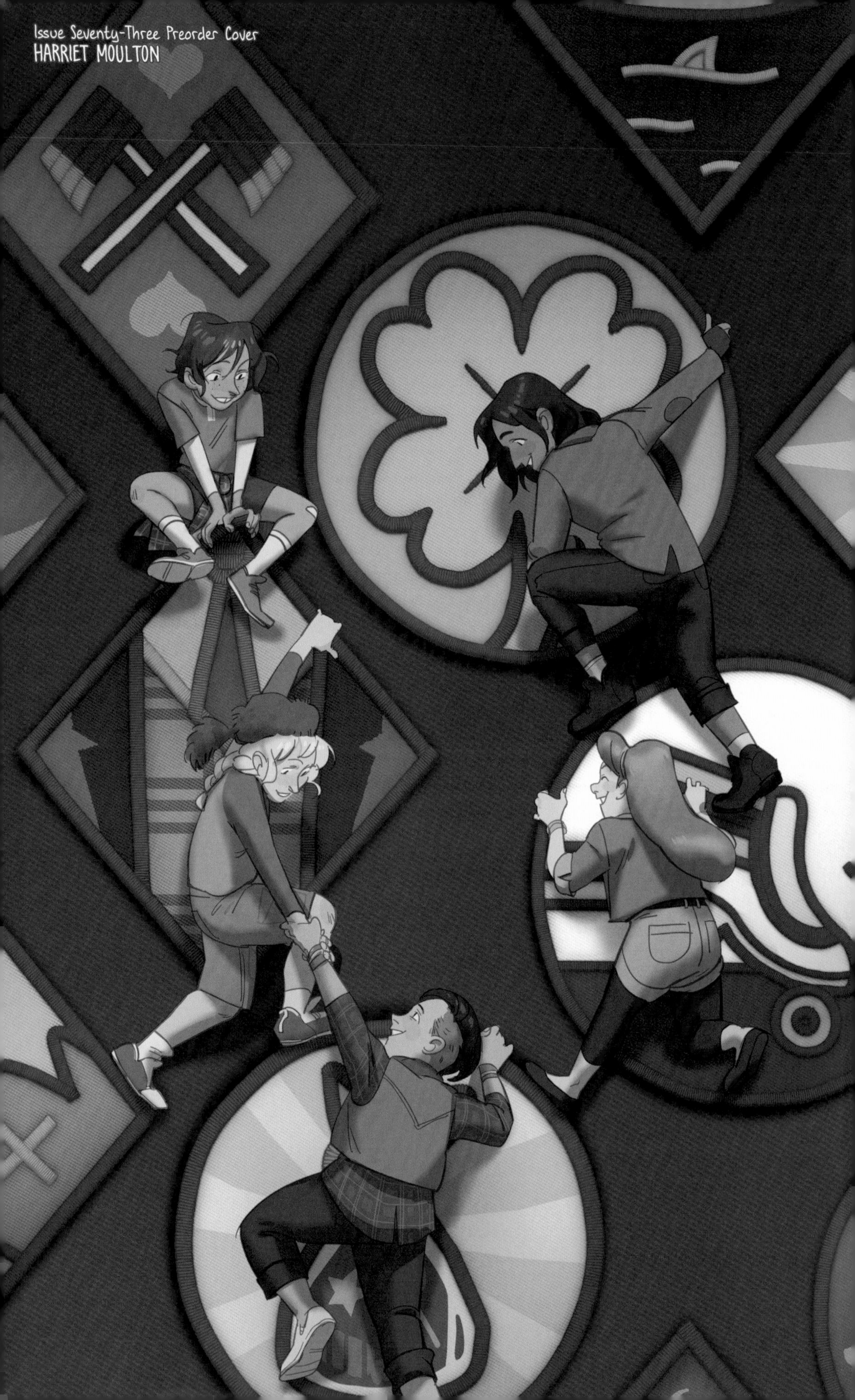

Issue Seventy-Four Cover
KAT LEYH

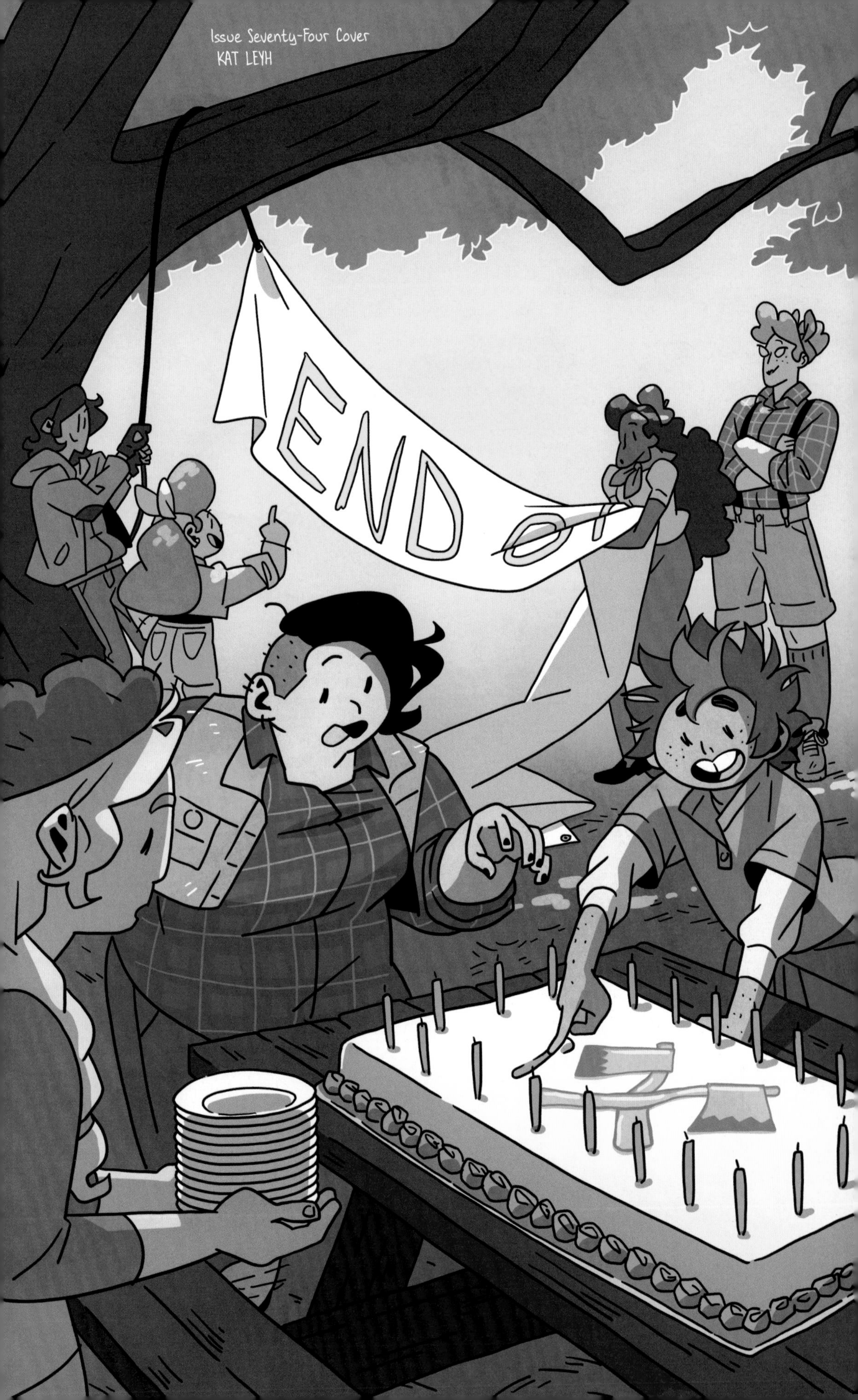
END

Issue Seventy-Four Back Cover
KAT LEYH

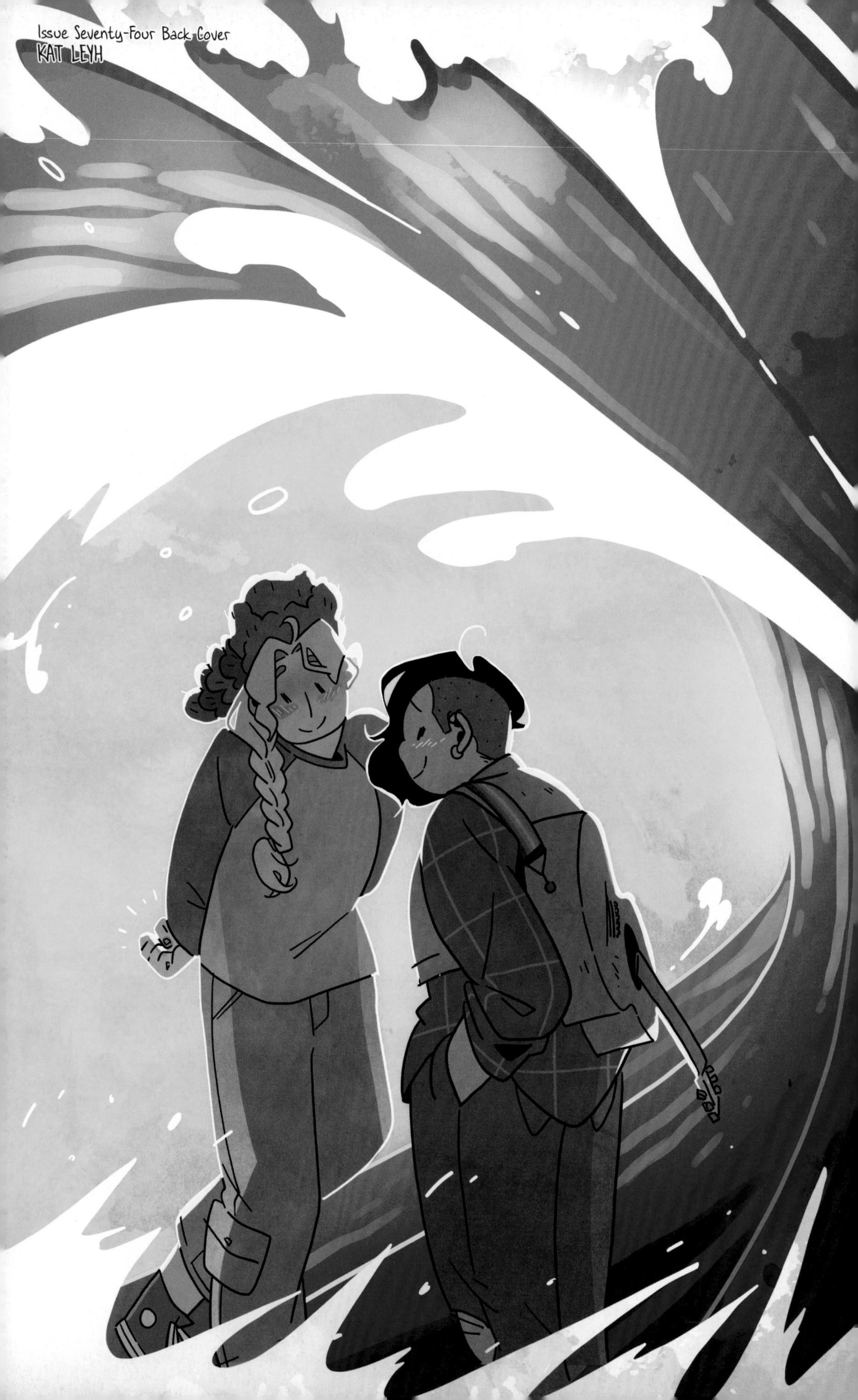

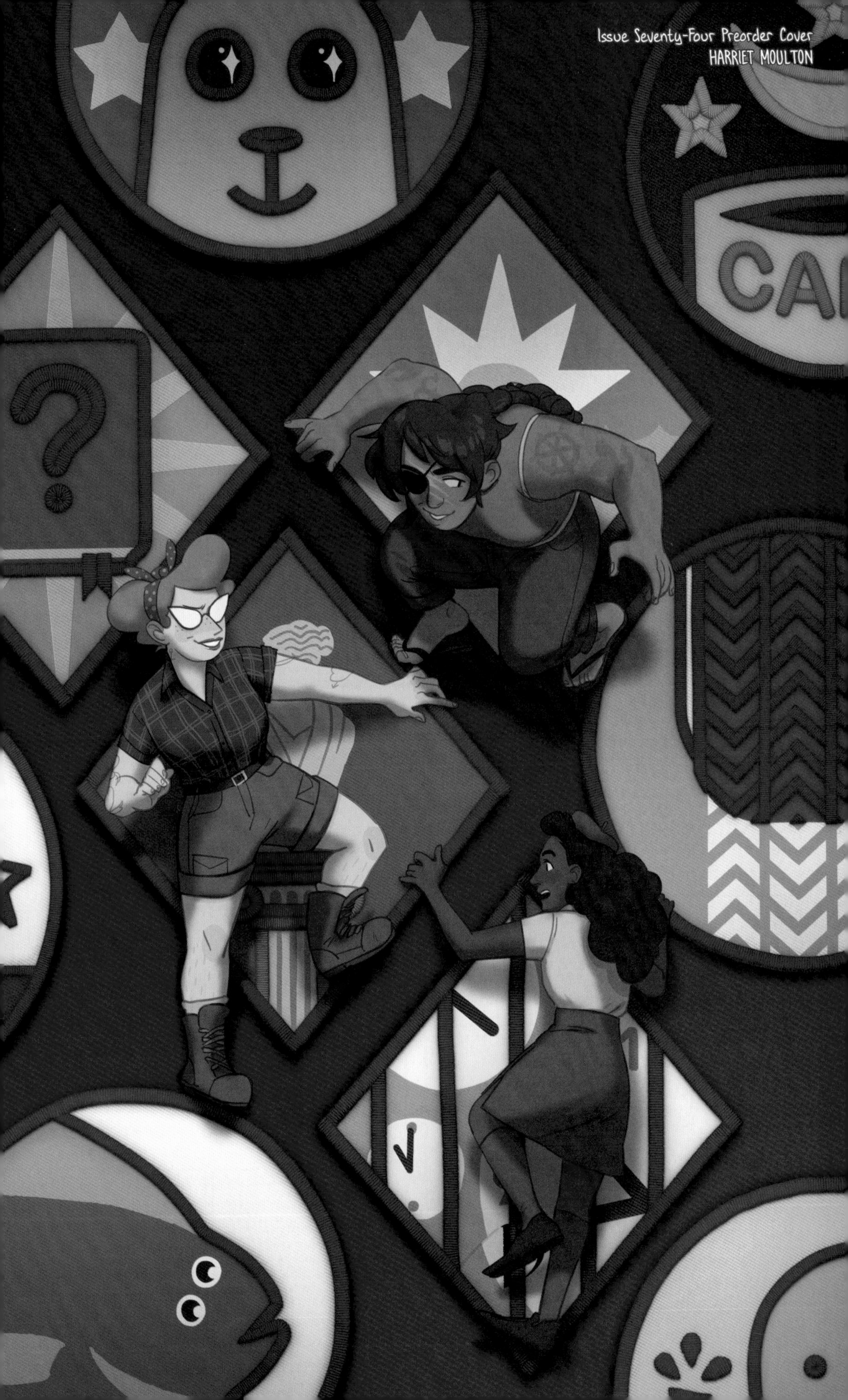

Issue Seventy-Four Preorder Cover
HARRIET MOULTON

Pencils by KAT LEYH

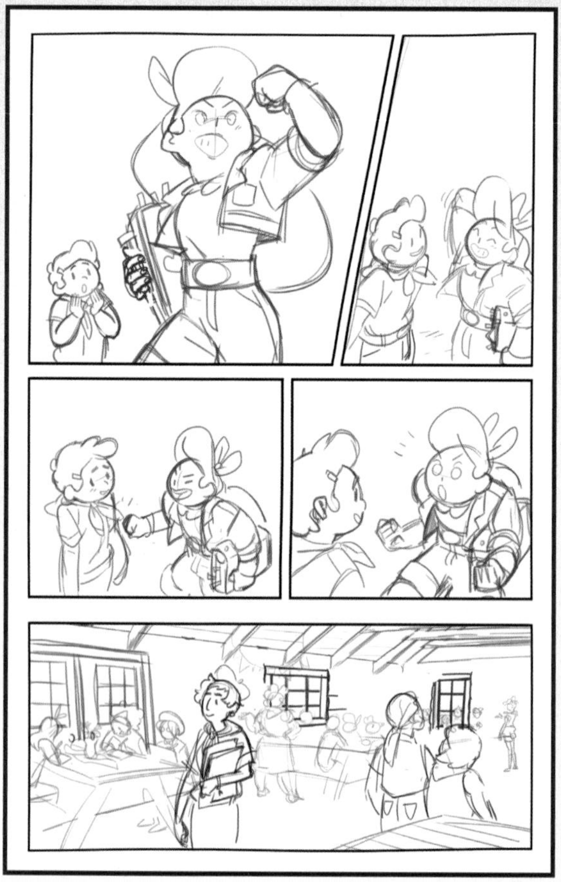

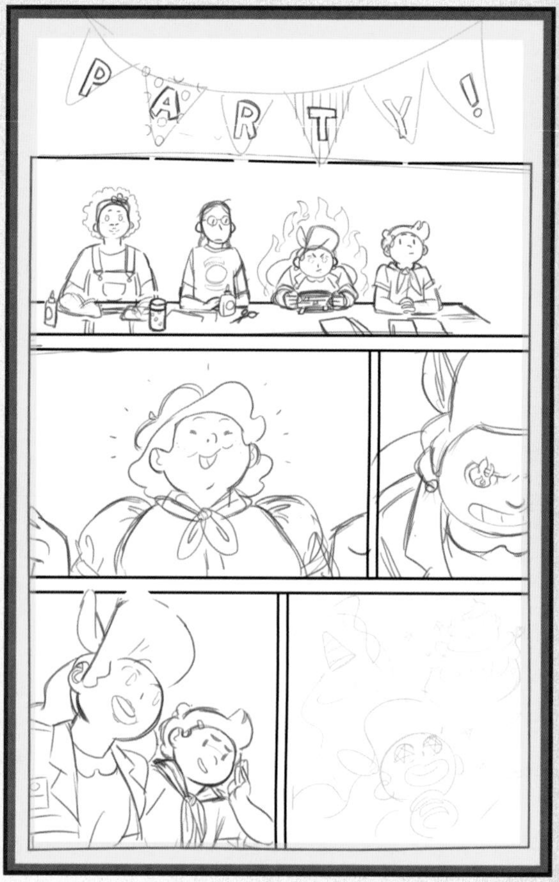
PARTY!

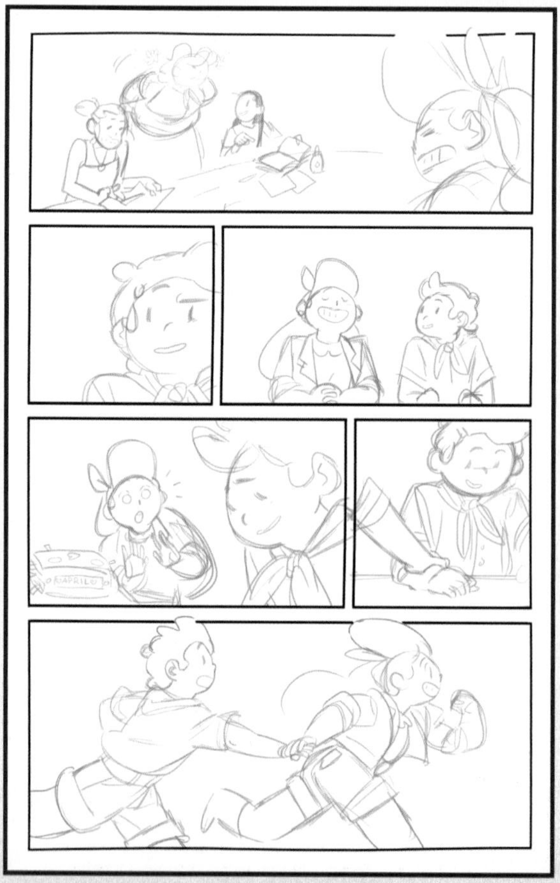

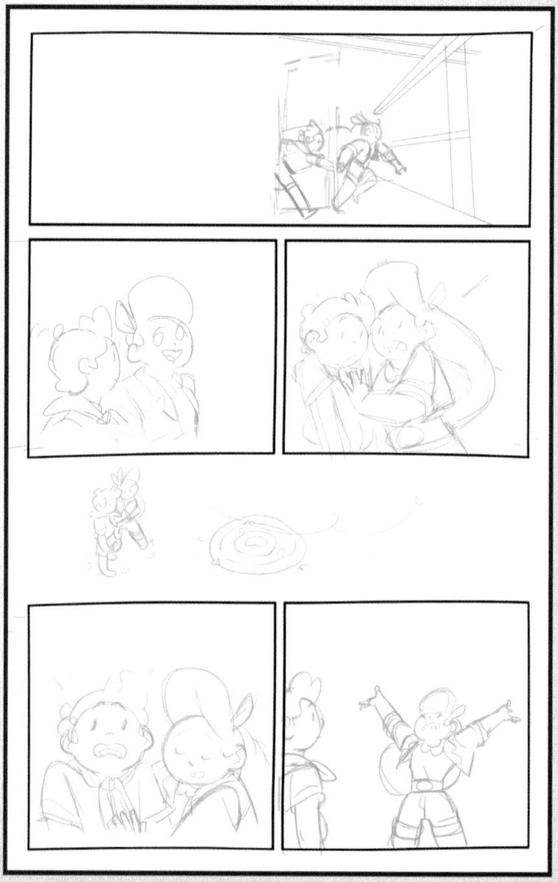

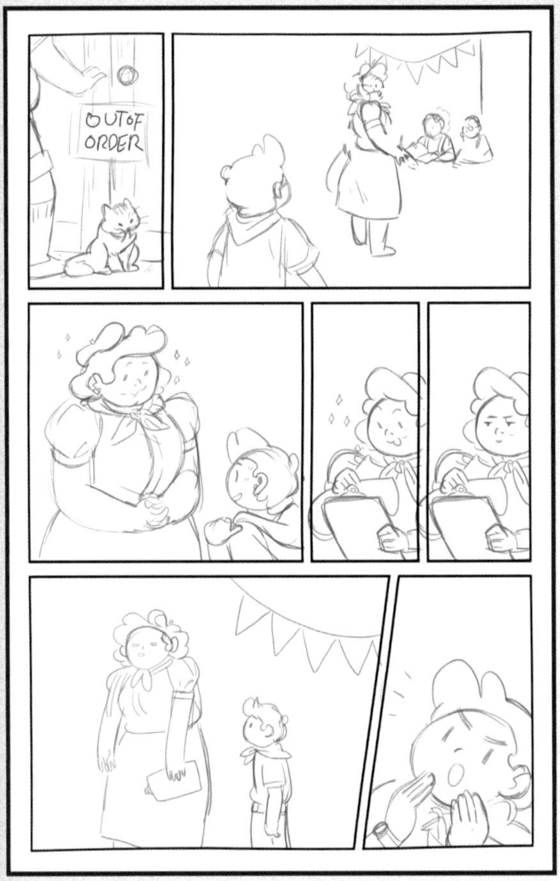
OUT OF ORDER

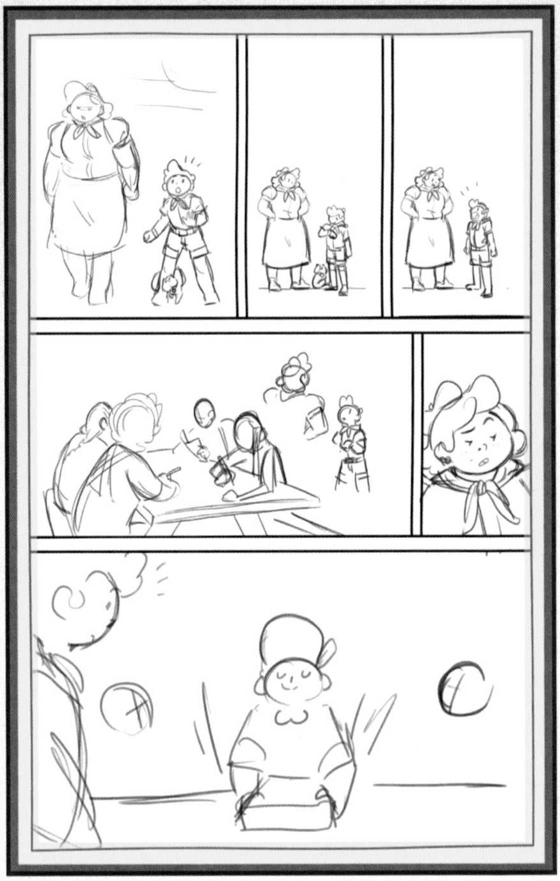

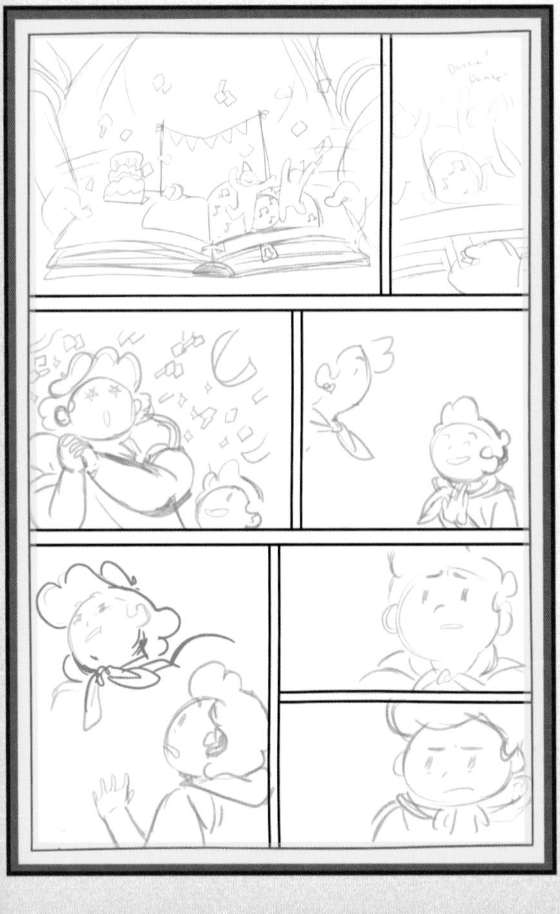
Dance! Dance!

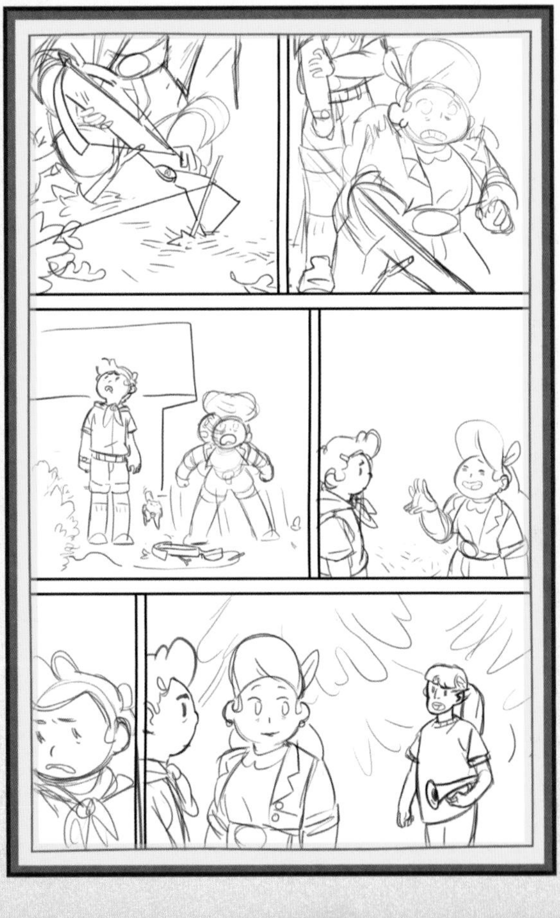

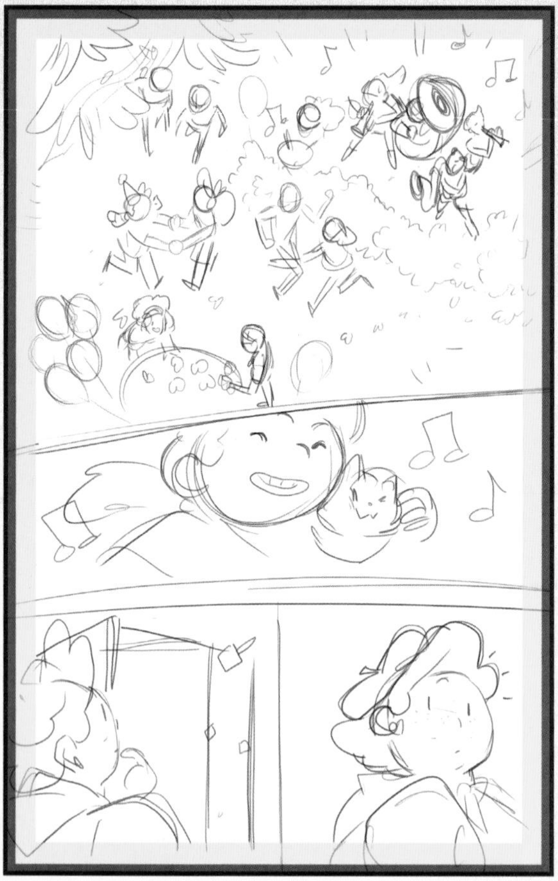

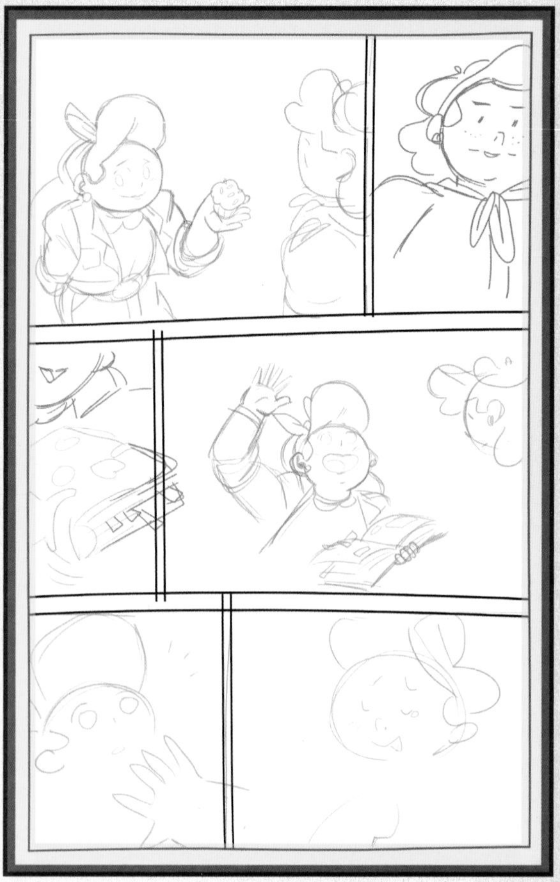

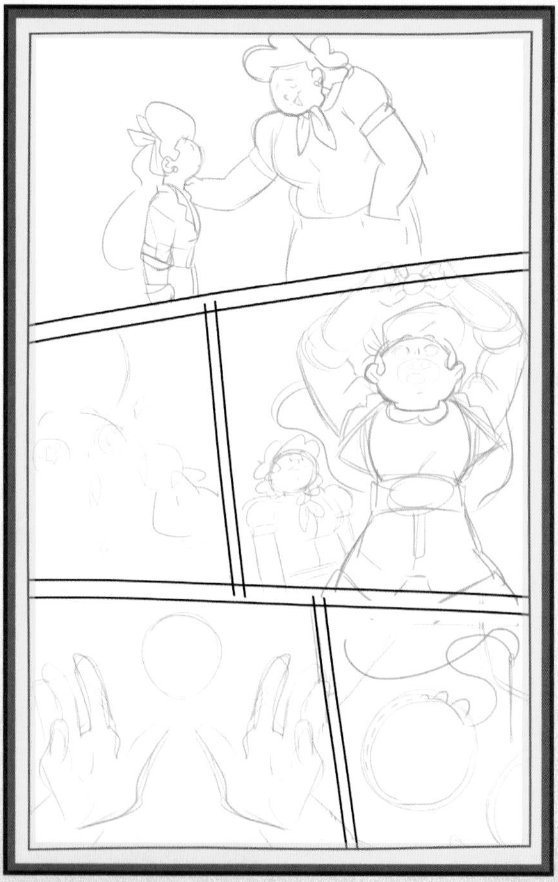

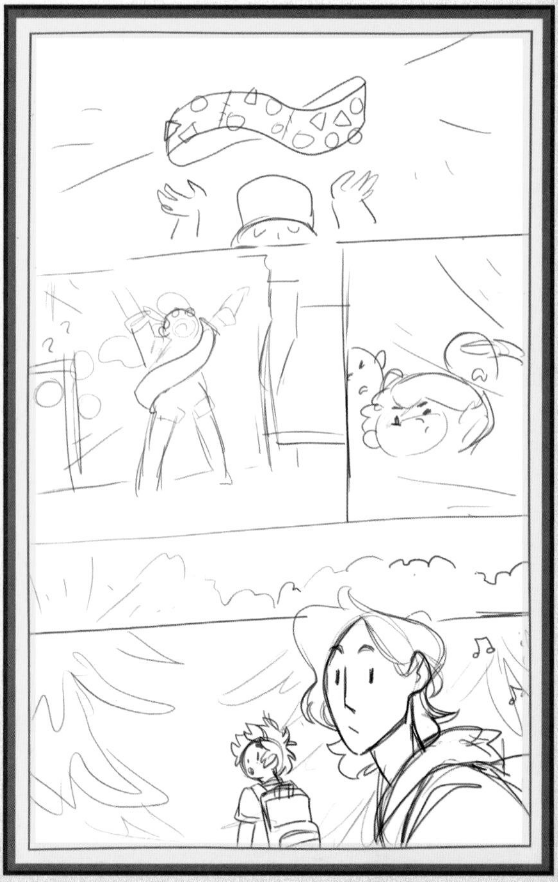

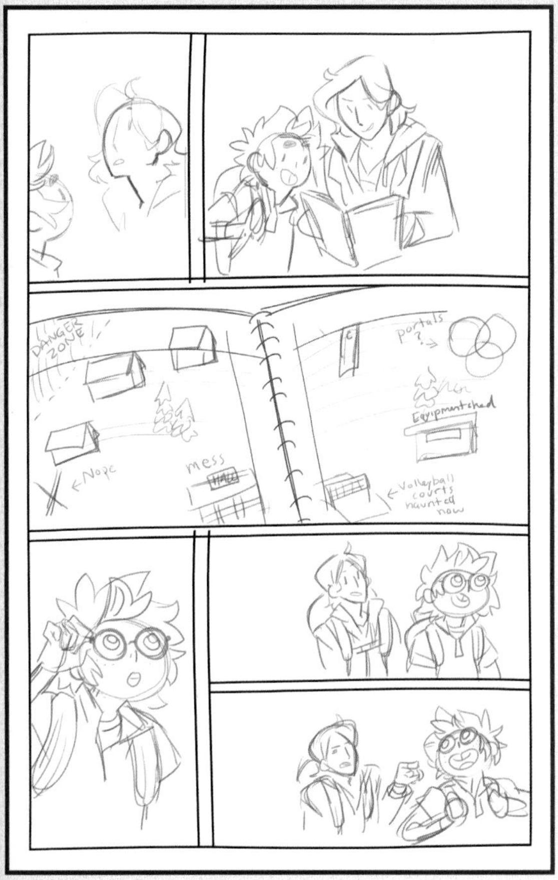
DANGER ZONE
portals ?
Equipmentshed
← Nope
mess HALL
← Volleyball courts haunted now

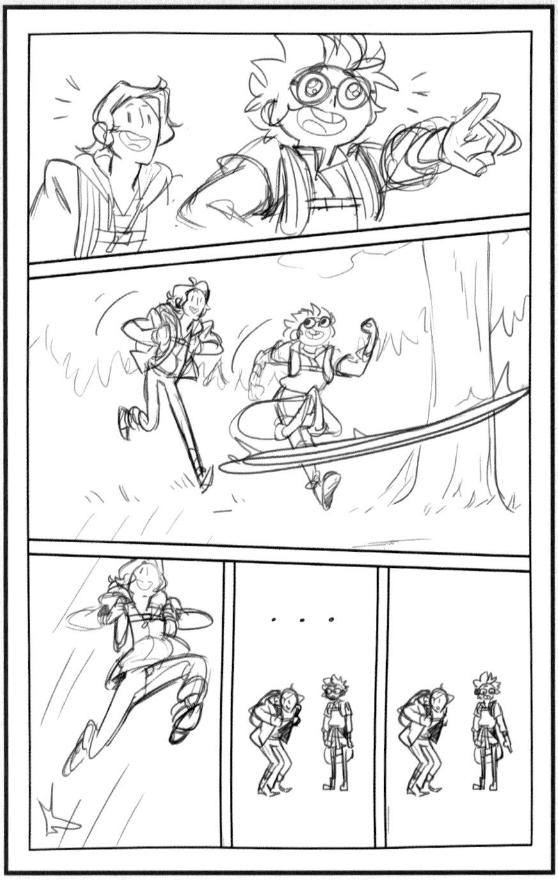
. . .

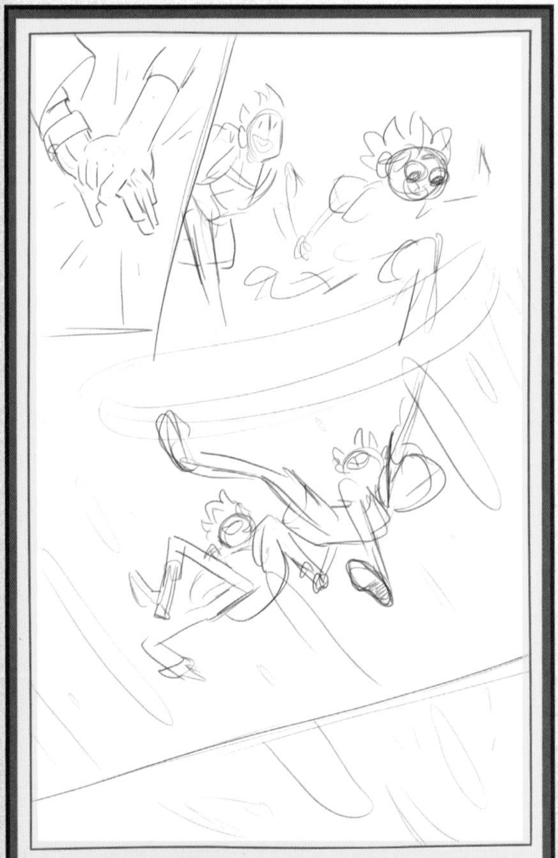

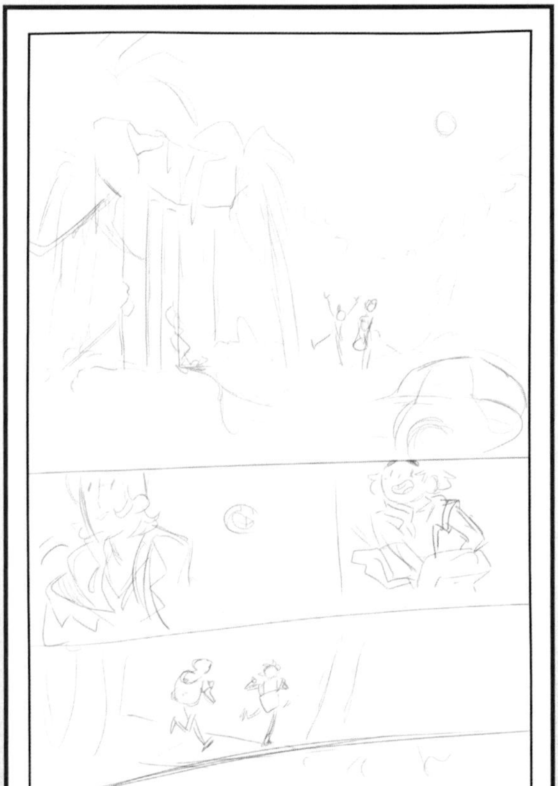

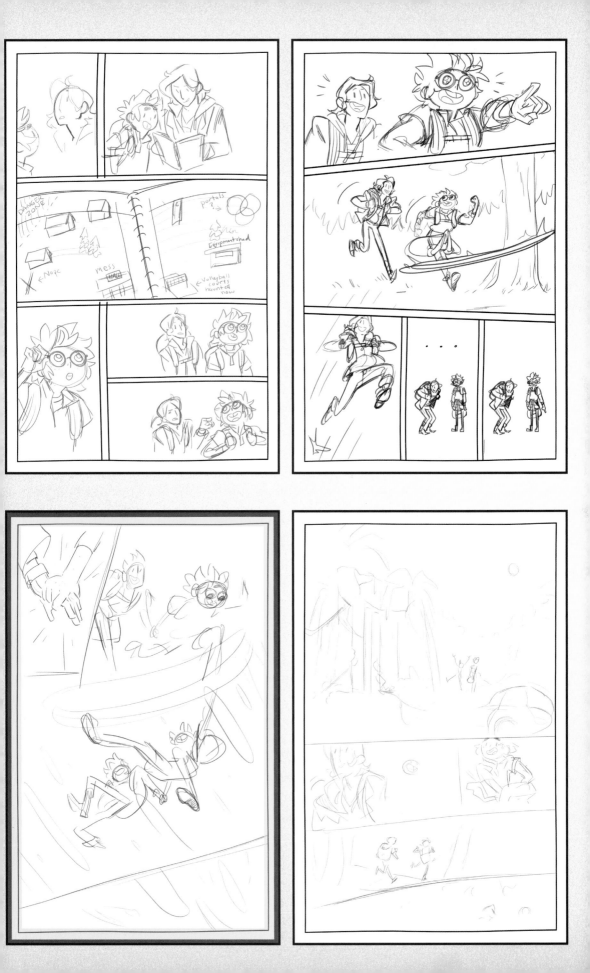

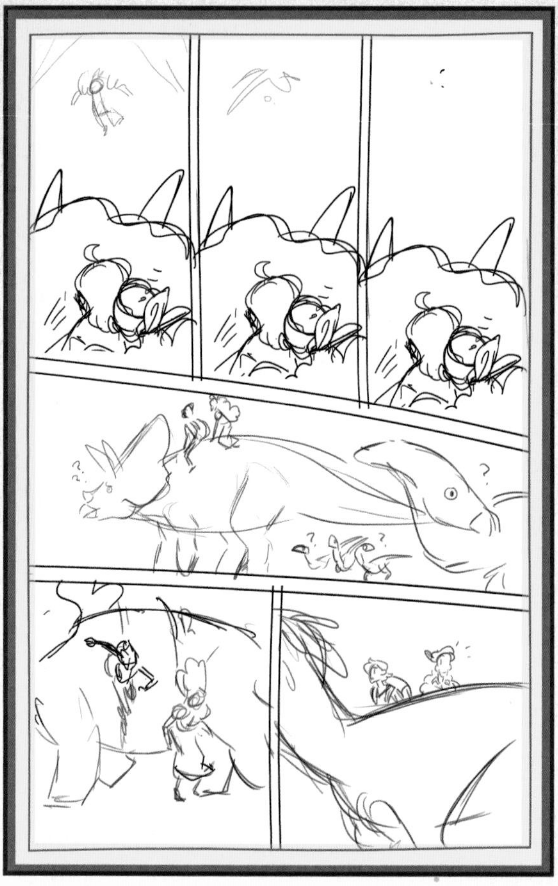

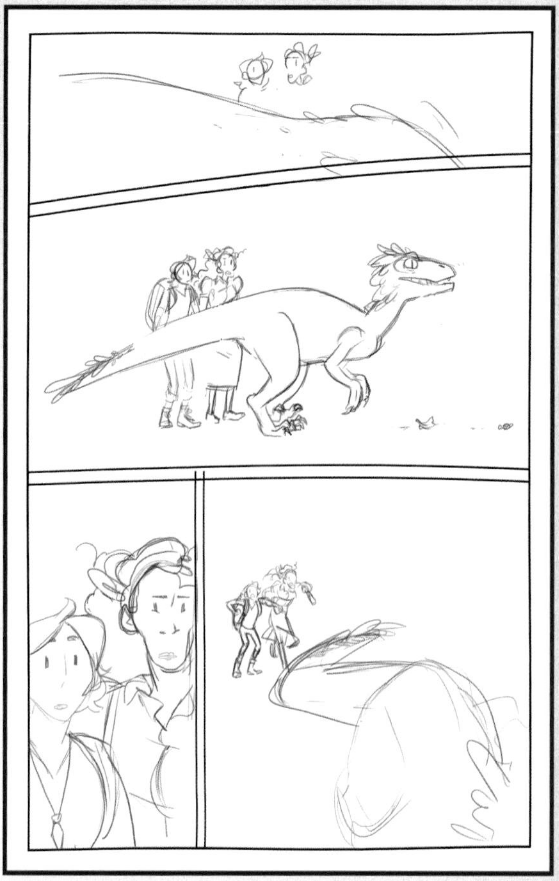

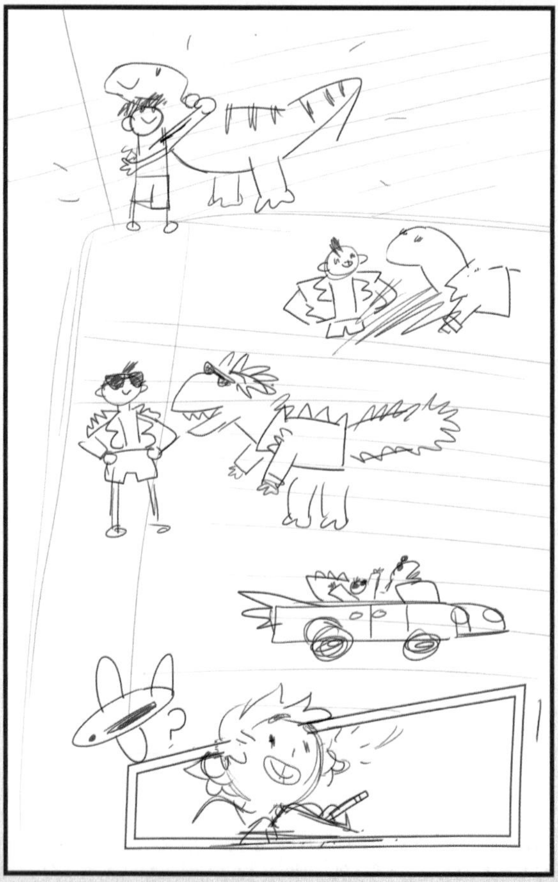

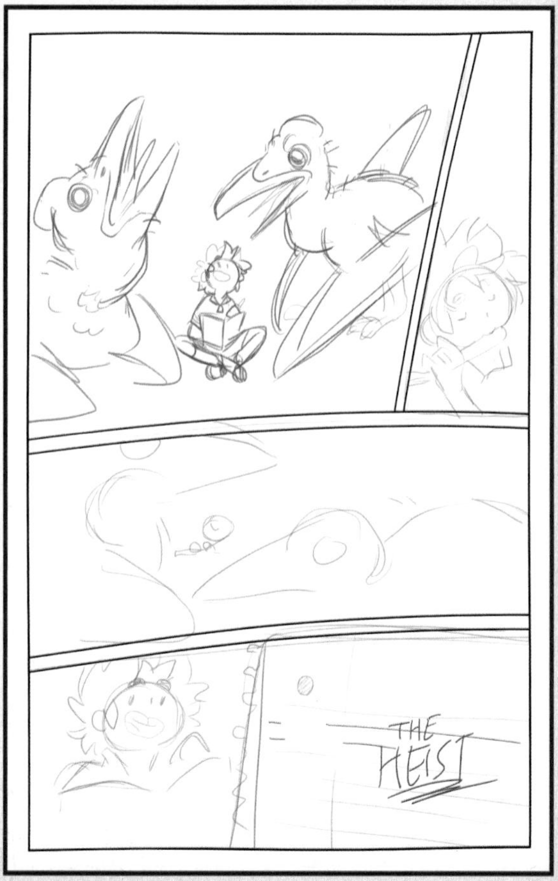
THE HEIST

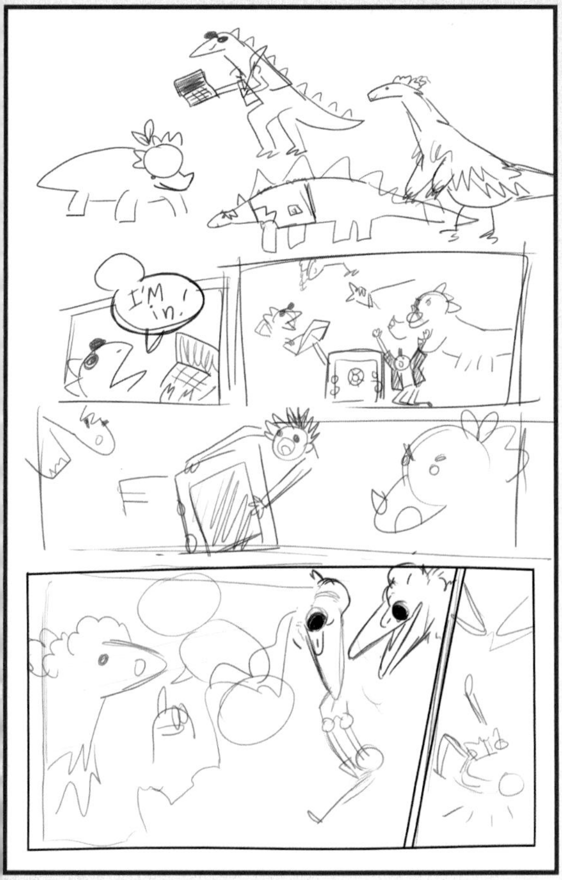
I'M in!

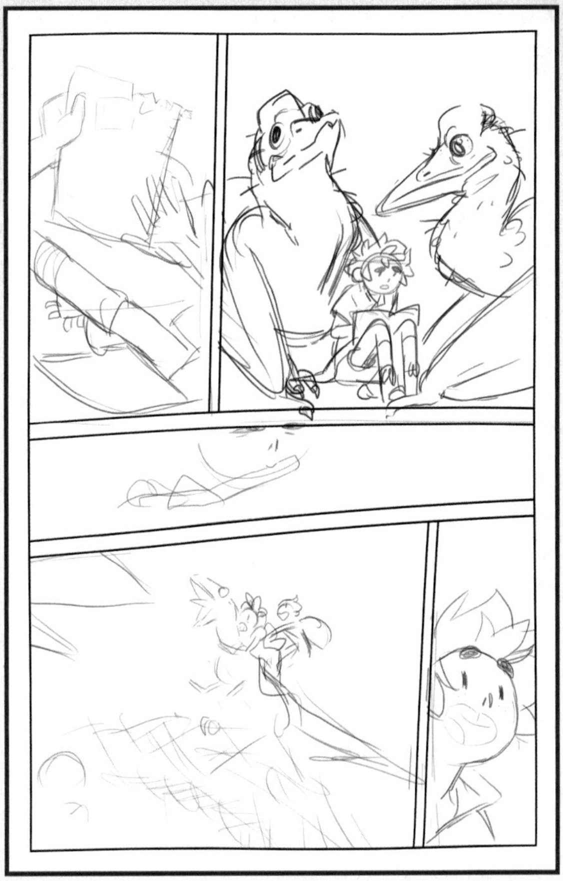

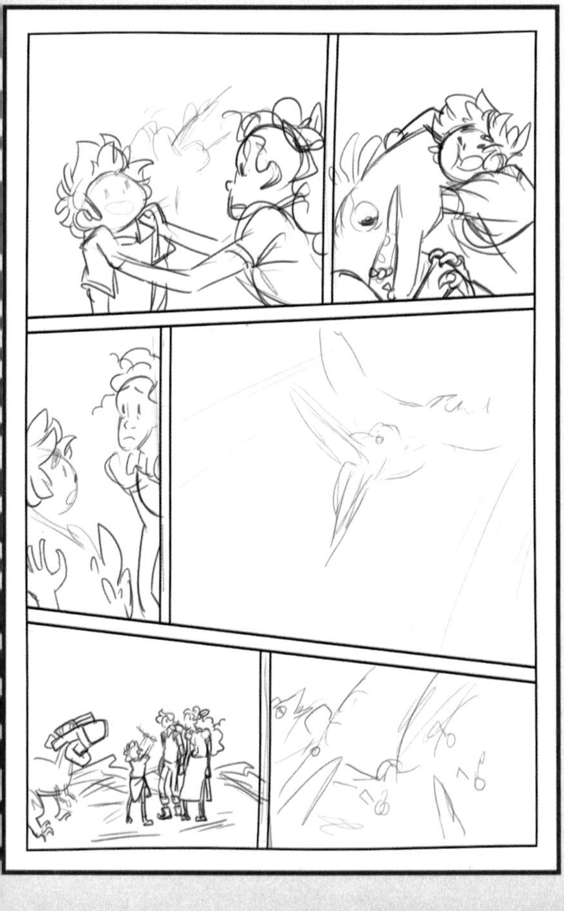

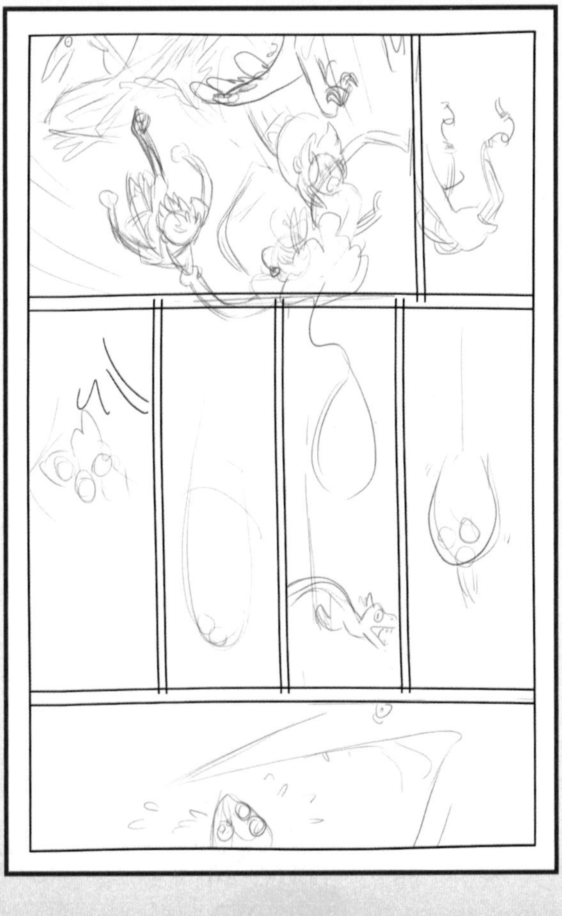

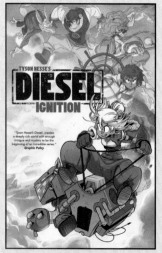